silencing of a witness

Stopping in front of Room 317, his gloved hand slowly turned the knob and he entered, quietly closing the door behind him. He could hear the old woman snoring softly. She was silhouetted in the moonlight. The intruder approached the bed and stared down at her for a moment. Her head was on a pillow. He reached over her and picked up a second pillow. His body tensed when she shifted her position. Her breathing became regular again, but as he lowered the pillow to her upturned face, her eyes opened. She tried to scream, but it came out as barely audible mewing, stifled by the force of the pillow. Her body thrashed soundlessly and her hands, twisted by arthritis, beat wildly at his arms. . . .

PariAh

brian vallée

BANTAM BOOKS
New York   Toronto   London   Sydney   Auckland

PARIAH

A BANTAM FALCON BOOK / MAY 1991

FALCON and the portrayal of a
boxed "f" are trademarks of Bantam Books,
a division of Bantam Doubleday Dell Publishing Group, Inc.

ISBN 0-553-28866-0

Published simultaneously in the United States and Canada

Bantam Books are published by Bantam Books, a division of Bantam Doubleday Dell
Publishing Group, Inc. Its trademark, consisting of the words "Bantam Books" and
the portrayal of a rooster, is Registered in U.S. Patent and Trademark Office and in
other countries. Marca Registrada. Bantam Books, 666 Fifth Avenue, New York, New
York 10103.

PRINTED IN THE UNITED STATES OF AMERICA

OPM   0 9 8 7 6 5 4 3 2 1

1
the
old
man

prologue

JULY 7, 1976

The late-model ranch wagon skirted Middletown, New York, and headed west on Interstate 84 toward the Pennsylvania state line. It was after midnight. The wagon's cruise control was set at the speed limit. The driver lowered his window a couple of inches. The woman beside him knew he preferred the air conditioner, but the wind whistling through the narrow opening made normal conversation impossible. It was his way of telling her to shut up.

She studied his face as they drove through the darkness. She thought about the boy. Without him, they might not have stayed together.

The man repeatedly checked the rearview mirror, which was tilted at an angle to allow him to see the interior of the car. The seats were collapsed flat and covered with a thin foam mattress on which a gaunt old man lay, a blanket tucked around him. His sunken eyes were closed. His head rested on a small pillow, wispy gray hair spreading over the blanket to his waist. His breathing was barely discernible. The driver rolled up his window and switched the air conditioner to low. He wanted a truce. He wondered if they would ever regain what they once had together. He squinted at the mirror until he was satisfied the old man was breathing. The woman wished the breathing had stopped long ago.

The Pennsylvania border was behind them. They were past Scranton and Wilkes-Barre, heading west on Interstate 80. Near Lime Ridge they crossed the swift, shallow Susquehanna River. It was two-thirty A.M. by the clock on the dash. The woman studied the map on her lap with a penlight.

"New Columbia's coming up next. There'll be a turn-off to Highway 15 north. It should be another twenty or thirty minutes to Williamsport. It's just a few miles from there."

The man checked the odometer. Eighteen miles since the turnoff. He was tense. In his mind he went over the checklist for the third time. He'd removed the bulb from the overhead interior light. The wheelchair; the blanket; everything was in order.

Williamsport was behind them. He turned off the highway at Hepburnville. The nursing home, on the outskirts of the town of Cross River, was a mile away.

He turned off the headlights fifty feet from the stone arch entrance. He wished the moon weren't so bright. "No fence," whispered the woman. "It's bigger than I imagined. It reminds me of the Staatsburg house."

"Good. He'll be right at home."

They turned slowly under the arch and stopped in the wide driveway just inside the entrance, sixty yards from the front door. The three-story building, framed in the moonlight, was surrounded by expansive lawns and a black wall of trees at the rear.

Effortlessly, the driver pulled on a pair of surgical gloves, opened his door, and unlatched the wagon's rear gate. He removed the wheelchair and set it up on the driveway. The woman was at his side as he gripped the mattress and slid the old man toward them. They lifted him to the wheelchair and tucked the blanket tightly around him. Leaning down, the man put his ear close to the old man's face. He couldn't hear over the pounding of his own heart, but he could feel the warm breath against his cheek.

Pushing the wheelchair ahead of him toward the building, he saw a nurse sitting in the lighted ground floor office. When he was ten yards from the double wood entrance doors, a dog growled in the shadows to his left. A chain jangled and the growls became loud, resonant barking. He saw the silhouette of a German shepherd straining at the end of its chain. He pushed the wheelchair hard to the right, off the pavement, and followed it behind a neatly trimmed dense hedge. The front door opened. The nurse squinted into the darkness as the dog continued to bark.

"Fred," she shouted. "You stupid mutt. Always barking at nothing. Quit your yappin' before you wake up everybody in the place."

The dog whined and moved back into the shadows. The door closed. The man rolled the wheelchair from behind the hedge to the front of the doors. He snapped down the brakes on each wheel and returned to the station wagon. The dog growled but stayed in the shadows.

"Did you see her?" asked the man.

"Yes. My heart's been in my throat. I thought she'd spot you or the car."

"Damn dog. I didn't expect a damn dog."

He shifted to neutral. The wagon rolled down the driveway to the road before he started the engine. "Now we go back to Williamsport and make the call."

"I've got the number here. My hands are sweaty. I hope I can still read it."

"Damn dog."

It was three-thirty A.M. when the woman called the nursing home from a telephone booth on Williamsport's main street.

"Corky here. What is it?"

"I'm sorry to trouble you, but we were just passing by your place and we noticed one of your patients in a wheelchair outside the front entrance."

"Lady, have you been drinking?"

"I'm quite serious."

"First of all, we don't have patients. We have residents. Secondly, they don't sit around outdoors at three-thirty in the morning. And thirdly, I just looked out a few minutes ago and there was nobody there."

"We're quite certain we saw someone."

"I think you're seeing things, but hang on a minute while I take another look." When Corky returned the woman had hung up.

1

People who only knew Ellen McKinnon as a business-woman found it incongruous that she drove a white Rabbit convertible and wore bright colors. A dark sedan and severe business suit would have seemed more fitting. Her preference was flowered dresses and when she did wear a skirt and jacket they were never black or gray. Navy, maybe, but even then she dressed it up with a white silk scarf tied in a loose, floppy bow around her neck. When, at thirty-six, she took over as director of the Gentle Care Nursing Home in Cross River, state health officials and municipal politicians and her own board of directors soon learned that youth, sex, attire, and cheerful disposition didn't mean a thing when it came to business. She bristled at her first board meeting when the stodgy, white-haired chairman ad-dressed her as "dear" and said how lucky they were and what a pleasant change it was "to have such a lovely young thing running the operation." She might have let it pass and corrected him later in private, but his leering smile put her over the edge.

"My name is Ellen McKinnon, not 'dear' and not 'lovely young thing,' " she said, rising to her feet. "You would not describe a male director in such personal terms. The company sent me here from California because I'm good at what I do and if we keep that in mind, I'm sure we'll all get on just fine.''

Her words were clipped and cold. The color drained from the chairman's face. He stumbled to his feet.

"I'm . . . I'm . . . sorry. No offense intended.''

"Offense taken,'' she said as she sat down.

Ellen was as good as she claimed and within six months of her arrival, Gentle Care Nursing Home was no longer a marginal operation—it was a solid money maker. The previous owner had let the home, then under a different name, fall into disrepair and the residents were regularly abused by the staff. A disgruntled worker went to the press, and the public outcry that followed had forced a state investigation. The owner and two senior staff members were fined and jailed. In 1972, the home was closed and forced into receivership. The Gentle Care chain, based in Long Beach, California, purchased it and spent two million dollars on renovations and landscaping. A year to the day of its closing, the home reopened with a highly qualified, well-paid nursing staff, many recruited from big city hospitals. To entice them to move to rural Pennsylvania, the chain advertised respite from high rents, increasing crime, dirty air, and intolerable traffic. Furthermore, after three years nurses could transfer to another home within the chain, which had fifteen locations in California and twelve others around the country.

It took the Cross River home a year to live down its past and fill all of its beds. When expected profits didn't materialize after the second year of operation, the director was transferred and replaced by Ellen McKinnon. The chain's practice was to appoint prominent local business, medical, and political people to its boards of directors, but they functioned as little more than a sounding board for the director.

A resident's health and ability to pay determined how and where he or she lived at Gentle Care. There were private and semiprivate rooms and four-bed wards on each floor. Those requiring around-the-clock care, the senile and the chronically ill, were on the third floor. Some locals called it the Wacky Ward. The second floor housed disabled residents, many of them stroke victims who used wheelchairs, walkers, or canes. The first floor seemed more like a hotel than a nursing home: Residents could come and go as they pleased, although they had to check in and out with the front desk and notify staff if they planned to stay away overnight or longer. The more private the accommodation, the higher the cost. Wealthier residents, or their families, hired private duty nurses or "companions" who attended them daily. Many had their own stereos, televisions, and telephones. Some paid extra for specialty diets. Excluding administration, cleaning, and kitchen staff, thirty people—nurses, nursing assistants, and orderlies—looked after the home's hundred and eighty residents. There were long waiting lists for accommodation on all three floors.

Ellen McKinnon parked in her reserved space in the lot on the hill above Gentle Care. There was staff parking below, adjacent to the building, but she preferred the upper lot for the view and the climb up the long cement stairway at the end of the day. She considered it a built-in exercise program, good for the heart, lungs, and leg muscles.

The night supervisor, Mary "Corky" Cavanaugh, looked up from behind the nursing station counter where she was standing when Ellen arrived at seven A.M. The director always arrived early, before the seven-thirty shift change, to hear firsthand how the night had gone. She never worried when Corky was in charge. Corky was a registered nurse from the old school—tough, crusty, and decisive in crisis situations. Ignoring the protestations of the board members who complained that Corky was stubborn, insubordinate, and, at sixty-four, too old for the job, Ellen promoted her from assistant head nurse to night supervisor.

Corky had been in her late forties when she began deploying dye to beat back a blitzkrieg of gray hair.

While the roots went white below, she remained a brunette, her hair cut in a short perm.

"Yeah, it's a dye job," she would declare. "But it has nothing to do with vanity. I know I'm no spring chicken, but when they see snow on the roof they think there's snow inside. They treat you differently and never take you seriously. To hell with that."

More than once Corky appeared before the home's disciplinary committee for refusing to awaken and administer medication to elderly, chronically ill residents during the night. That was her rule and the only exception was for those with life-threatening illnesses, such as those requiring regular insulin injections.

"Dammit, when they're sound asleep," she said, "I'm not going to wake them up to give them shots or pills they can get in the morning. They should be allowed some dignity in their last years. If the doctor doesn't like it, he can damn well get off his ass and get up in the middle of the night and administer the medication himself."

On this day, Ellen saw concern in Corky's eyes.

"A problem?"

Corky nodded.

"Mrs. Smithers?"

"No, she's hanging in there. She had a good night."

"Well, what then?"

"Somebody abandoned an old man in a wheelchair on our front lawn in the middle of the night."

"What?"

"Fred started barking, but when I went out, I didn't see a thing. A little while later a woman called. She said she was driving by and saw someone sitting out front in a wheelchair. I went out to look. He was there all right, but she hung up before I could ask her any questions. She's probably the one who left him out there."

"Where is he?"

"On the cot in the emergency room. He appears comatose. I don't know why they didn't leave him at the hospital. . . . I guess they would have been seen."

"Any marks on him? He wasn't beaten or anything, was he?"

"No, no. There were bruises on his arms and a fresh bandage, but it wasn't abuse."

"Intravenous?"

"Yeah, unless he's an addict. A lot of puncture marks. The one under the bandage suggests he was probably on an I.V. just before they left him out front, but I could be wrong. I've got him on dextrose and water. It was hard to find a vein. He's pretty feeble, but he seems stable. His pulse is faint but regular."

They walked along the corridor to the small emergency room that served as a holding place for deceased residents awaiting removal to a funeral home, or the morgue, and for those with serious medical problems awaiting transfer to the County Hospital, twelve miles away. The staff called the room Limbo and when no bodies, warm or cold, were around, they took coffee and cigarette breaks there.

Ellen pushed open the wide wooden doors and entered the room with Corky close behind her. They crossed to the cot and stared down at the old man, who was covered to the neck with a sheet and blanket. An intravenous tube ran from a clear plastic bag on a stand to his exposed arm, its loose, pallid skin covered with bruises and puncture marks. Talonlike nails protruded from the long, slender fingers frozen in a half curl. His cheeks were sunken, his complexion waxen.

"He looks like a corpse," said the director.

"He's breathing, but he hasn't moved. The hands look rigid, but they're not. He was wrapped in blankets and wearing a bathrobe and diapers when I brought him in. The diapers were wet. I cleaned him up and changed his pajamas. They were Mr. Bernardo's . . . his family didn't want them and he sure as hell doesn't need them anymore."

Ellen smiled slightly. "Did he have any identification at all?"

"Nothing, not even a label on the bathrobe."

Ellen pulled back the blanket and noticed the hair for the first time.

"I thought it was an old woman at first," said Corky.

"Christ almighty, it hasn't been cut in years. He's clean-shaven. . . . You'd think they'd cut his hair while they were at it," said Ellen.

"Why would anyone abandon such a feeble old man in the dead of the night?" asked Corky.

"His family probably couldn't cope—or maybe they couldn't afford to put him into a hospital or an institution. But that's no excuse for dumping him on us. We're not operating a charity here."

"What do we do with him?"

"Get an ambulance over here from County Hospital. He doesn't look like he's long for this world. I'll call Martin Butler. We'll see if we can track down the poor man's family."

Captain Martin Butler, of the Pennsylvania State Police, Williamsport Detachment, had a lot of time for Ellen McKinnon. He met her when he moved his seventy-six-year-old father into Gentle Care a few weeks after she was appointed director. Butler and his family were regular visitors even though his father no longer recognized them. He was impressed by Ellen's professionalism and compassion and by her ability to instill those qualities in her staff. Ellen and Butler discovered they lived only four houses from each other in a rustic wooded subdivision a half mile from Gentle Care. Ellen became good friends with Butler and his wife, Elaine, and her comforting presence made a difference when his father died in his sleep four months after his arrival at the home. One of the Butlers' two married sons lived in Williamsport with his wife and three children. The children spent a lot of time with their grandparents, and through them met Ellen. They were fond of her and called her "auntie."

Butler was six years from retirement. He was six feet five and two hundred and fifty pounds, a gentle giant who walked like an awkward teenager and did not use his size to intimidate. A career cop who joined up right after high school, he was even-tempered, with a soft, measured way of speaking.

Because it was Ellen McKinnon, Butler personally took on the investigation. He and two of his officers, one from the identification branch, met the ambulance at County Hospital. They photographed and finger-printed the old man before driving out to Cross River to interview Corky. Butler talked to her in the director's office while his men went through the old man's bath-robe and the blankets he had been wrapped in when he arrived. They also checked the home's driveway and entrance.

Butler had met Corky once before and he was chuck-ling when the director walked in to reclaim her office. Butler rose from the chair behind her desk.

"Do you need more time?" she asked.

"No, no." Butler smiled. "We've covered all the facts. Now Mrs. Cavanaugh is giving me her theories. She thinks the Mafia might be involved in this."

"Don't laugh," scolded Corky, her small, wiry body dwarfed by the policeman's. "I've been thinking about this. A family wouldn't just dump him like that. And I don't think they were poor. That bathrobe and those blankets—they're good quality. Somebody went to a lot of trouble. Somethin's fishy."

Butler placed a large paw on her shoulder. "There may be something fishy, Mrs. Cavanaugh, but I think your Mafia theory is a little farfetched."

"Well, I've told you all I know; now I've got to get the hell home and get some sleep. I'm beat."

"Thanks for staying late," said the director. "Put in for an extra half shift."

"No, I wouldn't do that. I just wanted to help."

Ellen made a pot of tea and she and Butler sat in facing leather chairs which gave them a view of the home's lawns and stone arch entrance, where Butler's uniformed men were walking slowly, heads down, as they scanned the driveway.

"I doubt they'll find anything," said Butler. "I think our only hope is the prints and the photographs."

"You know, Corky was right about the bathrobe and the blankets. The quality is excellent."

"I know, I took a look at 'em."

"Did you see where the label was cut off the bathrobe? Corky noticed that."

"And the blankets," said Butler, nodding, "and the serial number on the wheelchair. Under the seat of one of the supports. It's been scratched off. We're gonna take it in to check for prints, but my guess is it's clean."

"It's a very expensive chair. Some of our wealthier residents have them here. Top of the line, other than the motorized models."

"Expensive bathrobe; expensive blankets; expensive wheelchair; and I'd say this here's a pretty exclusive nursing home. Good taste, wouldn't you say, Ellen?"

"Except nobody's offered to pay his keep and we're sure not going to give him a free ride."

"I think you'd better contact the state to take him off your hands; Health Department, or whatever. He's just lying there in a coma and the hospital won't keep him. They're doing blood work and a brain scan. He'll be there another day or two, but that's it. They're tight as hell for beds."

"Thanks for the good news, Martin."

He smiled. "We might turn up something with the fingerprints. If not, we'll run his photo in the local papers and whatever major papers will run it."

"It was awfully nice of you to get involved in this. You didn't have to come all the way out here."

"It gets me off my butt and out of the office for a while, and since I'm already out here, I'll just go straight home. Besides, you sounded a bit upset on the phone."

"Things like this bother me. I think of what my mother went through . . . and your father. You were here almost every day. What's happened to the concept of family?"

Butler shrugged. "I suppose we could have found him wrapped in a plastic garbage bag."

"I really don't want to see him back here."

"Well, you might be stuck with him. The hospital sure don't want him."

Butler was right. After three days of tests, the hospital returned the old man to Gentle Care. A scan revealed no apparent brain damage and nothing more serious than mild anemia showed up in blood tests. There was no evidence of drug use. They estimated he was between seventy-five and eighty years old. It was impossible to determine how long he'd been in a coma, but it was doubtful he would come out of it. He wasn't expected to live more than a few weeks, more likely a few days.

Ellen McKinnon was on the offensive the day before the old man arrived back at the home. She drove to Williamsport and had lunch with Martin and Elaine. In the afternoon she hammered out an agreement with the state. Gentle Care would take the old man in for a month, with the government paying two-thirds of the normal fee charged by the home for disabled residents. If his family wasn't located and he lived beyond the first month, the state would find a place for him in a chronic care hospital or pay the full rate for the remainder of his stay.

Despite the lengthy waiting list, a third-floor private room was found for the old man. Its previous occupant, Samuel Bernardo, an elderly diabetic, had died of a heart attack. Corky had made up the bed and tucked the old man in when Ellen came into the room.

"He's wearing Sam's pajamas; he might as well have his room too," said the nurse, fluffing the pillow.

"He looks almost serene lying there like that."

"He looks pretty scary to me. He gives me the creeps."

"That doesn't sound like you, Corky."

"Oh, I feel sorry for him, all right. But there's something about him . . ."

Ellen would never admit it, but that kind of talk bothered her. Corky was definitely superstitious, but too often her instincts and predictions proved correct. For years the local funeral home had been donating surplus flowers to Gentle Care. They were displayed in the front lobby or divided into small bouquets to brighten up the tables in the dining room. The flowers didn't go to waste and they brought pleasure to the residents. It was a fine system until the day Corky recoiled when she saw several bouquets of red and white carnations.

"When you see red and white carnations together, it means someone is going to die," she had said somberly. Ellen had told her she was taking her silly superstitions too far. But that night a resident on the first floor died in her sleep. The director maintained it was pure coincidence—after all, red and white carnations had been delivered many times in the past. "I'll bet somebody died then too, but you didn't realize there was a connection," persisted Corky.

Red and white carnations were delivered together on three occasions after that and each time there was a death in the night. Two residents died in their sleep, one unexpectedly. The third to die was a young janitor who worked at Gentle Care. He had stopped at a bar on the outskirts of Cross River on his way home after work, and later, at two A.M., lost control of his car and struck a tree. After that, Ellen discreetly removed either the red or white carnations when they arrived together. The deaths affected her profoundly, but Corky, as obdurate as always, accepted them as one might accept the law of gravity. The director's fondness and respect for her eccentric night supervisor wasn't diminished, but there was a subtle change in her feelings toward her. It wasn't quite fear; more an uneasiness, something intangible. That feeling resurfaced now as Corky talked about the old man.

"I don't know what it is," Corky said. "But looking at him makes my skin crawl. I know he's alone and helpless, but I feel something evil around him."

"The nails . . . the nails and the hair don't help," said Ellen. "I'll get an orderly in here to cut them. What rotten luck. No family; no name; and a vegetable to boot. He's so thin. I don't see how he can last much longer."

"We've added Berocca to his I.V. like the hospital recommended. That will at least get some vitamins into him."

"Well, Corky, now that we're stuck with him, we'd better give him a name."

"I've got one for you."

"You do?"

"Yeah. Uncle Dudley?"

"Dudley?"

"Yep. He looks just like Uncle Dudley. Back when I was in nurses' training in a hospital in Pittsburgh, everybody kept talking about Uncle Dudley. When I asked who he was, they said he was an old guy who hung around the hospital and slept in a closet. I was a dumb rookie. I opened the closet and this skeleton came right at me. I must have jumped ten feet in the air! It was a skeleton they used in the teaching program. They kept him on a stand with wheels and whenever they needed him, they just wheeled him out of the closet. It was an old place—the floor was on a slant and if you opened the door, he rolled right out. That was Uncle Dudley."

"Well, this guy's the closest thing to a human skeleton that I've ever seen." Ellen laughed, feeling her tension melt away. "Okay, Corky, from now on it's Uncle Dudley."

Three weeks after he was abandoned, Dudley's identity remained a mystery. Pennsylvania State Police did not find a match for his fingerprints in their files. His picture appeared in several newspapers, but the four resulting leads proved negative.

Martin Butler was not a big fan of the FBI. He thought they were overrated and the agents he'd worked with over the years tended to be arrogant, treating members of the local forces like country bumpkins. He didn't go to them for help unless it was an absolute necessity. And when it was their investigation on your turf, the attitude was, "Give us the support we need, but stay out of our way." They didn't care that you had a wall full of citations. Oh, he'd met some decent agents, but they were a minority. Butler believed the FBI was a dog-eat-dog bureaucracy steeped in politics, a bunch of lawyers and accountants running around with guns.

But when it came to fingerprints, you often had no choice but to deal with them. The bureau was the main clearinghouse and the only game in town for checking prints you couldn't match in your own files. Identifying an old man abandoned at a nursing home wasn't big or sensitive, but Ellen McKinnon was his friend and Butler helped his friends. Butler used the FBI's fingerprint service for routine investigations, but when he had something big or something sensitive, he did have one alternative.

2

Vince Oliverio was balding, slightly overweight, and very Italian. He stood maybe five feet ten, with perfect white teeth and an engaging smile. He was a dapper dresser, but give him a white apron and he'd pass for the corner grocer. The appearance was deceiving. Oliverio was a tough New York cop. He was respected and popular when he walked the beat, but he hadn't seen the street in fifteen years. Now he was considered the best fingerprint man in North America, some would say the best anywhere. His tenacity, responsible for jailing a host of petty thieves, murderers, armed robbers, high-profile mobsters, and a few crooked politicians, earned him the nickname Bulldog. Prints were his job; his hobby; his passion; and along with family, his life. His private fingerprint collection of the famous and infamous was legend within the fingerprint fraternity.

Oliverio's roots were in the hillsides of Reggio di Calabria, Italy's southernmost mainland province, separated from Sicily by the narrow Strait of Messina. Both his paternal and maternal grandparents raised large families while scratching out a living on land visited with more than its share of epidemics, earthquakes, and droughts. The families cultivated olives, oranges, and lemons, and kept a few sheep and goats. Oliverio's father, Anthony, moved to Reggio, the provincial capital, after his parents and five of his eleven brothers and sisters were killed in the 1908 earthquake. There he lived with an aunt and uncle and worked as a tailor's apprentice. In 1921 Anthony got on a boat for New York with his wife, Florence, and two young daughters. He was thirty-four. Like thousands of Italian immigrants before and after them, they settled in Brooklyn. A boy, the third of their four children, was born ten days before Christmas in 1922, and was christened Vincenzo Luigi Oliverio. For four years Anthony worked long hours in the building industry under the oppressive authority of the *padroni,* the construction bosses. At home, in their cramped tenement, Florence took in sewing and looked after the children. Eventually they saved enough to open a modest tailor shop in a rented building on 86th Street near 21st Avenue in Bensonhurst. The family moved into a run-down four-room apartment above the shop. Another daughter was born there.

Family was everything to Florence and Anthony and the well-being of their children came first. Even through the worst days of the Depression they found ways to provide food and proper clothing. Vince was thirteen before the years of scrimping and hard work enabled his parents to purchase a home in a middle-class, predominately Italian and Irish neighborhood on a tree-lined street in Dyker Heights in the Bay Ridge area of Brooklyn. There was a small vegetable garden at the rear of the house, a veranda in front with ornate wrought-iron railings, and in the basement, a summer kitchen where Anthony made his own wine with grapes from California. There was also a cold room for storing the wine and preserves and for hanging homemade sausage.

Vince was a frail, introspective child who loved books. At the public library, when he was sixteen, he came upon an obscure little volume: *Fingerprints: His-*

tory, Law and Romance, written by George Wilton,
B.L., "One of His Majesty's Counsel in Scotland, and of
the Middle Temple, Barrister-at-law." It intrigued him
to learn that every fingerprint was different from every
other one, with its unique lines and patterns—and that
crimes could be solved with powders, brushes, and
magnifying glasses. He searched for other books on the
subject and read all the Sherlock Holmes stories.

At seventeen, Vince began writing to the New York
Police Department and pestering the local precinct
about joining the force. He was told to apply again
when he finished high school. He graduated second in
his class, but his application was rejected because the
police department considered him too frail. Through a
family friend, Vince took a construction job to help
build up his muscles. In the evenings he hung around a
local gym, lifting weights and occasionally sparring
with friends when serious boxers weren't using the
ring. He was preparing to reapply to the police department when World War II came along. The Japanese attacked Pearl Harbor one week before Vince's nine-
teenth birthday. Two days later, over the protestations
of his parents, he joined the U.S. Army. He felt immense relief and pride when Sicily fell in July 1943. In
every town, village, and city the Americans were
warmly welcomed by the local population. Mussolini
was arrested and Italy signed an armistice and joined
the Allies.

D-Day came less than a year later and Vince was
among the twenty-three thousand American troops who
landed at Utah Beach on the French coast. Three weeks
later he was shipped home with shrapnel wounds from
a German grenade. The wounds, to his upper back and
right shoulder, were painful but not serious. He recovered quickly in the hospital and at home, where he was
pampered by his family. Florence Oliverio was relieved
to have her only son home again. His father and sisters
proudly displayed his decorations and embarrassed him
by telling friends, neighbors, the mailman, the milkman,
anyone who came near the house, that he was a hero.
"The real heroes are the guys who were killed and the

guys who were blinded or lost limbs," complained Vince. But his father ignored his protestations and continued the lavish praise. Among the Italians in the neighborhood, a visit to the Oliverio house was like a visit to a sacred shrine, his uniform and decorations the icons. It was as if Vince had single-handedly liberated Italy and wiped out Mussolini, *mano a mano,* in a David and Goliath confrontation.

In the spring of 1946, despite Florence Oliverio's pleadings that he'd seen more than his share of guns and killing in the war, Vince Oliverio joined the New York City Police Department. He was twenty-three. His first postings were to precincts in Lower Manhattan and the South Bronx. His rise, in six years, from walking the beat, to squad cars, to plainclothes, to homicide detective was storybook. He was an analytical investigator with a photographic memory and the faculty to pick up leads that others overlooked.

By 1961, at age thirty-eight, Vince had earned his second grade Gold Shield and twenty-two citations and awards, including a Medal of Honor, two Merit Medals and a Combat Cross. He'd been shot at four times and had killed two men in shootouts, including a contract killer. Once, during a scuffle with a pimp, he was stabbed in the thigh. Vince was promoted to Lieutenant and allowed a say in his future. "Write your own ticket, Vince," they told him. Down the road he would be in line for supervisor of detectives and, eventually, headquarters. But back then Oliverio wasn't seeing things the way they were. Three months earlier, at age seventy-four, his father had died of bowel cancer after a long, painful time. He and Vince talked a lot toward the end. Of course, Anthony said, he would prefer to live longer, but he wasn't afraid of dying. He wasn't a religious man. Many of the Italian men weren't. Religion, they believed, was for women and children. They thought the church was too interested in money, and mocked the parish priest for the poster he put up in the vestibule. On it was a pie, representing parishioners' wages. It was divided into two unequal portions, a thin slice with the label 10% and a much larger slice marked 90%. Beneath the pie was the priest's favorite slogan: 90% FOR YOU, 10% FOR GOD. When they did attend church, the men sat at the back, the better to make a quick exit. Once a year, when the men showed up en masse to fulfill their Easter Duty, the priest railed at them, warning them not to wait until they were on their deathbeds "and then come running to God."

Now Anthony was on his deathbed. He believed in a Supreme Being and hoped he would be kindly looked upon in the next world. Over and over Anthony told Florence and Vince not to worry. He was at peace with himself and he'd lived a full life. All three daughters had good marriages. He had nine healthy, intelligent, grandchildren. Who could ask for more? There was only one regret. Not a big thing, he told Vince, but his only son wasn't yet married and raising a family. It wasn't that he was worried about the Oliverio name enduring. His concern was that the important things in life were passing Vince by because he was so immersed in his work. "In old age you'll get no satisfaction from plaques and newspaper clippings," Anthony would say. "You're trying to make a better world for other people, but there comes a time when you must think of yourself."

Vince carefully weighed his father's words while deciding whether to remain in homicide or transfer to another department. His choice surprised everyone. "I want fingerprints," he declared. "It's what I've always wanted." "That's a zero, Vince," they told him. "You'll bury yourself. There's nowhere to go from there." Oliverio was adamant. In all his years with the NYPD he had never lost the desire to be a print man. His years of reading and study made him more knowledgeable on the subject than most of the college-educated officers who worked at the job full-time. As a homicide detective he spent a lot of time at the white brick Police Academy on 20th Street between 2nd and 3rd avenues, across the street from the Cabrini Medical Center. The academy's top floor, the eighth, housed the ballistics and narcotics labs and the fingerprint section. When Oliverio was working a homicide that required print work, he could usually be found hanging over the shoulder of the technicians. Most of them didn't mind, but the price he paid was a lot of good-natured chiding. Someone would shout across the room: "Hey Carl, you sleepin' or what? You got a fuckin' Bulldog hangin' on you with his teeth in your neck."

Now the Bulldog was prowling and growling among them all the time. Vince Oliverio was home. Home was a large, fluorescent-lit room with a worn, dull-brown linoleum floor and row upon row of drab, olive-green metal filing cabinets and gray metal desks. Within eight years he became deputy supervisor of the department.

With the promotion, Oliverio was given his own office adjoining the main room. In the seven years since then, it had come to look more like an eccentric professor's study. A floor-to-ceiling bookshelf along one wall was filled to overflowing. Newspapers were stacked in sloppy piles on the floor. Some citations and awards hung on the wall; the rest were stacked in a mound on top of a row of battered green cabinets filled with fingerprint cards and case files.

For fifteen years, before his father died, Oliverio had lived in a small, pleasant walk-up apartment in Little Italy. Sunday he spent with his parents. Sunday dinner was a tradition, with his sisters, brothers-in-law, nieces, and nephews gathering for what they fondly called Florence's Feast. Anthony bragged that his wife's homemade pasta was the best in all of Brooklyn. After the death of his father, Vince moved back home to Dyker Heights to be with his mother, but he spent most of his waking hours in his cluttered office. At work, he wore scruffy leather slippers that his mother would have tossed out long ago. His oak desk and matching swivel chair, salvaged during his days as a construction worker, were as beat-up as his slippers. The top of his desk was covered with magazines, reports, fingerprint cards, case files, and empty Styrofoam coffee cups. To the visitor it was chaos. But he knew where everything was.

Oliverio was so good at what he did that his supervisor, John Sadowski, worried that the entire department would be paralyzed if anything happened to him. If you had a major technical problem, you took it to the Bulldog. His former buddies in homicide always asked for him first when print work was involved in their investigations. Over the years he had developed trusted contacts around the country, including the FBI's identification divisions in New York and Washington. And although he worked long hours, often on his own time, Oliverio could never overcome the backlog. Sadowski knew the Bulldog would scream and yell, but in 1973 he wrote a memo ordering Oliverio to take a partner. He was ready when the Bulldog charged into his office, slamming the door behind him and waving the memo in Sadowski's face.

"You can't do this to me," he snarled. "I've always worked alone. I like it that way."

Sadowski was known for his quick temper. His permanent flush and piercing blue eyes made it seem that much worse. He was quickly on his feet and standing nose to nose with Oliverio. He was two years older, slightly taller, but with the same square build and paunch as his deputy.

"Goddammit, Vince," shouted Sadowski, his flush deepening, "it's too much for one man. You need some help."

"I've never complained."

"That's not the point, for Christ's sake. You're killing yourself. You might as well fucking move in here. You're here all the time."

"Is that it? I'm putting in too much overtime?"

"Cut the bullshit, Vince. I'm not saying that."

The glass partition and flimsy paneled walls of Sadowski's office did little to muffle the sound of their shouting. Work stopped and every head in the place turned. Most of the other members of the department had never seen the Bulldog angry. There was an embarrassing silence for a moment before they returned to work.

"It's for your own good and the good of the department," continued Sadowski, sweat pouring from the tight curls of his white hair. "Just think about it. You're eligible to retire whenever you want. Or the way you're going you could drop dead from a heart attack. Where the fuck do you think that would leave us?''

Oliverio's anger began to subside; he could see the logic in Sadowski's argument. Sadowski returned to his chair. The Bulldog drew a deep breath and sat down facing his supervisor.

"Who do you want mè to take?" he asked quietly.

"It'll be your choice. There's only one condition."

"What's that?"

"It can't be one of your cronies."

"You mean I've got to take a Suit." Suits were young college-educated officers, with a good chance of making headquarters.

"All the new guys are Suits these days, Vince. That's the way of the world."

Oliverio rose from the chair. "Gimme a few days on this," he said softly.

"No sweat, Vince."

The man Oliverio chose was Officer Alfie Morrow, a graduate of Michigan State University with degrees in political science and police administration. His family wasn't wealthy and when he took a term off school to work, he was called up in the Selective Service draft. His grandfather had lost a brother in World War I and a son in Korea. Morrow was sent to Vietnam, where he was twice wounded, neither time seriously. On his return, he completed his education and married Anne Goodson, a woman he had met while on leave in Australia. By the time he had joined the NYPD in 1972, they had had two children. He'd been in fingerprints for two years when he became Oliverio's partner.

Morrow was affable and eager to learn—not like most of the Suits streaming into the department in the wake of the much-despised Knapp Commission hearings, the corruption scandal that shook the NYPD to its foundations. Morrow was in awe of Oliverio's achievements and felt privileged to be learning the print trade at the slippered feet of the master. Between their offices, accessible to both, was a small cubicle with a fingerprint comparator.

•   •   •

Morrow and Oliverio had been together two years
when a brown envelope from the Pennsylvania State
Police was added to the overflowing INCOMING tray on
the deputy supervisor's desk. Each morning, Morrow
scooped up the pile before Oliverio arrived, leaving personal mail and sifting through the rest in his office.

"What's this shit, Vince?" said Morrow, entering Oliverio's office with a print card in hand. "We're up to
our ass in murder-ones and they want us to I.D. some
old fart dumped in a nursing home."

"Lemme see."

"It's from a Captain Butler with the Pennsylvania
State Police. He's got a note in here for you."

Oliverio smiled as Morrow handed him the note and
print card.

"Martin Butler! He's an old pal. My fishing buddy. A
real decent guy."

"Why didn't he send it to the FBI?"

"Hates their guts. They stole one of his collars. A big
drug case in Williamsport. He set up the bust and arrested the guy. The bureau was supposed to be helping
out, but they walked in, put the suspect in a federal car,
and drove off. The guy was a kingpin and they took the
credit. Martin's never forgiven them."

"Can't say I blame him. But this isn't exactly the
crime of the century."

Oliverio read the note. In it, Butler apologized for
sending him such an inconsequential request.

"It's a favor to the woman who runs the nursing
home. She's a good friend of Martin and his wife. She's
a young widow, apparently a real knockout, too. He's
been bugging me about her for a couple of years. Wants
to fix me up."

"Why don't you take him up on it? If you're not too
old to get it up."

"Fuck you, Alfie. Let's put the print up and have a
look."

They entered the cubicle. Oliverio straddled the padded swivel stool and switched on the comparator, two

small parallel screens encased in a gray metal hood. Morrow stood behind him and watched over his shoulder. Oliverio inserted the card with the old man's prints. The comparator enlarged the prints fivefold. They stared at the screen for a few moments.

"Jesus, I think I know this guy," said Oliverio.

Permanent characteristics in a fingerprint, furrows and ridges, are formed in the twelfth and thirteenth week of a human's fetal life and remain constant until a body decomposes after death. The only changes are creases caused by a buckling of the skin as a person ages. The older the person, the more apparent the creases. There were plenty of creases in the print projected on the screen.

"You amaze me, Bulldog."

"Don't fucking call me that. I swear I've seen this guy. Run a file check on it for me, would you? The computer should be able to narrow it down some."

Oliverio knew Butler expected him to send the prints on to his FBI contacts if he came up empty, but he was reluctant to do so. It wasn't anything serious and it would piss them off to circumvent normal channels for something so trivial. Besides, the old guy wasn't going anywhere. It wasn't a case of life or death and he was certain he'd seen the prints before. It would come to him.

3

Although Ellen McKinnon expected Dudley to die soon, she insisted on strict adherence to the medication and intravenous ordered by County Hospital and confirmed by Dr. James Brooks, who made the rounds at Gentle Care twice weekly and responded to any emergencies. She and Corky thought each night would be the old man's last. But he survived the first month and a half, still lying perfectly motionless. Every night, after he'd been changed and monitored, Corky stopped to look in on him for a few minutes. At the beginning of the seventh week, she was sitting beside him at the foot of the bed, a nightly ritual, talking to him in soft, soothing tones.

"Come on, now, Uncle Dudley. Apparently you don't really want to die, so why don't you come out of this?" She could feel the protruding shin bone and knee cap beneath the blanket as she gently massaged his legs. "You know, your name suits you in other ways. You are a 'dud' when you just lie there like this. We can't do anything more for you; you've got to help yourself."

Exasperated, Corky patted the blankets and rose to leave the room. She was a step from the door when she heard the sound: a low, wheezing moan. She whirled in disbelief and returned to the bedside. She stared down. He was motionless. She wondered if she'd really heard anything. She was sure she had, plain as day. She leaned closer.

"Again, Uncle Dudley. You can do it again. I know I heard you. Try again. You've got to try."

The eyelids! Did they flicker just then? Now she wasn't sure. How many times had this happened to her at funeral homes, with friends or family at rest? *At rest* my rear end, she thought. *Dead* is what they were. She would begin to imagine there was life when she stared long enough at a corpse: a barely discernible rise and fall of the chest; a twitch of the mouth; a flicker of the eyelids. Gently she shook his knee.

"Prove to me it's not just my imagination." There was no sound or movement. She glanced back several times as she left the room.

Three nights later, she was sitting in her usual position on the edge of his bed when she felt his left leg twitch beneath the blankets. She switched on the bedside lamp and as she leaned in to speak to him, his eyes suddenly opened, wider than she'd seen any eyes open, ever. They closed as quickly—violently, a door slammed shut. In that split second she saw a rolled-back eyeball, obscuring all but a sliver of the iris and revealing the bloodshot sclera which, belying its common name, was more pale yellow than white. It was like the exposed edge of a dark planet in a murky, jaundiced sky crisscrossed by a tangle of raw red streaks of lightning.

"Holy Mother of God," whispered Corky, stumbling in her haste to move away from the bed. "That sure as hell wasn't my imagination." Her pulse quickened when the old man moaned, flat and forlorn, a distress call from a faraway ship adrift in an impenetrable fog. Corky's practical side took over. She moved closer to the bed. His eyelids fluttered rapidly for several seconds, then he blinked once. The eyes opened. The dark brown irises were in their normal position, much to Corky's relief.

"Are you with us, Uncle Dudley?" she whispered.

He stared straight ahead vacantly for a few moments, then closed his eyes. Corky stayed with him for an hour, but his eyes remained closed and he didn't move. She assigned a nurse to check on him through the night.

"He gave me an awful fright," Corky reported to Ellen in the morning. "His eyes rolled right back into his head."

"He actually moved his legs?"

"Twice while I was in his room and again when Janice was there about an hour ago."

The listless eyes, apparently not registering what they saw, were open more often than not in the days that followed. Movement of Dudley's spindly legs became more pronounced. Dr. Brooks examined him thoroughly.

"Nothing seems to be registering with him," he said. "But he's definitely out of coma. We can take him off the I.V. and get some real food into him."

In medical terminology it was called "indwelling nasogastric tube feeding." Liquid medication and pureed food were poured through the glass barrel of a syringe attached to a plastic tube that had been passed through his nostrils and into his stomach, and secured to his face with adhesive tape. During feedings, the head of his bed was elevated to a thirty-degree angle. A small amount of sterilized water was injected into the syringe to clean the tube, which was changed every four days.

Corky personally fed Dudley every morning before shift change. To her, he was an orphan abandoned by his loved ones. She had given him a name and now she adopted him as her own special patient, spending every spare moment with him. But her sympathetic feelings were tempered by a nagging sense of menace. There were times when his blank stare so unnerved her, she had to get out of the room.

Dudley had been in the home for nine weeks. The sun came pouring through his window. Corky was unusually chipper as she sat on his bed, chattering incessantly,

urging him to break free of his nether world. He was
lying still, eyes closed and arms at his side. Without
warning a gnarled hand reached up and wrenched the
tube from his nose, tearing the adhesive tape from his
face as he did so. Corky let out a yelp. The hand
dropped to his side, still clutching the feeding tube.
Brownish mush sprayed his neck and chin and several
droplets soiled the top of the white sheet. He made no
sound and his eyes remained closed. Corky, now on her
feet, reached down with a trembling hand and shook
his shoulder gently.

"Uncle Dudley, can you hear me?"

There was no reaction. She pried his fingers from
around the feeding tube, which she cleaned and replaced, using new tape to hold it in place. She used
tissues to wipe the sheet as best she could. Again the
hand rose and violently jerked out the tube, showering
himself, the bed, and Corky's crisp uniform. She
scolded him as she cleaned up the mess.

"I know you're awake, dammit. Now, knock it off."

When his hand went for the tube a third time, she
was ready. She grabbed his thin wrist, surprised at his
strength as she wrestled the tube from him, and held
on until the clenched fist relaxed and opened.

"This won't do, Uncle Dudley." She glanced at her
watch. Seven-fifteen. The director would be in.

Ellen could tell by the determined walk that Corky
had something on her mind as she approached the reception desk in the lobby.

"You wouldn't believe what that old bugger did."

"Who?"

"Uncle Dudley. He tore the tube right out of his nose.
Twice he did it. I caught him before he made a mess
the third time. Look at my uniform."

"Did he say anything?"

"Not a sound out of him. Except for the hand, didn't
move a muscle. Never once opened his eyes. It was like
the devil himself was in control of his arm."

"And he didn't make a sound?"

"Nothing. His strength was incredible. Look, I'm still
shaking."

They walked toward the elevator. "Calm down, Corky. You've seen a lot worse than a bit of food spewed around."

"That's for damn sure. I've been puked on and shat on and bled on, but I just didn't expect this. Up to now he's been nothing more than a vegetable."

"Maybe all that time you spent talking to him is finally bringing him around." Ellen smiled, pressing the third-floor button.

"You can laugh all you want, but there's something strange about this bird."

"I'm not laughing at you, Corky. It's just unusual to see you so flustered."

They entered the old man's room to find the tube lying across his chest. "Look at that, he did it again," declared Corky. "The sheets will have to be changed for sure, now. I tell you, he's possessed."

"You haven't been very nice to Miss Cavanaugh, have you, Uncle Dudley?" said Ellen, her tone brisk. "She's been very good to you. This is no way to show your appreciation."

"He just lays there, like he's sound asleep. But he knows what's going on, all right."

"You're pretty amazing, Uncle Dudley," continued the director. "You weren't supposed to be long for this world. You certainly fooled everyone around here."

"What are we going to do with him? We can't keep food in him if he's going to pull the tube out every time."

"If he persists, there's only one thing we can do—go to spoon feeding," said Ellen, leaning over the old man. "Did you hear what I said, Uncle Dudley? If you don't want the tubes in your nose, that's fine with us. We can be civilized. We'll switch to good old-fashioned spoon feeding." She leaned in closer and clapped her hands loudly, inches from his face.

"He blinked," exclaimed Corky.

"Probably reflex."

"I don't trust him."

Ellen gently rolled back Dudley's eyelids with her thumbs. The eyes stared ahead as if focused on something beyond the room. "Same as always," she said. "He's there, but he's not there. I don't believe he's trying to fake anything. He seems to be semiconscious . . . in some sort of stupor." She removed her thumbs and stepped back from the bed, surveying the mess. "Can't say I blame him for not wanting to ingest that muck. It's certainly not very appetizing."

"So what do you suggest we do?"

"You're off shift now. I'll get the day staff to clean this mess up. We won't put the tube back in until his eyes are open. If he pulls it out then, we'll try spoon feeding."

It was ten-thirty A.M. before the old man opened his eyes. Ellen was summoned to the room. The head of his bed was raised to a sitting position and a young nurse, with the help of an orderly, inserted the plastic feeding tube through his nose and into his stomach. Dudley remained still.

"It's eerie how he just stares straight ahead like that," said the nurse, taping the tube securely into position. His hands, palms up, lay limply at his sides, but as she began the feeding his right hand flew up, knocking the glass syringe to the floor, where it shattered. The startled nurse was almost to the door by the time the surprised orderly reached out too late to stop Dudley from pulling the tube out.

"Look at the grip the old geezer's got on this," said the orderly, wresting the tube free.

"His expression never once changed," said Ellen, "and nothing moved except his right arm. Just as Corky described it." She had trouble suppressing a smile as the orderly surveyed the havoc the flying food had wreaked on his hospital whites.

"This boy's a definite slob," he said, shaking his head.

The director calmed the young nurse and instructed her to get help to clean up the mess and to notify her when they were ready to resume feeding.

"Forget the tubes," she said. "We'll try spoon feed-

ing. If that doesn't work, we'll be forced to use
restraints.''

"Gladly," said the orderly, who went off to change
his soiled clothing.

To their surprise, the old man adapted to the new
feeding method. It wasn't necessary to chew the paste-
like food, but he chewed away unconsciously, unaware
of the nurse feeding him or of the other people in the
room. As soon as the spoon touched his lips the me-
chanical motion would begin. But he appeared to have
no control over the movement of his tongue, so half the
food mixture came back out, dribbling down his chin to
the waiting towel, tucked like a bib into the neck of his
pajama top.

"He's chewing and swallowing by rote," said Ellen.
"He doesn't have a clue what he's doing or where
he is."

"It's like feeding a robot," said the nurse, running
the side of the spoon along his lips and chin in a vain
attempt to catch the overflow.

The nurses who fed Dudley were initially intimidated
by the vacuous eyes staring through and beyond them,
but they soon grew accustomed to him. So oblivious
was he to movement, so unwavering was his sight line,
that some thought he might be blind. Dr. Brooks assured them he wasn't.

Corky fed Dudley before she went off shift on mornings when his eyes were open. Deserved or not, she
was credited with inducing him out of his coma by her
long hours of one-way conversations. Some said her
babble probably bored him so much that his eyes had
glazed over and he was in a permanent stupor, awake
or asleep.

Three months to the day of his arrival at Gentle Care,
Corky threw what she called a "foundling party" for
Dudley, complete with balloons, streamers, and cake.
He lay in bed staring straight ahead, unaware of the
activity around him. But two days later Corky noticed
a change in his eyes. She had just pulled the spoon away
from his mouth when his head slowly turned toward
her and his eyes seemed to focus on her. Goose pimples

formed on her arms. He stared at her quizzically, as if wondering who she was. Hesitantly she moved the spoon toward his mouth. *Slap!* The back of his age-freckled right hand knocked the spoon from Corky's grip. She ran for the emergency telephone in the third-floor hallway. It wasn't quite seven A.M. and the director hadn't arrived. "Tell her to come up to Uncle Dudley's room as soon as she gets in."

Ellen arrived on the third floor fifteen minutes later. Corky, distressed, was pacing back and forth outside the room. "He . . . he knocked the spoon right out of my hand. Scared the hell out of me. His eyes. They're different. He's awake. I mean really awake. He looked right at me."

They entered the room. The bed was in the upright position for feeding. Dudley was leaning forward, both fists tightly clenched, panic in his eyes. He was like a cornered animal.

"Now, now," said the director soothingly. "There's no need to be afraid. You're with friends. You're in a nursing home. You've been in a coma for a while." He looked around frantically. When he spotted the open screened window, he cowered against his pillows. "You've had a tough go of it, but you're getting stronger. You had no identification when you came here. Perhaps you can tell us your name and we can contact your family."

As they moved closer, he shrunk farther into the pillow.

"We're here to help you," offered Corky. He stared at them with a look of absolute loathing.

4

Other than his office, Vince Oliverio's favorite place was his den in the basement of the Bay Ridge family home. When he moved there after his father's death he replaced the old oil furnace with electric heat, making space for a den next to the summer kitchen. During the wine-making season, the odor of fermenting grapes permeated the room, which pleased him. The den was his inner sanctum, his womb. It had a rustic look, with pine-paneled walls and a bar built into one corner. He'd salvaged and painstakingly restored the three old barber's chairs which fronted the bar. One of the chairs, his favorite, swiveled to allow him to watch television.

On the side wall, opposite the bar, hung mementos from Oliverio's days in the army, including two miniature flags, American and Italian. There was also a framed biblical quotation sent to him by the British Fingerprint Society, of which he was an Esteemed Fellow. The quotation was from Job 37, verse 7. It read: "He sealeth up the hand of every man so that each may know his work." The society sent it to him after he, in jest, told a London conference that it was Mark Twain who first heralded the use of fingerprints to nab criminals. (Twain's stories did give impetus to the use of fingerprint identification, but he borrowed ideas for his fictions from factual articles written in 1880 by Henry Faulds, an Englishman.) Oliverio was well aware of the history, but he would never admit it to a British audience.

It was the end wall of the den that Oliverio treasured most. It contained row upon row of fingerprints of the famous and infamous, in uniform black wood frames. He was a member of the Canadian and American Identification Societies and the International Association for Identification. Through these organizations, he developed lasting friendships and an invaluable source of prints for his collection.

English policemen officially adopted the system of identification by fingerprints in 1901 and one of the prints from that first year had been sent to Oliverio as a gift from the British Society. His collection also included an original from Sing Sing prison dating back to 1903, the year fingerprinting was introduced to the United States; and an FBI print from 1924, the year the bureau inaugurated its identification division. His most prized print was a copy of an original from an 1892 murder case in Argentina in which the world's first conviction based on fingerprint identification was registered. The story was that a woman killed her children with a knife and then slashed herself. She accused a neighbor of the crime but bloody fingerprints were found on a doorjamb and police ordered samples of both the woman's and her neighbor's prints. Her prints matched those on the door and she was convicted and jailed.

If fingerprints were Oliverio's first love, fishing ran a close second. He'd been addicted to fishing since 1968 when Martin Butler convinced him it was one of life's finer offerings. Since then, they made annual week-long treks to a rented cabin in northern Michigan, where they fished for speckled trout and smallmouth bass.

There were other sports. Vince was a young boy when his father inadvertently introduced him to baseball. It came about because his father began bringing

him along to Dyker Beach Park for weekly bocce outings. Bocce, the traditional Italian form of lawn bowl-
ing, was as much a social event as it was a sporting
contest. Every Sunday, weather permitting, Italian immigrants poured out from a dozen Brooklyn neighborhoods to congregate at the park, just as they had once
gathered in village squares in the old country. It was
the boys' afternoon out, a private men's club. The
games were important but the conversation covered the
week's local gossip, politics, sex, and sports. Oliverio
remembered the neatly folded dark suit coat on the
grass beside the sand pitch. His father wore suspenders
over his white dress shirt, open at the collar. With shirt-
sleeves rolled up, he aimed and launched the heavy
bocce balls with a measured underhand throw. Like
most of the players, he tied a white handkerchief, like
a bandanna, over his head to protect against the hot
sun. Jutting from the rear pocket of his suit pants was
his own carefully whittled measuring stick, used to
check the distance between the balls thrown and the
smaller target ball. Older men, in their best Sunday
suits, sat on benches and chairs and passed judgment
on the games. Some of them leaned on canes, puffing
deliberately on pipes or thin Italian cigars. Vince sat on
the grass with the other boys, bribed into good conduct
with the prospect of a double-decker ice cream cone on
the way home. But after a few trips to the park, friendships were established and the boys wandered off to
nearby fields for pickup baseball or softball games. As
he grew older, Vince began to play the game at school
and he became a rabid Brooklyn Dodger fan like every
other kid in the borough.

Vince was thirteen when he convinced his father to
take him to his first professional game, at Ebbetts Field .
It was 1934—Babe Ruth's last year with the hated New
York Yankees, perennial winners of the American
League pennant and the World Series. Vince fell in love
with the Dodgers, but it wasn't until 1941, with Billy
Herman, Pee Wee Reese, Joe Medwick, and Cookie La-
vagetto in the lineup, that a pennant flew over Ebbetts
Field. The joy of that achievement was soured when

the Yankees eliminated them in five games in the World Series. The Yankees were to take the Series from the Dodgers four more times as the Brooklyn fans' cry of "wait till next year" grew increasingly hollow. It wasn't until 1955 that the threat of World Series revenge became reality, when the Dodgers scored two runs, enough for southpaw Johnny Podres, who pitched a shutout to win the seventh game. The affair of the heart between the Dodgers and their fanatical followers, including Vince Oliverio, ended in 1958 when owner Walter O'Malley, lured by the prospect of television megabucks, jilted them and moved the team three thousand miles away to Los Angeles. The wounded Brooklyn faithful never forgave and for most, the Dodgers replaced the Yankees as the most hated team in baseball. Now Oliverio's baseball team, was the New York Mets.

On this October night, sitting in his barber's chair in his den, he scanned the *New York Times,* a luxury he granted himself only because the Rangers, his favorite hockey team, had a three-goal lead over the Chicago Black Hawks. A two-goal lead or less and his eyes would be glued to the television set. He lowered the newspaper to the bar as a commercial interrupted the game. His eyes wandered to the far wall. Suddenly he pushed himself from the chair. "Jesus Christ!" he said aloud, striking his forehead with the heel of his hand. "Elliot Brodie! Goddamn it! Elliot Brodie!"

Three hurried strides, and he was at the wall reaching for one of the framed fingerprint sets on the top row. "The scars threw me off. The goddamn scars."

He heard the door open at the top of the stairs. "Vincenzo?" called out his mother.

"Yeah, Ma."

In Italian, she asked him who he was speaking to; who was down there.

"It's just me, Ma. I'm yelling at the television. It's okay."

She mumbled something he couldn't make out and closed the door. Oliverio removed the framed prints from the wall and wiped the glass with his shirtsleeve.

He walked to the bar and studied it under the lamp, shaking his head in disbelief. Deep diagonal scars ran across all four fingers of both the right and left hands. On the left hand appeared a second, parallel, smaller scar below the first. It sliced through the ring and middle fingers; there wouldn't be much left to compare on the left hand. And on the right, the scar had severely distorted the ridges on the print pattern area of the little and index fingers, but it ran below the flexion crease separating the tip joint from the middle joint in both the middle and ring fingers. That was all he needed. He had two clear pattern areas on those fingers. The longer he stared at them, the more certain he was that, minus the scars, they were a match for those of the old man from the Pennsylvania nursing home. But if they did match, then Elliot R. Brodie was alive, and that simply couldn't be. He telephoned Alfie Morrow.

"I know it's late, but I want you to meet me at the office right away."

"For Christ's sake, Vince, it's almost ten o'clock. The kids are acting up. They aren't ready for bed yet."

The door at the top of the stairs opened again.

"You speak again to the TV, Vincenzo?" his mother yelled down.

"No, Ma, I'm on the telephone," he said impatiently, his hand covering the mouthpiece until he heard the door close. "Listen, Alfie, I wouldn't bother you at home if it wasn't something important. Unless I'm mistaken, and I could be, I've got something unbelievable here. I need to meet you at the office right away."

"Okay, okay. Anne will have to deal with the kids. I'll leave in five minutes."

Oliverio had removed the prints from their frame and had them set up on the comparator by the time Morrow arrived. "Where did you put the prints of the old guy abandoned at the nursing home? They're not in my pile and they aren't in your basket. You had them last."

"They're in my FBI files," replied Morrow sheepishly.

"What the fuck are they doing there?"

"When I couldn't find anything in our files and you

didn't come up with anything, I figured I'd try the bureau. You said the guy was a good friend of yours. I thought I was doing you a favor."

"All right. All right. What did you get from them?"

"Negative. They drew a blank too. The guy wasn't a criminal. He lived a clean life."

"Get the prints, would you?"

Morrow returned with the old man's prints and Oliverio inserted them into the comparator and switched it on. They appeared on the left screen. The other set appeared on the right screen. The comparator enlarged both sets to five times their size. Morrow saw the name ELLIOT R. BRODIE at the bottom of the print card on the right screen. He turned to Oliverio. "Elliot Brodie. What the hell is he doing up there?"

"Take a look."

"At what? This one's all scars. What's there to compare? Are you fucking with me, Vince? You brought me all the way down here for this, at this time of night?"

"Just take it easy and have a look. We've got two clean areas on the middle and ring fingers of the right hand."

A delta in a fingerprint is like a delta at the mouth of a river: the first point where two strong lines or ridges, which had been running parallel, diverge and surround a pattern area. In the middle of the pattern area can usually be found the core, similar to the center of a whirlpool.

Using a red felt pen, Oliverio carefully drew a line on each screen between the delta and the core of the pattern area of the right middle fingers. Morrow sensed his partner's excitement. When the Bulldog was closing in on something, his movements became jerky, his speech clipped.

"Okay," said Oliverio, taking a deep breath, "you can see both patterns are in the loop category, ulnar loops." He counted aloud the number of ridges between the delta and core on each of the areas he'd marked. "See that, Alfie? Seventeen on each of them. And here we've got a ridge ending up right at the point of core. The same on this one. Here's a bifurcation on the third ridge to the left of point of core. Identical. Another one to the right of the core. Identical. A ridge dot above that bifurcation with a sweat pore in a furrow. Identical. I can go on and on, Alfie. The only difference that I can see is the age creases on the prints from Pennsylvania.''

"But this is all bullshit. Elliot Brodie has been dead for five or six months. The fucker's six feet under, so how can he be alive in a Pennsylvania nursing home?''

"That's what I'd like to know, Alfie.''

"And if the FBI gave you that copy of Brodie's prints, why couldn't they find a match for me when I sent the new version?''

"I'll tell you why. There were no scars on the prints you sent them. Brodie's prints would be in their Permanent Scar section. They had no reason to look there.''

"How did he get those scars in the first place?''

"I'm told that in his glory days, before he became a recluse, he was a damn good pilot. He tested his own planes. One of them crashed, sometime in the late forties; '47 I think. He got burned and his hands got cut up pretty good. He almost didn't make it.''

Oliverio wiped the red markings off both screens on the comparator and turned to Morrow. "Look, I want you to check these out yourself.''

"It's an obvious match, Vince.''

"Let's be a hundred percent sure. This is too big to fuck with. Don't you see the implications?''

Morrow nodded.

"If you can get me twenty points of comparison within those pattern areas, there'll be no doubt whatsoever. While you're doing that, there's something I want to check with the bureau.'' Vince went into his office and called Washington.

Morrow photographed the pattern areas that Oliverio had marked out on each set of prints on the screens. When the photos dried, he inserted them in the comparator, enlarging them an additional fivefold. Sitting on the swivel stool, he took measurements with a clear plastic ruler and used the red felt pen to mark the screen and make notations on the scratch pad beside him.

Oliverio returned to the cubicle, shooing away two

detectives who wandered in from the squad room wanting to know what the Bulldog and his partner were doing in so late.

"Did you get what you wanted?" asked Morrow, not looking up from the comparator.

"Naw, my buddy wasn't working. I didn't think he would be; he's a nine-to-five man. I tried him at home, too, but he was out. A party or something. I'll get him tomorrow."

"What is it you were after?"

"I want to know if they have prints of Brodie taken before his plane crash and, if so, was there a recent request for them from the Pennsylvania State Police."

Morrow's shoulders sagged and his head bowed before he turned to look up at Oliverio.

"Are you telling me this whole thing is a practical joke? That there is no old man?"

"It crossed my mind while I was sitting in my office. Martin Butler could be trying to put one over on me. If he is, it's working. I'm fucking around down here when I should be at home watching the Rangers."

"*We're* fucking around down here." Morrow picked up both print cards and studied them for a moment.

"But if the FBI has prints from before his hands were scarred, they wouldn't have these age creases," he said. "He would have been in his forties. This guy's a lot older than that."

"Could Martin have doctored them, though?"

"This is just a copy, but it sure as hell doesn't look to me like it's been tampered with. Why don't you just call him up and ask him?"

"If it's a hoax, I don't want to give him the satisfaction. What I will do is call that nursing home right now. What is it?"

"Ahh . . . Gentle Care in a place called Cross River."

Oliverio made the call, identifying himself as a police officer, and was assured an old man had been abandoned in front of the home in mid-July. He returned to the cubicle.

"There's an old guy there, all right, and they have no idea who he is."

"Well, if this is legit, this guy is definitely Elliot Brodie. I've got twenty-three points of comparison. More than enough to hold up in any courtroom in the country."

The men were silent for a moment.

"We've got to stop and think about this," said Oliverio. "Without the originals from Pennsylvania, we can't rule out a hoax. But I've known Martin Butler for a lot of years and it's just not his style. He likes to kid around, but he's not a practical joker."

"Another thing, Vince. He couldn't have doctored early prints because there are none. If there were, the bureau would have found a match to the copy I sent in."

"You can't count on that. They miss more than their share. I'll check that out in the morning."

"Let's assume that the prints are legit. That it's Elliot Brodie. Where does that leave us?"

"It leaves us at the center of one of the biggest scams of the century. He was a fucking billionaire. He stayed out of the country and moved around from hotel to hotel because he was under grand jury indictment for criminal fraud and stock manipulation."

"This could be fucking dynamite, Vince. What are we going to do with it?"

"We're going to keep it to ourselves until we find out what the hell is going on here. You got it? You say nothing. Not to your wife. Not to anyone, especially the jerks around here."

Supervisor Sadowski sauntered into Oliverio's office the next day, a Wednesday.

"Good morning, Bulldog," he said with a wry smile.

"Come on, John, you know I hate that."

"I hear you were in here until the wee hours last night."

"That's right, just helping out a buddy."

"It took two of you."

"Don't worry, there's no overtime."

"Just checking, Vince. I like to keep tabs on what's going on around here."

"I've never held out on you, John."

"Hmmm. . . . helping a friend?"

"That's right, John, he's got a missing person."

"Two of you," mumbled Sadowski, rubbing his chin as he walked off toward his office.

"What's his problem?" asked Morrow, entering Oliverio's office from the cubicle.

"Just being nosey. I told him I was helping a friend and you gave me a hand. . . . on our own time. For the record, we're looking for a missing person."

"Did you call Washington?"

"No. I was about to when Sadowski walked in. I'm going to cover by asking for help on the Lazaro hit. You're still on that, right?"

Morrow nodded.

"You keep the file handy and I'll tell them you'll be sending the pics and prints over."

Oliverio closed his office door and made the call to Washington. He got through right away and twenty minutes later he was in Morrow's office.

"They did have earlier prints on Brodie, from the late thirties when he needed security clearance. His company was filling a military contract for the Pentagon. They did a lot of that over the years."

"So the old prints were destroyed when they took new ones after the plane crash?"

"No. That's what I thought, too. But the old prints weren't destroyed."

"Then why couldn't they match them for me?"

"Because they weren't in the main reference file. I should have remembered. When a person reaches the age of seventy-five, whether they're criminals or not, their prints automatically go to a file called Presumptive Dead. You don't have to be dead to make it. The thinking is that in criminal terms, anyone over the age of seventy-five is generally inactive. It's pretty basic."

"Who were you talking to?"

"Joe Marsh. He's the one who sent me copies of the Brodie prints and quite a few others. He's pretty boring and he talks a lot, but he's always helpful. He's waiting to hear from you on the Lazaro case. I slipped Elliot Brodie into the conversation as if it were an afterthought. I didn't want any bells going off over there. He said there's never been a single request to pull those early Brodie prints. And he confirmed Brodie was fingerprinted again right after he died. There was no doubt it was him.''

''Why print him once he's dead?''

''The IRS. With all that wealth, they wanted to be sure it was him.''

''It would be hard to miss those scars.''

''Problem is, Joe Marsh was working from a copy, not the originals.''

''What are you getting at, Vince?''

''Think about it, Alfie. Copies of Brodie's early prints were never sent to Martin Butler. And even if they had been, where would the age creases have come from? Even you admit, it would be next to impossible to doctor a print that way.''

Morrow nodded in agreement.

''So if we operate on the assumption that these prints are legitimate, there can be only one conclusion: Elliot Brodie is alive and rotting in a Pennsylvania nursing home.''

''But they proved he was dead.''

''We don't know that for sure. Marsh told me specifically, he compared the prints using a copy they wired to him. I think he thought I was fishing for the originals for my collection.''

''So you're suggesting the guy who died on the plane from Mexico City to Houston wasn't Elliot Brodie?''

''That's right. With all that money involved, anything is possible. Put yourself in his position. Nobody's seen you in public for years. You've got billions but you're facing a stretch in the federal pen if you show your face in the U.S. So you fake your death using a substitute corpse with a few scars on his hands—probably a dime a dozen in Mexico—and pay off persons unknown to switch the dead man's prints with your own before they get to Washington for comparison.''

"You know what you're saying? The persons un-known would include a cop or a revenue agent."

"You don't exactly have to go to the moon to find a crooked cop," said Oliverio.

"Say for the sake of argument that your assumption is correct. How come he ends up comatose and penni-less at a Pennsylvania nursing home?"

"His insiders are fundamentalist Christians. Trust-worthy, that's why he hired them. Say the plan is suc-cessful, and then he takes seriously ill and goes into a coma. For moral reasons, they can't knock him off, so they dump him in an isolated place, convinced he's about to die."

"I suppose—"

"There's another scenario," interrupted Oliverio. "He could have been in a coma all along and his aides orchestrated the whole scam from the start after skim-ming off a bundle."

"I'm getting a headache thinking about this."

"Well, there is a way to answer some of the questions. . . ."

"It's a little late to exhume the body."

"Actually, that's a thought. You certainly wouldn't get a print, but you might get something from the dental records. But that's not what I was thinking about. The original prints from the body purported to be that of Elliot Brodie should be with the autopsy file in Houston. If they're not there, or if it's only a copy, then we know a switch was probable."

"I suppose you've got contacts in Houston, too?"

Oliverio smiled. "There's somebody there I can call."

The call to Houston was worthwhile. The original prints taken from Brodie before the autopsy were on file. Was there any chance a copy could be sent for my collection? asked Oliverio. "No problem," was the response, "I'll copy the whole damn autopsy file and send it to your home." Oliverio went to Morrow's office to report his success, but his partner was in a black mood.

"Cheer up, for Christ's sake. Houston's sending me a copy of the complete autopsy file."

"But Vince, even if we discover the old guy is Elliot Brodie, it doesn't explain the lack of scars. I've tried to think of every combination and each one comes out totally fucked, unless, for whatever reason, his prints were doctored as far back as the forties."

"You mean there never were any real scars?"

"Right."

Oliverio pulled out the Brodie prints he'd brought from his collection. "They sure as hell don't look doctored," he said.

"Then we're fucked, Vince."

"Hang on. My guy in Houston has the originals from the dead guy at the airport. If they match the ones in my collection, then we know they're not fakes."

"That still leaves you trying to explain why the Pennsylvania prints have no scars. And even if they are fakes, how do you explain the matching pattern areas on the middle and ring fingers of the right hand? See what I mean, Vince? We're going in circles."

Oliverio bowed his head and squeezed his temples. "This is a fucking nightmare."

"The only answer is no answer at all."

"And that is?"

"There are, or were, two guys out there with the same prints. One with scars and one without."

"And all that means, of course, is that the cardinal rule for this whole fucking so-called science goes right out the window. Come on, Alfie, we've got to do better than that. No two individuals on this planet have the same fingerprints. Not identical twins. Not anyone. Do me a favor. Go home and relax with your family. Leave all this shit with me and I'll give you a call later tonight."

Morrow readily accepted the suggestion.

"And remember, not a word," said Oliverio.

"Don't worry, I don't want the boys in the white coats chasing after me with butterfly nets."

For two hours Oliverio sat at the comparator check-ing and rechecking both sets of prints. It was nine-thirty when he telephoned Morrow.

"I compared two more pattern areas that weren't scarred: the left thumb and the heel part of the palm. Perfect matches."

"Except for age creases?" asked Morrow.

"Except for age creases. Somebody's fucking with us and I'm going to get to the bottom of it. I'm taking Friday and Monday off. I've booked a flight to Williams-port tomorrow night. When I get back, we're going to try to find out who printed Brodie the first time around, who printed him after he crashed the plane, and who printed him in Houston after he died. In the meantime, I'm going to get a firsthand look at this asshole in Penn-sylvania and bring back my own prints."

"You're actually going to fly out there?"

"I told you, it's already booked."

"I guess you'll be seeing that foxy widow who runs the place, right?"

"Fuck you, Alfie."

"Good luck, Vince."

5

The seizure occurred the day after Dudley seemed aware of his surroundings. It was prolonged and frightening to watch. The day shift nurses thought he might be having a stroke or heart attack, so he was rushed to County Hospital in an ambulance. Ellen McKinnon, believing she would never see him again, was left with mixed feelings—relief that he was no longer her responsibility, but sadness that he would die alone among strangers. In the hospital over the next three days the seizures recurred, between nine-thirty and eleven every morning. It wasn't a heart attack or stroke, nor was it epilepsy. The doctors didn't know what it was. The old man seemed to revert to a semiconscious state during the seizures, and he remained exhausted for a time afterward. But he demonstrated surprising recuperative powers and struck out at anyone who came near him. He refused to eat and restraints were used to prevent him from removing the I.V. On the fourth day he was returned to Gentle Care without a diagnosis for the seizures. He arrived strapped into a stretcher with a portable I.V. in place. In Dudley's room, the director, convinced he could understand her, pleaded with him to cooperate.

"We mean you no harm. We want to help; but we can't if you won't let us. I can see you're afraid of people and you don't like them near you. I can understand that. We're all strangers to you and that must be a bit overwhelming. But you must understand, we didn't force you to come here. Your family, or somebody, left you here with us. You've been here more than three months now and we haven't heard from them. We've heard you moaning and mumbling in your sleep, so I'm sure you could talk to us if you wanted to. Can't you tell us who you are so we can contact your family? And if you don't want that, if you don't want us to get in touch with them, just let us know."

He glowered at her.

"Well, you've obviously decided not to cooperate, so I'll tell you exactly what we've got planned for you. First of all, I'm going to have these restraints removed, along with the I.V., and if you don't fight the nurses when they bathe and feed you and change your bed pan, they'll remain off. But if you give them a hard time, you'll be restrained and we'll put tubes through your nose and into your stomach to feed you. It's a very unpleasant way to get food into you, but that will be your decision.

"In addition, the doctors tell us that your muscles have atrophied, but there's no reason why you shouldn't be able to walk again with proper therapy. So I'm assigning a therapist to come in and work your legs and arms and we'll get you into your wheelchair so you're not confined to these four walls all day. We'll also be installing an exercise bar over your bed so you can work your arms on your own. You don't seem to like us feeding you, so with a little effort you should be able to feed yourself."

It was Dudley who backed down. He offered token resistance for a few days, but once the restraints were deployed, as the director had promised, he was soon cooperating. Ellen was convinced he had understood every word she had said. It was as if he were suddenly resigned to his fate but damn well didn't have to enjoy it. The director didn't object when Corky asked to switch from night supervisor to third-floor head nurse on the day shift. Left unsaid was the reason for the change—her desire to comfort and nurse Dudley.

There was no letup to Dudley's daily seizures. It distressed Corky to watch him. Dr. Brooks experimented with several types of antiseizure medication, but none worked. Corky looked on helplessly, wiping the old man's brow with a cool cloth. She didn't know what else to do. With no medical explanation forthcoming, she was convinced he was possessed by the devil and the daily thrashings were his body's attempts to exorcise the demon. The one positive side effect of the seizures was that he involuntarily exercised many muscles. Combined with therapy, the result was marked improvement in the old man's general condition. He was soon able to feed himself, then able to stand for the few seconds it took to get into the wheelchair. The physical improvements were not paralleled by behavioral improvements, however. He remained silent, morose, and antisocial. Corky knew he detested her but carried on as if they were best of friends. Once Dudley was able to feed himself, Ellen instructed Corky to begin wheeling him into the dining room for his meals. He rebelled initially but, faced with the renewed prospect of the feeding tube, capitulated. The first time they bundled him up and wheeled him out to the wide veranda to get some sun on a crisp autumn day, he caused such a ruckus they were forced to strap him into his chair.

Dudley was most obstinate when forced to attend the daily exercise period in the games room, where residents confined to wheelchairs attempted to swat a large beach ball about. He looked upon the others with contempt and sat with arms folded tightly, making no attempt to join in. He cringed and flushed with anger when the ball inadvertently came his way and bounced off his head, much to the delight of the others.

What troubled Ellen most was the old man's aversion to dust and germs. Gradually, she realized that it explained his fear of other people and the panic he went into whenever his window was opened to air the room. Twice Corky caught him, barely able to stand, trying to close the window with one hand while the other held a tissue over his nose and mouth. He went through box after box of tissues, wiping everything within reach over and over again. There was always a box of tissues on the table beside his bed and another in his lap whenever he was in his wheelchair. Before every meal in the dining room, he wiped his eating utensils with three thicknesses of tissues.

"I've told you, you've got to stop wasting tissues or we won't give you any more," warned the exasperated director. "Our place is clean. We spend a small fortune paying people to keep it that way." Dudley ignored her.

Corky was wheeling Dudley past the front desk on a bright afternoon when he lurched to the side, almost tipping the wheelchair. Corky righted it and was scolding him when she noticed he was craning his neck toward the front desk. She turned the chair toward it and stopped.

"What is it you were trying to look at?"

No one was at the desk and the surface was cleared off except for a small calendar which displayed the date: October 17, 1976. Corky could see he was staring at the calendar with a look of confusion and anguish. She had no idea why the date so upset him, but she realized for the first time that he knew how to read. Later in the afternoon, she left a copy of a short article on his night table. It was the story, accompanied by his photograph, that appeared in the local newspaper a few days after he was abandoned at Gentle Care.

Dudley was soon able to wheel himself around the home, freeing him from Corky's mother-hen presence. She went about her business but kept an eye on him from a discreet distance. He wheeled quickly away one afternoon when Ellen spotted him trying to read a newspaper article over an elderly woman's shoulder in the bright reading room off the main lobby.

"We know you can read, Uncle Dudley," she called after him. "It's nothing to be ashamed about."

Three days later he was first to the front desk when

the *New York Times* arrived in the morning. He reached for a copy from the middle of the pile. It became part of his daily ritual. Like an addict awaiting a fix, as soon as the bundle was snipped open he would grab a copy and wheel off to an isolated corner of the reading room, making it clear he wanted to be left alone. He deliberately folded newspaper sections in half lengthwise, making them easier to handle. It seemed to give him a sense of purpose. Corky never saw him so contented as when he was reading. Whenever she offered him a magazine from one of the racks, he glared at her and folded his arms tightly, burying his hands against his chest. After watching him remove newspapers only from the middle of a newly opened stack, she realized he was turning down the magazines because others had touched them first, contaminating them.

Dudley was reading the *Times* in his corner on the last Sunday in October when his body began to tremble uncontrollably. The neatly folded half-page rattled in his hands as he drew it closer. The two-column headline had vaulted to his brain:

ELLIOT BRODIE WILL TO BE CONTESTED

The item ran only a few inches. His eye caught the words "Brodie died" in the last paragraph. He read it over and over.

> On April 5, 1976, Brodie died aboard a private jet taking him from Acapulco to Texas. He'd been living in Mexico for several weeks before his death.

He squeezed his eyes shut and gripped the arms of the wheelchair until his knuckles went white.

6

The lone motel between the towns of Cross River and Cogan Station wasn't much to look at, accurately reflecting what travelers could expect once inside. The spartan room with its soiled, threadbare rug, peeling walls, and lumpy mattress added to Vince Oliverio's depression. He'd stayed overnight at a comfortable hotel near the Williamsport airport after the connecting flight from Scranton. Friday morning he rented a car and went directly to the state police detachment, planning to surprise Martin Butler. But his friend was off with his wife on a long-promised trip to visit his sister and her family in Virginia. Oliverio had an open invitation and he'd been looking forward to staying with them. Now he was stuck in a shabby motel, without so much as a TV for company. He was upset with himself for not calling ahead. It was shortly after two P.M. when he checked in. He called Gentle Care Nursing Home from the telephone booth outside the motel. He felt a tightness in his stomach as he waited for his call to be transferred to the director's office. Ellen McKinnon answered, her voice genuinely friendly.

"I . . . ah . . . You don't know me. I'm, ah . . . a

friend of Captain Martin Butler. Ah . . . Vince Oliverio from the New York City Police Department.''

"Yes, of course. Martin and Elaine have told me all about you. He sent you the fingerprints. Is that what you're calling about?''

"Yes. That's right. I'm in town and, ah . . . I thought I might come out . . .''

"You're here, in Cross River?''

"Yes. I just drove up from Williamsport.''

She gave him directions to the home, just minutes from the motel. He was too embarrassed to mention where he was staying.

Oliverio's first thought when he saw Ellen's warm smile from across her desk was that he should have heeded Martin Butler's advice and met her long ago. He blinked and saw a look of happy confusion on her face. Maybe she was thinking the same thing. He cleared his throat and said he was impressed by the building and grounds.

"How does such a place survive in the middle of nowhere?'' he asked.

"That's the appeal,'' she explained. "It's a wonderful rural setting with every modern convenience. If you've got all your faculties and you truly want to commune with nature, it's ideal. And there's a wide range of recreational and social programs, including a weekly dance with a live orchestra. We've got people here from seventeen states. There are quite a few from New York. We're part of a chain and it has an excellent reputation.''

"That was quite a pitch.'' Vince smiled.

"Now I'll give you the down side. I'm afraid we're also a dumping ground for the monied elderly, suffering dementia or other infirmities that often go with old age. Their families ease their own guilt by paying to keep them in a safe, comfortable environment where they'll be well cared for. But the truth is, they want them here because it's as far away as they can possibly get. They pay the bills, but they really don't want to see them. They might visit once or twice a year.''

"Do you get many like our guy?''

"Uncle Dudley. No, I'm glad to say he's the first—and, I hope, last. Mind you, he's won a special place in our hearts. A tremendous will to live. Strange bird, though, as one of our nurses keeps telling me."

"Uncle Dudley?"

"That's what we call him. We had to call him something."

"If you don't mind, I'd like to get a quick look at him while I'm here and then return tomorrow to take another set of fingerprints."

"That's fine with me. You know, of course, he's no longer comatose?"

"No, I didn't know that. You mean, he's conscious? He's okay?"

"He doesn't speak. He just sits there, always looking very angry. We thought he would die within hours or days, the condition he was in when he first arrived. But he surprised everyone. It's been more than three months now and his progress has been amazing. His major problem now is that he goes into some sort of seizure every single morning. We've been unable to diagnose the cause. We thought it was epilepsy, but that's been discounted. Perhaps it's psychosomatic. We have a superstitious nurse who thinks some evil spirit, or the devil, has possessed him. It's a frightening thing to watch. He thrashes around violently for several seconds and then he tightens up like a spring. It goes on like that for an hour, sometimes longer."

"This happens every day?"

"Every morning around nine-thirty or ten, right on schedule. Except for that, though, he's doing quite well. He's able to wheel himself around in a wheelchair and we've gotten him to eat with the others in the dining room. Mind you, we had to use restraints on him and threaten to force-feed him to get him to that point. We've even got him standing on his own for a few minutes a day."

"But he doesn't speak?" asked Oliverio, distracted by the director's warm green eyes.

"Nope. He reads and I know he understands us, but he refuses to speak. We had a terrible time with him.

He hates being around people. I think it's some sort of germ fetish. He goes through several boxes of tissues a week, wiping everything around him. If only he would speak, tell us who he is." Ellen checked her watch. "You should be able to get a peek at him from the kitchen if we get over there right now. Dinner is served at five-thirty."

Oliverio accompanied her to the kitchen. She positioned him near the door to the dining room and opened the door a few inches. They heard the growing buzz and jangling of silverware as residents quickly filled the room.

"Keep your eye on that small corner table near the entrance," whispered the director. "He always comes in after everybody else and sits there. He doesn't want anyone around him and they all know it. He can look at you with such hatred. . . ."

The old man wheeled his chair into the room, oblivious of those around him. On his lap lay a box of tissues and his own silverware carried in a glass. He pulled two tissues from the box and smoothed them out over the tablecloth. Deliberately, he placed the knife, fork, and spoon on the tissues. He set the glass on another tissue.

"We've given up trying to get his glass and silverware away from him," said Ellen. "He washes them himself in the sink in his room and wipes them over and over with tissues. The glass is his second one. It's heat resistant. He broke the first one by running it under water that was too hot. Trying to kill any stray germs, no doubt. When they bring his dinner, you'll notice it's the only one covered with clear plastic. One of our nurses, Corky, started that to get him to eat. I guess it puts his mind at ease, knowing germs can't jump onto his plate during transportation from the kitchen."

Dudley's craggy features were accentuated by deep forehead furrows that gave him a permanent scowl even when his face muscles were relaxed. Could this be Elliot Brodie, the famous recluse billionaire? wondered Oliverio. He hadn't been seen in public in twenty-five years, which made definitive visual identification all but impossible. But the policeman thought he detected some similarities: the square jaw, the dark eyes . . . his height. "How tall is he?"

"About six-three. When he's sitting in that chair it doesn't seem like he's that tall, but he is."

"He seems awfully thin."

"You should have seen him when he first arrived. He's gained nine pounds since then." Dudley quickly ate his dinner of chicken, mashed potatoes, peas, and gravy, washing it down with tomato juice poured into his glass by one of the servers. Dessert, also covered, was brought to him before the others. When he was finished, he wiped his glass and silverware over and over. Leaving the soiled tissues on the table, he wheeled himself out of the room.

"You can see a lot more of him tomorrow," said Ellen as they left the kitchen and returned to the lobby.

Faced with the prospect of returning to his dreary motel, Oliverio haltingly invited Ellen McKinnon to have dinner with him. She accepted. "I'm afraid you'll have to suggest a place," he said. "I've been here twice before, but I don't really know my way around."

"As you can imagine, there's not a lot of choice. Did you notice Harry's Roadhouse on the way out here?"

"Yeah, I wondered about that place."

"I'm afraid that's it. Not that bad, really. It's our one and only night spot. All types eat there: locals, truckers, traveling salesmen, and even the occasional biker. The people are friendly and the food is good. Probably not what you're used to in New York, though."

"Cops in New York can't afford fancy restaurants. Greasy spoons and delis—that's our speed. Can't you tell?" he said, patting his belly. He blushed when Ellen McKinnon smiled. She was awakening emotions he hadn't felt in many years.

In the washroom at Harry's Roadhouse he found himself smoothing his shirt and tucking it tightly into his trousers, in a vain attempt to keep it from bulging in front. He tried buttoning his suit jacket but decided it made him look like a sausage about to burst its casing. He combed his hair, covering the spot that was thinning in front. He left the washroom cursing the greasy spoons and his mother's pasta.

Oliverio was surprised at how easy Ellen made him feel, and in the next hour he found himself, under her gentle probing and with the help of a couple of scotch-and-waters, pouring out his life story. He reached across the table and placed his hand on hers. "You know, I've had a partner now for three years and I just realized you know more about me than he does. You'd make a great interrogator. You could play the role of Good Cop."

"Is it really like that? I thought that only happened in the movies."

"It happens."

"And it works?"

"Sometimes."

"Listen," she said suddenly. "We don't have to eat here. Why don't we go to my place and I'll cook dinner. I've got a fridge full of goodies and I promise not to poison you. I'm just down the road, four lots over from the Butlers. You can follow me in your car."

It was dark when they pulled into the long driveway leading to Ellen's house, which was hidden from the main road by the trees.

"This is more like a fancy chalet than a house," Vince said admiringly of the rustic two-story cedar home. Ellen switched on exterior lamps that lit the high windows running across the front above the porch.

"I fell in love with the place as soon as I saw it," she said, unlocking the front door.

"I guess it's safe, living out here by yourself?"

"It's pretty quiet around here. I've got very good neighbors on both sides, and with a state police captain living almost next door, there's not much to worry about."

A fire was soon crackling in the wide stone fireplace in the living room with its high paneled ceiling. Sitting in an overstuffed chair and staring into the flames, Vince, nursing a scotch, began to feel very comfortable. Ellen returned from upstairs, where she'd changed into jeans and a sweatshirt. He quickly lowered his eyes when he caught himself looking at her full breasts.

"You've got a choice," she said cheerfully. "Steak, fish, or chicken."

"Anything is fine with me."

"Chicken, then. I do it Chinese style and I've got bean sprouts, snow peas, and rice to go with it. It's a little spicy."

"Sounds great to me."

This is a hell of a lot better than that crummy motel, Vince thought. The fireplace was double-sided and they ate in her cozy dining room with candlelight, French wine, and the flames of the fire a few feet away.

"What a great meal," said Vince.

"This is a treat for me," said Ellen. "I get tired of cooking for myself. Most of the time I don't bother. More often than not, it's frozen dinners or out of a can."

"I know what you mean. That's pretty much how I ate when I lived in my own apartment."

"The last time I cooked for anybody was two weekends ago when Martin and Elaine were here. They come over once in a while for dinner. Or I'm over there. They do a lot of barbecuing right up until the snow falls. I just love their grandchildren. They're darling."

"Did he tell you about our annual fishing trip to northern Michigan?"

"Oh yes. That's why I feel I know you so well. He talks about you a lot and I've seen the pictures and slides. Where did you two meet? Wasn't it at a conference or something?"

"That's right. We hit it off right away. I never fished in my life before I met him. He was after me for three years before I finally tried it. He was right. There's nothing in the world like it."

"Quite a switch from the hectic pace in New York, I'll bet."

"It's so relaxing. I couldn't believe the silence and I didn't know there were so many stars in the sky. You can't see them when you're in the city."

"Now, there's no way you're going to stay in that dump of a motel," said Ellen. "There's lots of room here. Martin would kill me if he knew I let you stay there." Vince objected feebly.

"I don't usually go in on Saturdays," she said, ignoring him, "but I'll take you over and show you around. You can watch Uncle Dudley in action."

Oliverio had almost forgotten the reason for his trip. "That's very kind of you." He was feeling light-headed. Perhaps it was the scotch. "You know," he said, "I've told you all about me, but you haven't told me a thing about yourself."

"I'm sure Martin's told you something."

"A little. You're a whiz kid from California, you're a great person, and you're a widow. That's about it."

"He told you I was a widow?"

"Is that bad?"

She thought for a moment. "Not really. It's just that nobody around here knows anything about my private life—except Martin and Elaine—and I want to keep it that way."

"I promise on my father's grave, your secrets are safe with me," said Vince, placing his hand over his heart. She smiled.

"So . . . am I allowed to pry?"

"I pried. I guess you're entitled."

"What happened to your husband?"

"Martin didn't tell you?"

"No, just that you were a widow and there were no children."

Her voice became dry and staccato. "His name was Paul. He was a wonderful man—a grade school teacher. He loved children. He played the guitar and the piano and he wrote songs. Then he got multiple sclerosis. He was very strong in the beginning. We fought it together. He continued teaching for a while but eventually had to give it up."

Vince saw that her eyes were misty. He wanted to hold her.

"The shaking got so bad, he could no longer do anything for himself. He felt guilty about me having to look after him like a child. He said I should be out living my life. I told him he *was* my life."

"I'm sorry," said Vince, taking her hand in his.

"He said those things . . . said them before he . . .

died . . . before he took an overdose. He left me a taped message. He told me he loved me and he was sorry, but he couldn't go on living like that any longer. He said it wasn't fair to me.''

"How old was he?''

"He was thirty-one. That was seven years ago.'' She wiped her eyes and sat erect as if she'd given herself a mental pep talk. "But that's all in the past. I went back to my maiden name, and I was engaged for a while, but it didn't work out.''

"How did you get into the nursing home business?''

"I don't know if Martin told you or not, but I was originally a teacher in California. That's how I met Paul—we taught at the same school. When he was sick I joined an MS support group. After he died I quit teaching and went back to the university. I was just sort of drifting, but I thought at the time I wanted to get into some kind of social work. Then my mother became ill.'' Ellen paused and sighed. "I don't know if you want to hear all this. It's pretty depressing.''

"No,'' said Vince firmly. "It's our past that makes us what we are. I want to hear about your family. I told you all about my father. I still go back to the bocce games I told you about. Some of his cronies are still alive and it keeps him alive for me. I don't see anything wrong with that.''

"You win,'' Ellen said, smiling. "So. My brother Dean and I were the only children. He's a career navy man. We were a close family, but then my father died after a second heart attack—he was quite young, only fifty-eight. I was living and working in Huntington Beach and I convinced my mother to buy a townhouse a block from my apartment. I don't know what I would have done without her. She gave me tremendous love and support through Paul's sickness and she helped a lot with him. After he died we grew even closer. We cried together, took vacations together, even went to parties and bars together.

"Then slowly she began to change—she became erratic, and was finally diagnosed as suffering from presenile dementia. Some people are calling it Alzheimer's disease today. It's a terrible illness—half the time she didn't know who I was. I had to keep an eye on her all the time. She'd forget the simplest things. I went out for half an hour one day and in that time she went to the market around the corner and bought a ten-pound bag of potatoes. I returned to find she'd peeled the whole ten pounds. I asked her why she'd peeled so many and she looked at me as if I were crazy. Another time I came home to find she'd turned all of the furniture upside down and piled it in a circle in the living room. Even the television. She wasn't a big woman and I don't know where she found the strength. She was sitting in the middle of this mess and had lit a fire with newspapers and magazines. It was terrifying. She started screaming and cursing me when I put the fire out.

"It was then that I started checking out nursing homes. The place I settled on was Gentle Care Nursing Home in Cross River. It was close by and I was very impressed with the people who ran it. It's the flagship of their chain. I spent a lot of my time there to be close to my mother and eventually they hired me as a social worker to help out with troubled patients and counsel their families. It was great for me. It was a new career and I was able to be close to my mother. She had a stroke and died there when she was sixty-seven. It was hard for me to be there after that. The company sent me back to school for a few more courses and then transferred me to their home in San Francisco as assistant director. When the director's job opened here, they offered it to me and I accepted."

Perhaps it was the fire, or the candlelight, or the wine or Ellen's soft, mesmerizing voice and stunning eyes. Whatever it was, Vince was captivated. More so, he realized, than he'd ever been in his life.

Impulsively, Ellen leaned over and kissed him softly on the lips. A feeling of incredible warmth washed over him.

"There, Mr. Detective," she said. "You've got the whole story."

"It's deputy supervisor, ma'am."

He felt the softness of her tongue when she kissed him again as they said goodnight at the door to his room.

7

Dudley refused to eat dinner. He left the dining room early and wheeled his way, unnoticed, to the emergency room, where he removed a packet of surgical gloves from an unlocked supply drawer. He returned to his room and lay awake for several hours in the darkness.

Clutching the side of his mattress, Dudley pulled his naked, scrawny body to a sitting position. He switched on his lamp, then reached into the bottom drawer and removed a pair of surgical gloves from the packet. He pulled on the gloves and stood on his spindly legs, like a foal taking its first tentative steps. Shuffling unsteadily to a chair at the foot of the bed, he pulled on his flannel pajamas, bathrobe, and hospital-issue canvas slippers. His breathing was heavy as he made his way to the door. Bony hands gripped the door frame as he looked both ways and pulled himself into the dimly lit hallway. The night nurse had completed her rounds and wouldn't return, barring an emergency, for two hours. Dudley grasped the wooden railing that ran the length of the hallway and began a grueling journey, resting every few steps. It took him ten minutes to reach the elevators at the end of the hallway. He pressed the DOWN button. On the ground floor, in her glassed-in office, the night supervisor heard the elevator start up and glanced up from her Jackie Collins novel. She listened for a moment and continued reading. Dudley, his breathing labored, entered the elevator. He pressed the basement button and gripped the interior metal railing with both hands. The supervisor heard the elevator start up again but didn't look up from her book. The elevator shuddered to a stop in the basement and the doors clanked open. Dudley winced at the noise. He crossed a wide corridor to a heavy black metal door on which the word RECYCL-ING appeared in large white letters. He tugged at the door but it didn't budge. He pulled again with both hands and it opened a few inches. Then he wedged in a slippered foot to keep it from closing. His breath came in short gasps from the exertion. He leaned his body against the door, relieving the pressure on his foot and allowing him to squeeze into the room. In the darkness he found the light switch next to the door. He flipped it, and the room was bathed in a harsh fluorescent glow.

Resting on a chair by the door, Dudley massaged his calves. He surveyed the three-deep rows of bundled newspapers stacked in four-foot piles stretching several yards in both directions. He stood and walked among the stacks, straining to read the dates of the top bundles. Each bundle contained a full week's papers. Halfway along, he stopped and pulled a bundle from the top of the first row. It landed on the floor with a muffled thump. He pulled a second bundle from the same row. It bounced off the first and flipped over on the floor. Dudley looked around and walked gingerly to a wall where a pair of scissors hung on a pegboard beside a large ball of twine.

He was bewildered and then angry as he scanned and clipped out more than a dozen articles from the several local and out-of-state newspapers. He folded them neatly and tucked them into the pocket of his bathrobe. Leaving the remains of the newspapers strewn on the floor, he returned to the chair, again massaging his calves. He replaced the scissors on the pegboard, switched off the light, and leaned into the door, which opened more easily than it had on entry.

The entire operation took just over an hour. Returning to his room, Dudley collapsed face down on his bed. Later, he sat up, placed the newspaper articles in a drawer in the night table, and peeled off the surgical gloves, dropping them into the wastebasket. He removed his dressing gown and pajamas and crawled under the covers. In the darkness he vigorously rubbed his thighs and calves. He dozed off until he heard the night supervisor making her four A.M. rounds. A few moments after the sound of the supervisor's footsteps receded, Dudley switched on the light, pulled on a new pair of surgical gloves, and unfolded and arranged the newspaper articles on the bed.

His hands trembled as he carefully read each of the articles, some of them a full page in length. Many of them duplicated each other. All of them concerned the life and death of Elliot R. Brodie. An Associated Press article with a Houston dateline was typical:

> Billionaire recluse Elliot Brodie died as he lived—in mystery that begat controversy. The 77-year-old former playboy pilot died yesterday a very emaciated man, on a flight from Mexico to Texas for emergency medical treatment. His private Learjet landed in Houston 30 minutes after Brodie died during the flight. The billionaire apparently said earlier he wanted to be buried in Houston, the city of his birth where his parents are buried.

It went on to say Brodie died childless and his two-billion-dollar estate would likely go to advance space technology and medical research. In addition to his vast business holdings, the articles dissected his love life; his exploits as a daredevil pilot; his life as a Hollywood movie mogul; the considerable backroom political power he exercised; and the weird isolation and eccentricity of his last twenty-five years.

The articles were contradictory about the cause of Brodie's death: one concluded he died of a stroke, another said he died in a diabetic coma.

Dudley banged his fists into the mattress over and over when he read that Elliot Brodie's will would be probated within ten days. "No . . . no . . . no . . ." he rasped, his upper torso rocking back and forth. He laid back on his pillow and closed his eyes for a few moments before reading on. An account of the funeral told of Brodie being buried beside his parents with a small group of mourners in attendance. Dudley, grinding his teeth, crumpled the article into a ball and resumed rocking. He stopped abruptly and smoothed the article over his knee. Sitting motionless for several moments, he stared at the story, before suddenly tearing it to pieces and flinging it toward the wastebasket . He looked pathetic, defeated, as he pulled another full page into the light from the bed lamp. He smiled ruefully when he saw the double row of thumbnail photographs of Brodie's ex-wives and Hollywood paramours. He lingered over the photo of Joan Gantry, the last of Brodie's wives.

Wearily, Dudley folded the articles and placed them in the drawer under the packet of surgical gloves. He switched off the light and slept fitfully. After two hours he awakened with a start and reached for the lamp. He held his hands under the light and stared at them. Over and over he rubbed the palms and fingers.

8

In the morning, Vince bounced out of bed like a kid. Ellen had left two folded thick towels on the pine dresser in his room. He could smell bacon frying as he went into the adjoining bathroom. The large window facing north afforded him a view of the sun-splashed woods at the rear of the house. It was late October and most of the leaves had fallen, but those surviving provided a muted gold-brown backdrop for clusters of stately evergreens. The shower was glass-walled and he didn't lose the view as the water poured over him. He whistled under his breath as he dressed and went down for breakfast.

They drove to Gentle Care in Ellen's car, arriving shortly before nine. Since she seldom worked on weekends, she took some good-natured teasing from the nurses in the front office. She introduced them to Vince before escorting him to the elevators. A nurse was already with Dudley when they entered his room. He glowered at them from his bed.

"He won't let me near him," said the young nurse.

"You'll just have to wait until it starts," said the director, walking toward the bed. "Uncle Dudley, this is

Vince Oliverio. He's with the New York City Police Department. He's here to try to help us find out who you are. You won't talk to us, perhaps you'll cooperate with him." Dudley closed his eyes and turned away.

Vince and Ellen had chatted for twenty minutes in a bright waiting room at the end of the hall, beyond the elevators, when the nurse advised them that Dudley's seizure was beginning. When they entered his room, they saw that Dudley's eyelids were flickering.

"It always starts the same way," said Ellen. "Rapid movement of the eyelids and then the eyes roll back in his head."

The nurse pulled up a chair beside the bed and applied a cool cloth to Dudley's forehead. The eyelids stopped flickering and remained closed. His body was motionless.

"Now he'll go into some sort of trance," said Ellen, moving to the bed. "Move closer and watch when I pull back the eyelids. See that? Only white, they've rolled right back."

"How long does he stay like this?" asked Vince.

"Several minutes, maybe ten, before the seizures begin."

Vince unpacked his identification kit and camera from a leather case the size of a shoe box. "This might be a good time to get a photo and fingerprints."

"Go ahead. Once the seizures start, he won't be very pliable."

Vince snapped three pictures of Dudley with an automatic flash camera. With Ellen's help, he pressed and rolled the fingers and palm of the old man's left hand on an ink pad and transferred the prints to a card. He repeated the operation on the right hand and used a cleaning solution and cotton batten to remove the ink from Dudley's skin.

"If you think you've got the time, you might want to give his hands a quick wash," said Vince. Ellen soaped a washcloth and wiped the old man's hands, finishing just as his legs began to twitch.

"Here we go," said the director.

Dudley moaned softly. The leg movements became

more violent. His back arched and his legs and arms went stiff. The moaning grew louder and his knees and elbows suddenly jerked tight against his body, leaving him in a grotesque fetal position.

"Just try to move him," said Ellen.

Vince, hardened by years of policing, was nonetheless apprehensive as he attempted to pry the old man's arms and legs away from his body.

"Christ! I can't even budge him." Vince's face flushed with exertion. He stood to get a better grip but gave up again after several seconds.

"That is unbelievable. His muscles are like steel."

"You'd better stand clear of him now," warned Ellen.

Vince moved to the end of the bed. A few seconds later, Dudley's legs shot straight out, his back arched and his arms stiff at his sides. His moans grew louder and became incomprehensible, guttural grunts. "We thought it might be some foreign language," said Ellen. "But it's sheer gibberish. Corky thinks he's speaking in tongues or some diabolical language from hell."

Dudley's body returned to the tight fetal position. "That's the complete cycle. He'll stay like that for a few minutes and then the whole process will be repeated several times. The doctors have never seen anything like it. They've ruled out epilepsy, but I still contend it's some form of it. Of course, why it happens daily at the same time is a real mystery."

Vince and Ellen had lunch at Harry's Roadhouse. He thought he might be able to connect with a late flight from Harrisburg to New York if he made it to Williamsport on time, but she invited him to stay the night and he accepted. He checked out of his motel and in the afternoon she took him on a tour of the surrounding countryside. They drove to World's End State Park where they stopped to take a long walk in the woods. It was dark by the time they returned to Ellen's house.

After dinner they talked long into the night, about politics, religion and abortion and capital punishment.

They were amazed at the number of areas of agreement. There was a divergence on the issue of capital punishment—although Ellen was surprised to learn that Vince didn't believe it was a deterrent.

"If it's no deterrent, what's the point in having it?" she asked.

"The answer is very basic. The key words are 'to others.' It's not a deterrent to others, but it's a definite deterrent to the guys you ice. They won't be around to do it again."

"But what about all those people who would never murder again? A guy who catches his wife with somebody else. Or a woman who kills her husband after she's been beaten up for years. Those are one-time situations."

"I'm not talking about them. They'd be charged with second-degree murder or manslaughter. I'm talking about killers who plan out what they're doing ahead of time or who carry guns in the commission of other crimes and are prepared to use them. They're the ones I'm talking about."

"Don't you think society is stooping to their level if it kills them? All nicely planned, right to the second. There's no morality in that."

"I understand what you're saying, but if you'd seen some of the things I've seen over the years, you'd feel differently. Morality is for human beings. Some of the people we're talking about are subhuman. They're lower than animals. I know the shrinks will tell you it's usually because they were abused in some way as children, and that may be true. But the fact still remains these guys are now twisted adults and there's nothing you can do to save them. You could sit there and tell them you cared about them, give them money, whatever, and they'd blow you away without batting an eye."

"I still say it's wrong for anybody to take another's life. And if you've read anything about it, you know that over the years some innocent people have been executed by the state."

Vince smiled. "Now you're hitting me where I'm

most vulnerable. Here's another one for future reference. What troubles me most is that a guy with big bucks can bring in a battery of the best lawyers and cop a reduced plea to keep him out of the chair; or he may even get off altogether. But a guy with no bucks doesn't have a chance. He's gone.''

"With holes like that in your argument, how can you sit there and continue to defend capital punishment?''

"Fix the system and eliminate those inadequacies.''

"What are the odds of that happening?''

"Okay, okay.'' He chuckled, raising his hands in mock surrender. "Let's put this one on hold for now. But just remember one thing: Trying to convince a cop to oppose capital punishment is about as tough as convincing a redneck that communism is good for him.''

It was four A.M. when they blew out the candles and Ellen invited Vince to her bed. He awoke in the morning to find her still in his arms, curled against his body. She was an inch or two shorter than him and he thought they made a perfect fit. He had never known such passion, tenderness, and absolute contentment. When she awoke they made love a third time. They stayed in bed until early Sunday afternoon and Oliverio accepted when she asked him to stay over one more night. She agreed to visit him in New York for a few days before Christmas. From there, she would go on to California to spend the holiday with her brother and his family. On the flight home, Monday night, Vince understood his father's warning about missing the important things in life. He'd been attracted to a few women in his time, but it had never never been like this. This was ecstasy.

Oliverio was still floating when he went to his office Tuesday morning. Even Alfie Morrow's inevitable teasing didn't break the spell; nor did the backlog of work piled to overflowing on his desktop. He sorted through the mess until he found the package from the Houston Police Department. Morrow came into his office as he was reading through it.

"Look at this—my guy in Houston has sent me everything. He copied the whole file and even sent a couple of Polaroids of the body. He said they took three or four dozen of them. You can see the guy was a junkie. He's got tracks up and down both arms and thighs.''

One glance at the fingerprints and Oliverio knew they matched the set from the wall of his den. He pushed them toward Morrow. ''There's the scars. You sure can't miss them.''

''But it looks like there are a lot more age creases than on your set,'' said Morrow.

''Which is the way it should be if the dead guy at the airport really was Elliot Brodie.''

Oliverio studied the photos of the corpse. ''I took a couple of photos of the old guy at the nursing home. They're in the soup right now. They should be ready in about a half-hour. He doesn't have a beard and mustache like this guy, but I think there's similarities in the shape of the head, the cheekbones, and the forehead.''

He passed the photos across the cluttered desk to Morrow, who studied them for a few moments.

''You're right, Vince, he's got more fucking tracks than Grand Central. Did you notice the hands? In one photo the palms are down and in the other, where you can see the needle tracks on the arms, there's a sheet over the hands.''

''So?''

''So we don't get to see the scars.''

''If there are three dozen Polaroids, there's probably a shitload of them with the scars. The autopsy was conducted by the department of internal medicine at the Houston General Hospital. They issued this medical bulletin at the time: 'Renal means kidney, two of them. Chronic means a long time. And failure means that they don't work so well. The kidneys have the responsibility of getting rid of waste products the body makes, and they come out in the urine. The kidneys are marvelous organs and when they don't function very well, the waste products accumulate. And unless something is done about it, the patient will die. And this is what we think happened.' He also sent us copies of the X-rays taken at the autopsy. Here, have a look at them. You can see fragments of hypodermic needles broken off in his arms. This guy really had it bad.''

It was a foregone conclusion, but they checked the Houston prints against the set from Oliverio's den. Except for the age creases they were identical. The Houston prints were on a standard FBI form. The name of the agent who took the prints was listed as Charles Bowman, from the Washington, D.C., office.

''Why wouldn't they use a local agent?'' asked Morrow.

''When it's big cheese, fuck the locals. You know how it works.''

Morrow made a note of the FBI agent's name and the name of the coroner who conducted the autopsy.

9

Ellen McKinnon had been to New York City only once before, when she was a child on vacation with her parents. She didn't remember much—only the tall buildings, the big park in the middle of the city, and the animals at the zoo. For years she'd wanted to see the great city decked out for Christmas and now that dream was coming true. She wasn't entirely comfortable with Vince paying for the hotel, but he'd insisted. It was his treat. This was his city and the four days they would spend together was his Christmas present to her. She gave up the argument when he insisted that she bill him for three nights' lodging and for the meals he'd eaten at her place while he was there.

"You also took me on a tour of the countryside, so I owe you for that, too," he'd argued.

As he waited to pick her up at La Guardia Airport, his stomach was in knots, but at the same time he felt as light as Ebenezer Scrooge on Christmas morning. The feelings were new to him, or if he had experienced anything similar, it would have been when he was a teenager on his first date. It couldn't have been this intense, he decided.

On the drive in to the city he sensed she was as excited as he was and it pleased him. When she asked what hotel he'd booked them into, he told her it was a surprise. She was stunned when he pulled up in front of the Waldorf-Astoria.

"My God, Vince, this is too expensive." Vince felt giddy. He winked at her.

"I know the manager," he said. "I got a deal."

While Vince checked in, she sat staring at the art deco sculptures on the high ceiling.

"This is incredible," she said when Vince rejoined her. "But I'm surprised there aren't more Christmas decorations. There's still two weeks, so maybe it's too early."

Their room was large, bright, and tastefully decorated. A lush poinsettia was on a round glass table by the window overlooking Park Avenue. The bellman arrived with their luggage. Vince tipped him and when he left, the couple embraced and fell to the bed. They made love and afterward, showered and changed.

"I can't believe I'm actually in the Waldorf-Astoria," said Ellen.

"It's a first for me, too. It's something I always wanted to do. But until now there was no one I wanted to do it with."

"Flatterer." She smiled, thumbing through her guidebook. "Boy, we're traveling in pretty elite company. Did you know that every president since Herbert Hoover has stayed here? And royalty and generals . . ."

"And don't forget Winston Churchill, Nikita Khrushchev, and Ginger Rogers. Did you ever see the movie *Weekend at the Waldorf*? She was in that."

"I think I've seen it on late-night television. I love old movies."

"I think *The Eddy Duchin* story was filmed here and Cole Porter's piano is still here in one of the lounges—Peacock Alley."

"This is so exciting. You read about a place and you

see it in the movies and then suddenly you're right in the middle of it. It says here there's a coffee shop downstairs called Oscar's, after the chef who invented the Waldorf salad.''

"Speaking of food, we've got reservations."

"Where?"

"Not far," he said smiling.

It was dark but still early in the evening when they left the hotel. The air was crisp and a light snow was falling. They walked up Park Avenue with thousands of tiny white lights shimmering on the trees.

"The people who live along here pay for these lights themselves," said Vince. "It's been a Christmas tradition for twenty-five or thirty years."

They crossed Park Avenue and walked along 59th Street, past the Grand Army Plaza, to Central Park South. The winter air was laced with the aroma of roasting chestnuts from the vendors' carts and over the sounds of the traffic they heard the resolute, rhythmic clopping of iron-shod hooves against pavement as the horse-drawn carriages transported bundled-up tourists through Central Park. Ellen looked up to see the Plaza Hotel, that grande dame, in all its holiday glory, the familiar double-peaked front standing like two stately sentries.

"Any movies pop to mind?" Vince asked.

"Jane Fonda and Robert Redford in *Barefoot in the Park* and what's that other one? It was also a Neil Simon movie . . . Don't tell me . . . *Plaza Suite*! Walter Matthau and somebody."

"You win the prize."

They entered the hotel and, after waiting a few minutes for a window table, had a drink in the dark-paneled Oak Bar. Vince sat facing the bar, his back to one of the large windows. Ellen sat in a leather chair across from him, looking onto the street and the park beyond. The waiter placed a bowl of mixed nuts between them. Vince pushed them toward her. "Keep them away from me," he said. "They're addictive as hell. I don't want to spoil dinner."

She smiled and reached into the bowl.

"I've got one more little movie quiz and then I'll ask you about Dudley," said Vince.

"I'm ready."

"Okay, what famous actor appeared in a scene filmed right here in this bar?"

Ellen shrugged.

"I'll give you a hint. It was an Alfred Hitchcock movie."

"I don't know . . . *Vertigo*?"

"Nope. *North by Northwest*."

"Cary Grant?"

"Right. There's a scene of him walking right in here."

"How do you know all this? Are you a real film buff?"

"No. I brushed up before you got here. I wanted to show off."

"Well, you're doing a great job."

Vince caught himself eating the nuts. He pushed them away again. "So tell me about our Uncle Dudley."

"Well, he's as obstreperous as ever. He keeps entirely to himself except when we force him to participate. He's gained a couple more pounds and he seems to be getting healthier and healthier.

"Has he talked?"

"Not a word. But I'm still convinced he could if he wanted to. I think that's why he hates me so much."

"What do you mean?"

"You can see it in his eyes. He gives me these . . . these vile looks. It's sheer hatred. I think it's because I keep telling him I know he understands and I know he's capable of speaking if he wants to. But I just can't figure out why he refuses to."

"Still no idea who he is or who abandoned him?"

"No idea at all. Have you been able to find anything more?"

"We're still checking out a few leads."

"By the way, Martin was very upset that he missed you when you came up to Cross River."

"Yeah, I know, he called me. Gave me hell for not

telling him I was coming. He would have left a key for me."

"But he's just tickled that we finally met."

"So am I," said Vince, taking her hand in his. "I should have listened to him a long time ago."

10

Corky couldn't decide if the change in Dudley was for the better. He wouldn't allow anyone to touch him or his wheelchair. Initially, it was a struggle for him to wheel the chair on his own, but he was soon moving about with apparent ease. She noticed a new look of determination as he propelled the chair forward with his bony hands. He always wore surgical gloves, which explained why supplies had been dwindling more rapidly than usual. Once a week she dropped off a packet of six pairs of gloves in his room so he wouldn't have to steal them from the supply drawer in the emergency room.

Corky also noticed an increased intensity in Dudley's eyes when anyone came near him. It made the hairs on the back of her neck and her arms stand straight up. The anger and hatred were most obvious in the daily games sessions. Other residents feared him and never batted the beach ball in his direction. When an orderly or nurse, conducting the session, directed the ball his way, he would lash out viciously with a gloved hand. After one of his whacks sent the ball into the face of an elderly woman, knocking off her glasses and leaving her in tears as a red welt formed on her cheek, even the staff refrained from directing the ball to him again. He functioned as a reluctant observer, sitting sourly in his wheelchair on the periphery of the circle.

It didn't surprise Corky when the orderly who usually bathed Dudley in the bathtub in his room reported that the old man was now bathing himself. As the orderly explained, he had arrived in Dudley's room one morning to find him already in the tub. When he went to help him from the tub, Dudley pushed him away and proceeded to pull himself out and dry off on his own. It was obvious he wanted to be left alone.

"He sits in his wheelchair while he fills the tub and he's able to undress and stand on his own while he gets into the water," explained the orderly. "He's a nasty old bastard. He doesn't want me to touch him. I just watch to make sure he doesn't hurt himself." After two weeks the orderly stopped watching.

11

In the morning, Ellen and Vince had breakfast in their room and were on their way early to join the rush of holiday shoppers. He left his car at the hotel and they took a taxi to Macy's. It was Ellen's introduction to the madness of driving in New York. She clutched Vince's arm and wondered if they would live through it, as their yellow cab lurched, swerved, and careened through traffic, coming to a jolting stop in front of the department store.

They were loaded down with parcels when they returned to the hotel in the early afternoon.

"Where are we going for lunch?" asked Ellen.

"The Russian Tea Room. A lot of New Yorkers think it's just a tourist trap, but it's kinda fun. Have you heard of it?"

"Of course. Not another movie quiz?"

"No, but keep your eyes open, you might see somebody famous."

"Before we leave I would like to extract a promise from you."

"What kind of promise?"

"I want you to let me buy lunch."

"But we have a deal."

"The deal was for the hotel only. I'm having the time of my life, but I'm beginning to feel very badly about not paying my own way. I'm not used to that. You must have spent a fortune last night and it's just not right."

Vince smiled nervously.

"I'm serious, Vince. I don't want to go if I can't pay my share."

"Okay, I give in. I certainly don't want you to feel badly."

"I'm well paid," she said, smiling.

"Probably better than me, but remember, I live at home."

"The big bad cop is a mama's boy."

"Yeah, right." He laughed.

The lunch crowd had all but cleared by the time they arrived at the Russian Tea Room on West 57th Street. Everywhere she looked, Ellen saw glistening antique brass samovars, which no doubt once held tea for aristocrats in days of imperial Russia. The walls were dark green and overhead gold tinsel hung from the chandeliers.

"So New York cops eat in delis and greasy spoons, hmm?"

Vince smiled. "When we're on duty. I'm off for four days. To tell you the truth, I'm not crazy about this place. It's great to look at but I'm not big on Russian food. I can take the pickled herring, the bread, and the vodka, but that's about it." He ordered a toasted club sandwich and a beer and she had borscht and a glass of white wine. Vince left the table to use the telephone during lunch.

"You're always on the telephone," said Ellen on his return. "Who do you call? Are you on a big case or do you have a girlfriend hidden away someplace?"

"You're right. That was my girlfriend. My dear old mom. She's all excited. Oh, I didn't warn you yet. Tonight you get to meet my whole family. We're having one of Florence's famous feasts tonight. They're all anxious to meet you. I hope you won't be too overwhelmed."

His announcement caught Ellen by surprise. She was flattered and just a bit terrified. "How many will be there?"

Vince thought for a moment. "Including you and me, there will be twenty adults and six kids. Don't worry; you'll feel right at home in no time."

"Does your mother know we're staying together?"

He smiled sheepishly. "Kind of."

"What do you mean, kind of?"

"Well, she knows we're in the same hotel. I made the mistake of telling her we had separate rooms. She said if that was the case, why didn't we stay at the house. There's plenty of room. I told her the hotel was special and it was convenient for shopping and sightseeing."

Ellen grinned and shook her head in disbelief.

"I know, I know," he said. I'm fifty-three years old and I'm still afraid of my mother. It's not really like that. She knows damn well what's going on. She's no fool. It's a game. Remember, she's from the old country and she follows a lot of the old traditions. I keep telling her, 'Ma, you're an American, you've been over here for more than half a century.' It doesn't do any good. But she knows I'm no angel. I got on her bad side when I was sixteen."

"What did you do?"

"It's a little embarrassing."

"I'm a big girl."

"Well, I was a virgin . . ."

"At sixteen," she said in mock disbelief. "Boy, did you miss out. A real late bloomer."

"All right, all right. I'm having a hard enough time telling this."

Ellen clasped her hands in front of her on the table and suppressed a grin. Vince smiled and shook his head.

"Anyway, there was a girl in Dyker Heights who was always chasing after me. And I mean that literally. Her name was Bernice. Well, one day I quit running, and we did it in the back lane. She'd had previous experience. As I remember it, there was a lot of groping around and all she did was giggle. The upshot was I . . . I . . . Christ, this is embarrassing."

"You can tell me; I'm not a prude. You got her pregnant?"

"No . . . no . . . I got crabs. Can you imagine? My very first time and I get crabs. I'll tell you, I thought God was punishing me. In my naïveté I told my mother and she went nuts.

"Like a lot of Italians who came from poverty in the old country, my mother was a neat freak. Our house was always spotless. She would wash and wax the floors at least once a week. There was a time when she even used a toothpick to get the dirt out of the nail holes on the hardwood floors. It wasn't until I moved back into the house after my dad died that I convinced her to take the plastic off the living room furniture. I told her the couch was made to be sat on but nobody did because the plastic made it seem like a museum piece.

"Anyway, when she saw those little bugs she took me by the ear to the doctor, where I got the old blue ointment treatment. And I think she sent every bit of my good clothing to the cleaners and sterilized the rest by washing them three or four times. She did the same with all my sheets and blankets and she took the mattress outside and vacuumed it and beat the hell out of it. Then she dragged me to church and told me to confess my sins to the priest. There were two priests there and one of them spoke only Italian. I went to him. All the kids did when they had something to confess that they thought was serious. We spoke in English and he didn't understand a word. I'll tell you, my mother didn't let me forget that escapade for a long time."

They left the Russian Tea Room and continued their shopping excursion at Bloomingdale's and Rizzoli's Bookstore; its walls adorned with Ruth Orkin photographic studies.

"I could stay in here forever," Ellen whispered as they wandered through the narrow aisles with the high wooden shelves.

12

Night after night, Dudley pulled out the newspaper clippings one at a time, smoothed them on the bed, and read them over and over. For a time he'd thought he must be insane or in hell, but now he was convinced it was all a plot. He didn't die six months earlier as the articles said he had. He was very much alive. He was Elliot Robard Brodie, self-made billionaire and founder of Centra Corporation. He was seventy-seven years old and somebody had left him here to die. He hated this place, but he must not act rashly. He had to plan a course of action . . . and revenge.

Every night, once the clippings had been returned to the drawer, Dudley lay in the darkness trying to make some sense of what had happened to him. He'd heard them, those shitasses downstairs. They said he had been abandoned in July. That would have been two months after his supposed death.

His last memories before awakening from a coma in this place were blurred. He was in his suite at the Acapulco Princess in Mexico. He'd reached for the codeine syringe but he couldn't remember the needle puncturing his arm.

He couldn't believe his trusted employees, the Christians, were involved in this nightmare—but they had to be. There was no other explanation. Hadn't Marvin Snow, the leader of the eight of them who worked as personal aides, nursemaids, and bodyguards, become more and more demanding in recent years? More days off. More money. But the money didn't go to Snow and the others. It went directly to the sect's headquarters in California. They weren't supposed to care about money. Their reward would come in the afterlife. That's the bullshit they believed in. Why would they want to get rid of him? It would mean an end to their gravy train. Unless . . . unless somebody at Brodie's headquarters, at Centra Corporation, was manipulating them, promising a huge payoff for removing Elliot Brodie from the scene. How long had he been sick, *really* sick? It started in London, a good two years before that night in Mexico. He remembered the benign tumor on the side of his head. He had first noticed it in London, and then there had been the fall at his suite in the Bahamas, when the tumor had split open. He rubbed the side of his head. No trace of the tumor now. Too many drugs. He cursed himself for being so blind. The Christians controlled the drugs and if somebody in the corporation controlled the Christians, they could have been slowly poisoning him.

Dudley was enough of a realist to know that it was money rather than affection and admiration that attracted people to Centra Corporation. He bought loyalty as he would any other commodity. He had no friends and he was sure most of his senior executives hated him for the way he played them off against each other. Face-to-face meetings with Brodie had become as rare as an audience with the Pope. Even his most senior executives could communicate with him only through memos or by telephone. They found it demeaning that all calls to Brodie's inner sanctum were screened. He remembered listening in as Robert Marlin, who was in charge of the Paper Lion and several other Las Vegas casinos Brodie owned, alternately begged and threatened the Christians when they refused to put calls through to him. Marlin wrote several memos a day to Brodie, but they went unanswered. Marlin's ostracism continued for nine weeks, during which another executive, Hugh Mallot, was having daily conversations with Brodie and bragging about it. Finally Marlin, who had been with Centra for fourteen years, threatened to quit. Two days later Brodie called him, feigning that he was deeply hurt by Marlin's conduct, stroking him until the executive agreed that he had been rash and would stay on with Centra. Two weeks later Brodie fired him, claiming in a press release that Marlin had stolen millions from the corporation. Marlin sued for libel and wrongful dismissal. The case was still before the courts; Dudley concluded it would no doubt help Marlin's lawsuit if Brodie were out of the way.

As for Hugh Mallot, Brodie had humiliated him for years by undermining his authority. He would order Mallot to negotiate a major business deal and when, after months of delicate bargaining, it was ready for closing, Brodie would change his terms, forcing Mallot to start over again. Often, Mallot would be ordered to join Brodie at one of his hotel hideouts, thousands of miles from Centra's Las Vegas headquarters. Mallot would wait for days or weeks, never getting to see his boss. Though he sulked and raged at the impassive Christians, his telephone calls wouldn't be put through and his memos piled up unanswered. When he threatened to return to Las Vegas a memo from Brodie would appear, instructing him to stay put.

In Vegas, Mallot lived flamboyantly. Brodie called him at all hours of the day and night to complain about it. Mallot was, in effect, Centra Corporation's chief executive officer, but Brodie never made the position official—as he had once promised he would. For years he dangled the CEO title before Mallot, meanwhile always finding excuses for putting off the decision. With Elliot Brodie gone, there was a good chance Mallot finally would become the top man at Centra. Yes, Dudley decided, Mallot had a motive.

He thought about Edith Hall, his faithful secretary. She had been with him longer than anyone at Centra, his eyes and ears at corporate headquarters. She knew more of Brodie's secrets and dealings than anyone. He had often thought she might be skimming off profits, but he never accused her. He wasn't perfect; he didn't always operate within the law and she knew it. She knew too much.

13

Ellen was nervous when she and Vince arrived at the Oliverio house in Dyker Heights early in the evening. She brought flowers for his mother. The welcome was warm and noisy, and soon she was at ease. In all, there were twenty adults and six children in the house. There was a lot of good-natured teasing and it became quickly evident to Ellen that Vince Oliverio was loved and admired by his sisters and their children and grandchildren and that his mother doted on him. His mother and sisters called him Vincenzo. To everyone else he was Uncle Vince. The children were all over him. Vince's brothers-in-law—an accountant, a clothing salesman, and a construction company manager—seemed content to sit back and watch the confusion around them. Their wives would appear from the kitchen, from time to time, yelling orders at the children. In the kitchen, however, Florence Oliverio was the sole boss; her strong voice could be heard over the others as she barked out instructions. Ellen offered to help, but Florence would have none of it. A table had been set up in the kitchen for the children and there were twenty settings at the long oak dining table covered with a white crocheted tablecloth. Florence brought out her best china and silverware and sent Vince to the basement for two bottles of red wine. When the food was ready and when everyone was seated, they bowed their heads and one of the older children said grace. Ellen noticed Vince didn't cross himself like the others.

"All these are special dishes my mother prepares for Christmas," said Vince. "Everything is homemade. She makes her own pasta, her own bread, everything."

Vince explained each dish as it was passed around: pizza rustica, strufoli, and Florence's special cassata, a ricotta cheese sponge cake covered with vanilla icing and topped with glazed fruit.

After dinner, while the table was being cleared, Florence took Ellen by the hand and asked her to go with her to the basement to see "Vincenzo's things."

"No, Ma," complained Vince. Florence scolded him in Italian, to everyone's delight, and proceeded to the basement. She showed Ellen her son's war decorations and memorabilia and his citations and awards from the police department.

Ellen and Vince stayed on to help clean up for a while after the others left. Florence gave her a hug at the door when they finally said goodnight.

"I'm so full," said Ellen as they drove back to the hotel. "You weren't kidding about your mother's cooking. She's incredible. It was just a wonderful evening. Everybody was so nice and so friendly. You're lucky to have such a warm, loving, normal family."

"I was a little worried the noise might get to you . . . with all those people and the kids."

"Those kids really love you."

"Probably because I spoil them."

"No . . . even the older ones. They look at you with such affection and admiration. And your mother . . . well . . . she thinks you walk on water."

"But what do you think?"

"Oh, I guess I'm in your fan club. Especially now that I find out that you're a war hero. And a modest one at that. I thought all your scars were from your job. You didn't tell me you were wounded.''

"It wasn't very serious. My family always made a big deal out of it. I guess my mother was trying to impress you.''

When they returned to the hotel there was a message for Vince to call his mother.

"Is something wrong, Ma?'' he asked. He listened for a moment. "Just a minute.'' He held the phone away from him, his hand over the mouthpiece. "Did you leave a couple of presents in the hallway for my mother?''

"Her name is on them,'' said Ellen, smiling. Vince removed his hand from the mouthpiece.

"Yeah, she did, Ma.''

"Tell her it's for Christmas and for her warm hospitality.''

Vince relayed the message and talked to his mother for several minutes.

"You rascal,'' he said to Ellen as he replaced the receiver in its cradle. "You know you didn't have to do that.''

"I wanted to. The gifts were in my purse and I put them out while you were in the bathroom.''

"What did you get her?''

"Just a silk scarf and a pretty brooch. I hope she likes them.''

"I know she will.''

After they made love, Ellen lay on her side, her breasts against his back. She ran her hand over his chest.

"I love the hair on your chest,'' she said, nibbling on the edge of his ear. "I'm just glad you don't have any on your back. I hate that.''

"I have a tough time shaving it. It's hard to reach.''

She punched his arm playfully. "You know, Vince, I can't remember having such a wonderful time. The last two days . . .''

"We've still got two and a half to go.''

"I don't know if I can stand it. It's been so good.''

Vince rolled over to face her and took her in his arms. He pecked at her nose and cheeks, running his hands down her back to her taut full buttocks. He pulled her tighter to him and her mouth opened to meet his.

"I think I'm falling in love," said Ellen.

"Ditto."

They spent Saturday morning at the Metropolitan Museum, where in the massive, dimly lit Medieval Sculpture Hall, they were part of a hushed crowd awed by the thirty-foot "Angel Tree," topped with a star that looked like the core of a gold fireworks burst. Fifty eighteenth century sculptured angels, in suspended flight, hovered in the tree, all eyes gazing rapturously downward to the Christ child lying on a bed of straw in an elaborate Neapolitan crèche.

"I'm not religious," whispered Vince, "but every time I see this, it really gets to me."

Afterward, they ate lunch at the museum's restaurant and took a taxi to complete their Christmas shopping at F.A.O. Schwarz.

When they returned to the hotel, Vince refused to disclose his plans for the evening. "All I'll tell you is that dress isn't casual. I'll be wearing my best suit."

"Please tell me I've got time to soak awhile in the bath."

Vince checked his watch. "We've got loads of time. It's only five-thirty." A few minutes later he knocked on the bathroom door.

"Can I join you?" he asked.

"Of course."

He sat behind her in the wide tub and nuzzled the back of her neck. His arms went around her and he caressed her breasts. She could feel his erection and knelt forward in front of him. He pulled himself to his knees and entered her. Afterward, he leaned back in the tub, and she put her head on his chest. She could feel his heart beating.

"Are you sure you're fifty-three?" she asked.

"Don't tell me you believe that men reach their peak at eighteen."

"Well, if that's the case, you're certainly an exception."

"Listen, I've been saving up for a long time."

It was close to seven when the taxi dropped them on Columbus Avenue. They ate a hearty meal in a modest Cuban restaurant. "Don't worry, it wasn't this place that we dressed up for," said Vince.

Later, they walked south along Columbus, smelling pine and spruce; vendors were selling Christmas trees on the street.

"Where on earth are we going?" asked Ellen.

"Right there," he said, pointing down the street to Lincoln Center. A banner announced the New York City Ballet's annual performance of *The Nutcracker*. She put both arms around his waist and hugged him tightly.

"You know," she said, "I've never seen it. It's something I've dreamed about since I was a little girl. How can you be so perfect? It's as if you're plugged in to my mind and know just the things that please me." Vince leaned over and kissed her lightly on the lips.

"Have you seen it before?" she asked.

"You saw all the kids at the house—so you can guess how many times."

14

Dudley was obsessed with the thought that a stranger, most likely a derelict, had been buried beside his parents in Houston. How dare they? A tramp. A bum. In the family plot reserved for him—Elliot Robard Brodie—and his dear parents. It was profane. A sacrilege. When he thought too long about it, his jaw ached from the clenching of his teeth and his hands squeezed into such tight fists that he broke the skin with his long fingernails and blood trickled into his palms.

It was the middle of the night and he was sitting up in his bed in the darkness, unable to sleep. When the anger had passed, his shoulders slumped and his head bowed. He was motionless for a few seconds and then switched on the bedside lamp and wearily pulled one of the newspaper articles from the small drawer. This was his other obsession: Joan Gantry, the last of Elliot Brodie's three wives. He had scissored out the photographs of the other wives and lovers and discarded them. Night after night his emotions took the same roller coaster ride, from longing and regret to sadness and anger, as he dissected their relationship in his mind.

. . .

Elliot Brodie had pursued Joan Gantry relentlessly until, in 1961, she agreed to marry him. He had just sold off his largest oil company for more than half a billion dollars in cash and was considered the richest man in America. The reclusiveness of the wealthy, handsome Brodie created an aura of mystery; his marriage to the beautiful young actress caught the public's imagination. What the public didn't know was that, despite the marriage, he was already well on his way to complete personal isolation. He and his new wife moved into separate bungalows in an exclusive hotel in Beverly Hills. They didn't make love after their first year together and Joan Gantry was not allowed to see her husband except by appointment. She was alarmed at Brodie's deteriorating physical and mental health. His germ fetish was consuming him. His windows were sealed with masking tape and heavy drapes kept out light during the day. He kept an oxygen tank in his bedroom for medical emergencies, but he sometimes turned it on to freshen the air in the room.

In 1964 Joan Gantry stormed into his bungalow and ranted at the Christians until they put her husband on the telephone. He relented and allowed her into his bedroom.

"I can't take it anymore," she said angrily, tears in her eyes. "You've locked yourself in here like an animal. You're killing yourself. This room is fetid. You've got to have light and fresh air."

"No, no," he screamed, pulling himself from his bed as she moved toward the windows and pulled back the drapes. He was naked. He cringed as sunlight splashed into the room for the first time in three years. In a voice cracking with fear and anger, he called to his aides.

"Get her the fuck out of here, Marvin," he shrieked, as she began tearing masking tape from one of the exposed windows.

Marvin Snow, with two other Christians at his heels, ran into the room.

"Please, Miss Gantry. Please leave."

Brodie had retreated to his bed and lay cowering under a sheet. Joan Gantry ran from the room in tears, slamming the door behind her. Their marriage lasted another seven years on paper, and although she did not see her husband again, he telephoned her several times daily and kept her under surveillance. In the summer of 1966, he told her he was taking her advice and seeking a full medical assessment at a Boston hospital. He traveled across the country in two specially refurbished Pullman cars, one for him and one for the Christians. He left the hospital after one day and holed up for the next four months. From there he headed for Las Vegas, where he began to invest millions in casinos and real estate.

Elliot Brodie had decided Nevada would become his private kingdom. He took over an entire floor of the Roman Palace Casino and Hotel. Shortly after his arrival he purchased a seven-hundred-thousand-dollar mansion and a four-hundred-acre ranch for his wife. For months he called her daily, begging her to move to the new house. She said she would, but only if he agreed to move in first. Joan Gantry knew Brodie was beyond making such a compromise.

His madness, manifested by his fear of germs, was devouring him. He had developed a ritual of "purification" for his aides: Whenever they entered his room they were required to wear surgical masks and sterilized white cotton gloves, which they donned after washing their hands four times with a disinfectant. Anything delivered to Brodie had to be wrapped in several layers of tissues to protect him from contamination. Paradoxically, the Christians were not allowed to clean his bedroom—the floor of which was covered with dust, used tissues, and discarded memos.

Brodie was usually naked and spent most of the time lying in bed or sitting in a leather chaise longue. On a small table beside the chair sat a movie projector. Four television sets and a movie screen were lined up along one wall, facing the bed and chair. He used the televisions to watch movies and to keep up with world and local news. With the movie projector he watched old movies over and over again. Brodie suffered from chronic constipation and he sometimes spent hours at a time on the toilet in the bathroom adjoining his bedroom. It defied logic that such a pathetic figure, living in his own filth, had the power and money to manipulate politicians at every level and orchestrate multimillion-dollar business deals—but nevertheless, he did.

The long-range marriage to an eccentric husband she never saw, but who tried to control her every move by telephone and a cadre of spies, became too much for Joan Gantry. Over Brodie's pleadings, she moved out of the Hollywood bungalow he had provided for her and began seeing Calvin Ritchie III. In 1971 she filed for divorce.

Dudley stared at Joan Gantry's photograph with growing anger. Beneath was an abbreviated account of her marriage to Brodie, their divorce, and her remarriage to Calvin Ritchie III. "I felt sorry and sad when I learned of Elliot Brodie's death," she was quoted as saying. The old man had stared at the picture and read the article a hundred times. Always his reaction was the same: the sadness and guilt over his self-imposed isolation which had kept them apart, followed by outrage over her refusal to move to the Las Vegas ranch. More than that, he hated the thought that she had rejected him and chosen someone else. She didn't understand.

No one understood. You must protect yourself from the germs—the viruses, the bacteria. They were everywhere, especially here. He had to get out of this place before it killed him. They were forcing him to breathe contaminated air and associate with sick people. It was that bitch, the director, and her lackey head nurse.

15

A thin blanket of snow fell overnight, and on Sunday morning Vince and Ellen rented ice skates at Rockefeller Center's sunken outdoor rink. A giant spruce tree studded with lights dominated the rink and the street above. Ellen, who had been on skates only twice before, spent most of her time clinging to the low walls of the rink while more accomplished skaters glided by. In Vince's mind, he was the great Andy Bathgate, stick-handling smoothly through opposing players on his way toward the opposition's net. In reality, he was barely able to keep his balance, skating almost on his ankles, arms flailing wildly to keep from falling. In the center of the rink, oblivious to her fellow skaters, and wearing more mascara and rouge than a brothel madame, a well-past-her-prime figure skater, in a flesh-colored body stocking and a short pink skirt, entertained the crowd with shaky pirouettes.

Vince and Ellen returned to the Waldorf and took a taxi to Central Park, where they had lunch in the glassed-in Crystal Room at the Tavern on the Green Restaurant—

so called because it was once an enclosure for two hundred sheep and their shepherd. With the help of a snow-making machine, the restaurant's outdoor terrace garden had been transformed into a winter wonderland.

In the afternoon they took a long walk through Greenwich Village, SoHo, and Little Italy. In the evening they were back uptown at Il Vagabondo, a boisterous neighborhood Italian restaurant on East 62nd Street. The place didn't accept reservations and Vince and Ellen had to push their way through patrons, packed into a long, narrow bar, to check their coats and list their names for a table.

"This is my favorite place," said Vince, as they made their way to the bar.

"Is it always this crowded?" asked Ellen.

"It's the weekend. This isn't that bad. I've seen it a lot worse."

The manager walked by and greeted Vince with a broad smile. A short, spirited conversation in Italian followed. Ellen heard the word *bocce.*

"What was that all about?" she asked.

"Come with me for a minute. There's something I want you to see." At the rear of the restaurant was an enclosed indoor dirt-floor bocce court. Two couples were engaged in a match.

"This is bocce," said Vince.

"I can't believe it, right in the restaurant."

"Yeah, some people play while they're waiting to eat."

They went back to the bar and had a drink while they waited for their table. Once seated, they ordered a bottle of Chianti and studied the menu. "Everything is delicious," declared Vince. They agreed on a garden salad with house dressing and ravioli as their main course. When the wine was poured, Ellen touched her glass to his.

"I'm glad we came to someplace casual and homey like this. I'm completely satiated. It's been so great, but I don't think I could absorb anything more at this point."

"Do you think we did too much?"

"No . . . no. There's been so many good things, I just want to sit back and savor them one at a time."

"I'm glad you're enjoying it," he said, taking her hand in his. "It's going to seem very strange, not having you around after tomorrow morning. I'm certainly not looking forward to returning to work."

"I don't see how I can feel the Christmas spirit in California after all of this. But I'll be thinking of you with your family on Christmas morning."

Vince excused himself and went to the washroom. When he returned there were two wrapped gifts beside his plate.

"What's all this?"

"The smaller one is for Christmas. You can open the other one now. It's for your birthday."

"How did you know about that?"

"Your mother told me."

The birthday present was a copy of E. L. Doctorow's novel *Ragtime*. The other gift Vince promised not to open until Christmas.

When their plates were cleared away, Vince said something in Italian to the waiter. Again, Ellen heard the word *bocce*.

"Did you ask him if we can play a game of bocce?"

"No," he said with a laugh. "I ordered dessert, the house specialty."

The waiter returned with two dessert plates and a few minutes later placed a large chocolate ball at the center of the table. Ellen moaned.

"That's the specialty," said Vince. "One bocce ball."

The waiter halved it for them. Beneath the chocolate coating was Italian ice cream with a cherry in the center.

They were lying on their backs after making love, Ellen's head resting in the crook of Vince's arm.

"I'm crazy about you," he said. "I love touching you. I love making love with you. I love listening to you talk. I love looking at you. I love everything about you."

"Wow, what brought that on?"

"I dunno. I guess because you're leaving in the morning and I'm going to miss you."

"I'm going to miss you, too."

"I hope you don't mind, but there's something I want to ask you."

"Of course not, silly."

"I've never felt like this about anybody before, and I want to see a lot more of you, but I just wonder . . . does my age bother you at all?"

"No." She laughed. "It's just your rotten personality that I can't stand."

"I'm serious."

"I've thought about it. I doesn't bother me. You've probably got two or three good years left in you."

Vince shook his head in disgust. "You rat. I figure at least twenty."

"No, your age doesn't bother me. All right?"

"A sixteen-year difference. I guess it's not so bad."

"It would be a lot worse if you were twenty-eight and I were twelve. Your friends might arrest you."

On Monday morning Vince picked up a set of photographs from a roll of film he'd given to the hotel concierge to develop. The photos chronicled Ellen's visit and she was in most of them. He arranged them in a mini-album and had them gift-wrapped along with a book of Ruth Orkin's photographic studies of New York. He handed Ellen the gifts from his briefcase as they said their goodbyes at La Guardia.

"Vince, the hotel and everything else was your Christmas present to me," she complained.

"Listen, I realized the other day, I can't remember how long it's been since I gave a Christmas present to a woman, other than my relatives. And it will give you a reason to think of me at Christmas too."

"I don't need a gift to help me think of you."

They kissed and he watched her walk through security. Once through, she looked back and he waved. He watched her until she was out of sight.

16

After work, Vince Oliverio and Alfie Morrow went to P. J. Reynold's Tavern at East 20th Street and 2nd Avenue. It was a hangout for cops from the Police Academy just up the street. They watched the assortment of colorful fish swimming in a large glass tank behind the bar while the bartender poured draft beers. The walls of the narrow room were covered with framed photographs of sports figures, mostly boxers and baseball players, including Babe Ruth and Joe DiMaggio. Oliverio nodded to a detective sitting at the bar as he and Morrow made their way to the rear of the tavern. They sat at a table near the fireplace.

"We've got to set out some rules," said Oliverio. "And we need a plan of action."

"I'm for that."

"Okay, the first thing is, our file is growing and I don't want it in the office. I'm labeling it DUDLEY, since that's the name they've given him and it keeps Brodie's name out of it if somebody should happen to see it.

Sadowski is getting too curious and there's too much traffic in there.''

"So I guess we're agreed that we're not going to the department with this at all?'' asked Morrow.

"You know what happens if we do. It's so big they'll panic and call in the feds and that will be the end of it for us. The fucking feds will take all the credit. I don't need that aggravation at this stage of my career. And you're just starting out. If we should happen to prove that the old man, Dudley, really is Elliot Brodie . . . well, you can just imagine. You'll be famous, Alfie, movies and the whole bit. It'll be bigger than the French Connection. But that's all a big if. The point is, if we turn over what we've got now, we'll be squeezed out of the picture. Do you agree?''

"Right.''

"Now, I'll keep the file at home in my den—unless we're doing something with it, when it will be here in my black briefcase. I've got an old comparator in the basement at my place. It's not fancy, but it works. I think from now on we do as little as possible on it from the office. If we have to look at prints or whatever, we'll do it at my place. You're not that far away. And when we discuss it at work, or here, if anybody's within earshot, the operative word is *Dudley*. Never any reference to Brodie.''

"You don't think we're overdoing it?''

"Listen, I keep telling you. We don't know what we're into here. This was one rich, powerful fucker. He owned a lot of politicians at every level. He was up to his ass in Watergate. It's still coming out. He had an army of private dicks. We don't have any idea who the players are in this and until we do, you're goddamn right we're going to overdo it.''

"Okay, Vince. I was just playing devil's advocate.''

"My cover story with Houston and with the FBI in Washington seems solid. They think I'm an eccentric and I'll play that for all it's worth. Plus I've done a lot of favors for Joe Marsh and the bureau in Washington, so I'm not worried about him. I was worried about Houston, but they've been very good to us.''

"So what's our next move?"

"Well, Houston tells us today that the coroner who conducted the inquest on Brodie is—"

"Dudley," interrupted Morrow.

"Smart-ass. Okay, you're right . . . Dudley. Anyway, they tell us the coroner is dead—a suicide. So we can never talk to him. But why would a sixty-two-year-old guy, with a reputation like his, off himself?"

"They think it might have been his health. A fatal disease or something. The guy wasn't too clear on that."

"Well, I think something stinks and you should pursue it. The locals should be able to help you with that. The guy was high profile in his own right. You don't have to mention Bro—Dudley. And I'll check with my guy about the photos. When I called Houston to thank him last month he said he was glad to help with my collection. I told him I was thinking of donating it to a museum and I'm looking for all the background material I can lay my hands on. I'll suggest I return the two Polaroids he sent and ask him to send me one with the scars visible. I'll also call Joe Marsh in Washington and ask him about the agent . . . what's his name?

"Charles Bowman."

"I'll ask if he can put me in touch with him so I can get a firsthand account of his experience with Brodie and his entourage in Houston—"

"You mean *Dudley* and his entourage."

Oliverio shook his head in disgust. "I won't fuck it up again," he vowed. "If we can talk to Bowman, it may shed some light on this."

"So when we're dealing with Dudley, we meet here?"

"Yeah, as long as it isn't a zoo. You know how it can get in here. We'll play it by ear."

Four days later, they popped their heads into P. J. Reynold's after work and it was a zoo. Cops stood three-deep at the bar. Several yelled to Oliverio and Morrow to come in for a drink.

"We're outa here," said Oliverio, pulling Morrow back by the shoulder and closing the door. They walked over to 3rd Avenue and up a block to 21st Street, then walked west to the Gramercy Park Hotel. The policemen found a window table in the piano bar. "So tell me the big news," said Morrow anxiously.

"You tell me what you found out about the coroner first."

"Okay. As I said, it was an apparent suicide—an overdose while his wife was away for the weekend. But she doesn't believe he killed himself. He did have a bowel tumor, but it wasn't malignant. She told the investigating officers that he wasn't morose; on the contrary, he was excited about a trip to the South Pacific they were planning. There was no evidence of an intruder, but get this, there were no prints on the pill bottle and they found him on the kitchen floor."

"Where were the pills?"

"In the bathroom. His wife said she'd never seen them before. They were in a plain bottle with no prescription or name."

"In my experience, when a guy O.D.'s with pills, he does it in bed, not in the kitchen."

"I agree, but they're calling it suicide. So what do you have?"

"Your hunch about the Polaroids was right. There's not a single shot with the scars visible. Whenever the palms are up, the sheet covers them. And guess who took the shots?" Morrow shrugged. "Bowman," said Oliverio.

"The FBI agent?"

"Right. But wait, this will blow your socks off. I asked Joe Marsh if he could put me in touch with Bowman and he said it wasn't possible because Bowman's dead. And that's only the half of it. They sent Bowman to take the prints because he knew Brodie—Dudley—from the old days. He's the same guy who took Brodie's prints in '48, a year after the plane crash. And get this. He volunteered to go to Houston before they even assigned anybody. He was right there, front and center, and the bureau thought it was a great idea."

"Jesus! And he's dead too? What the fuck happened to him?"

"Hit and run. Off the record, the bureau is convinced it's a homicide. He was hit as he stepped out of his car on a street in Washington. He was dragged eighty feet. The car was found abandoned—stolen, of course. He was fifty-eight. He could have retired a long time ago, but he'd decided to hang in until he was sixty. They put a lot of men on the investigation but haven't come up with a thing."

"When was he killed?"

"Last July, three months after he took the prints in Houston."

"So what do you think, that he was on Brodie's payroll?"

"It adds up. The dead guy isn't really Brodie—he prints him but brings back a set of Brodie's prints instead. And, officially, Brodie is dead."

"What about the coroner?" asked Morrow.

"Probably in on it too. It's too much of a coincidence that in three dozen photos you don't once see the scars."

"So to keep the secret safe, Brodie, or whoever, ices Bowman and the coroner?"

"Right. It's a great theory; now all we have to do is prove it. And with both suspects dead . . . "

"Where do we even begin?"

"We've got to check out how they lived. If Brodie was paying them, it should somehow show up in their assets, lifestyle, or whatever. I might be able to get some help from the IRS."

Morrow was silent for a moment.

"What's on your mind, Alfie?"

"The scars. If the old man in the nursing home is Elliot Brodie, what happened to the scars? Did they magically heal?"

"We just have to keep picking away at it and hope we come across something that will give us some answers."

They were preparing to leave when Oliverio changed his mind and ordered another drink.

"I almost forgot," he said. "I'm wondering if we

shouldn't fill in Ellen McKinnon and Martin Butler on this.''

''But I thought—''

''Let me finish before you get all hot and bothered.''

''You're the one who's hot and bothered, Vince.''

''Fuck you, Alfie. Dudley is our only real live link in this thing and we sure can't keep an eye on him from here. I saw him and I think he knows who he is and what's going on. We don't know if he's been double-crossed. But eventually something's got to give. He seems to be getting healthier and if he's who we think, he's not going to live that kind of a life if there are billions stashed away somewhere. When Ellen was in New York she kept asking me why I was so interested in a case involving a helpless old man so far away. She said she appreciated our interest but it was no big deal, since the state's paying his keep. If we let her know what was going on, she could inform us immediately if there are any changes in his status and I won't have to keep bullshitting her. But I could never tell her without telling Martin. The point is, I trust them both implicitly and I think they might be able to help us down the road if they know what's going on. So, what's your feeling?''

Morrow shrugged. ''I would never second guess you on something like this, Vince. And by telling them who we think he is, it might trigger something in their minds that could be helpful.''

''I'll kick it around some more, but basically, I think it's a good idea.''

17

The stooped figure, leaning heavily on the black cane, walked slowly across the lush lawn toward the woods. Ellen McKinnon and Corky watched his progress from the office window.

"He moves damn slowly, but I'll tell you, Corky, it amazes me that he's mobile at all. To think that a few months ago he was nothing more than a vegetable."

"It's just too bad he's such a sourpuss."

"God knows we've tried. I like our residents to feel at home. If we're one big family, he's definitely our black sheep."

"It's so sad. He hates everybody. It's not healthy the way he always sits alone."

"I know he understands us." Ellen sighed. "He's so . . . so bitter."

•   •   •

Gentle Care Nursing Home sat just below a steep ridge that stretched west beyond the main highway to Williamsport and to the east behind Cross River, Cogan Station, and Warrensville to the Tiadaghton State Forest, where the ridge reached its highest point at Stimets Knob. The ridge cradled the nursing home and the homes on the wooded lots adjacent to it, including Ellen McKinnon's and the Butlers'.

A driveway had been cut into the ridge at the west side of the nursing home. It led to a large paved visitors' parking lot above the home, screened from view by a dense hedge. Disabled or elderly visitors were allowed to park in front of the home and the staff had its own parking lot below the hill on the west side of the building.

Beyond the lawns on the east side, nature trails had been cut, winding through the woods at the base of the ridge. Cedar benches and small picnic tables dotted the trails. For the more energetic, one branch of the trail, with the aid of strategically placed cedar platforms and stairways, went to the top of the ridge where a raised platform provided a fine view of the surrounding countryside. Adventurous hikers could ignore the viewing platform and walk for miles in either direction along a former deer run on the top of the ridge.

Dudley glanced behind him. He was out of sight of the home and there was no one around. He straightened his shoulders, tucked the cane under his arm, and walked along the paved trail at a brisk pace. He'd been walking on his own for more than two weeks, extending his range each day. The first four days, accompanied by Corky, he shuffled a short distance into the woods and sat on one of the cedar benches. She left him alone after that, but each afternoon she anxiously watched the trail entrance until he returned.

The first three times Dudley climbed to the top of the ridge, his breathing was labored and he was forced to rest every few feet. But now the walk was effortless. Reaching the crest of the ridge, he glanced at the viewing platform but proceeded west along the dirt trail, well hidden from below.

Dudley checked his watch and, with his cane under his arm, set off along the trail. He covered half a mile in less than twenty minutes. The previous Saturday he had peered through the trees from the ridge down at the houses below. He'd seen a white and blue state police car in one driveway adjoining a house with a wide wooden rear deck. A propane barbecue stood covered in one corner. He'd noticed a grown-over path running from the trail on the ridge down toward that house. Four houses to the west, he'd recognized Ellen McKinnon's white Volkswagen Rabbit. On this day, he stopped on the ridge above her house. He checked his watch and moved a few feet off the trail. Pulling aside the branches of a dense evergreen, he squinted down at the house. He glanced at his watch again and headed back toward the nursing home.

At the bottom of the paved path below the ridge, Dudley positioned his cane in front of him and, with shoulders stooped, resumed his shuffling walk. Corky, staring out from the director's office, was relieved when she saw him emerge from the woods.

"There he is," she said. "Fifty-two minutes. I've told him if he stays out more than an hour I'll send somebody to look for him. He's been staying out longer and longer every day."

"Don't you worry," said Ellen. "He won't stay out beyond your deadline because he can't stand anyone near him."

18

Vince Oliverio could hear the excitement in Alfie Morrow's voice when his protégé called him at home on a Saturday morning.

"I've got to come and see you, Vince."

"Dudley?"

"Yes."

"Okay, come on over. I'm not going anywhere."

"And Vince . . ."

"Yeah?"

"Dust off your comparator. We're going to need it."

Morrow was at Oliverio's house in twenty minutes. They went straight to the den in the basement, where the fingerprint comparator was plugged in and ready to go.

"Okay, whaddya got?"

Morrow pulled a barstool up to the comparator and inserted a print card. The prints didn't mean a thing to Oliverio.

"So, who is it?" asked Oliverio. "It's nobody that I know."

"Oh, yes it is. They're mine."

"Well, what's your point?"

Morrow reached into his briefcase and inserted another card, magnified on the second screen. Deep sets of scars, similar in size and position to those on the Brodie print cards, cut across both palms and fingers.

"They're yours. How did you do it?"

"They look legit, don't they?"

"As good as Brodie's. How the fuck did you do it, Alfie?"

"Let's have a beer."

Oliverio opened two beers and they sat facing each other across the bar, Morrow relishing his discovery, Oliverio anxious for answers but doing his best to appear nonchalant.

"What was Brodie into in a big way in his prime?"

"Is this a fucking quiz, Alfie?"

"No, no. What was he into?"

"Aircraft manufacturing, oil drilling, flying, defense contracts, aerospace, gambling casinos . . ."

"You forgot one thing."

"Backroom politics?"

"No, that came later. The movies."

"Movies?"

"Yeah, movies. And who are the people who help put movies together? Producers, directors, actors, cameramen, sound engineers, editors, and, in many cases, special effects and makeup people."

Morrow retrieved his briefcase from beside the comparator and returned to the bar. He reached in and pulled out two purple strings of molded rubber.

"Here are my scars," he said, smiling broadly and passing them to Oliverio. "I went to a Manhattan special effects company and they made them up for me. They can stick them onto you and anyone who saw them would think they were real."

"That's good work, Alfie."

"I kept racking my brain, trying to figure out those fucking scars, and suddenly it hit me. This guy ran his own movie studio and had access to every type of gimmick going. It's the only possible explanation. A few years later, when things get too hot with the law and he wants to disappear, out come the exact same scars. He cements them to his hands, and presto, there are the prints, with age creases and all.

"What it means," Morrow continued, "is that Bowman was taken in by the scars and, if they were as good as these, I can understand why. Or else he was in on it. I read somewhere that it was after the plane crash that Brodie started to go a little funny. So he could have decided back then that someday he might want to disappear."

"Maybe he just snowed Bowman," said Oliverio. "He was being printed as part of routine security, not because he was a criminal. He nearly died in that crash. Let's say he calls the FBI and says, 'Look, the prints of mine you have on file aren't much good to you, I was scarred up pretty good in that plane crash. I plan to be doing a lot more business with the Pentagon, so maybe it would be wise if you had a new set."

Morrow nodded vigorously in agreement.

"So the bureau says, 'My, what a responsible corporate citizen we have here!' " continued Oliverio. "And they send one of their men out."

"Bowman."

"Right. And he's weak-kneed around all that power and money."

"A lot of people would kiss ass on main street at high noon for just a smell of that kind of money."

"You got that right," Oliverio said. "I think Brodie puts Bowman on the payroll right then and there, because you don't just walk in thirty years later and strike up a deal to switch prints with those of some poor dead anonymous fucker."

"I wonder if Brodie was actually on that plane with the dead guy?" asked Morrow.

"Too big a gamble. The feds could have seized it for half a dozen reasons. I think he was probably already in the country. And remember, it was Bowman who volunteered to go to Houston. I think it was a setup.

But I don't know if the coroner was part of it or not. When are you supposed to hear back about his money?"

"The IRS told me a few days," Morrow replied. "I'll call next week if I don't hear anything by Wednesday."

"I don't have all the dope on Bowman yet, but he did live in Georgetown in pretty fancy digs and that's a start. He had to be in on it. There's no other answer. I guess I don't have to tell you that you should be proud of yourself. Judging by your shit-eating grin, I'd say you've come to that conclusion on your own."

19

"Just half a worm, Vince," said Martin Butler. "Otherwise we'll run out before we catch enough for our dinner."

"I break it off once I get it on the hook."

"Don't bullshit me. You were going to use the whole worm. You can't seem to get it through your head—if there's a lot of overhang, they'll just eat away at it without touching the hook. A free lunch."

Butler smiled as he watched Oliverio force the hook through the squirming worm and pinch off most of the overhang between his thumb and index finger.

Their argument about how much worm to use had become a ritual over six years of Michigan fishing vacations.

"Just check the live-net, Martin," Oliverio said with a laugh. "That'll tell you who has the biggest and the most." He cast smoothly toward the rocky shore.

"Nice cast," said Butler. "You should get one in there if you don't get a snag."

It was their fourth day on the lake and the best fishing they'd ever had together. Their rented cabin was on an island at the quiet end of a clear lake near the town of Grayling. White birch trees along the shore of the island gave way to a mixed forest of maple, cedar, spruce, mountain ash, and tall hemlocks which rose around the cabin like a cathedral.

"There's a hit!" exclaimed Oliverio. "Get the net! It feels like a good one."

"Take it easy, now. Reel in slow and steady. Keep your rod tip up and don't give him any slack."

Butler quickly reeled in his own line and grabbed the net. The fish pulled the tip of Oliverio's ultralight rod sharply downward. Suddenly, his line began moving out from the boat.

"It is a good one," said Oliverio. "He's going to jump."

"Just keep reeling."

"Christ, he's big. Listen to the drag."

The reel's drag whined as the smallmouth bass spotted the net and with a surge ran straight out from the boat.

"There he goes!" said Butler.

The bass exploded high out of the water, body twisting and tail snapping in the sunlight. Unable to throw the hook, it plunged back deep below the surface.

"It's a good three to four pounds," said Oliverio.

"Just don't lose him. That's the rest of our dinner."

The fish jumped once more near the boat as Oliverio reeled in. It was tired from the struggle and Butler netted it cleanly. "You're actually getting the hang of this," he said.

The bass felt heavy and cool when Oliverio lifted it from the net and removed the hook. He tightened his grip, respecting the power for which smallmouth were famous. From beside the boat he lifted the wire mesh live-net halfway out of the water and added their latest catch.

"Let me see them," said Butler. Oliverio lifted the net, displaying half a dozen bass. "That last one has them all beat."

Over a fire in a sand pit a few feet from the shore

below the cabin, they cleaned and skinned the bass and pan-fried the filets. They ate boiled potatoes and slices of tomato and cucumber with the fish, which was cooked in butter with freshly ground pepper, paprika, and thin slices of lemon and Spanish onion. Then they loaded enough wood on the fire to keep it going while they went up to the cabin to wash the dishes.

Oliverio stirred the embers with a solid driftwood branch. Sparks rose, caught the light wind, and drifted over the water into the night. Butler filled his pipe from the worn leather black pouch he carried in his shirt pocket. Oliverio gazed at the stars.

"I think of her all the time, Martin."

"I know she's sweet on you. She told me as much. I knew you two would hit it off."

"I've never met anyone like her."

"How serious is it?"

"As serious as can be. For me, at least. I was worried about the age difference, but she put me at ease on that. Everything seems so damn right with her."

"So, are you planning to do anything about it?"

"Well, I'm sure as hell ready. But I don't know if she is."

"You won't know until you ask."

"You're a real Cupid, Martin."

Butler smiled.

"The way she's been talking about you, I think she'd be pretty receptive to some sort of commitment. You wouldn't have to get married."

"You mean live together. How could I expect her to give up her job?"

"She's damn bright. She could get a job anywhere. But what about you? You're eligible to retire. I could get you something with us with no problem."

"That would never work, Martin. I like getting away from New York once in a while, but it's in my blood. I could never leave. Besides, Ellen had a great time when she came to visit. She loved it."

"I know. I saw the pictures and that was all she talked about for weeks."

"She's invited me to stay with her a couple of days when I go back with you. I think I'm going to ask her if she wants to get engaged. If she accepts, I'll give her a ring when we drive to the Hamptons later in the summer. I know it seems awfully fast, but it just feels so right, so natural, when I'm with her. And it would sure save on telephone bills."

"I have a feeling she'll accept. When would you get married?"

"Whenever she wants to. The way she talks, I think she'd like to have children, so the sooner the better. Christ, I'm jumping way ahead of myself."

"You both like kids. You'd make a great father."

"Jesus, Martin, I'm old enough to be a grandfather."

"Don't knock grandfathers, Vince," Butler said with a laugh.

They sat a while longer, sipping scotch by the fire. There was no moon and the flickering light from the coal oil lantern in the cabin window became more intense as the night darkened. Butler checked the time on his pocket watch? "It's gettin' on near midnight," he said. "I think I'll call it a day. We should be up early if we're going to do a little trolling for pike." He stood up stiffly.

"Martin, before you go, there's something I've been wanting to tell you," Oliverio said.

Butler sat back down. "You haven't got Ellen pregnant, have you?"

"No, no. It has nothing to do with that."

"Well, what, then?"

"It's the old man at the nursing home. My partner and I have discovered some pretty startling things about him."

"You mean you found out who he is?"

"That's part of it. Before I go on, I want your word that what I have to say is absolutely confidential. I know I probably don't have to say that to you, but this is very

big. Our own department doesn't know a thing about
it.''

"You don't have to worry about me, Vince.''

"I know, I know. Martin, we're convinced that old
man is Elliot Brodie.''

"You son of a bitch!'' said Butler, laughing. "You're
just trying to get back at me because I whipped your ass
in cribbage.''

"No. I'm very serious.''

Butler could see he wasn't joking. The cop in him
surfaced, and he leaned forward, his face suddenly serious. "You mean the prints matched.''

"Not exactly.''

Oliverio related the whole story to Butler, who
shook his head in amazement. "I didn't want to tell
you,'' Oliverio said, "until we were sure. At first I
thought you were trying to put one over on me. Because there were no damn scars on the prints you sent
me, it drove us crazy trying to figure it out.''

"Ellen told me his condition has improved a lot and
he's a real pain in the ass. Doesn't talk and won't cooperate with anyone.''

"That's right. Did she tell you about the seizures he
has every morning?''

"Yeah.''

"Ellen is convinced he understands exactly what's
going on. He watches television and reads a lot, so I
think she's right.''

"Does she know about this?''

"No. I wanted to tell you first. I'm going to tell her
when we get back there, but we've got to keep it quiet
until something gives.''

"For Christ's sake, don't give it to the feds.''

"Don't worry, this is our baby. We're still checking
out the Houston coroner and Bowman, the FBI agent.
After that, all we can do is keep a close eye on him.
That's where you and Ellen come in. Any strangers coming around, any unusual calls, anything at all, we would
like to know.''

"She can put in a twenty-four-hour telephone moni-
toring system. It would be considered a normal security

measure and you wouldn't need a judge's order. A lot of hospitals use them."

"I'm sure we wouldn't have to worry at all about Elaine, but I think the fewer people who know, the better. Nobody in my family knows and my partner isn't telling his wife."

"Elaine and I have a deal. I never bring my work home—we both want it that way."

"I wouldn't tell Ellen, but it's important we have somebody on the premises who can keep an eye on him. She's pretty damn smart, too. Now that we've been seeing each other, she's been wondering why I'm so interested in the old man."

20

Dudley had béen sleeping fitfully for two hours when the names came crashing out of his subconscious. *Frank Clifton! Maria Brazao!* He fumbled frantically for the lamp, almost knocking it from the bedside table. He switched on the light and stared at his trembling hands. *No Scars! Impossible!* His mind went back to 1947. Elliot Brodie, test flying an experimental fighter plane that he had designed and his company had built. A propeller malfunctions. The plane loses power and crashes into a warehouse near Beverly Hills. Brodie is pulled unconscious from the burning wreckage. He survives but suffers burns to his chest and hands. The hands are also cut and he is left with permanent scars.

Dudley continued to rub his hands. The skin was smooth. He didn't understand. He felt the side of his head. No tumor. No tumor and no scars. Frank Clifton. Dr. Frank Clifton. How long had it been? More than two years since he'd last seen him. He said everything was all right with Maria. Beautiful Maria, with the mysterious dark dancing eyes. And the child. Where was the child?

Dudley's mind raced, his head pounded. There were so many questions. So much confusion. He looked again at his hands. No scars. He thought he must be insane. Perhaps he *was* dead. Perhaps he was in hell.

21

As was their custom on the drive back to Pennsylvania from Michigan, Oliverio and Butler stayed overnight at a motel outside Cleveland. They kept their fish iced down in a cooler and the cleaned fillets were white and firm when the fishermen arrived at Butler's home Sunday afternoon. Elaine Butler prepared asparagus and rice and they cooked the fish in tinfoil on the barbecue on the rear deck. Ellen McKinnon joined them for dinner. Afterward Vince went to her place and they shared a bath. It was then that he told her about Dudley. She found it difficult to believe that Dudley and Elliot Brodie were one and the same, but the more she thought about it, the more plausible it seemed.

"It's peculiar, you know," said Ellen. "I thought, fleetingly, of Elliot Brodie when Dudley first arrived. But I knew he was dead. I had read a while back that he was a weird recluse with long hair and nails, and that's just how Uncle Dudley was when he came to us. And he certainly has a fetish about germs and dust and keeping his distance from other people."

"If he's not amnesiac and does in fact know what's going on, then I expect he's going to want to contact the people who left him there, or somebody in his organization," said Vince. "That's why it's important that you keep close tabs on him. Only you and Martin know anything about it around here. What amazes me is that he's alive at all. We're not really sure how the equation works, but we believe Brodie himself was involved, initially at least. When he went into a coma or whatever it was, it must have shocked the hell out of whoever was working the deal with him. They obviously decided to carry on without him. We think they had the coroner and the FBI agent killed. But why not kill Brodie as well? That's the part that doesn't fit. Why go to all the trouble of finding a secluded place out here? Then again, we can't even begin to fathom the dollars that could be involved. We know Brodie was a billionaire, but who knows how much he may have secretly stashed away? My own feeling is, there are two camps involved in this and one of them is keeping Brodie under wraps as insurance."

"This is all too amazing for words."

"All I'd like you to do is to keep an eye on him. That's the most important thing. Martin will always be available if you see or hear anything at all suspicious. Just look for anything out of the ordinary. And, in the meantime, try to think back to anything unusual that might have happened since he arrived here, or even in the period immediately prior to his arrival."

"I won't tell Corky about this, of course, but she has a special interest in him. I've got her back as night supervisor. She checks on him regularly, so we'll have that covered. And during the day I'm always around."

After they made love in Ellen's bed later that night, Vince told her that he loved her so much and felt so close to her emotionally, physically, and spiritually that it actually hurt.

"I know it sounds corny," he said. "But it's true. It's like a deep aching. It's something I've never experienced before, but it feels so good."

Her hand lightly brushed the hair on his chest. She raised herself on one elbow and leaned in closer.

"Do you remember when you asked me whether your age bothered me?" she asked.

"Of course," he replied, alarm in his eyes.

"Well, there's something I want to ask you."

"Yeah?"

"Do you ever wonder if I compare you with Paul? You've never asked about him after I told you what happened."

"I just didn't think it was my place."

"Do you ever wonder?"

"I suppose, yes. The way you talked about him, I knew you loved him a lot and I'll admit I was envious— which, of course, I have no right to be. But I don't think I've ever thought of myself in any sort of a competition, if that's what you mean."

"When you and I first started going out and telephoning back and forth, I used to think about him a lot. I don't know why, but I did. But lately I haven't thought of him at all."

"What brought this on?"

"When you told me how you felt. It sounded like something he would say. And I suddenly realized I hadn't thought about him in a long time. You're so different from him. I guess you surprised me. I didn't expect to hear anything like that from you. He was the sensitive, gentle songwriter and you're supposed to be the tough, burly cop. But you're not like that at all. I felt the same way when I got to know Martin . . . I don't mean in a romantic sense. But neither of you fit the image that I had of the typical policeman."

"What did you think, that all cops get their jollies bashing heads under a bare light bulb to get a confession?"

"Something like that, I suppose. . . . I guess what I'm trying to say is that initially I *was* consciously comparing you and Paul. But now it doesn't matter. I know I'll never forget him, but somehow, it's no longer important. Do you understand?"

"I think so. When you told me about him, I could see it was still very painful for you. I thought a lot about it and it's my feeling that you were deeply hurt—*betrayed* is probably a better word—when he took his own life. You were both going through hell because of his suffering, but looking after him was something that you wanted to do because you loved him. Maybe when he killed himself you felt that he really didn't love you as much as you loved him."

Ellen was silent.

"I know I probably shouldn't be talking this way," said Vince.

She moved closer. "I love you," she whispered. He smiled and turned on his side to kiss her.

"Will you marry me?" she asked.

"I'm supposed to ask that," he said, smiling. "Have you been talking to Martin?"

"No. Have you?"

Vince blushed.

"The boys go fishing and brag about their conquests?"

"No, no. All I told him was that I was crazy about you and wanted to marry you."

"I love how easy it is to embarrass you," she said, smiling.

The four-hour drive back to New York went quickly for Vince, as he planned how he would give Ellen an engagement ring when they drove to the Hamptons in August, and how they would be married in the spring.

22

The investigations concerning FBI agent Bowman and the Houston coroner were inconclusive. The coroner lived lavishly; he was called a jet-setter by the local news media. But his wife was from a very wealthy oil family, which could account for their wealth and lifestyle. And in Bowman's case, it would take a team of accountants to determine if the European sports cars and the expensive Georgetown real estate were the result of illicit payoffs or legitimate, shrewd dealings in the stock market.

Oliverio decided to play a hunch. He telephoned Ellen McKinnon.

"This is a switch, calling me at work. You're going to end up in the poorhouse if you continue calling so often."

"This time it's business."

"That's a different story."

"We're drawing blanks with the coroner and the FBI agent, so I want you and Martin to try something. It's just a hunch, but it might work. I want you to put it to Dudley directly.''

Oliverio paused. ''What's wrong?'' asked Ellen McKinnon.

''Is the tape on?''

''Oh yes, I forgot. . . . There, I switched it off.''

''When Martin comes by, have him erase the first part of our conversation.''

''Okay. I love all this cloak-and-dagger stuff.''

''It's not as glamorous as you think. Anyway, I want you and Martin to tell Dudley you know he's Elliot Brodie. That should get to him. Let Martin do the talking. Authority figure and all that.''

''What do you think will happen?''

''Your guess is as good as mine. Let's hope he starts blabbering or makes some kind of a move.''

''This is exciting. I'll contact Martin right away.''

''Tell him to wear his uniform and hat; the more intimidation, the better. And be sure no one overhears you when you and Martin are in his room.''

''I love you, darling.'' She visualized Vince smiling.

''Did you get all that?''

''I got it.''

''By the way, I told my mother we're getting married.''

''You did!''

''Yeah. She started laughing and crying. She's already making preparations, but I told her she'd better consult with you before she does anything. She became indignant, and told me it was all right to plan her cooking. I said, 'Yeah, Ma, you can plan your cooking.' ''

It was a sunny late June afternoon when Ellen McKinnon and Martin Butler, wearing his gray state police uniform, entered Dudley's darkened room. The drapes were drawn and the only light in the room came from the small television which Dudley was watching from his bed. The director switched on the overhead light and turned off the television. Dudley, scowling as usual, glanced warily at Butler, who was wearing his trooper's hat and seemed to fill the room. The policeman closed the door behind him.

"Mister Dudley, this is Captain Butler of the Pennsylvania State Police," said Ellen. "When you first came to us in a coma, his men photographed and fingerprinted you. He has spent a lot of time trying to find out who you are and who left you here. Now he has something to say to you."

Butler moved from behind Ellen, closer to the bed.

"The director here tells me that you refuse to speak to anyone, but you can understand things real good," he said. "I'm going to get right to the point. They've given you the name Dudley, but you and I know that's not your real name, now, is it?"

Dudley's breathing quickened. There was panic in his eyes.

"You're a long way from your usual stomping grounds, now, aren't you?" continued Butler. "And it must be a bit embarrassing for you, living here off the state when you're worth all that money. You're Elliot Brodie, aren't you?"

The question seemed to startle and confuse Dudley. His eyes darted back and forth between the director and Butler.

"The deception with the phony scars didn't work. We know who you are. Fingerprints don't lie, even when you try to doctor them. Now, why don't you just tell us all about it? We think whoever it was who dumped you here might be responsible for the death of a coroner in Houston and an FBI agent in Washington."

Ellen removed a lined yellow legal pad and a pencil from the briefcase she was carrying. "If you insist on not talking," she said, placing the pad and pencil on the bed beside Dudley, "maybe you could write down anything you want to say."

Dudley eyed her coldly.

"I've been told you read the newspapers regularly around here," said Butler. "You must be able to see what they're doing to your financial empire. All the restructuring, the lawsuits, and the phony wills. Don't you care about that?''

It was as if Dudley had abruptly turned off. He clasped his hands in his lap and closed his eyes.

''I know you can hear me, Mr. Dudley,'' said the director. ''I'll leave the pad and pencil with you.''

Ellen telephoned Vince at home that night and gave him a verbatim account of their encounter with Dudley.

''So he definitely reacted?''

''For a moment I thought he was going to jump up and try to run right out of there. He seemed very upset, but just like that he closed his eyes and shut us out.''

''It's important that you keep a close eye on him from now on. He has to make some sort of move—send a letter, use the telephone, whatever.''

''Oh, before I forget. You told me to try to recall anything unusual since he arrived . . .''

''Or immediately before.''

''Well, two week's after Dudley arrived here we received an anonymous donation for twenty thousand dollars.''

''*What?* Twenty thousand dollars?''

''Now, hang on, it's not unusual for us to get large donations, but it is unusual that the donor wants to remain anonymous even to us.''

''And you have no idea where it came from?''

''It came in the form of a bank draft from a Philadelphia law firm. I called them after I talked to you today, but they refused to disclose much. They said the money came to them from an out-of-state law firm representing the donor. They told me they have no idea who the donor is and they refused to name the other law firm.''

''What's the name of the Philadelphia firm?''

''Gilmore and Coleman. It never crossed my mind that the donation might have something to do with Dudley.''

''It may not, but it's certainly worth looking into.''

The following afternoon, Oliverio and Alfie Morrow met in P. J. Reynold's. Oliverio brought him up to date and asked him to press the Philadelphia firm for the name of the out-of-state firm which had forwarded the money to the home.

23

JULY 1977

Corky was relieved when she saw the first light of dawn. Maybe, for once, it wouldn't happen. She'd been anxious since midnight, when she spotted the bouquet of red and white carnations beside the couch in the lobby. She figured they were delivered after Ellen Mc-Kinnon had left for the day. During her stint on the day shift, Corky had once seen the director intercept a hearse driver at the front door before he could enter the lobby with several bouquets of flowers. She thanked him and said she would look after them from there. He drove off and, when he was out of sight, she plucked out all of the red carnations from one of the bouquets, leaving only white ones. It wasn't the first time the director had intercepted and destroyed red carnations. But now they were in the building. Corky doubled her rounds through the night. None of the residents was in apparent difficulty and she began to breathe easier as dawn broke.

•　　　　　•　　　　　•

Dudley felt the comforting warmth of the sun on the back of his neck as he sat on the bench on the hill at the rear of the nursing home. His chin rested on his hands, clasped over the curved handle of his cane. He watched wistfully as the home emerged from the mist being gradually burned away by the sun. He tensed when he heard the whine of Ellen's Volkswagen as it climbed the hill to the parking lot. Her parking spot was a few yards from where he sat.

The director was startled to see Dudley sitting stiffly on the bench, gazing straight ahead. Rather ominous, she thought, amused. Like a mangy old buzzard.

"We're up rather early, aren't we, Uncle Dudley?" she asked cheerfully as she approached him and the long cement stairway leading down to the home's rear entrance. "That's pretty heavy going, getting all the way up here on your cane. We must be getting stronger." Dudley remained impassive.

"Sixty-five steps. You must be careful not to overdo it."

He turned away as she approached him.

"Come on, Uncle Dudley. It's a nice day . . . a beautiful day. Why not smile for a change? Is today the day you're going to talk about who you really are?"

Dudley stared straight ahead. Exasperated, Ellen shrugged and turned toward the stairs. She heard the sharp crack of Dudley's cane as it fell against the cement, but her back was to him and she caught only a glimpse, a black blur, as he lunged at her, hands open and arms outstretched. She was unable to sidestep the swift-moving form. Her head snapped violently from the force against her back. One white high-heeled shoe popped free of her foot and came to rest on its side on the third step from the top. There was no scream as her tumbling, spinning body thumped down the cement steps. Dudley watched calmly as the twisted form came to rest at the bottom of the stairs, blood flowing over her white suit. He retrieved his cane and walked down the stairs. A pool of blood was seeping outward around Ellen's head. Dudley leaned over to look at her face. She was breathing, but convulsively. Her eyes were glassy, unfocused, and blood was running from her mouth and ears. Dudley heard a raspy, gurgling sound as he walked casually toward the home.

As he neared the entrance he looked up to see a flat, pasty face, its whiteness accentuated by parallel slashes of heavy red lipstick and broad strokes of mascara, staring down from a third-floor window. The elderly woman seemed incapable of releasing the curtain she'd pulled aside to check the morning sky; it was as if she were paralyzed by Dudley's venomous glare. He kept his eyes on her until he disappeared into the building. He went to his room and lay fully clothed on his bed. It was twenty minutes before he heard the first screams and shouts. Ten minutes later, he heard the sirens. There was confusion and hysteria in the main lobby when he limped in a few minutes later. Solemn nurses and orderlies wept as two ambulance attendants wheeled Ellen McKinnon on a stretcher toward the front entrance. Blood had already seeped through the heavy towel wrapped around her head. Her stomach rose and fell in rapid spasms. Dr. Brooks rushed ahead of the stretcher to the ambulance. Dudley watched from a comfortable stuffed chair near the entrance.

There was the trace of a smile on Dudley's lips when he heard the ambulance pull away, siren shrieking. He had a clear view of the corridor leading to the elevators and he scanned the faces of each resident who passed him, paying particular attention to the women.

"She always parked there and came in through the rear entrance," said an orderly to a state trooper. "It was the same every day. The rest of us park in the front lot, but she always used the one up above. I . . . I just can't believe this has happened."

"Why didn't she park with the others?"

"Exercise. She did it for the exercise. She liked to keep fit. She felt the climb up the stairs was good for her, was healthy."

The police cordoned off the cement stairway while they took photographs and measurements. Tears streamed down Corky's cheeks as she ripped apart the bouquet of red and white carnations, stuffed them into a plastic garbage bag, and took it out to the trash bin. Her shift was over, but she decided to drive to the County Hospital to see if she could do anything to help her director.

Dudley remained in the lobby chair long after the ambulance departed. He watched intently as residents began streaming by him in small subdued groups on their way to breakfast. Three elderly women, two using canes, rounded the corner to the corridor from the elevators. Behind them a solitary figure, the woman from the third-floor window, peered around them. She was mildly senile, but she recognized Dudley and cowered behind the others. He limped after her into the dining room and kept her in view during breakfast. Later, he was watching from behind a plant in the third-floor lounge when she stepped from the elevator and walked down the hall to her room.

Within two hours of Martin Butler's telephone call, Vince, his face ashen, was at Newark International Airport, where a private charter jet waited to fly him to Williamsport.

"Get here as quickly as you can," Butler had told him, his voice cracking.

In the air, Vince, alone in the eight-passenger cabin, struggled to control his emotions. He found himself praying, begging, that Ellen not die. She had brought so much to his life. She was too good and too young. She must recover and live. She must have her children. It had been painful when his father died. But he'd been ill for a long time. His death had been expected. Vince had been able to deal with that loss. This was different. The thought of losing her was too overwhelming. At that moment he believed that if she died, he would not survive.

A police cruiser was waiting beside the runway. Vince hurried to the car. Butler, his face grim, turned on the siren and flashing lights as they sped off to the County Hospital. "She's still alive, Vince. She's on a life support system." There was nothing more to say.

With Butler leading the way, the men went directly to the Intensive Care Department at the hospital. Vince's stomach churned when he saw the intruding tubes and the intravenous. Ellen had not regained consciousness and she looked pale and fragile. He wanted to hold her and rock her in his arms. He walked to the bed and placed his hand over hers. After a few minutes, Butler approached.

"The doctor's in the next room, Vince. I asked him to have a word with you. He's a good friend of Ellen's. He's the doctor for Gentle Care." Vince followed him to the adjoining room and was introduced to Dr. Brooks.

"I'm afraid it looks very bad," said Brooks. "She lost a considerable amount of blood and she's in a coma."

"Is there any hope at all?"

The doctor looked at the floor. "It would take a miracle. And if she did stabilize and recover, we believe there is considerable brain damage."

Vince stayed at Ellen's bedside continuously from three in the afternoon until she died shortly after midnight. Corky and the Butlers were also in the room.

"It's just not fair," said Corky, tears streaming down her face as she ran from the room.

Vince sat slouched over with his head bowed. He didn't look up as Ellen's body was moved to a stretcher and wheeled from the room. His right fist clenched and he slammed it repeatedly into his knee. Behind him, Elaine Butler signaled to her husband with a nod of her head. Butler placed his hand on Vince's shoulder.

"Let's go home, Vince," he said wearily.

Long after the Butlers retired for the night, Vince sat on the rear deck in the darkness, staring at the stars. He hadn't cried since he was a boy of twelve, but he gave in to the silent sobs and the tears when they came. Reflecting a few weeks later on Ellen's death, he was convinced it was the tears which kept him from walking into the woods and shooting himself with his .38.

●   ●   ●

Corky was still weeping when she completed her two
A.M. rounds. Dudley waited for fifteen minutes after she
left the third floor. His slippered feet made no sound as
he made his way along the corridor and through the
heavy swinging doors where the senile residents were
housed. The evenly spaced, muted lights caused his
shadow to distort and overlap on the corridor walls like
a frenzied pagan dance. Stopping in front of Room 317,
his gloved hand slowly turned the knob and he entered,
quietly closing the door behind him. He could hear the
old woman snoring softly. She was silhouetted in the
moonlight. Dudley approached the bed and stared
down at her for a moment. Her head was on a pillow.
He reached over her and picked up a second pillow. His
body tensed when she shifted her position. Her breathing became regular again, but as he lowered the pillow
to her upturned face, her eyes opened. She tried to
scream, but it came out as barely audible mewing, stifled by the force of the pillow. Her body thrashed
soundlessly and her hands, twisted by arthritis, beat
wildly at his arms. He pushed harder and held the pillow against her face long after the thrashing ceased.

Low-lying gray clouds moved in before dawn. By noon
a light rain had turned to a steady downpour. Vince
Oliverio couldn't remember feeling so awful, so empty.
He wanted to stop thinking—about what would have
been, what should have been. Ellen's brother, Dean,
would arrive in the afternoon from California. He
stayed overnight at an airport hotel in Chicago. It was
there, at two A.M., that he learned his sister had died. He
would bring her home to be buried beside their parents.

Shortly after lunch, Butler's office called to tell him
an elderly resident had died in her sleep at the nursing
home.

"How elderly?" he asked.

"Eighty-four."

"What time did she die?"

"She seemed all right when the nurse checked during
the two o'clock rounds. There's usually another check

at four A.M., but it didn't happen last night. They were all pretty shook up over the director's death. They discovered she was dead during the six A.M. rounds.''

"All right. Get the particulars and contact the next of kin.''

Oliverio had to keep occupied. He asked Butler to drive him to the nursing home.

"I know your people checked out Ellen's death, but I'd like to have a look myself.''

"Of course, Vince. I went over the scene myself after they took her to the hospital. I know what you're thinking. We tell Brodie we know who he is and two weeks later Ellen is dead. That was the first thing that crossed my mind. But there was no sign of a struggle. No sign of anything. And no strange cars entered the grounds.''

"Where was our friend?''

"As far as we can tell, Dudley—or Brodie, or whoever the hell he is—was in his room.''

"What do you mean, as far as you can tell?''

"Well, no one actually saw him at the time of the accident. But Corky, the night supervisor who you met last night, saw him sleeping in his bed when she made her last rounds shortly after six A.M. and he was seen coming out of his room when my men and the ambulance arrived. Besides, he just barely gets around and that's a climb of sixty-five steps.''

They drove to the parking lot on the hill above Gentle Care. Oliverio suppressed the urge to vomit when he saw Ellen's car. They parked beside it and walked through the drizzle to the top of the stairway. The cop in Oliverio was taking over, relieving some of the pain.

"You can see it's pretty wide open up here,'' said Butler. "It's at least fifty yards to the woods back there, so she would have seen anyone coming at her. And there were no signs of a struggle at the top of the stairs.''

The cement steps were six feet wide, with a black steel railing running along the right side.

"Was she near the railing?'' asked Oliverio.

Butler could sense his friend's anguish, evident in the irritable tone of his question.

"Are you sure you want to go through this now, Vince?"

"I've got to do something, Martin. I have to know if Brodie is involved. If he is, then I signed Ellen's death warrant."

"I think your logic is backwards, Vince. Let's assume that the old man in there is Brodie and he knows we know who he is. The last thing in the world he would want is the police crawling all over around here."

Oliverio was silent for a moment. "I guess it's hard for me to accept that a healthy, vigorous young woman would die that way. I could see it if there were ice or even rain to make the surface slick, but yesterday it was sunny and dry. You said she was wearing high heels. Did one of the heels catch a step and break, or what?"

"I looked for that," said Butler, moving down to the third step. "Her right shoe landed on its side here. The left one stayed on. Neither shoe was structurally damaged. There were scuff marks on the left one from the fall, but the right one was clean."

Oliverio eyed the bench, a few feet back and to the left of the top step. He studied the wet pavement directly in front of the bench.

"My men went over this whole area with a fine-toothed comb," said Butler.

With the sleeve of his light raincoat, Oliverio wiped the water from a section of the bench and sat down. "Can you just stand at the top of the stairs with your back to me for a moment, Martin?"

Butler complied. Oliverio lunged toward him and grabbed him with one hand on his shoulder and the other on his chest.

"Two and half strides and no more than a second," he said.

"But that would probably mean the person sitting there would have known her," said Butler. "Ellen didn't have any enemies."

They descended the stairs, Oliverio in the lead, closely checking each step. Butler knew there was no use telling Oliverio that his men had been over the steps thoroughly.

"How many times did she strike her head?"

"Five, including the sidewalk at the bottom," said Butler. "The first contact was on the eighth step, right about where you're at."

Oliverio counted down eight steps and looked up to the top.

"That's a hell of a long way, Martin. Unless you were taking a run at it."

"She probably put her hands out when she stumbled and that protected her head initially. Her right wrist was broken."

"Or a violent shove from behind could have propelled her out that far."

Butler shrugged. "It was an accident, Vince," he said resolutely. Oliverio was thinking of the hit-and-run "accident" that killed agent Bowman and the suspicious suicide of the Houston coroner. They stopped at the bottom of the stairs. Oliverio had lost count of the number of murder and death scenes he'd attended over the years—but when he saw this bloodstain, he had to turn away. He looked up at the nursing home and the two windows above the rear entrance.

"Nobody saw anything?" he asked.

"Nope. The nursing staff helped us check with all the residents. I got a call just before we came out here. Nobody saw a thing. It was too early. Most everyone would have been asleep. It's only a skeleton staff on at night and their offices are at the front of the building."

"Can we go inside?"

"Sure," said Butler, checking his watch. "We should leave for the airport to pick up Ellen's brother in another hour or so."

At the entrance, Oliverio turned and looked back toward the stairs. They walked through the first-floor corridor to the main lobby. The atmosphere was subdued and residents in small clusters spoke in hushed tones. Butler was surprised to see Corky through the glass of the main office. There were dark circles under her eyes. She came out of the office when she saw them.

"You met Mary Cavanaugh last night at the hospital, Vince." Oliverio nodded. "I thought you came back here last night, Corky."

"Yes, I did. But after finding poor Mrs. Jasper dead, on top of everything else, I couldn't sleep when I went home this morning."

"You were here the night before, too, weren't you?" asked Oliverio.

"Yes. I'm the night supervisor. I work every night except Saturdays and Sundays."

"Martin, would you mind if I have a word with Mrs. Cavanaugh?"

"Corky," she said.

"With Corky?"

"No. Go ahead. I'm going to grab a coffee from the cafeteria. Do you want one?"

"No thanks, I'll wait 'til the airport."

Oliverio asked Corky if there was a quiet place to talk.

"There are small visitor's lounges on the second and third floors. They're usually empty."

They took the elevator to the second floor, where they had the lounge to themselves.

"I still can't believe that Ellen's dead," said Corky.

"She spoke very highly of you."

"She confided in me sometimes. She told me she would be leaving in a few months. I guess it was you she met in New York. She seemed awfully happy. She was the fairest, nicest person—the best administrator I ever worked for. And I've been around a long time. I just don't understand it—she used those stairs every day, for exercise. But I know what really did it."

"You know what?"

"It was those damned flowers."

"What flowers?"

"They bring them in from the church and the funeral parlor. Most of them are all right. But when they bring in red and white carnations together, somebody always dies. That's the first time two people died, though."

Oliverio remembered Ellen telling him that Corky was superstitious.

"The flowers were here when I came on shift Tuesday night. They must have come in after Ellen left for home because she never allows red and white carnations to come in here together. I thought for sure one of the patients would die. I never thought it would be her. I threw them in the trash yesterday morning. Too late by then, though."

"Captain Butler tells me that no one saw a thing?"

"We asked everybody. Most of the residents were asleep, but they couldn't see the back stairs anyhow. Most of their windows don't face that way and the ones that do have big trees blocking the view. Some of the kitchen staff were in, but their windows face the front, like our offices."

"What are those windows just above the rear entrance on the second and third floors?"

"Oh, I forgot about those. They're the only two. They're the rooms at the end of the halls on those floors."

"I saw curtains on the windows. Do residents live in them?"

"Yes, they do."

"And they didn't hear or see anything?"

"No. Mr. Domnus, on the second floor, is a deep sleeper. Most days we have trouble getting him down in time for the ten-thirty breakfast deadline."

"And on the third floor?"

"We didn't get a chance to ask her. That's Mrs. Jasper's room and she died herself last night. We would have tried to talk to her this morning. Poor soul, she was quite old and a bit senile—out of it half the time."

Oliverio straightened in his chair.

"You mean nobody talked to her?"

"No. Like I said, she died. I made my rounds at two A.M. and she was fine then. I always check to make sure they're breathing, especially when they're as old as she was. We were crying and talking about Ellen in the office, and I missed my four A.M. rounds. I don't usually do that. We're not required to make three rounds, but I always do. I found her dead when I went back at six A.M. Just stopped breathing and died in her sleep. I hope that's the way I go. Just fall asleep and never wake up."

"Can you show me her room?"

"Sure."

Once in the room, Oliverio went straight for the window and pulled aside the curtain. He had a clear view of the stairway and the end of the paved lot where Ellen's car was parked.

"Was Mrs. Jasper suffering from any serious illnesses other than her senility?"

"She had a lot of ailments. But you have to remember she was eighty-four. She had very bad arthritis and a touch of diabetes."

"What about in the past week or two?"

"She just went along from day to day, but they haven't had to rush her to the hospital in the past six or seven months, if that's what you mean."

Oliverio turned from the window.

"Dudley's room is on this floor, isn't it?" he asked.

"Yes, just down the hall. The state police still haven't found out who he is."

They returned to the second-floor lounge.

"Do you know for certain that Dudley was in his room at the time Ellen was injured?"

"I looked in on him about six-fifteen. He was asleep then. The accident happened about half an hour after that. There were sirens and a lot of confusion after they discovered Ellen lying out there. I saw him come down from the elevator with his cane. So the noise must have woke him up. He usually comes down for breakfast at exactly eight, but on Wednesday he was down about half an hour early. He just sat there."

"Where was he sitting?"

"In the main lobby over by the elevators. Everybody, including me, was running all over the place, but he just sat there. I used to tell Ellen he looks like a vulture. He went in for breakfast and was back in his room by nine. He's always back by then because of his seizures. Did Ellen tell you about that?"

"Yes," said Oliverio. "I was there for one of them."

She talked as if Ellen were still alive. Each time she mentioned her name Oliverio felt despair. For some reason, he suddenly thought of his mother, and how difficult it would be to tell her.

"Why are you asking all these questions about him? You don't think he was involved, do you?"

"What's your feeling about it?"

"I know he hated her. He hates everybody. But I saw him sleeping in bed. He gets around a bit, but he's very feeble. He could never make it all the way up those stairs and have the strength to attack a woman as strong as Ellen."

Oliverio thanked Corky for her help and they returned to the main lobby.

On the drive to the airport, Butler said a memorial service for Ellen at the Cross River town hall was being planned for the next day and a huge turnout was expected. Oliverio didn't respond. He was thinking about Mrs. Jasper.

"Will there be a postmortem on the old woman who died . . . Mrs. Jasper?"

"No. Dr. Brooks was called in and he signed the death certificate. He suggested there could be a postmortem because he couldn't pinpoint the cause of death. But the family refused. It was really up to them."

"But you could order one, right?"

"Only if there was a suspicion of foul play."

"I think you should have one."

"Why? Did you find something, Vince?"

"There are only two rooms that have a clear view of the stairway and hers was one of them." Butler looked over at him. "And she died before anyone had a chance to question her. We don't know if she saw anything at all. It could be just coincidence, but if she did see something she could have been killed because of it."

"If she did see something, she had all day Wednesday to tell someone about it."

"You said yourself she was old and sick and senile. Perhaps she was frightened or someone threatened her."

Butler thought for a moment. He didn't believe there was foul play, but his friend's theory wasn't unreasonable.

"All right, Vince, I'll contact the family and the pathologist when we get back."

•   •   •

The rain stopped in the early evening. After dinner, Ellen's brother, Dean McKinnon, and Oliverio sat on the deck of the Butlers' house.

"I've never seen Ellen as happy as she was when she came out to stay with us over Christmas," said McKinnon. "She told us all about New York and you, and she showed us the pictures you gave her at the airport. It doesn't seem possible that she's dead. . . ."

"I can't begin to tell you what she brought to my life," said Oliverio.

"She called me when you two decided to get married. She was so excited. We were planning to bring the kids out in September to stay with her and meet you."

"We planned to spend a week in the Hamptons just before that and I was going to drive back here with her."

"The kids don't know she's dead yet. They'll be devastated."

Elaine Butler brought out cold beers and she and Martin joined them.

"Vince, I just want you to know that you're welcome to visit us in California anytime," said McKinnon.

"Thanks," said Oliverio, knowing he never would. What he wanted most was to be alone. He had already decided he wouldn't go to California for the funeral.

In the morning, Dean McKinnon drove to the funeral home to see his sister's body before the coffin was closed and moved to the town hall for the memorial service. An executive from Gentle Care who had known Ellen when she was assistant director for the chain's home in San Francisco drove up from the airport in Harrisburg, arriving in time for the ten A.M. service. He and Dean McKinnon would fly out with the body at four in the afternoon.

Despite a light rain, it seemed the whole population of Cross River and the surrounding towns turned out for the memorial service. There were also civic leaders

and hospital executives from Williamsport in attendance. The respect, admiration, and love for Ellen was
evident in the outpouring of grief. Speaker after
speaker, including clergy from four denominations, eu-
logized her.

Several school buses had been used to transport most
of the residents and staff from Gentle Care to the service. Corky was one of those left behind. She knew that
Ellen usually sat through Dudley's morning seizures and
she decided to take on the task, allowing the duty nurse
to attend the service. She would drive over on her own
once his convulsions ceased. As she watched the familiar contraction and extension of his limbs, she was overcome by a sudden resentment.

"She tried so much to make things easier for you,"
she said, knowing he couldn't hear her. "And all she
ever got from you was your wicked glowering. And
now she's gone."

It was ten-fifteen when Dudley's muscles began to
relax. Corky wiped his forehead with a cool face cloth
and dried her hands. His eyes opened as she checked
her watch. "I should get there in time for most of it,"
she said, leaving the room without a backward glance.

Oliverio had mentally turned off the speeches. In his
mind he saw Ellen's warm smile, as he imagined the
two of them on the broad beach on the ocean near
Montauk on Long Island where he had once stayed. He
knew then that there would be no more tears but that
she would always be with him wherever he went. He
could have found an excuse to leave the service early,
but he was sitting near the front with the Butlers and
Dean McKinnon. And Martin Butler, in full uniform,
was to be the last speaker.

The hallway was silent when Dudley left his room. He
looked both ways and walked through the swinging
doors to the service elevator near Mrs. Jasper's room.
No one saw him leave the elevator or go out the rear

door of the building. He made his way into the woods and stayed a few feet inside the tree line until he reached the paved nature trails. With his cane under his arm, he followed his usual route to the top of the ridge, past the parking lot and the home. He followed the dirt trail until he was above the Butlers' house. He took a deep breath, and using his cane to push aside protruding branches, he worked his way down the overgrown path to the rear of the Butler property. He rested a moment and pulled on a pair of thin surgical gloves. He walked quickly across the lawn to the rear deck and climbed the exterior stairway. There were two doors to the house from the deck. One led to the kitchen and the other to a storage room and small workshop. Dudley peered through the kitchen window and tried the second door. It was unlocked. He leaned his cane against the house and entered. Standing on a rubber entrance mat, he closed the door behind him. He stepped around the barbecue, which Butler had brought in because of the persistent rain. Dudley looked around, his eyes adjusting to the darkness. He pulled aside the curtain of a small window. The room was filled with tools and machine parts. There was a gas lawn mower and an outboard motor against one wall. On the other, above a built-in work bench, there were two shelves filled with paint cans, cleaning fluid, and turpentine. On the floor beneath the bench were three red plastic five-gallon gasoline cans. He reached under and jiggled each can. Two of them were full, one half full. The propane barbecue stood in a corner by the door. He went to it and lifted the protective plastic cover. Placing his ear near the cooking surface, he turned the on knob until he heard a slight hiss. He used a wrench to open the valve on a spare propane tank on the floor beside the barbecue. He listened for a moment and tightened the valve slightly. Using a rag from a plastic pail, he wiped his wet footprints from the tile floor. He laid the rag on the floor, and stepping on it with one foot, he leaned up and pulled the curtains closed. He felt for the pail and replaced the rag. Standing on the mat, he opened the door and stepped out to the deck. He closed the door and retrieved his cane. The steady rain washed away his footprints as he left the deck and returned to the woods.

Martin Butler had tears in his eyes when he talked about the years he'd known Ellen McKinnon. Her kindness, compassion, and intelligence would never be forgotten, he told the crowd. Oliverio felt numb. The service had gone on for two hours and he was trying not to lose his composure. He tried to put himself in her brother's position, but that made him feel worse. He thought of all the bastards that he'd had to deal with on the streets of New York. Why were many of them still alive and she, in all her goodness, was dead?

After the service, a hearse carried Ellen McKinnon's body to the Williamsport airport. Her brother followed in a car with the Gentle Care executive from California.

After lunch Butler drove Oliverio to Williamsport in time for his three P.M. flight to New York. The gray sky and the drizzle deepened Vince's melancholy as he boarded his plane. He felt like he was in a dark cave and he would never get out.

The first explosion occurred at five A.M., and the second less than a minute later. Initially firemen could not determine whether the gas line servicing the Butler home had blown first, or if it was triggered by the explosion in his workshop. One witness said the blast sent a fireball two hundred feet into the air. It took several hours to put out the blaze, which continued to burn even after the gas company shut down the feeder line. The house was completely destroyed and the consensus was that Elaine and Martin Butler, whose bedroom was directly above the workshop, had died instantly.

2
robard

24

Robard pushed aside the sheet and comforter. Raising a hand to shield his aching eyes from the morning sun that streamed through the wide windows, he twisted his body and strained to reach the jar of codeine tablets on the bedside table. He grabbed a handful, counted out five, and dropped the excess back into the wide-mouthed jar. He washed down the tablets with flat soda from a glass on the floor beside him. Pushing himself to a sitting position, he swung his feet to the floor. He cursed the sun and his hangover as he went to the window and yanked the drapes closed. He stumbled back to the bed. The alcohol-induced throbbing in his head was tolerable; it was the other pain he dreaded.

It began, as always, with the twinge in his lower abdomen. As the pain intensified, he strained against the invisible vise forcing his body to a fetal position. It was a conflict he couldn't win. His soft moans became guttural cries as his eyelids flickered rapidly and he slipped into semiconsciousness. Then came the spasms: the knees and fists tight against his chest, and then the legs shooting out, rigid and fully extended, and the arms stiff at his sides. It was a drama played out daily and with it came the dreams he could never remember. Only fragments came back to him. Swimming frantically . . . deep underwater . . . suffocating. It was murky and he was disoriented. He couldn't see . . . couldn't see. Suddenly, the crimson snake knifing toward him . . . vile . . . putrid . . . deadly.

The duration of the seizures had lessened to twenty or thirty minutes, but they left him physically and emotionally spent, with a dull ache deep in his belly. He reached for his watch on the floor beside him. It was just after ten. He lay quietly for several minutes before getting out of bed. The room was empty except for the bed, a television set, and the small table. The drapes in the bedroom and the living room had cost him four thousand dollars, paid to the previous tenant.

In the bathroom, Robard splashed water on his face. Running his wet hands through his hair, he stared at the haggard face in the mirror. The alcohol and pills were taking their toll, but he was looking decidedly more youthful. He shaved, returned to the bedroom, and opened the sliding closet door. There were several dark suits on wooden hangers and shelves full of shirts, underwear, and socks, still in their cellophane wrappings. New ties, brown and navy, hung on a rack beside the suits. On the closet floor were fourteen pairs of shoes in boxes that had never been opened. He chose one of each item. Once dressed, he went into the spacious, carpeted living room which was devoid of furniture. Three empty vodka bottles sat on the fireplace mantel. The only light in the room came from a slit where the heavy drapes met. He tugged one aside and looked at the traffic fourteen floors below on Central Park West. Dropping the drapes, he went through the open French doors to the empty dining room and into the walnut-paneled den. It, too, was bare except for a couch on one side with a two-drawer end table and a floor lamp beside it.

Robard opened one of the drawers and removed a small cardboard box which he took to the kitchen. In addition to the five appliances that came with the apartment, there was a pine pedestal table and two matching chairs in the room. He sat at the table and opened the box. Inside were passbooks and withdrawal slips from twenty New York banks. He chose one book at random, flipped through it, returned it to the box, and picked another. It was from a branch of Chase Manhattan and showed a balance of thirty thousand dollars. He sorted through the withdrawal slips until he found one from the same branch. He printed in the name Robard Anthony Bryce, made the amount out for seven thousand dollars, signed it, and slipped it into his inner suit pocket with the passbook. From the closet in the front foyer he put on a dark blue cashmere overcoat and left the apartment.

"It's nippy out there," said the cheerful doorman in the front lobby. "Do you want me to call you a taxi?"

"No thanks," said Robard, pulling on a pair of black leather gloves and flipping up his overcoat collar. He left the building and walked several blocks south on Central Park West. He hailed a taxi in front of the Mayflower Hotel, near Columbus Circle.

At the bank in midtown Manhattan, the friendly teller was surprised when she saw from the passbook that the account hadn't had an entry in more than three years.

"Your book hasn't been updated in a long time, Mr. Bryce," she said cheerfully.

"No it hasn't, I've been out of the country."

She took the passbook away from the counter to update it.

"That's pretty good," she said on her return. "You've got more than six thousand in interest."

Robard nodded.

"I'm sorry, Mr. Bryce, but I have to ask you for two pieces of identification."

Robard eyed her and reached for a leather billfold from his suit pocket. He produced a social security card and a New York driver's license with the name Robard Anthony Bryce.

"Thank you," she said. "I'll get this initialed and I'll be right back." She walked into one of several offices in a row behind the tellers' counter, returning moments later.

"Do you want all of the seven thousand in large bills?" she asked.

"All but two hundred. Give me that in twenties and tens. And I want twenty new one-dollar bills."

25

The deaths of Ellen and the Butlers within days of each other had been too much for Vince Oliverio. The day after he returned to New York from the Butlers' funeral, he told John Sadowski he wanted an extended leave. His mother had always wanted to return to Italy for a visit and now was the time. It was either that or a mental breakdown. Oliverio had lost his appetite and he had trouble sleeping more than two or three hours a night. Sadowski had never seen his friend so exhausted. He told him to take all the time he needed. Oliverio asked for three months.

Three days before he and his mother departed for Italy, Oliverio huddled in his basement den with Alfie Morrow.

"I'm sure Brodie had something to do with this," said Oliverio. "It can't be coincidence. Ellen and Martin confront Brodie. They tell him they know who he is, and now they're dead. I might as well have pulled the trigger myself."

"Goddammit, Vince, you can't look at it like that. I

don't see how he could have been involved, but even if he was, you can't blame yourself."

"Just think about it. Ellen used those stairs countless times and the day she supposedly fell, the weather was perfect. The steps were bone dry. It doesn't make sense. And what about Martin and Elaine? I talked to the fire inspector this morning, and he's convinced a propane leak caused both explosions. Martin was extremely careful about things like that. He would never be that careless. More important, the night before the memorial service for Ellen he told me he hadn't barbecued for a few days because the weather was shitty. And I know he didn't barbecue the day I left because it was still raining. So if there was a leak he would've noticed it long before it ever blew."

"Maybe it didn't begin to leak until the night of the explosion."

"I just can't accept that. Look at what we've got here. The day Ellen is injured on the stairs, Brodie is in his bed but no one actually sees him there. And the woman whose room looks out over the stairs, the one person who might have heard or seen something, she's found dead in her bed. By the way, that postmortem report might not be out until after I leave, so I want you to stay on it. I'll leave you the name of the officer who's handling it. And where was Brodie during the memorial service for Ellen? The place was jammed to overflowing, but he wasn't there. The nursing home was virtually empty. He would have had more than two hours to get to Martin's, tamper with the tanks, and get back without being seen."

"But I thought he barely gets around?"

"That's the impression, but who knows? Maybe he moves around better than he lets on. Or if he's not directly involved, he could be pulling somebody else's strings."

"I guess it's like you said: With the sort of money that could be involved here, anything is possible."

The telephone call from Mary Cavanaugh came late the next afternoon.

"It's Corky," she said to Oliverio. "I'm glad I got you before you left for Italy. The state police told me you were taking your mother there."

"Yes, I have to get away for a while."

"I can understand that. If I wasn't so old, I think I'd hightail it the hell out of here myself. I think this damn place is cursed."

"Why did you call?"

"Oh yes. Uncle Dudley is gone."

"Gone?"

"Disappeared. I think he wandered into the woods and has gotten lost or hurt out there, but the police think different. They had tracking dogs smell his clothes like they do. Well, the dogs went right into the woods and all the way up to the top of the ridge behind the home here. He could never have made it way up there."

"They lost the scent up there?"

"Oh no, they're claiming he went along that trail up there all the way out to the highway to Williamsport. I don't believe that for a damn second. I think the dogs got their scents mixed up or something. Young people have a hard enough time getting up to the top of that ridge, let alone walking all the way out to the highway."

"How far is it from the home?"

"Well, it would be just about the same as the road down below. Probably close to two miles, maybe more."

"So they've found no trace of him?"

"I raised hell and raised hell until they sent out a search party. They were out all day today. I was with them. We just came in now. That's when I thought I should call you. I went out to the place where I used to watch him sit on the bench just inside the woods. We started from there, but there was no sign of him. I still think he's out there somewhere, but it's too dark to look anymore today. I'll go back out in the morning when I'm off my shift. It's pretty warm out, even at night, so except for bugs and mosquitoes, he should be all right as long as he's not hurt."

Oliverio thanked Corky and called the Pennsylvania

State Police in Williamsport. A desk sergeant confirmed Corky's story.

"She was like a mangy alley cat," he said. "We put a search team out to get her off our backs, but we're a hundred percent sure he's long gone. We put two of our best tracking dogs on it separately and they both went right up the path to the ridge and right out to the highway. There was no hesitation. We ran the dogs for half a mile in each direction along the other side of the highway with negative results. So either somebody was waiting there for him or somebody gave him a ride."

"Did you find depressions in the ground from his cane?"

"Funny you ask that. We picked them up on the ground leading to the pavement where the path starts into the woods but there were no marks up along the top of the ridge where the path reverts to dirt."

"That was it?"

"No. Once the trail came out of the woods near the highway, they reappeared again."

"Which means he didn't really need a cane. He only used it when someone might see him."

"Something like that. I found it very peculiar. I mean, this guy apparently was all but dead when they found him there a few months ago, and he was in a wheelchair until only a few weeks ago."

"Are you doing any follow-up?" asked Oliverio.

"The local newspaper and radio stations are asking anyone who may have seen or picked up an old man along the road there to contact us. There's not a lot more we can do. And in the morning we've got two men going out to lead a search in the woods behind the nursing home to keep that damn nurse happy. But that will be it unless we get some help from the public."

Oliverio called Alfie Morrow to tell him about Dudley's disappearance.

"I was right about that fucker, Alfie. I know goddamn well my friends were murdered and he was involved. They tracked him all the way to the highway. If he was able to get up that hill and get all the way out there, he was capable of anything. I'm sure he's working with somebody."

"You mean the people who left him there?" asked Morrow.

"Has to be. We've got to find out who made that anonymous donation. That's the key. I'm working on it through the IRS. It might take some time, though. The only way we can get at their records is if Revenue orders an audit. My contact says he's prepared to do that. It's the only way we can get a list of their clients. I want you to check with the Pennsylvania State Police in Williamsport from time to time in case they come up with something. I told them you'd be calling. Make the calls from your home. I don't want anybody fucking this up. We've got to get that bastard one way or another."

Oliverio left Morrow a schedule of arrival and departure dates for the hotels he and his mother would be staying at in Rome, Florence, Venice, and Reggio di Calabria.

"If something major breaks, send a telegram," he said. "I'll cut short my trip if it's something I have to move on right away."

Oliverio and his mother spent a few weeks in Rome, then went on to Florence and then Venice, where they stayed in a grand old hotel on St. Mark's Square. From there they were to travel by train to Reggio di Calabria and spend their last seven weeks visiting relatives and old friends, some of whom Florence hadn't seen in more than half a century.

It was while they were in Venice that Alfie Morrow's telegram arrived. It stated: POSTMORTEM RESULTS STOP CAUSE OF DEATH ASPHYXIATION STOP FOUL PLAY NOT SUS-PECTED STOP ALFIE.

Oliverio decided to continue the trip as planned. His mother was excited as a child readying for a birthday party; he could not bear to let her down. Besides, the vacation had worked wonders for him. He'd finally accepted the reality of Ellen's death. He missed her terribly, but he began to take pleasure imagining how she would react to the sights, sounds, and tastes he was enjoying in Italy. Sometimes he could feel her presence. Meeting relatives and watching his mother with some of her girlhood friends was like a rebirth for Oliverio. When they visited his father's and mother's relatives in the hills beyond Reggio di Calabria, it gave life to the stories his father had told him about the way his grandparents lived before the turn of the century.

By the end of their seven weeks, however, Oliverio was beginning to miss New York. He felt rested and energized, with a renewed appreciation of the importance Italians place on family. Ellen McKinnon and Elaine and Martin Butler were part of his family and he was determined to get the man who destroyed them. It was more than a matter of personal honor or vengeance—much more.

He and his mother returned from Italy in the last week of October. The next day, a Saturday, Oliverio phoned Alfie Morrow and asked him to bring the autopsy report on Mrs. Jasper, the woman who had been found dead in her bed at Gentle Care.

Morrow arrived in his partner's basement den to find several pathology and forensic medicine textbooks on the bar with sheets of paper protruding from some of them as markers.

"Jesus, you look good, Vince. I've never seen you so tanned."

"You can't avoid the sun in Italy, and I get dark in no time."

Oliverio told him about his trip and Morrow brought him up to date on the happenings and politics around the office before turning the conversation to Mrs. Jasper.

"So you don't want to believe the autopsy findings, right, Vince?"

"I didn't say that, Alfie. I just want to read the report."

Morrow handed him the report from his briefcase. Oliverio sat back in his favorite barber's chair and read through it.

" 'Death due to asphyxiation resulting from accumulation of fluids in the bronchial tree,' " read Oliverio.

" 'No evidence of bruises or abrasions in the region of the mouth or nostrils.' " He put the report down beside him. "Nowhere does he come right out and say whether her death was accidental or a homicide, Alfie."

"Come on, Vince. He as much as rules out foul play in the last part you just read. 'No evidence of bruises or abrasions.' "

Oliverio pushed himself out of the chair, went to the bar, and poured a drink.

"Listen, smartass, you know goddamn well injuries aren't always visible when somebody gets smothered. Especially when the victim is feeble, like an infant or an old person, and especially when something soft is used—like a pillow."

"All right, all right," said Morrow raising his hands. "So it's possible she was smothered. But it's not definitive."

"It's definitive enough for me. She saw him push Ellen down those stairs and he fucking killed her for it. And he killed Martin and Elaine, too. I feel it in my gut."

26

In the debilitating heat of the Spanish afternoon, Robard sipped an iced lemonade. The cool drink and the over-head umbrella at his cafe table in Ibiza's town square provided an illusion of respite from the white-hot sun. He tilted his wicker-backed chair deeper into the umbrella's shadow when he spotted two Guardia Civil, in their green uniforms and black hats, approaching on the wide brick sidewalk across the square. He wondered how they tolerated the heat. The Guardia, who always traveled in pairs, stopped for a moment to light ciga-rettes. They appeared relaxed and uninterested, but Ro-bard wondered if they were looking him over. Most of the summer visitors to the island were students; wealth-ier tourists came during the "season," in winter. On the other hand, although the island's artistic community, most of them foreigners, thinned considerably in July and August, there were a few who never left. One was a writer, a man named Ian Creighton.

When the sun dropped to the horizon, Robard re-turned to his inconspicuous hotel, near Bar Serra, where he'd registered as Ronald Powell, the name on his doctored passport. Two additional passports were sewn into the lining of his suitcase. In his room he changed from his sweat-soaked white sports shirt to a black cotton pullover. Black trousers replaced the white slacks he'd worn during the day. He stared several seconds into the cracked mirror in the small bathroom. He saw the face of a man in his late forties, his dark hair combed forward to match his passport photograph. Now he slicked it down with hair oil and combed it back off his high forehead, parting it on the left. He went to his suitcase, lying open on the worn blue chenille bedspread. He searched beneath his clothes until he touched the cold metal of the small World War II–vintage German officers' pistol. He had purchased it in Madrid.

When it was dark, Robard left the hotel through the rear door and walked along the rutted dirt road leading away from the town and the harbor. Earlier in the day he'd inquired as to the whereabouts of the American writer Ian Creighton.

"Our happy jailbird writer," an English-speaking barman told him, "lives up there on the hill beyond the town. He's alone and doesn't seem too happy these days. He doesn't come out to party like he used to."

Robard was breathing heavily from the steep climb to the house. Despite the bright moon, no one saw him come up from the town. A light was on in a rear ground-floor room. When his breathing slowed to normal, he moved in the shadows to the front door. He found the door ajar and entered. Sounds of Mozart wafted through the house as he pulled the pistol from his hip pocket. He could hear the staccato clacking of a typewriter. He moved through the kitchen and dining room to a long hallway dimly lit from the room beyond. He could see Creighton typing at a large desk. Raising the pistol, Robard was within touching distance before the writer sensed his presence.

"What the hell!" he blurted, jumping to his feet.

"Keep very still," said Robard icily. Creighton, eyeing the pistol, clenched his fists.

"Who are you?"

"Take a good look. You should know me. Aren't you my biographer?"

"But . . ."

"Go on, tell me. Who am I?"

"It's obvious who you look like. Is this a gag?"

"This is no gag, I assure you."

"What, then? A robbery?"

"Why would I want to steal from my biographer? You did such a wonderful job with the book. I'm here to repay you."

"You sure as hell look like him. Who are you?"

"I *am* Elliot Brodie."

"Brodie is long dead and you're much too young. Did he have a son after all?"

"There is no son. I'm Elliot Brodie. I've come back to get bastards like you."

Creighton could see that the man before him, whoever he was, was deadly serious. He could kick the chair at him, but it would be too slow. The pistol was aimed at his chest, no more than three feet away. Creighton was fifty-four and overweight; he doubted he could move fast enough to overpower the slender intruder without being hit. He'd have to talk, try to humor him.

"Look, if you are Elliot Brodie incarnate, don't you think I've paid for my sins. I mean, I spent two years in jail and now I've lost my wife and family. I only wrote the book to find out if you were alive. I thought it would bring you out of hiding."

"Who was hiding?" growled Robard.

"Well, incommunicado, then."

"Don't bullshit me. You're a greedy shitass leech."

"I didn't get a thing but jail."

"You made your so-called reputation at my expense. You and a lot of others. I'll get all you fucking bloodsuckers."

"Come on, man, what do you want from me? I've done my time."

"I told you, I'm here to pay what I owe you."

Robard's left hand went to his trouser pocket and pulled out a fresh American dollar bill. He held it out to Creighton.

"I want you to eat this," he said.

"What?"

"You heard me. Eat it! Eat it or you're dead."

"But—"

"Now," demanded Robard, moving the pistol closer to Creighton's chest. Creighton tore off a piece of the bill and began chewing. "Turn around. I don't like to watch people when they eat." The writer turned slowly. He didn't see Robard snatch the pillow from the divan beside him.

"Is it good?"

Creighton nodded.

"Make sure you swallow it."

Creighton, shoulders slumped, nodded again.

"Here's the balance owing," hissed Robard, squeezing the trigger. The pillow was held tightly against the pistol's muzzle. Creighton heard the muffled shot and felt a searing pain in his chest before he fell heavily to the floor. Robard leaned down and fired a second shot into his temple. The sounds of Mozart could still be heard as he left the house.

27

The killing of Ian Creighton in Spain was given prominent coverage by the media around the world. For Vince Oliverio and Alfie Morrow, it was the first indication that Brodie might be on the move.

"Who else would give a shit about getting Ian Creighton?" Oliverio had asked.

"But all he got out of that phony biography was a couple of years on the inside for ripping off the publisher," responded Morrow. "He sure didn't get rich like he thought he would."

"No, but he did something that must have been the ultimate piss-off for Brodie. He forced him to go public. To talk to the media to prove he was alive. Brodie's ego just wouldn't allow him to let somebody make money off him."

"If he had Creighton killed, the money was no doubt part of it. But from all we've read about Brodie, he was probably more upset because there was a lot of truth to some of the things Creighton said about his weird habits."

"He didn't have to show his face, but that telephone call to the press in California from his Bahamas hideout must have made him furious. Just think, the fucker might have been planning to fake his death a lot sooner, but suddenly he has to prove he's really alive."

"So you're convinced he's behind Creighton's death?"

"I'd bet a year's pay on it. Robbery wasn't the motive. Nothing was taken. It was straight revenge. Why else would he be found with a half-chewed dollar bill stuck in his craw?"

For two months after Ian Creighton's death, Oliverio and Morrow spent all of their spare time reading everything they could about Elliot Brodie. In the library and bookstores, they found dozens of magazine articles and six books about the billionaire's life, including four that came out in the two years since his purported death. Morrow copied hundreds of clippings about Brodie from newspaper libraries.

"I think we're going to hear more from him," said Oliverio. "We've got to get into his mind, find out who he loved and who he hated."

"I don't think he loved anybody but himself."

It took until late summer for Internal Revenue to complete its investigation of Gilmore and Coleman, the Philadelphia law firm, for the 1976 fiscal year. And it wasn't until the end of October that Oliverio's IRS contact sent him a list of the firm's clients. From the list, they were able to determine that the anonymous donation to the nursing home came from the New York law firm of Torgov, Adleman and Associates. Morrow and Oliverio went to P. J. Reynold's after work to consider their next move over a couple of draft beers.

"In a way, we're not a hell of a lot further ahead than we were before," declared Oliverio. "We still have to find out the actual source of the donation. We couldn't squeeze the Philadelphia firm for information and, sure as hell, these New York guys will scream lawyer-client privilege too.''

"So we'll have to go through another IRS audit to get the information we need?''

"That's what it looks like.''

28

At seventy-four, Edith Hall was spry and alert. She'd managed to keep herself busy in the two years since Centra Corporation terminated her employment. She had been Elliot Brodie's trusted private secretary, following him from Houston, to Hollywood, to Las Vegas. The relationship continued by telephone long after he went into permanent seclusion. She was convinced reports of his transformation to a raving madman, and then a bearded senile recluse, were media sensationalism and malicious gossip. Despite the Christian Curtain, she had regular conversations with Brodie right up to four months before his death. She was dubious about how he died. She didn't trust the Christians and they resented her unique relationship with Brodie. She'd dedicated her life to him and his empire, despite a meager salary—particularly in the first years of her forty-year association with him. She was a shrewd businesswoman and as her raises became slightly more generous, she invested soundly. She was active in Republican party politics at both the state and federal level. She also did considerable charity work and meetings were often held in her spacious, antique-filled Las Vegas home.

The spinster was knitting a scarf for one of her niece's children when the doorbell rang. She glanced up at the grandfather clock ticking soothingly beside the bookcase filled with leather-bound classics. It was ten-thirty. She wondered who could be calling on her at such a late hour. Setting aside her knitting on the white leather divan, she went to the front foyer and switched on the closed-circuit security system. She paled when she saw the tall, slim figure on the small screen. She must be dreaming, she thought. She pressed the SPEAK button, her eyes glued to the monitor.

"M-Mr. Brodie?" she asked, not trusting her own voice.

"Yes, Edith, it's me."

She felt like she was in a trance as she unlatched the double-chain lock on the solid cedar door. "But . . ."

"I understand, Edith," said Robard, standing before her. "I know it's difficult to comprehend, but you can see it's really me. I'll explain everything." He walked past her into the living room. She closed the door and followed him. Everything seemed right. The face, angular. The hair, thinning and combed straight back. The height, about six feet three inches. The weight, one hundred and fifty pounds. The clothes, a dark brown, loose-fitting sports coat, with a white shirt open at the neck, and tan gabardine slacks. Even the shoes, brown wingtips. He didn't appear much older than when she'd last seen him in person. It was as if the clock had been turned back twenty-five years. She didn't understand this, but there was no doubt in her mind—he was Elliot Brodie. The speech pattern, the voice pitch, so very familiar. If anyone were capable of coming back, from the dead or wherever, it was Elliot Brodie. He sat on a chair beside the divan. She sat staring at him expectantly.

"You can see I'm not dead, Edith. You're the only one who knows."

Edith Hall was flattered that, as in the old days, Elliot

Brodie would confide in her. But there was a sharp edge to his voice that made her uneasy.

"I didn't believe any of those nasty stories the newspapers wrote about you . . . just didn't believe them."

"And Ian Creighton?"

"As far as I'm concerned, they put him in jail where he belonged. All those lies he told and now he's been murd . . . murdered." My God. She shuddered, realizing. *He* did it. He killed him or had him killed.

"Not murdered, Edith. Executed. Executed because he was a lying, cheating bloodsucker. He was eliminated for the crime of greed, committed at my expense. At the expense of my reputation."

Edith was terrified. The initial calm and warmth had gone from the eyes, which now seemed to pierce her.

"I've come back to make them all pay, Edith. All of them!" His voice was rising, caught up in itself. Edith thought he might be in some sort of demonic stupor. He rose to his feet. "My organization was full of bloodsuckers. All of them greedy. *Greedy! Greedy!* You hear me, Edith?"

"Yes, yes, Mr. Brodie," she whimpered. "I tried to warn you. I never trusted them. They took over. Tried to warn—"

He ignored her and continued his harangue.

"Every one of them will pay!"

"Yes, Mr. Brodie. You should try not to upset yourself so."

Robard was on his feet, pacing back and forth in front of her, gesticulating with his hands. "I was always a good employer. I paid well. But it was never enough. They had to have *more*. And more and more! Wanted to bleed me dry. To destroy me. Now it's my turn. I'll destroy *them*!"

Edith Hall was wringing her hands. Robard's eyes seemed to soften and he stopped speaking, abruptly. He looked inquisitively at her, as if wondering what she was doing there. He sat down, his eyes warm, almost kindly.

"I'm sorry to bore you with all this, Edith," he said calmly.

"Oh no, it's quite all right," she said, relief in her voice.

"The reason I've come is that I desperately need your help."

The old woman nodded apprehensively.

"Did you keep the keys for Operations?"

"Yes, of course. I kept my extra set like you told me to. I didn't trust them."

"And my personal files? You had the only key."

"I still have it. They never asked me for it. I think they missed them. There were so many other files and documents to go through after you . . . you died. As far as I know, they're still there."

"And the sealed package I had sent to you."

"From that doctor at your cancer clinic?"

"Yes Edith, it was very important."

"I did just what you told me to do on the phone. Nobody saw me put it in with your personal files. I kept it sealed, just as you instructed. Of course, they may have forced their way in by now. But they never once asked me for the key."

"Thank you, Edith. You've always been very loyal to me. What I need now are both sets of keys. There are some important files I don't want to fall into the wrong hands. I only hope they haven't been removed."

Edith paused, confused. Surely this *had* to be Elliot Brodie, but what had he done to look so young? Perhaps a face-lift and dyed hair.

"I need the keys *now,*" said Robard, his eyes cold again.

"Yes, of course. I'll get them. They're upstairs in my bedroom safe." She hurried across the room to the wide carpeted stairway. Robard studied the spacious room and its rich furnishings as he pulled on his gloves. Upstairs, Edith removed the keys from her safe and paused over her beside telephone. She lifted the receiver, hesitated a moment, and replaced it in its cradle. Pursing her lips, she left the room. Downstairs, Robard picked up the black iron poker from beside the massive stone fireplace.

"I've got the keys," said Edith, descending the stairs.

Robard stood facing her, the poker behind his back. He reached for the keys with his free hand.

"Thank you, Edith." The old woman moved back to the divan. Robard dropped the keys into the inside pocket of his navy blue suit jacket. He looked at her coldly. "You know, Edith, I've always liked and trusted you. There was a time when you knew more about my private and public business than anyone."

"Yes, and I appreciated your trust in me."

"And you were well paid? Your pension is generous?"

"Yes. You looked after me very well."

"Tell me, Edith, how did you come to own such a large, expensive home . . . and all these lovely antiques?"

"I . . . I . . ."

"Tell me, Edith! I certainly didn't pay you enough for all of this," he said, swinging the poker in a sweeping arc, like a teacher's pointer. The old woman was frozen with fear when she saw the poker.

"*Answer me, Edith! Where did it come from?*"

"I . . . please . . . it wasn't from you."

There was a whooshing sound and then a loud *whack* as Robard brought the poker down on the white leather cushion inches from the terrified woman. She flinched and shrunk against the arm of the divan.

"Please. Please, Mr. Brodie. Why are you doing this?"

"*Where did you get it, Edith? Where?*" He struck the divan a second time.

"Investments. I made . . . made investments, Mr. Brodie. Please don't hurt me . . . please."

A dull ache in Robard's stomach became a fireball. His eyes glazed. "*Lies! Lies! Fucking lies!*" The poker struck again.

"I never cheated you," cried the hysterical woman. "Never cheated. Never."

She screamed as she saw the poker begin a high-speed downward arc directly in line with her head. She raised her hands to shield herself but the poker tore though them, crushing her skull.

"Kill it! Kill the snake!"

The poker rhythmically battered the lifeless body.

"Get it off! Kill the snake! Kill!"

Splattered blood, radiating from the pulp that was once Edith Hall's head, contrasted sharply with the white leather of the divan. The poker fell to the floor. Robard found it curious that one dangling, bulging eye had popped out of its socket. He managed to find Edith Hall's mouth, into which he inserted a new, folded dollar bill. He calmly surveyed the room, avoiding the divan, and walked to the front door. There was a look of ecstasy, of sublime peace, about him.

It was well after midnight when Robard approached the rear gate to Centra Corporation's downtown Las Vegas headquarters. The key turned effortlessly in the padlock on the high, chain-link gate. He opened it wide enough to slip through, closing it after him. He replaced the lock but didn't snap it shut. No security guards were visible. He crossed the paved parking lot to the shadows of the building, his black trench coat billowing behind him in the light wind like a cape. A gloved hand cradled a .22 revolver in one pocket. In the other was a foot-long lead pipe and the key to the building's metal rear door. He turned the key in the lock and, using it as leverage, slowly pulled the door open. He peered inside. There was no one on the dimly lit stairway or the landing between the first and second floors. He removed the key, left the door unlocked, and entered the building. Taking the stairs two at a time, he went to the second floor and entered a long, dark corridor. The only light came from beneath the door of one of the offices halfway along the corridor. A country song was playing faintly. Removing the revolver from his pocket, he moved toward the light. He tried the knob, turning it slowly and opening the door a crack. Ten feet in front of him, a uniformed security guard sat with his back to the door. He was munching on a thick sandwich and reading a copy of the *National Enquirer* spread on the desk in front of him. The music came from a transistor radio on the desk beside an open brown bag. A fringe of gray hair was visible below the guard's cap. Transferring the revolver to his left hand, Robard pulled the lead pipe from his coat pocket and lunged, striking the guard on the back of the head. The guard's forehead struck the edge of the desk from the force of the blow. Pocketing the pipe and the pistol, Robard rummaged through the desk drawers until he found a roll of masking tape. He used most of the roll to gag the guard and pinion his chest, arms, and legs to the chair.

In a dusty, unused office two doors away, Robard, using two of the keys from Edith Hall, opened a walk-in safe and a five-drawer metal cabinet. He spent several minutes rifling through a sheaf of manila folders. He removed several of them from the cabinet, along with a heavily taped rectangular package, and left the building.

29

Alfie Morrow was waiting at the bar at P. J. Reynold's when Oliverio arrived with the thick white envelope. He looked anxious. The bar was crowded and noisy and the stools around Morrow were filled. Oliverio stood behind him and ordered a draft.

"It finally arrived," said Morrow.

"Yeah, but we gotta talk."

Morrow looked around.

"Not here," said Oliverio sullenly. "Let's finish our beer and go to the bar at the Gramercy Park."

"What's wrong, Vince?" asked Morrow when they went out to the street.

"I can't believe this. Those stupid fuckers at Revenue audited Torgov, Adleman for three years."

"So?"

"*So* . . . so '72 to '75!"

"You gotta be shittin' me!"

"No, it's true. They missed 1976. The rest of it means shit to us. My contact apologized all over the fucking place. He doesn't know how they managed to screw up. He told them to do one year, 1976. Instead they do three years and miss the one we need."

"So now what?"

"So now we're fucked."

It was midweek and the hotel bar was nearly empty when they arrived. Morrow could feel his partner's frustration and anger as they sat at a table.

"I'm really sorry about this, Vince," he said. "All that time waiting. . . . Do you think maybe we'll have to go public with this now? It might be the right thing to do."

"Don't fucking tell me what's the right thing to do."

"Christ, Vince, you don't have to take my head off. I just thought after the death of that woman and the dollar bill shoved into her mouth . . . You said yourself it had to be Brodie."

Oliverio grasped Morrow's arm and leaned toward him.

"Listen, I didn't mean to snap at you. But that fucker destroyed a part of my life and I want him. I'm trying not to let that affect my judgment. I've thought a lot about what our responsibilities are. If the feds get involved, what will it change? Not a fucking thing. Think about it. They've publicly made the connection between the murder in Spain and the murder in Vegas, and they're saying it's probably a disgruntled former Brodie employee. What we're saying is not a hell of a lot different than that. No prints have been found at either scene, so they're no further ahead than we are. Telling them what we know wouldn't contribute a single fucking thing. If I thought for a second that sharing what we know would help nail that bastard . . ."

"I'm sorry, Vince. I just wanted to be sure we're doing the right thing. The only thing I wonder about is if the feds would be able to squeeze the law firm for the name better than we could at this stage."

"I thought about that after I opened this piece of shit this afternoon. You can be sure the feds will be interviewing every former Brodie employee they can find. They could come up with something tomorrow, for all we know. And remember Interpol is in this thing now, too."

"Do you go back to your contact and ask him to get the audit right?"

"He says he can't go back to them again because the firm was absolutely clean. If they tried another audit so soon, the company would cry harassment."

"The only way would be to skip the audit and go right in with a court order and seize their records. But that can only happen if we come forward with what we've got. And you know what that would mean. It would no longer be our case and Sadowski would come down on us like a ton of bricks for not coming clean a long time ago. He knows something's up. I can tell by the looks he shoots me every once in a while. The shit would really hit the fan. It would be a lot worse for you than me. I'm on my way out. I know we're at a stage where you probably think my judgment is being fucked over by my feelings, and you may be right. I promise you I'm not thinking about the glory. And there could be a lot of it if we crack this. I admit, the publicity possibilities may have been a factor when we first got into this. But after Ellen and Martin and Elaine . . . I just want that fucker. Worse than I've wanted anybody, ever. Obviously, though, we can't gamble with other people's lives. But I think if the feds know what we've got it will get into the press and Brodie will go underground, maybe for good. We've got one more card to play and if it doesn't work, then I admit we'll have to share what we've got."

"What's the card, Vince?"

"Telephone records. We've got the IRS list of all the employees who ever worked in a Brodie-owned company. Now, if we can get the 1976 telephone record for Torgov, Adleman and Associates, we might find a name that appears on both lists."

"Jesus, Vince, that will take us forever. We'd have no problem getting the telephone records, but it means converting each number to a name and then looking for a match."

"It will take a hell of a lot of work—maybe weeks, maybe months. But I think it's worth a shot. We wouldn't need the records for all of '76. Right off the top, we can rule out August to December. We would start with July and work back. My bet would be June or early July."

"But if this fucker was being so secretive that he used two law firms to hide his identity, he could have used a front or he could have used a phony name. If he did that, we'd be looking in a haystack for a nonexistent needle."

"I still say it's better than sitting on our asses and letting the feds fuck it up."

Morrow sipped his beer. "Okay, Vince. But Anne's been chewing my ass off for not spending enough time at home. And we've got so much shit piled up at work . . ."

"I don't want you screwing up things at home, Alfie. Just give me one night every week or so. I can work on it most nights at my place. Who knows? We could get lucky."

30

It wasn't yet midnight as Robard walked aimlessly down a garish, sleazy street near Times Square. Although it was a warm night, he wore a trench coat, black cotton gloves and a silk scarf wrapped high around his throat. He paused in front of a porno movie theater advertising *Debbie Does Dallas* on its marquee. He read the promotional posters and walked back and forth several times before entering. He glared at the friendly usher who took his ticket and found a rear aisle seat in an empty row. The explicit sex on the screen was both repelling and riveting. Halfway through the movie he'd had enough. "Leaving already?" asked the usher. Robard brushed by, mumbling something about Jane Russell's tits and the Catholic Legion of Decency.

To passersby, Robard, with the determined set of his jaw, his wild eyes, and hands jammed deep into the pockets, was just another crazy—a man with a twisted mission that even he probably didn't understand. He crossed the street and entered a porno shop offering live peep shows for twenty-five cents. Overcoming the stench of sex, sweat, and industrial disinfectant, he approached a thin, swarthy man with black, greasy hair and a thin mustache. A coin dispenser, strapped over his rumpled black suit, held a soiled yellow tie in place. He gave Robard eight quarters in exchange for two dollar bills. Off the dingy entrance foyer was a narrow passage with a row of booths along each side. There were red and green lights above the doors on each booth, indicating whether or not they were occupied. Robard entered one with a flashing green light. He found himself in a room the size of a small closet. He deposited a quarter into a slot and a sliding metal window, at eye level, slowly rose, revealing three naked woman reclining on an elevated mini-stage covered with thin worn mattresses. One of the women sidled up to an open window and Robard saw a hand emerge with a five-dollar bill. She took the money and allowed the hand to stroke her breasts, buttocks, and vagina. Robard's window lowered after a few seconds. He deposited another quarter and, as the window rose, a tall redhead approached. He left the cubicle. Wandering to another row of booths, he heard a woman's voice yell out the number nine. He entered number fourteen. Its slot required fifty cents. He deposited two quarters and the metal window rose. A naked young blond woman, with acne scars, came into view. A Plexiglas shield separated them. In its center was a hole designed to accommodate rolled-up bills. The woman, seated on a chair, spread her legs and stared dreamily at Robard. She began touching herself.

"Pull it out, honey," she said softly. Robard stared at her blankly. "It's okay, honey. Don't be shy. Take it out and play with it. Let's see what you've got. Why don't you give me a decent tip and I'll really show you something." Robard fumbled for the door. As he was leaving, he bumped into a well-dressed, heavyset man with a briefcase, exiting the booth beside his. "Number twelve," a woman's voice called out. In his panic, Robard turned in the wrong direction. He retraced his steps and watched with revulsion as a male attendant, with a mop and pail, entered the booth where the plump man had been and swabbed the floor.

Robard returned to his apartment and removed his shoes in the hallway outside his door. Inside, he spread newspapers on the floor, stood on them, and removed all of his clothes, except for his gloves. He rolled the clothes into the newspapers and placed the bundle into a plastic garbage bag. He retrieved his shoes and shoved them into the bag along with the gloves. After showering, he dressed and pulled on a pair of surgical gloves. He tied the garbage bag and carried it out to the garbage room at the end of the hallway. He dropped the garbage and the surgical gloves down the chute.

31

John Sadowski was smiling expansively when his deputy entered his office.

"Sit down, Vince. I've got good news. We finally convinced headquarters to take your advice. They want to take a close look at this new laser system you've been pushing."

"Now that the FBI has had it for over a year," said Oliverio sarcastically.

"Whatever. The main thing is, it looks like a go. And that means you're going. They want somebody from our department to go up to Toronto for a firsthand look at how this thing operates. It was your suggestion, so you're the natural choice. You'll go for a couple of days and file a detailed report when you return."

"I already filed a report."

"So, give us another one after you've had a look at the thing. You leave next Wednesday. Your ticket and expense check will be ready by late tomorrow. In Toronto you'll meet a senior forensic analyst by the name of Dalrymple. He's a civilian with the Ontario Provincial Police, the OPP.''

"I know him. He's one of the guys who discovered this thing. I met him for a few minutes up in Ottawa in June at the IAI annual convention. He won the Dondero Award. Too bad you didn't make it up there. It was quite a bash this year."

"Didn't you say it was held in some great old hotel?"

"Yeah, the Chateau Laurier near the Canadian Parliament buildings. It reminded me of Europe."

Oliverio left the office feeling vindicated but disappointed that the NYPD hadn't moved to get a laser system before the FBI installed theirs. He'd fought for the system after reading about it in the *Journal of Forensic Science*. Dalrymple and two Xerox Canada researchers developed the system in 1976. It was no surprise when the IAI, the International Association for Identification, awarded Dalrymple its prestigious Dondero Award, established in 1958 after the death of John A. Dondero, who in his day was highly regarded for his contributions in the fields of identification, investigation, and scientific crime detection. Dalrymple was in elite company. The first winner of the award was J. Edgar Hoover and only nine others, all Americans, had won it in the twenty years of its existence.

Oliverio had told Sadowski the laser technology was the industrial revolution of fingerprinting. The key element of the discovery was that some prints, without the use of chemicals, would luminesce under a laser beam. It meant latent prints that were weeks, months, and even years old could be picked up. One drawback was that the system wasn't yet portable and couldn't be used at crime scenes. Materials to be checked for prints had to be taken to wherever the laser equipment was set up.

Other than his trip to Ottawa two months earlier, Oliverio had been to Canada only once before, in the late 1960s, for a fingerprint conference in Montreal. He'd never been to Toronto, but he'd heard positive reports about it. He arrived at Pearson International Airport shortly after four P.M. and took a taxi south into the city on Highway 427 and east on the Queen Elizabeth Way, along the shore of Lake Ontario, to the Gardiner Expressway. It was a warm, sunny day and the lake was dotted with sailboats. The taxi driver pointed out Ontario Place and Exhibition Stadium, the home field for the Toronto Blue Jays baseball team. His hotel, the Sheraton Centre, was across the street from a broad concrete square with a reflecting pool at its center.

At the check-in desk, there was a message for Oliverio to call Dalrymple at the OPP office. An hour later the two men met in the hotel lobby. Dalrymple was a stocky six-footer with short, light brown hair pushed to one side in the front. He wore glasses and, despite a neatly trimmed mustache, looked much younger than his thirty-four years. They went out the hotel's south exit across Richmond Street to Hy's Restaurant for dinner. The maître d', wearing a tuxedo, greeted Dalrymple by name in the book-lined foyer.

"Can we get a table for two in Joe's section?"

"No problem. Wait here a moment, please, and I'll send him right over."

Oliverio was wondering how anybody working for a police department could afford to be a regular in such a formal, posh eatery. The thick carpets, the intimate lighting, and the dark, wood-paneled walls, adorned with large paintings on canvas with gilded wood frames, gave the place a feel of Victorian propriety. Oliverio thought it looked more like an art gallery or museum than it did a restaurant. They sat at a table against the back wall of a slightly elevated section overlooking the restaurant's main room and, at the far end, a glass enclosure where flames and smoke were rising as a chef turned sizzling steaks on a grill.

"Quite a place," said Oliverio, looking around.

"Not as pretentious as it looks. This place is known for its steaks, but everything on the menu is pretty good."

"I didn't eat lunch, so I'm pretty hungry."

Oliverio was carrying copies of the *Toronto Sun* and the *Toronto Star* under his arm. He dropped them on the table and pushed them toward Dalrymple. On the front page of each was a large, full-face photo of a taxi driver with a bandage on his head, the result of a mugging.

"I can't fucking believe this," said Oliverio, shaking his head. "A mugging. A cabby gets a few stitches and he makes the fucking front page. Unbelievable. We've had murders that don't even make the back pages."

Dalrymple smiled and shrugged. "Don't forget, your murder rate is out of sight compared to ours."

Over dinner, Oliverio questioned Dalrymple about the use of lasers and how the new system evolved.

"It's important to realize that this system is simply another investigative tool," said Dalrymple. "It's not a replacement for existing methods. A major plus is that it can pick up some prints that conventional methods would miss."

Dusting with powder was the usual method for finding fingerprints on hard surfaces. Porous substances, such as documents, were dipped in a ninhydrin solution, revealing prints in a magenta stain. Documents could also be treated with iodine vapor, as could some fabrics, light-colored leathers, and even human skin. A silver plate was then pressed against the exposed print to get an impression that could be photographed. Because the iodine was so dark, it was ineffective on dark surfaces. That was the problem Dalrymple had set out to solve.

"I was looking for a way to get the iodine to fluoresce so we could see prints on dark surfaces. My neighbor, who's also my fishing buddy, happens to work as a researcher for Xerox. I told him about my problem and he was able to get permission to look for a solution in their lab. We tried our damnedest, but we couldn't get iodine to fluoresce. Then we thought, forget the iodine, maybe there's something in fingerprints themselves that might be induced to fluoresce. I read and reread the properties in a fingerprint—water, inorganic salt, B complex vitamins, uric acids, urea, lipids, and up to twenty-one amino acids. You can find all of those and more in human sweat, but it can vary from person to person and day to day in each person. Another Xerox researcher joined the project, and we discovered that prints were excited by blue-green light. The second researcher was a laser physicist and he knew that the argon laser was the best source for that. In their work they had to be careful how they handled materials because they were inadvertently exposing their own fingerprints.''

"So their problem was really your solution?"

"Yeah. It was there all along, but they didn't know what they had. It was kind of like a farmer working his field and throwing out unwanted rocks, not knowing that the rocks happened to be gold. It was incredibly exciting. We were picking up our own prints on glass, on Styrofoam cups, even on a secretary's arm.''

"And your first success in the courts was a drug bust or something?"

"Yeah, that was great. Police in Kitchener recovered a small plastic bag full of dope. It was sealed with black electrical tape. They couldn't find any prints, but with the laser we found one on the sticky side of the tape. It belonged to a guy who wasn't even a suspect. He pleaded guilty.''

"But the laser doesn't always work?"

"That's right. We don't know what it is in a print that causes it to fluoresce under the laser, but sometimes it obviously isn't there. The good thing about it, though, is that when we scan a surface with the laser it doesn't disturb it in any way and it doesn't mess it up for dusting or iodine or whatever. Unfortunately, the reverse isn't true.''

As they were leaving the restaurant they met Al Dickie, a reporter with Canadian Press. He and Dalrymple were friends and he invited them for a drink at the Toronto Press Club on the third floor of the same building. Four men were playing snooker on the single table in a room across from the elevator as they entered the club. The bar was in a high-ceilinged room, with muted lighting, which ran the length of the building at the front. Dickie introduced Oliverio and Dalrymple to Michael, the bespectacled barman who was well read and grew roses as a hobby. They stood at the center of the bar and waited for their drinks.

Oliverio noticed an impeccably dressed short man with ruddy cheeks, a snow-white goatee, and a handlebar mustache standing at the corner of the bar. He was wearing a three-piece suit with a red silk ascot and matching folded formal handkerchief peeking out of his breast pocket. The man saw Dickie and called out to him with a pronounced English accent.

"How are you, Al?"

"Just fine, Desmond. And you?"

"Couldn't be better, old chap. Thank you." He smiled and went back to his drink.

"Is he a journalist?" asked Oliverio.

"No. A graphic artist."

"He tells great stories about his mother in England. She had nine husbands."

Dickie called Desmond over and introduced him to Oliverio and Dalrymple.

"I was just telling these gentlemen about your mother and her nine husbands."

"It's quite true," said Desmond, as he squeezed in between Oliverio and the reporter.

"Which one was your father?"

"Number three. But I never saw him or met him."

"What happened to him?"

"I haven't the vaguest idea. I didn't know any of them except the last one. Number Nine. I quite liked him."

"You used to drink with him or something?"

"Yes, I met him when I went to visit mother in England a while back. She had taken a job in a nursing home. That's where she met him—Captain Charles Seaton-Winton, Ninth Gurkhas, British Army. He received a minor leg wound when he was twenty-six and for the next sixty-five years he lived off a pension and did absolutely nothing. But he was a charming old gent. When my mother met him, they had taken away his tobacco and whiskey and he was quite put out. After a week, they left the place together. He was in his late eighties at the time."

"How old was your mother?" asked Oliverio.

"She was a mere child compared to him. Eighty-two

or three, I believe. They lived in sin for a couple of months and then made it legal. He was ninety when I met him. We would go to the pub in the morning and he would get quite fried. We would take a taxi back to mother's and he would pour each of us half a tumbler of neat gin before we ate. 'Cleans the palate, my boy,' he would say. Then we'd have wine with the meal. Needless to say, a sleep ensued after dinner.''

"What happened to all the other husbands?"

"The first two were killed in the First War. As for the others, if you've seen *Arsenic and Old Lace* it might give you some idea of their fate. It's the only conclusion I've been able to reach.''

A thin young man in a worn leather jacket and a baseball cap entered the room and looked around. Michael talked to him a moment and approached the group at the bar.

"Your taxi's here Desmond," he said.

"Thank you, Michael. Well, chaps, I'm off.'' He downed his drink in a single gulp and left the bar.

"Does he come here a lot?" asked Oliverio, who was sorry to see him go.

"Just about every day," said Michael.

"Michael, tell them about the time Alfred Hitchcock came to town," said Dickie.

"Oh, yeah," Michael said, laughing. "He was in Toronto to promote the movie *Topaz*. It was so bad, I guess even he realized he had to do whatever he could to sell it. There was a mass press conference up in his room, but Paul King, a magazine writer, had arranged for a private interview after the mob left. Hitchcock told him he was feeling lousy, a case of the flu. He said he'd heard there was a drink that would solve his problem: two-thirds vodka and one-third white crème de menthe. A bottle of each was ordered up to the room and King, Hitchcock, and the publicist finished them off. King came here to the club later and told the story. They decided they had to give the drink a name and Dickie came up with *Rear Window*. We've been pouring them ever since.''

Oliverio checked his watch. It was after ten.

"I'd like to walk around downtown before I pack it in for the night," he said.

"Yeah," said Dalrymple. "I've got to get home, too."

They parted in front of the hotel and Oliverio walked a couple of blocks to the Yonge Street strip. He was back at the hotel shortly after one A.M., surprised at how many people were still on the street.

In the morning, Oliverio walked the seven blocks from his hotel to OPP headquarters on Harbour Street. He signed in with security and Dalrymple met him in the front lobby. They took the elevator to his third-floor office, which looked out over the Gardiner Expressway and Lake Ontario beyond. They went to the coffee room, where Dalrymple introduced his coworkers to Oliverio.

The two men spent the day in the laser room, where Oliverio learned, hands on, how the equipment operated. Late in the afternoon they were back in Dalrymple's office.

"I really want to thank you for all the time you gave me today and yesterday," said Oliverio. "It's been very enjoyable and that laser is the cat's ass. Can you give me a ball park figure on the cost of installing something like your setup?"

"I'd say about thirty-five thousand with no frills and probably a hundred thousand if you get all the bells and whistles that go with it."

"Christ, that's cheap at double the price."

"I know, it surprises a lot of people."

"How long would it take to install?"

"If you've got the room, you can set up in a couple of days."

On the drive to the airport, Oliverio decided he was impressed with Toronto, but something about it bothered him. It was pleasant but perhaps a bit too sterile for his liking. It was squeaky clean, maybe too clean. Even with its imposing skyline and office towers, it had a small-town feel about it. He didn't know if that was good or bad.

32

Robard sat on the bed with manila folders strewn about him. He shuffled through them, checking each label, until he found the one with the name MARIA BRAZAO. He opened the file and studied several photographs of the beautiful olive-skinned young woman. He carefully read through the notes on the legal-sized yellow sheets attached to the file.

Robard waited patiently while the pleasant, overweight Portuguese butcher served the two women in line ahead of him.

"I'm new to the area," he said with a smile when his turn came. "Your place was recommended to me. Are you the proprietor?"

"Yes, since 1974,", the man replied cheerfully with a heavy accent. "Five years I've been at this location."

"It's very nice."

"Thank you. Thank you. Can I get you something today? I have some nice veal on special."

"What I'd really like is a half dozen filet mignons."

The butcher's smile broadened. At five dollars a pound that was a good order. He wiped his chubby hands on his blood-streaked white apron. They talked about the weather while he prepared the steaks.

"I'm told you have a large family," said Robard, smiling.

"Yes . . . yes, lots of children. Seven. Three young ones. Three in the university, and one already a lawyer."

"A lawyer?"

"Yes, my oldest daughter. She fights the pollution cases in the city."

Robard dumped the steaks in the nearest trash can when he was out of sight of the shop.

Not a week went by without Maria thinking about the birth of her son. Doug Bradford, whom she'd been dating for more than a year now and was thinking of marrying, often talked about having children. Always, it sent her mind back to the house in Staatsburg. It seemed like a lifetime ago. The boy would be five now, the boy she'd never seen. It was part of the agreement. She remembered the doctor and his wife and the painful birth. Average first-time labor was fourteen hours, but it could be a lot longer or a lot shorter, the doctor had told her. When it went beyond eighteen hours, he did his best to reassure her. He knew it was thoughts of the baby as much as the pain that kept her awake the night before the delivery. She saw the doctor almost every day for ten months and she had come to trust him and his wife completely. They were kind to her and they told her so much about the beautiful things outside her world of poverty and ignorance. In the beginning she didn't think much about the child, but as it grew and moved within her, she began to love it, to want it. She knew this wasn't possible, but she couldn't help herself. The doctor told her it was normal for a pregnant woman to become depressed, but his eyes told her he understood the real reason for her sadness. She would never get to see or hold her baby. He consoled her with the promise that the baby would be happy and well cared for, and she and her family would never again be poor. Only she and her parents would know how the family came to own their own home. And her father would get the butcher shop he had dreamed about since his arrival from Portugal in the early 1950s. Unable to find a decent job, he'd become disillusioned and angry. After years of welfare and menial jobs the anger turned to despair and the dream dissipated. But this baby would change all that. She and the other children could even go to college. Never again would she have to work ten hours a day at the laundry during the sweltering summer months. Never again would she have to fight off her sour-smelling boss who twice tried to rape her. She'd been too frightened to tell her parents about the attacks. Her father would think she was soiled. She told only her priest. He urged her to go to the police, but she refused. She couldn't bring dishonor to her family.

Before the tests and the pregnancy, the doctor and his wife drove Maria to the Staatsburg house. It was like a fine vacation. She'd never been out of the city. They provided her with a new wardrobe and helped her with her first-year college correspondence course. She'd always wanted to be a lawyer; now it was a possibility. Her room at the house was bright and cheerful and as large as her family's Bronx tenement flat. She had her own desk, vanity table, bookcase, and even a telephone to call her parents whenever she wanted to. Her bed was queen-sized and there was a terrace where she could sit outside when the weather was fine.

She missed her period three weeks after arriving at the house. As the days passed, she noticed the telltale signs the doctor told her about. Her breasts grew firmer and slightly enlarged, the nipples more prominent and sensitive. There was the morning nausea and sometimes she vomited. At eighteen weeks she felt the first fetal movements, reminding her of the fluttering wings of a butterfly gently imprisoned in cupped hands. Near the end, the flutterings became periodic pounding which caused her discomfort. The doctor reassured her con-

tinually. When it was all over her life would be better;
she'd marry a fine young man and have many babies of
her own.

But that was five years ago and Maria had neither
husband nor children. Her career had come first. She
studied diligently and graduated near the top of her law
class. She went on to specialize in environmental law
and at twenty-four she was working for a successful
firm which offered to take her on as a junior partner
when her tenure was complete.

Robard was into his second day of scanning the faces
entering and leaving the steel and glass lobby of the
Manhattan office building when he saw Maria Brazao.
She was taking the escalator during the lunch hour rush.
He followed her half a block from the building to an
intimate, crowded French restaurant. She went to the
front of a short line of people waiting for tables. A handsome light-haired man in a three-piece suit waved to
her from a table beneath a window. He stood and kissed
her cheek. Robard noticed she was wearing an engagement ring. The couple held hands and kissed several
times during their lunch. Robard found a seat at the bar
but left before they did.

Their lovemaking started slowly. Maria was trembling.
She couldn't understand this. Why? The question seared
her consciousness. Why in bed with him when she
loved another? She was engaged to be married. How
could she be with him? She couldn't understand the
compulsion that drew her to him. This man, this
stranger. There was no sharing, no love. It was as if she
were hypnotized.

For days she'd seen him following her, tracking her:
outside her workplace, in restaurants; near her apartment; at the grocery store. Twice she spotted him while
she was out with Bradford, but something within kept
her from telling him.

Today he had approached her as she left work. "My

name is Robard Anthony Bryce and I want you to come with me,'' he'd said. She felt fear and excitement as she followed him to the waiting taxi. She knew it was wrong, but she couldn't stop herself. They didn't speak on the way to his apartment.

Maria sensed she was in danger as his lovemaking became more violent, but still she responded. Their bodies were slick with perspiration. He grasped her buttocks tightly, his fingers forced rhythmically against the firm mattress as his movements intensified. Her body was no longer her own. The husky screams of pleasure couldn't be hers.

A hundred images bombarded Robard's mind, illusive images, never there long enough to isolate. There was a series of small explosions in his brain like patterned mortar fire. Persistent . . . moving . . . nearer . . . nearer . . . He was coming. *Mother . . . Mother . . .*

Maria knew she would be bruised, but didn't care. Her climax came with his. As his sperm convulsed into her, he squeezed her so tightly she thought her ribs might crack and she would never breathe again. The pressure eased as he moved off her and lay on his back, his chest rising and falling rapidly. She saw the wetness on the sheet from their bodies as she rolled onto her still heaving tummy. His eyes were fixed on the ceiling. She moved her hand to his damp chest.

''Please don't touch me,'' he said coldly, without looking at her.

She moved her hand away as if from a hot iron. He didn't look at her when she got out of bed and dressed in front of him. She left without a word, feeling confused and guilty. She was also relieved because she knew she would never see him again.

33

The Las Vegas Police Department concluded the powerful explosive had been left in the men's washroom at the Paper Lion Casino. It had a sophisticated timing device and the person who planted it probably left the building a few minutes before it exploded. Two patrons were killed in the blast and several others were injured. Damage to the casino, owned by Centra Corporation, was in the hundreds of thousands of dollars.

Robert Marlin wasn't surprised when the police arrived at his sprawling estate to question him about the bombing. The Paper Lion had been one of four casinos under his charge until Elliot Brodie fired him, charging that he had stolen millions. Now Marlin was involved in an ongoing, multimillion-dollar lawsuit against Centra, claiming he had been slandered, robbed of his livelihood, and dismissed without cause. When Centra refused to rehire him after Elliot Brodie's death, he continued to press his case, but the consensus among legal experts was that his prospects for winning were slim. Marlin was able to prove he was in San Francisco on the day of the bombing. When it was suggested he may have hired someone to do the job for him, he volunteered to take a lie detector test. He passed, convincing the police of his innocence.

There were a lot of people who believed Marlin was a crook. In his heyday of working for Elliot Brodie, he looked the part—with his slicked-down hair, diamond rings, and open shirts exposing a chest covered in gold chains. He always smoked big cigars and traveled in chauffeur-driven limousines with tinted windows. He was married but was seldom seen in public with his wife. More likely, he would be in the company of one or more high-priced call girls. Among his closest friends were known members of the mob.

Working for Elliot Brodie and Centra had opened a lot of political and financial doors for Marlin. The Brodie name was magic; even the mob bosses were impressed. Marlin was in effect a high-priced delivery boy for his billionaire boss. But he was treated with deference by politicians seeking Brodie's blessing, and his cash; and by bankers, realtors, and would-be tycoons promoting deals or seeking investment capital. Marlin had no qualms about using his position or Brodie's name to forge private deals that were of considerable personal financial benefit. Despite the claim in his lawsuit that his firing prevented him from earning a living, the private deals struck while working for Brodie left him a millionaire with substantial annual income from interest, mortgage, and dividend earnings. He owned a ranch, two miles out of the city, as well as condominiums in Florida and Lake Tahoe. It was Centra's contention that the deals Marlin made while working for Brodie should have been made on the corporation's behalf, not his own.

Marlin would never admit it, but what hurt him most about his firing was the loss of prestige. A lot of doors closed and his profile was diminished when he lost the aura of the Brodie name. He had lived a lavish life-style at Centra's expense, but now that he was paying his own way, he'd become much more frugal. He could no longer spend without thinking—especially after his wife divorced him, winning an expensive settlement which included hefty monthly support payments.

Secretly, Marlin was pleased with the publicity that came his way after the Paper Lion bombing. It was like the old days. He was a celebrity again. Out came the limo, the cigars, and the women. He booked the best tables at the nightclubs and the casinos, taking advantage while it lasted.

Robert Marlin's fifty-acre estate, formerly part of one of the largest cattle ranches in the state, was on prime land three miles from Las Vegas. His turn-of-the-century, fourteen-room brick house was considered an architectural gem. He had purchased the property at half its market value during his days with Centra, after convincing Elliot Brodie to bankroll a major development scheme in partnership with a local banker. Marlin's reward was the estate. The previous owner had defaulted on his mortgage, held by the banker.

For the third straight night, Marlin had drunk too much. He decided he was too drunk to continue the party at his place. When the limousine pulled up in front of the house, he peeled two hundred-dollar bills from the roll he was carrying and passed them back to the women in the backseat.

"Take 'em home or wherever the fuck they want to go," he said to the driver.

"Awww shit, honey," said one of the women. "I thought we were going to party."

"Tomorrow . . . tomorrow," said Marlin, waving them off as he staggered from the car. The driver leaned across the front seat and closed the door after him. Marlin fumbled for his house keys as he stumbled up the wide front stairway. The lights of the limousine had disappeared at end of the long driveway by the time he entered the house. He had sent his live-in girlfriend to visit her parents for a week in Los Angeles.

Marlin removed his clothes and left them in a pile at the bottom of the stairs.

"Fucking broads . . . fuck 'em," he said, lurching his way up the stairs.

The police believed there was a connection between the Paper Lion bombing and the murder six days later of former Centra executive Robert Marlin. He was found dead in his fashionable home, shot once in the back and once in the temple at close range. A new dollar bill was found stuffed into his mouth. There were no signs of forced entry and robbery was ruled out as a motive. The similarities between his murder and those of Edith Hall and the writer Ian Creighton were too numerous to be coincidental. As a result of the murder and bombing, security was expanded at Centra's other three casinos and FBI agents working on the case recommended that current and former Centra executives take steps to protect themselves.

Robard was relieved to be back in his New York apartment. He wore a powder blue silk bathrobe and sat on a hassock in front of a low circular glass coffee table in the living room. On the floor beside him were two thick manila folders. He placed them on the table and for two hours meticulously studied their contents. The names on the folders' labels were GENERAL WILLIAM MARVIN BOYD and SENATOR ELLIS COMPTON.

Robard called the *New York Times* city desk from a public telephone on 8th Avenue near the Port Authority Bus Terminal. He was carrying a large sealed brown envelope.

"I want to speak to Arthur Raymond," he said curtly.

"I'm sorry, but he's not here right now. Can I take a message?"

"No, you can't. When do you expect him?"

"Not until after three."

"Listen carefully to what I have to say. I have a very important tip for Mr. Raymond. It involves political and military wrongdoing."

"Can't you speak with someone else?"

"Listen, shitass, it's Raymond or the *Washington Post*. Now, don't interrupt. I'll call back at exactly four o'clock. If Raymond's not in, my information goes elsewhere. Got it?"

"I've got it."

Raymond was waiting when he called back at four exactly.

"You say you have something important?"

"I'll do the talking. If you have questions, hold them until I'm through."

"Whatever you say."

"In 1971, March to be exact, Centra Corporation was awarded a contract to provide the electronic systems for the new F-2 fighter planes. The reason they got that contract was because General William Marvin Boyd and Senator Ellis Compton, who was then chairman of the Senate Defense Committee, received kickbacks and other favors totaling over two hundred thousand dollars."

"How do—"

"Just fucking hang on."

"Okay, okay."

"Centra badly needed the contract because its aircraft division was in bad shape financially. There was a second part to the deal that didn't go through. The general and the senator were to push Centra to get similar contracts for the new B-series bombers but Centra fell so far behind on delivery of the fighter systems their participation would have been too obvious."

"This is—"

"No questions until I'm fucking finished," said Robard, waiting a few seconds before continuing. "I'll tell you how Centra Corporation got that first contract. The general and the senator were wined and dined by Centra executives, Hugh Mallot in particular. They were flown by company jet to Houston once and to Vegas twice. The whole tab, including booze and prostitutes, was picked up by Centra. In Houston, they attended a dinner and orgy at the mansion of Mafia boss Franco Nardini. In addition to the free trips, the booze, the broads, and the parties, they each received fifty thousand in cash and two hundred Centra shares. What did they do in return? They broke the law, lots of laws. They looked over all the bids from the competition before the official opening date and tipped off Centra. Centra came in at the last minute, five thousand dollars below the lowest bidder. To refresh your memory, that fighter contract was worth four hundred million. Do you think there's a story there?''

''Those are pretty serious allegations.''

''They're not allegations, they're facts.''

''You have proof?''

''Goddamn right! How about tape recordings? How about photographs of the general, the senator, and Mallot with Franco Nardini? How about photographs of them screwing the prostitutes? How about the—''

''You mean you've got—''

''How about Centra records with entries listing the fifty-thousand dollar payouts to Compton and Boyd and their signed receipts for the stocks.''

''You've got all of that?''

''You bet your ass I do.''

''How do I check it?''

''If you go to your front reception desk, you'll find an envelope with a key in it. It's for a locker at the Port Authority Bus Terminal. You'll find directions to the locker with the key. Everything you'll need is in the locker.''

''What if I hadn't been here?''

''I have two keys. I would have removed the material. It would have gone to Woodward at the *Post*.''

''If everything you've told me is true, how did you come by it?''

''Now you're getting into territory that's off limits.''

''Well, what's in it for you?''

''Never mind my motives. Let's just say I'm interested in justice. Why should you give a damn? You've got the fucking story.''

"Would I know who you are?"

"You might, but you wouldn't believe it."

"What does that mean?"

"I think you've pursued that about far enough."

"You'll never identify yourself? Off the record?"

"Fuck the record. Drop it. It's better for you. You can't be forced to reveal a source if you don't know who the source is."

"That's true, but I like to know who I'm dealing with."

"This is one time you're not going to know."

The New York Times headlined the story three days later, running photos of General Boyd, Senator Compton, and Hugh Mallot with Nardini. The night the story broke, the general shot himself at his Pentagon office. Two days later, the senator resigned and the Senate Judiciary Committee ordered a full inquiry into the contract with Centra. Hugh Mallot and other executives of the corporation weren't talking. The Justice Department announced it was launching its own investigation.

34

About the time the Pentagon scandal broke over the Centra Corporation contracts, Vince Oliverio and Alfie Morrow found what they were looking for. By putting names to the June and July 1976 telephone bills of Torgov, Adleman and Associates they found one that also appeared on the list of Brodie employees. The name was that of Dr. Frank Clifton. He was listed as director of a small cancer research center in Staatsburg, seventy miles north of New York City on the Hudson River. His position had been terminated by Centra Corporation in October 1976. The center was one of many Brodie ventures closed down by the corporation after his death.

The policemen traced the doctor to a private cancer clinic in White Plains, New York. His home was in Connecticut. With his wife and young son, he lived outside the small town of Ridgefield. After calling ahead, Oliverio and Morrow decided to visit him on a Saturday. It was a warm and sunny day and the drive was pleasant. The doctor's spacious, forest-green frame home sat on four acres of land with two large ponds at the rear of the property and a wide circular driveway at the front. The policemen could see the doctor was nervous when he welcomed them at the front door. He explained that his wife was upstairs in bed with a deep chest cold and his son, Bobby, was fishing for bass in the pond out back.

"I should have brought my rod," said Oliverio smiling. "I love to fish, but it's difficult to find the time. I make sure I get away once a year, though." He was suddenly overwhelmed by the image of Martin Butler, in his battered aluminum boat, fishing in northern Michigan. He suppressed the image and controlled his anger.

Clifton invited them to sit out on the deck behind the house. He offered them a drink. Both asked for cold beer. They noticed he poured himself a stiff scotch before settling in a chair across from them. After small talk about the weather, the lushness of the trees, and the baseball standings, they got around to the purpose of their visit.

"You told me on the phone this has something to do with my previous work?"

"That's right," said Oliverio. "Your old boss, dead though he's supposed to be, is causing quite a stir these days, as I'm sure you're aware."

"Those murders and the bombing," said the doctor, suddenly less nervous. "You think it might be somebody who used to work for him? That's what I've been reading in the press."

"It's certainly a possibility," said Morrow. "How long were you with him?"

"Ten years. I started with him in 1966 and stayed on until shortly after his death, when they closed the center."

Oliverio, content to observe the doctor, decided to let Morrow do the talking.

"You were in cancer research, I understand?"

"That's right. Mr. Brodie was concerned about the disease. He wanted to help find a cure. So he set up the center and hired me to run it."

"But it wasn't that big an operation, was it?" asked Morrow.

"Not really. Just my wife and I. She's—ah—a nurse."

The doctor was uncomfortable again, and grew more uneasy as Morrow questioned him about the specifics of his research. He responded with a lot of medical jargon that they didn't understand. Oliverio decided the time was ripe.

"I'll cut through the bullshit, Doctor," he said. "We've got a real problem here. We've got a set of fingerprints that belong to Elliot Brodie. The problem is, they were taken from a very live old man several months after Elliot Brodie was reported to have died."

Clifton's drink slipped from his hand and smashed on the deck, spraying ice cubes and broken glass in all directions. He apologized and went to the kitchen to pour himself another. On his return, he apologized again and scraped the broken glass into a pile with his shoe. Oliverio continued as if there had been no interruption.

"Shortly after Elliot Brodie was supposed to have died, an old man, almost comatose, was dumped in the middle of the night at a nursing home in a small town in Pennsylvania. He was never identified and now he's disappeared. But I went out there to see him before he disappeared and I was able to observe him and get a set of his prints. And do you know, they matched Elliot Brodie's prints perfectly. We're at our wits' end trying to figure out what's going on."

"Could . . . could you have made . . . perhaps made a mistake?" stammered Clifton.

Oliverio leaned in close to him. "Listen, you're a doctor. If you were operating on someone, would you know the difference between their appendix and, say, their heart?"

"Yes, of course."

"Well, it's the same for us, I assure you, Doc."

"But how do you think I can help you?"

"I'll put it this way, Frank. Do you mind if I call you Frank?"

"No. Not at all."

"Somebody from the New York area sent a twenty-thousand-dollar anonymous donation to the nursing home where the old man was dumped. And Frank, I

think that somebody is the only person who can help
us with this fingerprint thing.''

Clifton sat in stunned silence. His face was pale.

"I . . . I don't know what to say. I wish there was
something I could do.''

"Well, we've taken enough of your time, Doc,'' said
Oliverio, handing Clifton his card as they rose to leave.
"If you can think of anything that might help, just call
me at this number.'' The doctor led them silently
through the house to the front. As they walked to their
car he yelled out to them.

"The old man!''

They turned. "Yes, Frank, what about him?'' asked
Oliverio.

"Do you—ah—do you think you'll find him?''

"Dunno, Frank. We're looking. That's all we can
do.''

"Why weren't you tougher on him?'' asked Morrow on
the drive back to New York. "Why not tell him we
know he's the one who sent the money?''

"He's not going anywhere and I think he's basically
honest. He'll come around. We scared the shit out of
him as it was. Give him time to think it over. Let him
stew for a while. Besides, I want a little time to find out
more about him. I hired a guy, an old friend of mine,
name of Conway. He's working on it for me.''

"You brought somebody in?''

"He doesn't know a thing and he doesn't ask questions. He's doing a routine background check. That's
it.''

"How much you payin' him?''

"Five hundred. He's worth it. He's very thorough.''

35

After Anastasio Somoza Debayle was overthrown as president of Nicaragua in 1979, he complained that the "traitorous" United States was the reason for his downfall. Nevertheless, his first stop in exile was Miami. But the Sandinistas were screaming for his blood and he feared a second betrayal. The United States might allow his extradition to his former country and that would mean certain death. The safest haven for a man in his predicament was Paraguay, and he gratefully moved there at the invitation of a fellow dictator, Alfredo Stroessner.

Somoza set up house in a luxurious villa in a suburb of Asunción, the Paraguayan capital. He surrounded himself with cronies and bodyguards. His hoarded fortune was estimated at a hundred million dollars and his reluctance to invest any of it in his adopted country caused resentment. He further offended his hosts with his flamboyant social life and amorous escapades in Asunción. He knew he had created enemies, but enemies were not new to him. He was more worried about the ERP, the People's Revolutionary Army, a leftist Argentine guerrilla group with suspected ties to the Nicaraguan Sandinista revolutionaries who had overthrown the Somoza family's ruthless forty-three-year dynasty. The ERP were known to be operating in Paraguay. Somoza had received a lot of threats and his villa was an armed camp. He didn't know what to make of the envelope that arrived with an Asunción postmark. Inside was a crisp, unused American dollar bill. Folded around it was a single sheet of paper bearing the signature Elliot R. Brodie. He knew Brodie had been dead for years. Perhaps it was a prank. But he'd read about the murders and bombings. He would take no chances.

Somoza smiled, thinking back to early 1972, when Elliot Brodie arrived in Nicaragua after slipping out of the Bahamas to avoid an official inquiry. The glare of publicity following his telephone press conference had broken fifteen years of public silence and exposed Ian Creighton as a fraud. Somoza offered Brodie his personal protection. Brodie thought a couple of expensive gifts, a speedboat, and a fancy limousine would ensure the protection continued, but Somoza wanted much more. Through intermediaries he suggested the billionaire bail out Nicaragua's bankrupt steel industry, owned principally by Somoza himself. Brodie bought a third of its stock and took up residence in the capital city of Managua, situated on the southern shore of Lake Managua and flanked by the smoldering volcano Momotombo. The city's politics were as hot and sultry as its weather. The Brodie entourage was ensconced in the ultramodern, pyramid-shaped Intercontinental Hotel. Outside, ragged children slept in the city's doorways. After just a month, with Somoza urging him to buy into his family's lumber and real estate companies as well, Brodie decided it was time to leave. To protect the ten million dollars he'd already paid out, and to ensure he could return in an emergency, he decided to meet with Somoza personally. His voice had gone public; now it was his body's turn. He called in the Christians to get him ready. Hair, beard, and toenails were neatly trimmed for the first time in several years. He showered and dressed in a suit and tie. He invited Somoza aboard his private jet on a Managua runway and they talked for an hour and a half before Brodie flew off to a new hideout in Panama.

Elliot Brodie returned to Nicaragua eight months later and again took up residence in a hotel penthouse. His second visit wasn't much longer than the first, but this time it wasn't Somoza's greed that drove him out. Managua wasn't a stable place to live, notwithstanding its politics. On December 23, 1972, shortly after midnight, Elliot Brodie was lying naked in his bed and watching old movies when the city was hit by a devastating earthquake. The Christians carried him down ten flights of stairs in the darkness while the hotel heaved, cracked, and fell down around them. Brodie spent the night cowering under a blanket in the back of a limousine while fires burned and the city was rocked with aftershocks. In the morning, the Christians drove him through the shattered streets, which were littered with bodies, rubble, and thousands of homeless, numb survivors. More than ten thousand people were dead. Brodie and his entourage drove out of the city, through the squalor of thousands of flattened tar-paper hovels, to Somoza's country palace, left untouched by the earthquake. Brodie spent the day in a darkened cabana beside Somoza's pool and that night managed to fly out on one of his Gulfstream jets to London.

Until the recent murders, Anastasio Somoza hadn't thought much about Elliot Brodie. And now here was this envelope with a crisp dollar bill.

It was shortly before ten on a sunny morning when the fifty-four-year-old former dictator climbed into his white Mercedes-Benz 250 limousine. With him were his chauffeur and a business associate. They drove off from his suburban villa toward Asunción, escorted by a second car following close behind, carrying three well-armed bodyguards. They had traveled only five blocks when a Chevrolet pickup truck pulled alongside the limo and unleashed a hail of automatic rifle fire. The bodyguards returned the fire. Robard and a second man watched the action from the porch of a nearby house. As the Mercedes drew abreast of the house, Robard fired the bazooka rocket, scoring a direct hit. The force of the blast tore the roof from the car and killed its three occupants instantly.

Paraguayan police launched a manhunt, convinced the assassins were members of the Argentine guerrilla group ERP. They picked up sixty people for questioning but later conceded the hit team had made a clean getaway. In Managua, thousands of people poured into the streets. They sang and danced and set off a barrage of fireworks. Somoza had finally brought happiness to his people. The ruling Sandinista junta denied any direct role in the assassination. They issued a communiqué calling his death *adjusticiamiento*—justifiable execution, since Somoza had been responsible for the deaths of a hundred thousand Nicaraguans.

36

Alfie Morrow and Vince Oliverio bumped into each other in their eagerness to enter the new laser room. Morrow backed away and, with a sweeping motion of his hand and an awkward curtsy, nodded toward the doorway.

"I defer to your age and bulk," he said.

"Fuck you, Alfie."

"That's not very polite."

"Just give me the stuff," said Oliverio in mock disgust.

Morrow handed him two clear plastic bags, both sealed with tape at the top. "I couldn't believe it when Sadowski asked me to check these with the laser."

"It was shit luck, but we can sure use some," said Oliverio. "You say the head I.D. man in Vegas called Sadowski?"

"Yeah, they're old friends. He told the FBI they'd get it when we're through looking."

In one plastic bag was the dollar bill removed from the mouth of the former Brodie executive, Robert Mar-

lin; in the other was a pair of surgical gloves found in
a trash receptacle on a street corner, half a block from
the Paper Lion casino shortly after it was bombed. Las
Vegas police had used powder and chemicals on both
items, but had failed to come up with a print.

At Oliverio's insistence, and with Sadowski's backing, the NYPD's new laser room on the top floor of the
Police Academy had all the bells and whistles. In four
months the laser had become fully integrated into the
identification section. Four officers, including Oliverio
and Morrow, were fully trained to operate the
equipment.

"Ready?" asked Oliverio. Morrow nodded. They
wore white cotton gloves and safety goggles to protect
their eyes from the laser beam, which scattered when it
struck an object. The goggles were fitted with a special
orange filter, necessary to see a print under the laser.
The centerpiece in the room was a sixteen-watt, argon-
ion laser machine. Oliverio switched on the machine
and the room was bathed in a surrealistic blue-green
haze.

"They don't know if the surgical gloves are in any
way connected to the bombing," he said. "Even if they
are, we're not likely to see anything. I'm sure they've
overdone it with powder and silver nitrate. Same with
the dollar bill."

Using scissors, he cut open one of the plastic bags
and shook the dollar bill loose. He nudged it into place,
flat on the table, under the laser.

"A couple of smudges," said Morrow. "Nothing us-
able." With the corner of the plastic envelope and the
tip of a sharp pencil, Oliverio flipped the bill over and
slid it into place. He scanned it from end to end.

"Nothing there, either," he said. "Let's try the
gloves."

They scanned the outer surface of each glove
separately.

"Fuck all here," said Morrow. "One shot left—the
insides. If we can get anything at all, that's where it'll
be."

Carefully, they turned the gloves inside out. "Pop

the fingers all the way out, Alfie. It's slim, but I think our only hope for pay dirt will be in the tips."

There were streaks and smudges and ninhydrin residue on the inside of the first glove, but no fingerprints. Oliverio slid the second one, the left, into place.

"A couple of knuckle lines on the middle finger," he said. "Flip it."

The laser scanned the palm and the thumb. Negative. Fore and middle fingers. Negative. Ring finger.

"Bingo!" shouted Morrow. It was a partial print above the flexure of the last joint on the ring finger. Not perfect, but adequate for their purposes.

"Goddamn, we got it! Get the camera over here, Alfie."

Morrow photographed the print and they went to Oliverio's office, closing the door behind them.

"Get it developed and bring it over to my place tonight. We'll use my comparator. From what I'm seeing, I'm a hundred percent sure it's Brodie, but we may have a problem."

"What problem, Vince? It looks great to me."

"Use your eyes, Alfie. The print's fine, but look at the age creases."

"Jesus! This is insane, Vince. A perfect match but only about half the age creases. What the fuck is going on?"

Oliverio bit his lower lip and shook his head in bewilderment. "It might look better when we blow it up and get it under a comparator."

"There's no way, Vince. There are a hell of a lot less age creases than on the Pennsylvania print. And what happens when we send the glove on to the FBI?"

"They'll never I.D. it. It's not in their general file and they'll have no reason to check under Permanent Scar or Presumptive Dead."

"It gets more and more insane."

"Just print it up and come over tonight. My mother phoned a few minutes ago. I've got a parcel at the house. It has to be the report on the doctor."

"Report?"

"From the investigator, Conway. The guy I hired."
"Right, right. I forgot."

Oliverio got up from the comparator in frustration. A blowup of the partial print lifted from the surgical glove was on one screen. On the other was the corresponding section of the Pennsylvania print. There were twice as many age creases on the Pennsylvania print.

"This is making me crazy, Vince," said Morrow. "Every time we get somewhere, we get hit with a new twist."

Oliverio slapped at the air in disgust. "Let's just can it for now and go through the stuff that came today." He went to the bar, where he picked up a three-inch pile of legal-sized paper. He handed Morrow half the pile and they settled in the barber's chairs.

"So this guy's pretty good, Vince?"

"Conway? He's the best. He was a dick for years in Fort Apache. One day he decided he'd had enough and just up and quit. He moved to New England and went into business as a P.I."

"He's got a lot here on Clifton."

"We'll go through all this shit and then go out and sit on him. We can prove he donated the twenty thousand. He'll have to tell us who dumped Brodie at the nursing home. I'm sure he's a pawn. And he can't be feeling too good about these killings."

The door opened at the top of the stairs and Florence Oliverio appeared with a plate of homemade cookies and a pot of coffee. She placed them on the bar without a word.

"Thank you, Mrs. Oliverio," said Morrow.

"I make myself," she said, smiling.

"You're wonderful, Ma. You keep me nice and fat." Morrow laughed.

She poured them coffee and retreated up the stairs. They had been reading Conway's report for thirty minutes when Oliverio handed Morrow the thickest document in his pile.

"This is his thesis. You're the college boy. You plough through it. Here, I'll take some of yours."

Morrow sighed as he began reading the document, but he was on his feet by the time he got to the middle of the second page.

"Holy fuck, Vince! Look at this!" He thrust the document into his partner's lap. Oliverio read several lines. They looked at each other incredulously.

At work the following morning, Friday, there was a message for Oliverio to call Dr. Frank Clifton. He went into Morrow's office. "He's reading our mail," said Oliverio.

"The doctor?"

"Yeah. I was going to get him on the horn first thing today, but I come in to find a message from him. He called at nine last night."

"Good timing. We're going out to bust his ass and he calls us. Conscience?"

"Who knows? Is everything clear with Anne for tomorrow?"

"No problem. I promised we'd get a sitter for Sunday. We're going out for dinner."

"I still can't believe any of this."

The traffic was heavy, so it took them two and a half hours to drive to the outskirts of Ridgefield, Connecticut, where they'd arranged to meet the doctor at a bar. They'd driven in Oliverio's car. It was after seven when he parked in the lot beside the roadhouse. Oliverio had been silent during the latter part of the drive. Morrow could see the firm set of his jaw.

"Vince, I know you're pissed at this guy, and you've got good reason to be, but we need his cooperation. If this is what we think it is . . ."

Oliverio eyed his partner coldly for a moment, then his eyes softened.

"I know what you're saying, Alfie."

The bar was dark and dingy. There were two rooms, the larger of which had a small dance floor, a jukebox, and booths along one wall. Frank Clifton was in the smaller room, at a corner table where a candle burned in a red bell-shaped glass.

"I'm sorry this is such a dump," said Clifton. "It was the only convenient place I could think of. They call the other room the Sin Room. Friday nights are the worst. You see a lot of lawyers, accountants, and stock-brokers trying to make it with their secretaries."

The doctor was drinking a scotch on ice. Oliverio and Morrow ordered draft beers from the bored wait-ress, who was chewing gum at a record-setting pace.

"We read your thesis, Doc," said Oliverio noncha-lantly after their drinks were served. Clifton nodded. He wasn't as surprised as they thought he would be. "Is it true?"

"Initially I didn't think it was possible."

Morrow couldn't bear the suspense. His pulse was racing.

"Did you do it? Did you clone Elliot Brodie?"

The doctor was silent for a moment. "Yes," he said, shifting his weight in his chair. Oliverio sighed and shook his head. "When I wrote the thesis, I didn't really believe it. It was all hypothetical as far as I was con-cerned. I knew it was controversial and I just wanted to get their attention."

"So that wasn't a cancer clinic you were running over at Staatsburg?" asked Morrow.

"No."

"You actually cloned Elliot Brodie? I can't believe it."

Clifton nodded.

"This is fucking science fiction."

"How many are there?" asked Morrow.

Clifton appeared momentarily confused. "One," he replied, agitated. He reached down to pick up a thick accordion file, tied with a narrow ribbon. He placed it on the table in front of him.

"I'll give you everything I've got. It's all in here." He patted the file. "It's a nightmare."

"I'm sure the guy he killed in Nevada and a few oth-ers would go along with that," said Oliverio.

"Easy, Vince," said Morrow.

"For Christ's sake, he knew Brodie walked away from the nursing home. He fucking put him there."

"It's true. I did leave him there. But I didn't know he'd walked away. At least I didn't know when I last saw you. I had my suspicions, but I didn't know."

"You should've told us what you knew."

"I went into absolute shock when you came out to my house like that. I was confused and upset. I didn't know what to do."

"How did you do it?" asked Morrow.

"What?"

"The clone."

"As I told you, I really didn't think it was possible. I thought Brodie was insane, but he was willing to put up a lot of money. I thought it might lead to a breakthrough in cancer research. I worked at it for years. But there was a lot of parallel research going on and suddenly things started to happen. In the late sixties, a British researcher by the name of Gurdon successfully took a cell from the body of a tadpole, inserted its nucleus into a frog's egg, and created a genetic carbon copy, a clone. It grew into a normal adult frog. But nobody thought it would work with humans because human eggs are extremely fragile compared to the large, sturdy egg cells of frogs.

"Cloning is really asexual reproduction, involving just one parent, if you will. It happens widely in nature. It's the normal route for reproduction of bacteria and many plants and lower animals. In normal human reproduction, the male and female each contribute to the genetic makeup of their offspring. When the egg and sperm unite, the fertilized egg contains forty-six chromosomes, half donated by the mother and half by the father. The fertilized egg divides into two cells, then into four, then eight, and so on into the billions which make up the body. Now, each of these body cells contains in its nucleus all of the genetic traits that were present in that single fertilized egg.

"In cloning, an egg is removed from a woman and the nucleus of that egg is destroyed and replaced with a body cell from whomever you want to reproduce. The cell can come from any part of the body."

"Where did Brodie's come from?" asked Morrow.

"The roof of his mouth."

Oliverio and Morrow looked at each other.

"Because it's a body cell and not an egg cell, its nucleus already contains a full set of chromosomes. The egg senses the presence of the chromosomes and is fooled into reacting as if it had been fertilized. Then it divides over and over, forming an embryo, and eventually a child. There are three major obstacles in all of this: to remove the nucleus of an egg cell without harming the cell itself; to successfully fuse the nucleus from the body cell with egg cell cytoplasm; and to get the nucleus and cell dividing at the same rate. Since the cell divides more rapidly than the nucleus, it's necessary to find the correct medium to slow one down and speed the other up."

"I'm afraid you lost me there, Doc," said Oliverio. "I must admit we had a hell of a time understanding a lot of your thesis. There was so much technical gobbledegook."

"I know it can be pretty confusing. Let me put it this way. It was like searching for the exact extra weight that would burden a fast racehorse to the point it would cross the finish line in a dead heat with a much slower horse. If the cell and nucleus divide at different rates, the chromosomes shatter."

"And you solved those problems?"

"It was a long process. I was able to duplicate other scientists' experiments and successfully cloned carrots, sea urchins, frogs, and mice. Then I used an ultraviolet radiation technique to destroy the nucleus of an egg cell without damaging the rest of the egg. Next I isolated a virus that enabled me to effectively fuse a nucleus-free egg cell with a body cell nucleus. I won't go into the details, but I also found a way to successfully fertilize the new complete egg. It was fertilized for several hours and then transferred to a test tube."

"Are you telling us Elliot Brodie's clone came out of a test tube?" asked Morrow.

"Initially, yes. It keeps dividing in a test tube until it's a sixty-four-cell embryo. Then you implant it in a woman's uterus."

Oliverio eyed the doctor in disbelief. "Brodie's clone came out of somebody's womb?"

The doctor nodded. "That's how it works."

"Who was the woman?"

"She was an eighteen-year-old girl that Elliot Brodie found. He ran it like a military operation, with a whole slew of private investigator types. In his movie days he apparently used people like that to ferret out potential movie starlets. He gave these guys the same pitch—led them to believe they were searching for girls that he would mold and promote for the movies. He told them to search for the girls in poorer neighborhoods in New York. They had to be white, beautiful, and, preferably, virgins. I told him it didn't matter what they looked like because the clone would have only his characteristics and genes. The woman would be providing a host womb, so to speak. He didn't listen. He had dozens of secret files on these girls. He finally chose one from a Portuguese immigrant family. She was very bright—a lawyer now, I believe. Part of the agreement was that Brodie purchased a new home for the family in a middle-class neighborhood and set up education trusts for all the children. I think there were seven of them. A bank controls the trusts. And he set the father up in his own butcher shop. Something he'd always wanted."

Oliverio was agitated, squirming in his chair. "So you just casually walk up to this family and say we want to knock up your daughter so Elliot Brodie can have a clone?"

"No, of course not," said the doctor sharply. "We had to lie about a couple of things. Basically, I convinced her parents it was simply a case of artificial insemination to bring happiness to a childless, lonely old rich man. It was the morality that bothered them most. Old-country standards, I guess. But eventually, they agreed. The young woman spent her pregnancy with us at the Staatsburg house. We had the very best of facilities and equipment. Brodie saw to that. He told me over and over that 'this cloning thing,' as he called it, was the most important thing in his life. Nothing else mattered. The agreement stipulated that the girl wouldn't see the baby. And that turned out to be a good thing."

"Why's that?"

"It was at the birth that everything began to go wrong."

"I've got a million questions to ask you, Frank," said Oliverio, producing a notepad and pen. "We've got all the time in the world, so why don't you just start at the beginning and take us through this step by step? You say it's all in that file and that's fine. But I'd just like to hear it from you and take a few notes along the way."

3

the doctor

37

The thin, pale man was agitated when young Dr. Frank Clifton entered his private room at Massachusetts General Hospital.

"How many more of you are there? I feel like I'm on display in a goddamn zoo."

"We have a job to do," said the doctor. He smiled. "It's for your benefit."

"Too many of you involved. It was supposed to be kept quiet."

"Don't worry, we've been sworn to secrecy. And don't forget our good old sacred oath."

"I just want the hell out of here. Your goddamn sticking and probing. I hate this goddamn city. I don't know how you people can live here."

"I'm not from here originally, but it's not that bad."

"Why did you come here?"

"I'm doing postgraduate research at Harvard."

"Research. Not on me, I should damn well hope?"

"No, no. I just want a blood sample from you. Working here helps pay my way."

"You mean they're sending me goddamn part-timers? What the hell is going on here?"

"They tell me I'm very good at what I do."

"Are you now?"

"Yes, I am," replied the doctor, amused at the interrogation.

"What's your name?"

"Frank Clifton."

"I don't care much for doctors, Frank."

"I gathered that."

"I hate Boston and I hate this dump. And now the goddamn press is starting to snoop around. Somebody here must be talking. Some shitass."

So this is the famous Elliot Brodie, thought Clifton as he approached with the needle. Rather pathetic.

"That thing sterilized, Frank?"

"Of course, Mr. Brodie."

The billionaire turned his head away and closed his eyes as the needle was inserted. Clifton studied his face. Gray-streaked black hair, combed straight back. Angular features and a neatly trimmed thin mustache. He wore faded blue-striped flannel pajamas, obviously his own. Why not silk? The chart listed Brodie's height at six feet three and his weight at one hundred and twenty-five. He was as skinny as a rake.

"What's your research, Frank?"

"Genetics."

There was a marked change in Brodie's demeanor. He eyed the doctor intently. Clifton was ready to leave, but he sensed Brodie wanted to say something. He paused, but there was an awkward silence and he moved toward the door.

"Frank." Clifton stopped, his hand on the doorknob. "I . . . I don't hate *all* doctors."

Clifton pressed the button in the lobby elevator of the Ritz-Carlton Hotel. Two burly men in identical blue suits confronted him when the elevator doors opened on the fifth floor. They demanded identification. Satisfied, they escorted him to a suite at the end of the corridor. A fortyish, slight, pale man responded to the knock on the door. After a whispered conversation with one of the men, he released the chain and allowed Clifton to enter.

"So glad you made it," he said, closing the door as the escorts returned to their posts at the elevator. He picked up a telephone on a small desk in a makeshift office set up in the foyer. He dialed three numbers and spoke into the phone in a whisper.

"Mr. Brodie will see you now," he said in a tone that Clifton felt was supposed to make him feel eternally grateful. He was led through an empty adjoining room to another door. The pale man indicated with a nod that he should enter. Clifton shrugged and opened the door. The room was considerably darker than the others and it was stifling.

Elliot Brodie sat on an overstuffed white leather chaise longue near an unmade double bed. He was wearing a white bathrobe. Used Kleenex tissues formed a pyramid on the table beside his chair. The pyramid, Clifton noticed, had overflowed to the floor below. He also noticed Brodie was wearing a hearing aid, something he'd missed at the hospital.

"Come over here," whispered Brodie, motioning with his head to a straight-backed antique leather and wood chair beside the small table. The drapes in the room had been tightly drawn and the only light came from a small reading lamp on the table.

"It's hot in here," declared Clifton, loosening his tie. "Is the air-conditioning out of whack?"

"I don't believe in it. It's not healthy."

"Oh."

Big band music was playing on a radio beside the bed. Brodie got up and turned up the volume to a level Clifton found distracting. Brodie returned to the chaise longue and leaned toward the doctor.

"Sorry about the radio," he said in a hoarse whisper. "It's a precaution. We've swept this place for bugging devices, but you can never be too careful."

Clifton wondered who would care about listening to their conversation.

"I'm not worried about him," said Brodie, nodding toward the outer office. "He's some sort of strict Christian. I'm not religious myself, but I like to hire them. They don't drink or smoke. Very dependable. I don't know what the hell they believe in, but you can trust them."

Clifton was beginning to perspire from the heat.

"I suppose you want to know what this is all about, Frank?"

"I didn't expect to be seeing you again when I heard you left the hospital prematurely."

"I've arranged to stay here at night. You're liable to catch anything in a goddamn hospital. There are germs everywhere."

Clifton found it ludicrous that two grown men would be having a whispered conversation in a sweltering hotel room with music blaring in the background. He noticed Brodie continually wiped the arm of his chair with tissues, discarding them every few minutes.

"I've had you checked out thoroughly, Frank. Impressive credentials. Considerable research in genetics at Mount Sinai School of Medicine, and at Harvard. Married. No children. I must admit I like you, Frank. And I'm very interested in your research. I'd like you to come to work for me."

"But—"

"A hundred thousand a year."

The young doctor was stunned.

"Don't get the wrong idea. I've got my own quacks looking after me. It's your research. I want you to pursue it. I'll set you up in your own laboratory with the best equipment money can buy."

"I don't understand. I plan to go into cancer research. What aspect of my work are you talking about?"

"Genetics, Frank. Genetics. I read your thesis. You think it's possible to clone human beings and so do I."

"You want me to *clone* you?" said Clifton.

"That's right, Frank."

"What I wrote was a hypothesis. Just scratching the surface."

"But it's technically possible, isn't it, Frank?"

"Hypothetically. But practically, well, that's a different story."

"You take the nucleus from a female egg cell and replace it with the nucleus from a body cell. Fertilize it. Grow it in a womb, and bingo, you've got it. You said it yourself, Frank. Isn't that right?"

"That's a gross oversimplification. There is a myriad of extenuating factors that . . ."

"They've already done it with carrots."

"Human egg cells are minute. When you compare them with carrot cells, it's like comparing a pin to a railway spike."

"C'mon Frank," said Brodie, his tone taunting. "You've admitted it can be done. So why not give it a try? You've got nothing to lose. Anything you need, you'll get. It'll be your own show and you'll never have to work in a crummy hospital again."

"There are other ways to have a child, an heir, if that's really what you want."

"I don't want a goddamn child that way," said Brodie, anger rising in his voice. "He'd spend his entire life under a fucking spotlight just like I did. I wouldn't wish that on anyone. And I don't want any more involvements with women. They're all gold diggers. It would have been better if we could just fuck them through osmosis, and not have to live with them."

Clifton was taken aback by the outburst.

"If it was even remotely possible, who would look after the child? He would still be under the spotlight."

"I'd work that out. But one thing is certain. No one would ever know he was Elliot Brodie's son unless he wanted it that way when he was old enough to think for himself. I'd never burden him with that."

Brodie leaned back, regrouping. "Now listen, Frank, you've defined the problem and you know the solution. Now it's simply a question of putting the pieces together until they all fit. I know it won't be easy. I used to design airplanes. There's a lot of trial and error. You experiment over and over until you get it right. Until it's perfect."

Clifton found it incomprehensible that the skeletal

figure before him was once a dashing, daredevil pilot who built his own airplanes and flew them at record speeds.

"I don't know what to say."

"You don't have moral problems with it, do you, Frank? You're an atheist, aren't you?"

"Is there anything you don't know about me?"

"I don't take this lightly, Frank. If you accept, I'll put you on the payroll today."

"Where do you propose to set up an appropriate research facility?"

"It's all looked after, Frank. I've set aside a wonderful estate in upstate New York. You would live right there. You would be working directly for me and your cover could be cancer research, since you have an interest in that area."

"What if I tell you I'm not interested?"

"I'd be extremely disappointed, Frank. But there are others. You're my first choice."

"But you didn't know anything about me until a couple of days ago."

"And I never would have, without our chance meeting in the hospital. I believe in fate, Frank. The others on the list are very big names. To tell you the truth, I've been putting off talking to them because I think the fact they are high profile could cause a lot of problems. If it ever got out, there would be more bullshit in the press about me being a crackpot."

"I'm sure you can understand that this is all quite a shock to me. I'll have to have some time to think about it and talk it over with my wife."

"I thought you might. She's a registered nurse and that could be helpful, I suppose. Okay, Frank, you talk it over with her, but no one else must ever know, whatever way you decide. Is that understood?"

Clifton nodded.

"I know you're a man of your word. You must understand, none of my people will ever know what we're doing. This is special, Frank, and it's very important to me. The most important thing in my life. Cancer research. That's very good, Frank. I'll tell them it's cancer research. You'll get whatever you need. We'll never discuss it over the telephone. We can set up meetings on the telephone, but we'll meet face to face."

Frank Clifton wanted out of the steaming room. His shirt was soaked through. He was feeling weary and elated when he left the hotel.

38

NOVEMBER 1966

Margaret Clifton was a handsome woman, tall, with prominent cheekbones, strawberry blond hair, and golden skin. She grew up an only child on a farm near the town of Spillville in northeastern Iowa. Outsiders usually laughed when they heard the name, but the town did have its claim to fame. Czech composer Antonín Dvořák did some of his best work there while visiting one summer. A lot of Czechs, including Margaret's ancestors, settled in that part of Iowa. Not blessed with the rich soil and rolling plains of most of the state, northeast Iowa was grim, visited by destructive winter winds, oppressive summer heat, and violent thunderstorms.

Margaret was delivered by cesarean section and her frail mother nearly died. She couldn't have any more children, and Margaret's father wouldn't get the broadshouldered brood of boys he'd yearned for. He was forced to hire help to plant and harvest his corn and soybeans. Margaret often wished she were a boy. In her teens she worked as hard as any of the hired hands. By her last year of high school, she decided that farm life wasn't for her. Over her father's protests, she studied literature and social work at the University of Iowa. She was in her sophomore year when her parents were killed in a car accident on their way home from visiting her. For a time, she blamed herself. She sold the farm and dropped out for a term. A few years later, she was a graduate nurse working on a master's degree in social work at Harvard when she met Dr. Frank Clifton.

Like her, Clifton was an only child, although orphaned at a much earlier age. His mother had died of pneumonia when he was a six, and he was nine when his father died of a heart attack. He was raised by a kindly but stern aunt who dragged him to church every Sunday. Clifton and Margaret had a lot in common and quickly fell in love. She liked his thoughtfulness, brooding good looks, and easy sense of humor. Margaret was beautiful and clever, but what Clifton admired most was her fierce independence. She carefully weighed both sides of an argument before taking a position, but once she came to a decision she couldn't be swayed.

They'd been married for a year and a half when Elliot Brodie made his offer. Margaret had no hesitations.

"Fantastic," she said. "Take it. A once-in-a-lifetime opportunity."

They soon learned that Elliot Brodie did things in a hurry. Within three months of accepting his offer, they had moved into a spacious stone house on an estate in Staatsburg, on the Hudson River. Margaret thought they were living in a fairy tale. A fully equipped laboratory had been installed on the third floor and there was plenty of room left over for a delivery room and nursery.

Brodie's people had contracted with a landscaping firm to maintain the expansive lawns, flower beds, hedges, and small trees. Frank and Margaret came to love their new brick home with the white pillars in front. Inside, the floors were of polished hardwood, there were four stone fireplaces, and the rooms had high ceilings. The entire estate, five acres of woodland and yard, was surrounded by a black iron fence.

•   •   •

"What did he want this time?" asked Margaret as Clifton emerged from his study. She knew it was Brodie again; there was a separate telephone for his calls.

"Same old story. He's complaining about his doctors. 'Those shitass quacks,' to use his words. I'm sure they're perfectly capable, but he won't let them near him and he ignores their advice. He says he has to see me. He claims the press is hounding his people again."

"You told him you're staying put, I hope?"

"I protested, but as always, he had the last word."

"But Frank, Thanksgiving weekend is coming up and we've still got things to move in."

"I told him all of that, but he insisted I meet him. I'm sorry, but you'll have to supervise the rest of the move. He said he'd have a crew sent around to take care of everything."

"So you have to go back to Boston?"

"No, he's leaving there tonight. You won't believe it, but he's traveling by train. I have to meet him in New York tonight."

"Train? You've got to be kidding."

"He's got special cars all set up for him. I'd better get packed."

"Where is he going this time?"

"He wouldn't tell me over the phone."

"How long will you be gone?"

"Who knows? I'll call you the first chance I get."

The Union Pacific train came to a jarring halt. Clifton checked his watch. It was five in the morning, a Sunday. There was a slight chill in the air as the Brodie entourage left the private cars which formed part of the train. It was not a scheduled stop. They were in the desert, five miles north of Las Vegas. Brodie did not want to risk being seen at the station. He was bundled up and moved from the train on a stretcher. A small pickup truck, two cars, and a station wagon were waiting to meet them. The backseat of the wagon was folded down to allow room for the stretcher. Brodie asked Clifton to ride with him.

"I really appreciate your coming all the way out here, Frank," he said as the caravan snaked its way toward the city. "I know the train is slow, but you can't be too careful these days."

Clifton was silent. He'd slept fitfully on the train and he was in a sour mood. By now, he was familiar with Brodie's ploys. Always sounding so grateful. Like you were doing him a big favor. But the reality was, you had no choice but to go along or quit.

Once in Las Vegas, they drove directly to the rear of the Roman Palace Casino Hotel, where Brodie was ushered through a rear door to the service elevators. He'd reserved the entire ninth floor, where his personal twelve-room suite included a living room, dining room, office, dressing room, and bedroom, which, he decreed, was an 'isolation zone.' It overlooked the hotel's golf course and swimming pool.

"Could you give me a few minutes of your time before you go to your room, Frank?" asked Brodie after shooing his aides from the suite.

"Certainly."

"Have you noticed a difference in the air in here, Frank?" Clifton inhaled and shrugged. "It's much cleaner," said Brodie. "I had them install a purifier."

Clifton did his best to conceal his disinterest.

"Frank, I want to thank you again for coming out here with me. Your research is the most important thing in this world to me. I want you to know that. I hope you'll proceed as quickly as possible."

"Well, it would help if I returned as soon as possible. I would like to fly back tomorrow. As you know, we're still moving in."

"I realize it's an important time for you, Frank. But would you mind staying on a few days?"

A uniformed armed guard sat outside the battleship-gray metal door that sealed off Brodie's ninth-floor suite. Clifton didn't know it, but he was being allowed more access to Brodie than anyone other than the Christians. Sometimes called secretary-nurses, secretary-companions, or executive assistants, the Christians were loathed by Centra Corporation executives and anyone else seeking access to Brodie. They had little formal education and they were fiercely protective in their role as Brodie's shield. The billionaire had hired them on a whim, after reading about them in a newspaper. They belonged to a shadowy religious sect, called the Church of Christian Arians—a misnomer, since they were Biblical fundamentalists, while Arianism was one of the most divisive heresies in the history of Christianity. Its creator, Arius, was a fourth-century parish priest in Alexandria, who preached that before He created anything, God created a son, Jesus Christ, a demigod, not quite human and not quite divine. He was a supernatural creature who was neither equal to nor eternal with God. The founder of the misnamed Church of Christian Arians, a petty criminal named Hans Merluk, claimed that God had appeared to him in his prison cell and ordered him to found the sect.

Besides their fundamentalist reading of the Bible, the Christians, as Brodie called them, were white supremacists, which suited their boss just fine. Brodie feared and hated black people, as his father had before him.

There were always eight of Merluk's men, headed by Marvin Snow, working twelve-hour shifts around the clock. They spent much of their time going through Brodie's "purification" ritual to prevent germs from contaminating his "isolation zone." They were his runners, his keepers, and his protectors against the outside world. Frank Clifton referred to them collectively as the Christian Curtain.

The doctor heard nothing from Brodie for three days and when he demanded a meeting the Christians rebuffed him.

On the fourth day he decided to return to Staatsburg, whatever the consequences. He informed the Christians of his plans and a half hour before he was to leave, Brodie summoned him. He entered the "isolation zone" wondering if he was about to be fired.

"Sorry I couldn't see you sooner, Frank. I've been very busy. I appreciate your staying on like this. Have you visited Las Vegas before?"

"No."

"Are you enjoying yourself?"

"I want to get back to my work."

"Of course you do, Frank. Maybe you should fly out today. Everything seems to be under control here. I'll call you occasionally to see how things are going. We'll have to talk in a sort of code, in case our lines are bugged. You understand, don't you?"

"Yes, I understand."

39

Frank Clifton was in a deep sleep when the telephone rang in the bedroom at the Staatsburg house. It was the special phone. He hadn't heard from Brodie since he left Las Vegas four months earlier.

"Mr. Brodie?" he asked, his voice thick with sleep.

"Hello, Frank. How are things going?"

"Wha . . . what time is it?"

"It's three A.M. where you are, Frank. I'm sorry it's so late, but it's the safest time."

Clifton roused himself. "Is anything wrong?"

"Not at this end, Frank. I've straightened things out here. How are things proceeding there?"

"I've started—"

"Careful what you say."

"Okay. Yes . . . well . . . I'm, ah, well into that stage we talked about when I last saw you."

"I understand, Frank. That's very good news. How long before you'll be needing those other things we talked about?"

"That'll be down the road a bit."

"Not too long, I hope."

"These things can't be rushed, Mr. Brodie."

"I realize that, Frank, but I don't know how long I've got. That has to be a factor."

"Of course. I understand."

"You'll come to see me personally when you're ready to proceed with the next step?"

"Yes sir. If that's what you want."

"Thank you, Frank. I'll always be indebted to you."

"We're getting there."

"I had a few problems out here, but I worked them out."

Clifton was silent. He wasn't interested and he wanted desperately to get back to sleep.

"They tried to evict me from here at Christmas. Can you imagine the nerve of the sonofabitches?"

"Why was that?"

"They said we were costing them four thousand dollars a day because the Christians weren't gambling in their goddamn casino. The shitasses upped the rent by that much and they still wanted me out."

"What did you do?"

"I bought the fucking place, Frank."

40

Frank Clifton was appalled when he saw Elliot Brodie for the first time in three years. The Christians had warned him that the billionaire's health had been steadily deteriorating, which would account for the decline in late-night telephone calls. Despite the warning, Clifton was unable to mask his reaction when he saw the pitiful creature lying in the bed in the stuffy, darkened Las Vegas hotel suite. Piles of tissues were everywhere, with documents and memos scattered among them. Brodie was naked, except for a linen napkin covering his crotch. His weight had dropped below one hundred pounds.

"I know, Frank," he rasped. "I look like hell. These bastards are killing me. I agreed to let them give me blood transfusions because I'm anemic, but I think it was a mistake. I think there's something bad in the blood. I told them to find out where it comes from, but they say they can't do that. I've got somebody on it. A lot of Negroes sell their blood for money. That could be it."

"I'm sure there's nothing wrong with the blood. What you need is fresh air, sunshine, and a proper diet."

"I've got my air purifier, Frank, and I drink only Poland Spring water. I won't go out there. Too many people. Too many germs. And those goddamned nuclear tests out in the desert. The sonofabitches. I've spent a fortune trying to put a stop to them."

The tirade weakened Brodie. He took several deep breaths before continuing.

"I understand congratulations are in order, Frank."

Clifton looked at his boss blankly.

"Your son. You have a son, don't you?"

"Yes, yes. Bobby."

"How old is he now?"

"He was born in June. So that makes him five months on the seventeenth."

"That's very good, Frank. You and Margaret must be very happy."

"Yes, we are. He doesn't like us to sleep at night, but he's a real joy."

"And how are we doing with our project? I know I haven't called you for several months, but I've been very busy. From what you told me last time, you're ahead of the scientists cloning frogs at Oxford. Right?"

"I've been successful with frogs and mice. The mice were considerably more difficult. For a time I didn't think it would happen. I was ready to give up. But I'll soon be ready to proceed to serious human cell work."

The doctor's words had a dramatic effect on Brodie. He raised his frail upper frame, resting on his elbows, and Clifton could see the color rise in his face from the effort.

"That's good news, Frank. Good news."

"I'll be attempting to start embryos in a test tube to determine effective fertilization and maturation cultures. It's an essential step. There is a lot of work being done in that area in Italy, England, and in this country. It will be commonplace very soon."

"I'm sorry you're not getting the recognition you deserve, Frank. You'd be famous if they knew what you've already accomplished. But you'll never have to worry about your future."

"We've got a long way to go."

Brodie lay back on the bed, his shallow chest heaving. The doctor rose to leave. "Frank?"

"Yes, Mr. Brodie?"

"What happens to those things you grow in the test tubes?"

"They get flushed down the toilet."

41

Neither man knew it, but their meeting in Elliot Brodie's hotel suite in Nassau would be the last time they would see each other. Frank Clifton did not want to be there, with this dissipated, dying madman. Three months earlier, he had successfully implanted a sixty-four-cell embryo in Maria Brazao's uterus and he was reluctant to leave her, even for a short time. But Brodie, as usual, had his way. The billionaire had become more reclusive than ever as he stayed one step ahead of the law, in an odyssey that took him from Las Vegas to the Bahamas, Nicaragua, Canada, England, and back to the Bahamas.

Clifton had been with Brodie's entourage on that cold November night in 1970 when they carried him on a stretcher from his Las Vegas hideaway, through a fire escape exit, and down nine flights of stairs, to a waiting station wagon. Several black limousines drove off as decoys while Brodie was being driven to a nearby air force base. Clifton watched as his employer was carried aboard a four-engine Lockheed JetStar which flew off to Nassau International Airport. The doctor went back to his laboratory and Brodie went into new self-imposed isolation. The same immigration service that had chased Brodie from the Bahamas less than two years earlier was there to welcome him back in December of 1973. When he arrived in the middle of the night, resident and work permits were doled out to his entourage like flowers to arriving tourists in Hawaii. The top two floors of the Xanadu Princess Hotel had been cleared of guests and reserved for Brodie.

"I fixed things up," he bragged in a hoarse whisper. "It's a new government. It's amazing what doors will open when they think you're going to invest. I promised them a lot, but I haven't given them a goddamn cent and I never will."

Clifton was disgusted as he looked at the deplorable condition of Brodie's supposedly germ-free environment. The windows were sealed with masking tape and there was dust and filth everywhere. Lined up along one wall, stark testimony of his deepening depravity, were rows of capped jars containing his urine and feces. Brodie, his body emaciated, lay naked in the middle of the double bed. His unkempt gray hair had grown almost to waist length and his fingernails and toenails were the longest the doctor had ever seen on any human being. All that immense wealth and he's living in shit, Clifton thought.

Clifton was insistent about getting back to Staatsburg and Maria as soon as possible. Brodie seemed vague and confused until the conversation turned to the clone.

"I shouldn't be away more than a day," said Clifton.

"Do you realize the significance of your accomplishment, Frank?"

"I suppose."

"You estimate the birth sometime in June?"

"That's right."

"And you foresee no complications?"

"The heartbeat is strong. We could check the fetal skeleton, but I know how you're opposed to X rays."

"No goddamn X rays, Frank. If you've got a strong heartbeat, that's good enough for me."

Clifton was sitting on a chair beside Brodie's bed. Raising a skeletal arm, the recluse motioned him to move closer.

"Everything is in place for my son's future. But I want him to have something more than my money. I would like him to have my name, but at this point that's not possible. I can't call him Elliot Brodie, Jr. But I can give him my middle name. We'll call him Robard. Did you know that's what my initial stands for, Frank?"

"No, I didn't know that."

"Most people don't know and that's good. His name will be Robard Anthony Bryce. Don't ask me about the 'Bryce.' It came to me in a dream. We'll talk later about how I plan to have him raised. In the meantime I will give you some instructions that must be followed to the letter."

Clifton was apprehensive.

"A parcel will be delivered to you at the house in Staatsburg the day after tomorrow. Make sure you stay there until it arrives. Inside you'll find six hundred thousand dollars in cash. It will be divided into twenty bundles, with thirty thousand in each bundle. You will also find a white envelope. In the envelope will be twenty signed deposit slips, in the name Robard Anthony Bryce. Each slip is for a different bank or branch in New York and each is made out in the amount of thirty thousand dollars. You will open accounts and deposit all of the money at the banks stipulated on the slips. From each bank you will get a savings account passbook and several blank withdrawal slips. You will do that for all twenty banks. Then you will take the passbooks and the withdrawal slips and put them into a secure bundle, which you will send by registered mail to Elaine Hall at Centra Corporation headquarters. She is expecting the parcel. She won't know its contents. The package will be locked away in my private safe. Elaine has been with me a long time and she can be trusted."

"Six hundred thousand dollars is an awful lot of money."

"I chose that amount for a reason. That was the amount my father left to me. At least that was what his company was valued at when I took it over."

42

JUNE 1975

Maria awoke with a start. She screamed from the pain in her abdomen and lower back. Margaret Clifton went quickly to her.

"It's coming. Uh . . . *uhh* . . . I can feel it. It hurts so much."

"It's okay, Maria. Hold on. The doctor's on his way."

The girl clawed at her swollen abdomen. She suppressed a scream, her face contorted, as Frank Clifton entered the room.

"She's nearing second stage," said Margaret calmly. "The contractions are every three minutes."

"Get ready," said Clifton, flipping his wife a sterile scrub gown and mask from the enamel cupboard near the door.

"The membrane's ruptured," said Margaret.

"I can see that. Clean her up and we'll get her to the delivery table."

Maria's rich black hair was glued to her neck and chest like strands of seaweed. She eyed the hypodermic needle in Clifton's right hand.

"It's almost time, Maria. But first we'll do something about the pain." Margaret brought the girl a fresh gown and wiped her face, chest, and arms with a cool sponge. She helped Maria to a sitting position, hugging her shoulders to keep her angled slightly forward. Clifton pulled the gown from beneath the girl and injected the anesthetic into her lower spine. He felt her writhe, but she made no sound. They lowered her slowly and gave her ice chips to relieve the dryness in her mouth and throat. The doctor rolled the bed, silent on its black rubber wheels, to the delivery table. Maria's pubic hair was soaped and shaved before they shifted her gently to the table. Carefully lifting each leg in turn, Margaret helped Maria slide into sterile leggings, pulled to her groin like a ballerina's rehearsal warmers. Sterile sheets were placed beneath her buttocks and over her abdomen. Her feet were strapped into stainless steel stirrups, forcing her legs apart as if she were straddling an invisible vertical saddle. The contractions were down to two-minute intervals and Maria's groans became grunts. The doctor moved the anesthesia and oxygen cart to the delivery table.

"Okay, Maria, you're in second stage. It'll be just like we practiced." He applied the oxygen mask and she inhaled steady streams of nitrous oxide and oxygen to help the baby. "Bear down now, Maria. Give the baby all the help you can muster."

Grimacing, Maria braced her feet with each contraction, pulling as hard as she could against the hand grips at her sides, a sculler tugging at immovable oars.

"It's not my baby!" she cried. "Oh . . . the pain . . . Mother . . . Mother of God! Can't hate the baby . . ."

"Easy, now, Maria. The anesthetic should take effect soon."

"You . . . you lied. You said . . . said it wouldn't hurt much."

"You surprised us, coming along so quickly. It'll be over soon."

"I'm going to die, like my auntie in the old country. She died like this. Mama told me. Oh, God, I don't want to die."

"Now, now, Maria. You're not going to die. You'll be just fine."

Tears welled in the girl's eyes and streamed down her cheeks. Margaret glanced at her husband. Clifton lowered his eyes.

"Uhhh . . . the man with the money. It's his baby; make him suffer. *Damn him! Damn him!* No, no. Mustn't sin. Uhhh . . . uhh . . . Hail Mary . . . please, God, make the pain stop. Mama! Maaahhh . . ."

"The head's emerging," said Clifton. "Get the scissors." Margaret handed him the surgical scissors and he made a small cut to enlarge the vaginal opening. It would prevent undue tearing later. Margaret loved to watch her husband confidently working the instruments as if they were a natural extension to his strong, slender fingers. Clifton sensed her admiration and smiled beneath the surgical mask. Maria's pain eased as the anesthetic began to take effect. Margaret sponged the sweat from her forehead as the doctor pulled and guided the baby's emerging head.

"History in the making," he said, winking at his wife.

"And we can get back to living normal lives?"

"Normal lives. Absolutely."

The tiny head was making its final push through when the doctor shuddered and stepped backward half a step as if someone had shoved him violently. Margaret saw alarm in his eyes; then fear; then terror. His forehead went as white as his mask. She moved to see the baby.

"Stay back," he hissed. It was too late. Margaret saw the umbilical cord wrapped around the baby's neck: a livid, snakelike vein. But it was much more than that. It was the baby. The face. The hair. The skin. Margaret felt herself falling. Clifton grasped her elbow. His right palm cradled the baby's head and upper body. Margaret desperately wanted to look away, but something within kept her eyes fixed on the small form. Beneath the mucus and blood streaks she could see the wizened face of an old man. The hair was thin, gray, and almost shoulder length. There was a sickly pallor to the skin.

"Oh, my God!" she gasped. "No! No!"

"We've got a job to do here," said Clifton, struggling to keep composed. "Get a clamp and tend to Maria."

He was a professional with a string of degrees. He'd treat this as any of the hundred and fifty deliveries he'd made at the Bronx Free Clinic where he signed on to ready himself for this day. He couldn't understand this birth, but he wouldn't panic. He'd think it all through later. For now, he must continue. Maria was groggy from the anesthetic and he was grateful for that.

"We must continue this as if it were a routine delivery," he whispered. "Maria must not see it, nor must we alarm her in any way. This is our problem."

He pulled the remainder of the tiny body through the vaginal opening and clamped and cut the umbilical cord, unwinding it from the neck. He moved quickly behind the white portable screen, holding the baby upside down. He slapped the wrinkled, sagging buttocks. There was no normal baby's cry but a guttural wheeze as it drew its first breath. Working mechanically, Clifton washed the small body. Squeezing drops of silver nitrate solution into the dull eyes, he placed the baby into a crib with an overhead heat lamp. He checked the heartbeat and found it surprisingly strong. Returning to Maria, he avoided his wife's terrified, questioning eyes. He delivered the placenta and stitched up the small vaginal incision. He gave Maria a sleeping injection and without a word they moved her to the hospital bed and returned her to her room, lifting her to her own bed. The girl appeared frail and exhausted when they left her. Margaret went directly to the washroom along the hallway. Clifton could hear her vomiting as he returned to the delivery room.

43

More than three months had passed since Maria had left the Staatsburg house, but Margaret often thought about her. She never associated her with Robard; the girl had been an innocent participant. Margaret was thinking of Maria as she returned from grocery shopping with Ethel Bridges, their heavyset housekeeper, at the wheel of the family station wagon. She too had known Maria. The Cliftons had told the housekeeper that the girl was the daughter of an influential friend. When she found herself pregnant in high school, they took her in to allow her to have the baby discreetly. Ethel assumed the baby had been put up for adoption soon after the birth. In the few conversations she'd had with Maria, Ethel found her decidedly different from the daughters of wealthy people she'd worked for in the past. She wheeled the wagon through the last turn, where the dirt road left the dense woods and began its gentle descent through the meadow to the house.

"You miss her, don't you, Mrs. Clifton?"

"You knew I was thinking of her, Ethel?"

"I sensed you were, ma'am."

"Yes, I do miss her. At times very much. She was such a lovely girl, so innocent and trusting."

The Cliftons were pleased with Ethel. She seldom pried. She was standoffish in an appealing, shy sort of way—except with Bobby. She always had time for the boy and she relished Saturday mornings, when they settled into the family room to watch cartoons on television.

"She was so cheerful and happy most of the time," said Ethel. "I'm glad it's over for her. I don't think there'll be any permanent scars. You and the doctor were very kind to her. I think she rather liked being here. I'd be pleased if she paid us a visit one day."

"I doubt it, Ethel. I think she was happy here, but she'll want to forget about the baby. Perhaps when she's older . . ."

After Maria left, the nursery was closed and the door kept locked. Ethel wasn't given a key. The doctor told her he was using the room for storage of medical records. The entire third floor, including the laboratory, was now off limits. He was getting back into cancer research and he didn't want her exposed to any dangerous substances that might be lying around. He and Margaret would worry about keeping the lab clean. Besides, Ethel had plenty enough to do. She thought they were just being kind because of the extra work she did when Maria was there.

Margaret never thought of Robard as a human being, let alone a child. And although he wasn't in this world by choice, she loathed him. She glanced up to his room as the station wagon approached the rear of the house. A tremor surged through her body. She thought she saw movement in the window. A shadow? A face? *His* face? It wasn't possible. She wished Frank hadn't gone to the city for the day.

"The . . . apple trees are blooming beautifully, aren't they, Ethel?"

Ethel studied the orchard across the road from the house. She detected uneasiness in Margaret's voice. "Yes, ma'am, they're quite lovely. Anything wrong, ma'am?"

"No, nothing."

"You seem suddenly pale."

"The dip in the road. It sometimes gets to my stomach."

"Sorry, ma'am. I should drive a bit slower."

"No, it's all right. It only happens occasionally."

Margaret clasped her hands to prevent them from trembling. Robard was a vegetable. He'd never so much as raised his head from the pillow. Had she seen something at the window? Was it just her imagination? She wondered if she were going crazy. Why doesn't Frank do something before our small family is ripped apart? she asked herself. Ethel parked the station wagon in the garage adjoining the pantry and kitchen.

"Would you mind bringing in the groceries on your own, Ethel? I need a bit of air."

"Not at all, ma'am."

Margaret walked away from the house until she knew the window was in view. She whirled and looked up. Nothing. No face, no shadow, nothing unusual. She felt a prickling sensation at the back of her neck. The pressure of keeping Robard's unholy presence a secret from the rest of the world, from Ethel, from their own son, was taking its toll, she realized. It had been eight months since Elliot Brodie, sounding very unstable, had contacted them. It was only through the media that they were able to keep track of his whereabouts.

Margaret had become increasingly morose in the weeks following the birth. Initially, she thought the clone would die and the nightmare would end. But intravenous feedings alone kept him alive, nourished him, as he grew at a tremendous, abnormal rate. She had begged her husband to discontinue the I.V.'s, but he refused. "I respect your feelings," he said. "But it's my duty as a scientist and as a doctor to give him basic sustenance at the very least."

"He's a monster and a freak and it's your duty as a human being to let him die in peace and get him out of our lives before he destroys our family," she argued. But Clifton was adamant.

Robard grew taller and taller, like a skeleton being

stretched. He remained comatose, but emitted occasional groans and muffled grunts. Clifton kept the nursery spotless, but whenever Margaret was in the room she noticed a stale, foul odor. The door to the nursery, which adjoined the spacious laboratory, was always locked. The laboratory itself was off limits to Bobby, unless accompanied by his father, and he was told the nursery was now used for storage. Margaret watched her husband become despondent and short-tempered as months of intensive research left him no closer to solving the riddle of Robard's defective birth and abnormal growth. He turned to cancer research to try to keep his mind off the clone, which he treated as an experimental object, like a laboratory rat or frog. Twice a week he weighed and measured Robard, religiously recording every change in his diary.

Ethel was still putting the groceries away when Margaret returned to the house. The housekeeper was aware of the growing strain between the doctor and his wife. She liked them and enjoyed living at the Staatsburg house. She hoped whatever the problem was between them would quickly pass.

"You did the groceries, so I'll drive over to the Welch's to pick up Bobby while you're preparing lunch," said Margaret.

"But if you're not feeling well, ma'am . . ."

"I'm all right now. The queasy feeling has passed. It's a short drive."

It was Bobby more than anything that kept things together. He was an energetic, outgoing, and very bright child.

"Will the Welch boy be joining us for lunch?"

"Probably. Those two are inseparable. We're fortunate that Bobby was able to find a playmate living so near."

Bobby bounded into the house twenty minutes later.

"Where's Teddy?" asked Ethel.

"Had to go into town with his mother," said Bobby, heading for the table.

"Just a minute, young man. Wash those hands first. They're filthy." The boy retreated to the washroom off the front hallway. Ethel noticed Margaret was in a better mood when she came in from parking the station wagon, but she felt there was still something bothering her. During lunch Margaret was distracted and picked at the food on her plate.

"C'mon, Mom, you're not eatin' your food. You always make me eat everything."

Margaret wasn't listening.

"*Mom!*"

"What? Uh, sorry. What is it, Bobby? There's no need to raise your voice."

"You're not eatin' your food."

"I'm afraid my appetite is off today."

"Your mother's not feeling one hundred percent today," explained Ethel.

"She always makes me eat when I don't feel like it."

"You're a growing boy. You need it more than I do," said Margaret.

"Aw, sure, that's what you always say."

After lunch, the boy went to his room, where he was working on a model airplane his father had bought for him. It was meant for an older child, but he was progressing quite well. It was his third model and he'd completed most of it on his own. His father had helped him with the first two, but he was determined to make this one himself. Not even Teddy Welch would see it until he was finished. It was a World War II Spitfire— a famous fighter plane, his father told him. The boy was thinking of his mother as he worked. He hoped she wouldn't get too sick.

His thoughts were interrupted by a creaking sound outside his door. The sound of tiptoeing. He was about to call out but caught himself. Opening the door a crack, he saw his mother pass her bedroom door farther along the hallway and start up the third-floor stairs. Bobby followed her quietly, creeping up the stairway to the heavy oak door. He'd been up there often to see Maria, but he had been at Teddy's summer cottage when the baby was born and she took it away before he returned.

Bobby had never seen his mother go up to the laboratory alone. He watched as she crossed the room and stood on her toes, straining to reach something at the top of a cupboard. He heard a jangle of metal and saw a set of keys on a ring in her right hand. She moved toward the storage room which used to be the nursery for Maria's baby. He had promised not to tell anyone about the baby because Maria wasn't married and wasn't really supposed to have a baby. She was too young and it was an accident that she was having it. A nice married family would take the baby after it was born.

Margaret paused at the storage room door, listening, before inserting one of the keys. She opened the door and felt along the wall for the light switch. Bobby craned his neck but couldn't see into the room from his perch at the top of the stairway. His mother stared into the room and entered. The door closed softly behind her. The boy's stockinged feet were silent on the tiled floor as he moved toward the door. He pressed his ear against it. He could hear her moving around inside. Her footsteps grew louder and he scurried to the stairway. His mother locked the door and replaced the keys above the cupboard. She seemed relieved, almost happy.

Margaret hugged her son tightly as she tucked him in for the night. Hearing the study door close after she went downstairs, Bobby pushed aside his blankets and eased himself to the floor. He kept his eyes closed in the darkness but found the door with ease. It was a private game he often played: walking around with his eyes closed, to prepare himself if he should ever become blind. He moved silently up the stairway. His dad wouldn't like this one bit. Sucking in his breath, he pushed against the heavy door. It closed behind him and he flicked on the lights. The room was bathed in a harsh fluorescent glow. He usually enjoyed his visits to the lab with his dad, but now it seemed scary. He walked resolutely to the cupboard but couldn't reach the top where his mother had put the keys. He pulled a stool to the front of the cupboard and stood on it. He panicked, nearly falling, when the keys jangled loudly. Pressing them against his chest to muffle the sound, he stood motionless an eternity of seconds. Stepping gingerly from the stool, he moved across the floor to the door of the storage room. There were four keys on the ring. He found the correct one on his second attempt. The key turning in the lock sounded as loud as a metal Christmas noisemaker. Again he paused, chest heaving. The door creaked as he opened it several inches. Squeezing his eyes closed, he ran his hand flat along the wall in a wide arc, searching for the light switch.

"Geez, where is it?" he whispered. "Shoot! I can't find it." He opened the door farther. The glow from the overhead lab lights ended abruptly in the darkness of the doorway. Squinting, he strained to pierce the darkness. "It's so dark. I should get outta here."

Instead, he stepped into the room, one hand gripping the edge of the door, like a mountain climber clutching his lifeline. His breathing was like thunder in his ears. Pushing the door fully open, he dropped to his hands and knees. He moved to the right, one outstretched hand leading the way, his antenna. He touched something solid. Cardboard boxes in a row. They gave way to wood; first a leg and then a series of parallel vertical rungs. Stretching higher, he felt a row of wood beads. The crib! For Maria's baby. Why didn't they take it with them? He reached a corner and started along the back wall. More wood. This time a trunk or box. The lid was unlocked. He raised it slightly and felt inside. Toys. A stuffed animal. The baby's toys. He closed the lid.

Framed in the light from the lab he noticed something large and dark in the center of the room. He couldn't make out what it was. It obscured the lower half of the doorway. Maybe it was a table or counter like the ones in the lab. He crawled toward it until his outstretched hand felt something soft. A wool blanket. On a bed.

Suddenly, something cold and damp gripped his wrist. He pulled away, and heard a raspy, hollow moan—like something from the depths of an evil cave—something very close to him.

Margaret was reading in the study when she heard her son's scream. "*Bobby!* Oh, God! Bobby, I'm coming." She saw the light splashing down the third-floor stairway from the open door of the laboratory as she rushed to his room. The boy was in his bed, covers pulled tightly around him. His cheeks were flushed, his forehead dotted with perspiration. She hugged his trembling body, stroking the back of his neck.

"It's okay, Bobby. It's okay."

The boy began to sob.

"What were you doing up there?" Margaret asked in a soothing voice. "What upset you so?"

"Some . . . something in that room grabbed me. It was dark. I couldn't see. . . . I ran and ran."

"How did you get in there?"

Ethel Bridges arrived, out of breath, wearing a bright red dressing gown over her full-length flannel nightie. "What's wrong? I heard screams."

"It's okay, Ethel. Bobby's just had a fright."

"A nightmare?"

"No. He went up to the lab in the dark and was frightened."

"It was in the baby's room," blurted the boy.

"Okay, take it easy, now. You told me that. How did you get in there?"

"I saw you go in there this afternoon. I saw the keys. I'm sorry. I'm sorry."

This was Margaret's worst fear come true. An inquisitive six-year-old. What else would you expect? The anger toward her husband intensified.

"Tell me exactly what you saw."

"I didn't see anything. I couldn't find the light. I was crawling around and when I felt the bed or something in the middle, something grabbed my arm and made a scary sound. What is it? What's up there?"

"There's nothing up there, Bobby. It's a storage room. It was dark and you were frightened. That's what happens to little boys when they go into places they're not supposed to."

"But I felt it," he sobbed. Margaret silently cursed her husband for forcing her to lie to their son.

"How come the bed and toys for Maria's baby are in there? I felt them, you know."

"They already had a crib and lots of toys. We didn't know that when we bought them."

"I could have had them." The boy was feeling better.

"You've got enough toys. We've been meaning to give them to the Salvation Army or some other charity. I must remember to do that." Margaret smiled. "I'll prove to you there's nothing there. I'll go up and put the lights on and then I want you to come up and see for yourself. You'll see there's nothing there but an old hospital bed."

"Oh, no. I'm not goin' back up there."

"You just wait here. I'll come down and get you."

"I'll go and take a look if you like, ma'am."

"Thanks, Ethel. You stay with Bobby. I'll only be a few minutes." There was a sharpness in her voice that Ethel had never heard before.

Robard was in his usual position when Margaret entered the room. She moved to the crib, pulled it aside, and opened the door to the linen closet behind it. Inside, she pulled two blankets from a shelf and spread them as best she could over the floor of the small room. Moving quickly, she rolled Robard's bed to the narrow doorway. She pulled back the sheets from his skeletal frame and unhooked his I.V. from the metal stand, laying it on his stomach. She could tell from the odor his large flannel diaper was wet. She covered her mouth and gagged. With one hand supporting the I.V. bag, she pulled his bony legs over the side of the bed and eased his body to the floor, fighting the nausea that gripped her. She dragged him onto the blankets in the linen closet, the I.V. still resting on his stomach. Pulling another blanket from the cupboard, she covered him.

She closed the door, moved the crib back into place, and pushed the bed to the middle of the room. She made it up deftly, took a last look around, and went down for her son.

He entered the room, holding tightly to Ethel Bridges's hand. He frowned when he saw the empty bed. Maybe he *had* been confused in the darkness. But the grip on his wrist—that awful sound—they sure *seemed* real.

"It stinks in here, ma'am," said Ethel, crinkling her nose. "It needs a good cleaning. I could scrub it out in the morning."

"I've tried. I think odors from the lab get locked in here. There's only that one small window for ventilation. And you know how the doctor feels about people being up here when he's not around."

"Well, you were here today," said the boy.

"When your dad called this morning, he asked me to look for a book he's misplaced. He sometimes reads in here. He was mistaken. It wasn't here."

44

APRIL 1976

Margaret was planting spring flowers in the back garden when the telephone rang. By the time she reached the kitchen Clifton was replacing the receiver.

"Brodie?"

"No. His Christians. They want me out in Houston right away. They're flying him in from Mexico."

"You mean you'll finally get to see him again?"

"He's very ill. In a coma, they say. They've got a company jet waiting for me at La Guardia." He checked his watch. "I've got to get moving. He's supposed to arrive about six this evening. I'd like to know why the hell they wait until he's half dead before they decide to bring him home."

An anxious Christian, introducing himself simply as Maxwell, met Clifton at the Houston airport and ushered him to a private lounge. "Mr. Brodie's plane should be arriving on schedule," he said solemnly. "We believe it's quite serious. We've been praying for him."

Maxwell's face was pale and drawn. The doctor wondered if it was Brodie he cared about or the potential loss of a very lucrative meal ticket. They left the airport lounge shortly before six P.M. A limousine took them to a secluded runway out of view of the main terminal. An ambulance, two doctors, a nurse and four company executives were already there. The billionaire's Learjet landed moments later and taxied to within a few yards of them. A door opened and the ambulance attendants clambered aboard with a stretcher. They emerged moments later with a sheet-covered form on the stretcher.

"He died about thirty minutes ago," an attendant whispered reverently. A gust of wind uncovered Brodie's face. Clifton glanced down. It was uncanny; except for the chestnut mustache and beard, the old man on the stretcher was an exact replica of Robard. The small troupe followed the ambulance to the hospital, where the body was removed to the pathology lab for an autopsy.

On day two, Brodie's aides and executives from Centra Corporation waited outside the autopsy room. Clifton waited with them while a police sergeant stood guard.

"What's he doing here?" said Clifton, nodding toward the guard.

"This is no ordinary body," replied Maxwell. "This is a corporate body. This man is worth billions."

"Even in death, he's got to have his security," said the doctor, shaking his head. As a courtesy he was invited to the autopsy, already under way.

Maxwell, who felt left out, was waiting anxiously when Clifton emerged from the room half an hour later. "Was it a stroke?"

"Kidneys. They say he died from a chronic kidney disease. There were a dozen other contributing factors, but they say that's what killed him. They were just wrapping up when they let me in. Apparently his heart was fine."

Three men in dark suits had arrived while Frank Clifton was in the autopsy room. "More cops?" he asked Maxwell.

"Yes, Internal Revenue, Customs, and the FBI. The government sent them. They want to take Mr. Brodie's fingerprints to be sure it's really him. Can you imagine? He had to die to prove he was alive."

"The body's not even cold and they want their cut," said Clifton.

"That's the government for you," said Maxwell. "They've been after him for a long time. Well, it won't matter to him now. He looked awful, didn't he? I hadn't seen him in person for several years."

"It was all that time he spent confined to bed in dark hotel rooms. His frame shrunk. His weight went down to ninety pounds. What a shame for a man of his position."

"When did you last see him, Doctor?"

"In London, a couple of years ago."

"How did he look then?"

"Not very good. But nothing like this. He had a lot on his mind."

"Will you be staying for the funeral?"

"I suppose I should. Yes. I hadn't really thought about it."

"He'd probably want you there. I'll send a car around to your hotel in the morning. It will be a quiet sunrise service. Very private. He'll be buried alongside his mother and father."

"Does he have family?" asked Clifton. What he really wanted to know was whether a will existed and if so, if there was any mention of Robard. He had no idea whether anyone else knew about Robard. He and Margaret knew and Brodie knew. But Brodie was dead.

"Some distant relatives. Nobody close that we know of. And we don't know if he's left a will. We're still searching."

"What happens to all of his interests?"

"You mean your cancer clinic?"

"The clinic. The casinos. Aircraft . . . oil . . ."

"I don't really know what will happen. Business as usual, I suppose. The lawyers will decide all of that."

There were fewer than twenty mourners at the cemetery. Clifton saw no tears when he scanned the solemn faces at the graveside.

"That's his closest living relative," whispered Maxwell, nodding toward an elderly woman sitting in a chair in front of the steel gray casket. "An aunt or something."

Clifton wondered if Elliot Brodie had ever talked to her during his years of seclusion. Maxwell nudged him with his elbow.

"The minister is from the cathedral where Mr. Brodie was baptized," he whispered. "Anglican, I believe."

". . . We brought nothing into this world," droned the minister. "It is certain we can take nothing out. In my Father's house there are many mansions. Remember thy servant Elliot, O Lord. Give him eternal rest and peace in Thy heavenly kingdom." And please, thought Clifton, no germs or air conditioners. The minister sprinkled dirt over the casket as it was lowered into the ground.

There was nothing final about the ceremony for Clifton. No will had been found and, back in Staatsburg, Robard was lying in an upstairs room.

45

Vince Oliverio and Alfie Morrow has sat spellbound as the doctor told them his story.

"Why did you decide to dump him, Frank?" asked Oliverio.

"This whole thing nearly destroyed our marriage. I couldn't bring myself to remove him from his life support system, and this was very upsetting to Margaret. She came up with the idea of a nursing home and she studied all the literature. I was against it at first and that made her very angry. The matter was settled for us when we received notice from Centra Corporation that they were closing the clinic. They gave us sixty days' notice. Elliot Brodie was dead and there was no will. As far as we knew, no one was aware of Robard's existence. Our child knew nothing about Robard and that was another sore point with Margaret. We couldn't very well cart him around when we moved."

"Why not go public?" asked Morrow. "Wouldn't you have been famous?"

"I didn't feel very good about what I'd done. I didn't

consider it an accomplishment. And, in retrospect, I'm sure it would have been a step backward scientifically speaking. People would have said, 'Look, he's created a monster.' A lot of moral questions would have been raised. Even Margaret, who considers herself an agnostic, has convinced herself that God is in some way punishing us for interfering with nature. You must also realize that the United Nations has been contemplating a worldwide ban on genetic experimentation. I think that would be regressive. If this came out, it would be used to play on people's negative emotions. And I'm sure there is also a selfish motivation—I believe I would have been universally condemned by my peers. On the other hand, if the birth had been normal, there is a strong likelihood that I would have come forward.''

''I take it, it was you who sent the twenty-thousand-dollar donation to the nursing home?'' asked Oliverio.

''Yes. It was part of the sixty-thousand-dollar severance package from Centra Corporation. Margaret and I didn't think it would be fair to place a burden on the home. I don't know where he got the will to survive for so long in such a dissipated state. When we left him there we thought he would die very soon and twenty thousand was more than enough to pay for his care.''

The policemen sensed the doctor was suddenly uncomfortable.

''Is there something you want to tell us, Frank?'' asked Oliverio. The doctor was silent for a moment.

''Yes, there is. But it's not something I'm particularly proud of and I believe it could get me into some legal difficulty.''

''I think we have the same interest here, Doctor,'' said Oliverio. ''We have to get him. If what you know will help us with that, then I think you should tell us. It's not you we're after at this stage.''

Clifton bowed his head, contemplating.

''Okay,'' he said finally. ''We ran into considerable financial difficulties. I won't bore you with the details, but I made some very bad investments. I made a lot of money in the ten years I was employed with Elliot Brodie. Not only was the salary generous, but he covered most of our normal day-to-day expenses as well. House-keeper, car, grounds maintenance. All of that. And Centra Corporation owned the property, so they paid all of the taxes. In effect, our personal expenditures were at an absolute minimum. We had a lot of money saved. It's embarrassing to admit, but most of that was lost. We were deeply involved in a company developing hydrogen as an alternative energy source. It looked like a sure thing with the world oil crisis. Oil prices soared and we thought they'd stay there. Needless to say, they didn't. We were faced with losing the house. I'm not trying to shift the blame to Margaret, but she suggested we use some of the six hundred thousand dollars that I had deposited for Robard on behalf of Brodie."

Clifton lowered his eyes.

"I had copies of the deposit slips to prove I made the deposits. I practiced the signatures over and over and attempted to withdraw small amounts from three different banks in New York. I was told the accounts had been closed. At first I thought Centra had closed them, but that didn't make sense. Brodie was always adamant that nobody but the three of us would know about this. He didn't trust anybody who worked for him. He probably didn't trust me, either, but he had no choice. At any rate, I decided to call the nursing home and inquire about the old man who'd been left there. I got the shock of my life when they told me he'd died of exposure in the woods. I thought they'd made a mistake. When we left him there he was comatose. But they insisted it was him."

"Who told you he had died?"

"It was a woman. I think she was some sort of supervisor. She said he walked into the woods and got lost."

"Corky," said Oliverio.

"Who?"

"It doesn't matter. The point is, he didn't die. He walked away."

"When you came out to see me, I thought you were trying to trace the money or something. Then when you told me he'd disappeared and wasn't dead, I didn't know what to think."

"Six hundred thousand, plus three years' interest," said Morrow. "If he's got it, it's no wonder he's able to get around like he does."

"He's got it, all right," said Clifton.

Oliverio leaned forward in his chair. "How do you know that?"

"I've seen him. He called me three or four weeks after you came out to see me. I met him at a hotel in White Plains."

"Jesus Christ! Why didn't you contact us right away?"

"I'm contacting you now. He threatened me and my family. I believe he's very dangerous. He didn't admit it, but I think he's behind those killings. The worst part is, he's not the same."

"What does that mean, not the same, Doc?"

"Please don't call me doc. It would be like me calling you a dick."

"I am a dick, Frank."

"For Christ's sake, Vince," said Morrow, turning to Clifton. "What do you mean, Doctor? He's altered his appearance?"

"What I mean is, for some reason that I have been unable to fathom, he's become considerably younger."

"Ahhh, what is this shit?" said Oliverio.

"I'm telling you, he's getting younger and younger."

"You expect us to believe that? I suppose he has a portrait in his attic."

"I don't expect you to believe anything. I'm just telling you what I know. I've gone through enough guilt and anguish over this and if you don't want to hear it, that's fine with me. I can just leave you this and be on my way."

Oliverio realized he'd gone too far. Morrow cast a disapproving glance his way.

"All right, Frank. I'm sorry. But you have to admit, this is pretty wild stuff."

"If he's getting younger, that would explain the reduction in age creases on the prints from Vegas," offered Morrow.

Clifton looked at Oliverio sullenly before continuing.

"He wanted to know why he wasn't born as a child. It was then I realized I was talking to Elliot Brodie. Obviously not the body, but certainly the mind. I attempted to clone his body. You can't clone a mind and a memory. It's a scientific impossibility. But here was the living proof, standing in front of me. Do you know what something like that can do to your sanity? The longer I talked to him, the more difficult it became to differentiate between Brodie, who was dead, and the clone. It was the same voice, the same eyes. The only difference between him and the Elliot Brodie I first met fourteen years ago was that he was younger and healthier and not lying naked in a sealed, filthy room. There I was, engaged in the same kind of weird conversations that I used to have with Brodie. He knew exactly who I was and what I had done. It was as if there'd been a total brain transplant. He was still an egomaniac. But there was one major difference. I never saw Elliot Brodie as a threat. He was eccentric and a bit depraved, but in my view a danger only to himself. Robard, on the other hand, was menacing. I felt fear all the time I was in his presence. He wanted to know when the reverse aging would stop and what had gone wrong in the first place. I told him I had no idea what was happening."

"Do you have any idea today?" asked Morrow.

"I have no understanding whatever on the mind and memory side of it. As I said, scientifically it shouldn't have happened. I asked him all sorts of questions about Brodie's past and he looked at me like I was insane. He knew all the answers. He did say that he forgets some incidents that happened to Brodie in his later years. Now, I don't know if that means his memory is shrinking in concert with his age or if it was because Brodie was in such a drug-induced daze all those years. As for the reverse aging, in the past few weeks I've pored over every scientific text and article that I could find. As far as I can determine, he is suffering from a reverse form of a very rare disease called Cockayne's syndrome. It's an accelerated aging disease that usually affects young children. They die very young but with all the symptoms of a very old person. In effect, they die of old age.

It has to do with DNA. That's the molecules that carry your genetic code, the instructions for the production of your particular body characteristics. Somewhere along the line, his became defective. They seem to have repaired themselves but are operating at an accelerated pace in the wrong direction.

"There's been fewer than fifty known cases of Cockayne's syndrome since it was first discovered in the 1930s. The last reported case was about a year ago in California. A five-year-old girl died. She was the genetic equivalent of a ninety-year-old woman. She had cataracts, hearing problems, decaying teeth, wrinkles, dry brittle hair, and high blood pressure. She even had arthritis in her hands. Scientists think the disease is caused by the inability of the DNA to repair itself."

"And the cure?"

"None to date, and because it's so rare, I don't think you'll see a lot spent on research."

"So what happens to our friend?" asked Oliverio.

"Well, in that little girl's case, it was estimated the disease caused her to age at the rate of fifteen to twenty years for every year she lived. Brodie—er, Robard—seems to be reverse aging at about the same pace."

"You're saying he'll get younger and younger and then just die?"

"I don't know. I have no yardstick to go by."

"What did you mean when you said he seemed menacing?"

"He seemed very sure of himself. And the impression I got was that because Elliot Brodie was dead and he himself didn't officially exist, he could get away with just about anything he wanted to. I don't know if I did the right thing, but I told him at that point that the police were after him—that you were out to see me, and that you had his fingerprints."

Oliverio bowed his head and massaged his temples.

"When I told him that, he got very angry. He had me go over and over our conversation and warned me not to talk to you again. It was then that he threatened me and my family."

"What did he say?"

''To use his words, he said that a lot of people had fucked him over, and now he was going to do the fucking over. He said that I should stick to my work and find a quick solution to stop his age reversal and if I should tell the police anything more, he wouldn't be responsible for any harm that came to me or my wife and child.''

''Has he contacted you since?''

''Once by telephone, to check on my progress. I told him what I told you about Cockayne's syndrome. I told him I was searching for a solution. Even with massive funding, it would take years of study and research to accurately define the problem and come up with an answer. I didn't tell him that, of course. He said I was being watched and that he would contact me again in a few weeks.''

''Can you give us more on his description when you last saw him?'' asked Morrow.

''All you have to do is dig out an old photograph of Elliot Brodie when he was about forty-five or so. That's exactly what he looks like. There's one other thing: He told me he had daily seizures that last about a half an hour. The way he described it, it sounded like epilepsy, but he said it wasn't.''

''He's right,'' said Oliverio. ''They tested him extensively. I saw him go through a seizure when I went to the home. It lasted more than an hour. He would curl into a ball and it was impossible to pry him loose. Then his legs and arms would shoot out, stiff as a board. His strength was unbelievable.''

''He talked about recurring dreams and a huge snake chasing him underwater. I'm not a psychiatrist, but I believe the snake is symbolic of the umbilical cord. He was born with the cord wrapped around his neck. The dreams could be based on actual womb memories.''

''What you're saying, Doctor, is that we've got a modern version of a Frankenstein's monster on our hands,'' said Morrow.

''Yes, and I'm the mad doctor who created him. If he looked like a monster, you'd have no trouble finding him. Unfortunately, he looks absolutely normal. And I can't stress enough how extremely paranoid he is. He went on and on about his enemies. He called them bloodsuckers who stole from him.''

"He probably won't harm you as long as he thinks you can help him.''

"I'll do whatever I can to help you get him. All I would ask is that you give me sufficient notice to get my family into seclusion if my role in this must be made public.''

"That's fair, Frank," said Oliverio. "What we want you to do is to contact either one of us the moment you hear from him. And try to delay meeting him until we've had time to get out here. He will probably assume you're under surveillance, so we'll be very cautious.''

"This has been like a millstone around our necks and I want it purged from our lives. I would obviously implore you to keep us out of it, but if that's not possible. . . . Well, we'll just have to face it as best we can.''

The doctor pushed the thick folder across the table toward Oliverio. "All of my notes and documents are in there, as well as my personal diary. I've removed or blacked out personal sections that had nothing to do with Elliot Brodie. It will give you a complete account of everything that has transpired since the first day I met him in Boston.''

4

robard

46

Robard could see the meeting was about to break up and he didn't wait for the waitress to return with his change. He slipped out the side door and sat in his rental car, parked in the shadow of the building. He followed Oliverio's dark brown Plymouth out of the lot.

It was after two A.M. by the time Oliverio dropped Morrow at his car at the Police Academy and arrived on his deserted street in Bay Ridge. He parked, as he always did, on a side street around the corner from his house. An old, full maple tree blocked out the street lamp and put the car in deep shadow. He was carrying his briefcase and Frank Clifton's thick file. As he leaned down to press the lock button on the driver's door he felt the steel silencer against his ribs.

"Keep very still or you're dead, Vince," commanded a flat, controlled voice.

"I don't have much cash."

A hand frisked Oliverio, removing his .38 service revolver from its holster under his jacket. He could taste fear. He was also felt humiliated. In all his years with

the department, he had never had his gun taken from
him. He felt further violated when his wallet was removed from his hip pocket.

"Open the briefcase and set it on the ground."

Oliverio complied. Robard dropped the revolver and
wallet into it and snapped it shut. "Now put the file on
the ground and get in the car and keep both hands on
the steering wheel."

When Oliverio was behind the wheel, Robard ordered him to look straight ahead. He held the pistol to
the back of the policeman's neck, at the base of the
skull, and placed the briefcase and the file on the rear
seat. He reached behind Oliverio and unlocked the rear
door.

"If you turn your head, or move your hands one
inch, you're dead," said Robard, removing the pistol
from the back of Oliverio's neck and closing the door.
In an instant, he was sitting directly behind him.

"I want you to drive to the shopping plaza in the
next block. Keep it very smooth. If the speedometer
goes above fifteen, I'll pull the trigger."

They parked near a light standard in a deserted corner of the plaza's parking lot, out of view of the street.
There was one other car in the lot, parked several yards
from them. Must be his, thought Oliverio. It wasn't a
high crime area and Oliverio knew it was only lightly
patrolled by the NYPD. Robard, wearing a pair of black
leather gloves, saw the gold detective shield as he
looked through the wallet.

"You're the clone, aren't you?" asked Oliverio
evenly.

"I'll do the talking. You'd be some big shitass hero
if you brought me in, wouldn't you, Vince?"

"What do you want from me?"

"If I'm not mistaken, it's all right here. Why haven't
you gone public before now, Vince? I have a feeling you
and your partner are the only cops who know anything
about me."

"Hell, no. The FBI. Interpol. They're all looking for
you."

"I think you're full of shit, Vince. They're looking

for somebody, but they don't know it's me. The fingerprints never crossed my mind. I had no idea they would
be the identical."

He began thumbing through the contents of the briefcase and the file. Oliverio was angry with himself for
taking Robard's file with them when they went to see
the doctor. Everything he had on the case was in there.

"This is a real bonanza, Vince."

"Did you kill Ellen McKinnon?"

"That shitass bitch. I hated her. Just a friendly push
to help her on her way."

Oliverio's knuckles turned white as he squeezed the
steering wheel.

"What about the old woman?"

"She was a mental case. She saw me do it. I had no
choice. Nobody really cared." Robard, Oliverio sensed,
was enjoying himself. Then the businesslike tone
returned.

"Frank shouldn't have talked to you like he did. I
warned him. He'll have to pay for that."

"We went to him."

"I don't care. He told you everything. He was helpful, though, giving me your names. It wasn't difficult
finding out where you and your partner lived. I've been
watching the two of you."

"Are you going to kill us and the doctor, like you did
the others?"

"Not Frank. He's not as smart as I thought he was,
but I still might need him. But the boy . . . their precious son. They dote on him."

"Why don't you let it go? Get help."

"Fuck you, Vince. I know what would happen to me.
Come and see the freak. No, thank you. I'm going to
get every shitass that ever fucked me over. They were
all greedy. But now I don't exist and no one can stop
me."

He removed all of the cash from Oliverio's wallet and
tossed it over the seat to floor on the passenger's side.
This is it, thought Oliverio, the bastard's going to waste
me right here in the car. He heard the rear door open
and in the instant that Robard moved the pistol around

the door frame to step out of the car, the pressure of the silencer eased from the back of his neck. Oliverio slammed down on his door handle and dropped his body sideways with all the force he could muster. The door struck bone and the metal of the revolver. Oliverio rolled over once on the pavement and began to run in a half crouch. He could hear Robard cursing behind him.

He heard a muffled pistol shot. The bullet hit him in the left hip, shattering the bone. His momentum carried him several feet forward before he fell to the pavement, writhing in pain. He struggled to get to his feet, but his leg buckled and he fell again. He could hear Robard running toward him. He was on him quickly and Oliverio instinctively turned his head to the side when he felt the cold of the silencer against the back of his head.

"Shitass bastard!" hissed Robard as he pulled the trigger. He ran back to Oliverio's car and retrieved the wallet and the service revolver. A light came on in one of the townhouses beyond the parking lot as he ran back to the prone form. He dropped the wallet to the pavement beside Oliverio, and, lifting the policeman's shoulder, replaced the pistol in its holster. Another light came on and he heard voices as he ran toward his rental car, the briefcase in his hand and the file under his arm.

Alfie Morrow was in a deep sleep when John Sadowski called at four-thirty in the morning. Morrow was dressed in minutes. The call awakened his wife, Anne. She could see his face was ashen.

"Who was it?" she asked.

"Sadowski. Vince has been shot."

"Oh, my God!"

"He's had emergency surgery at Victory Memorial in Dyker Heights."

"Where did it happen? Who—"

"He was robbed. That's all John told me. I've got to get over there. They don't know if he'll make it."

"Oh, no."

Morrow kissed his wife and left the bedroom. It was

still dark as he walked quickly to his car parked in the driveway beside the house. Robard, who had been crouching down behind the passenger side, suddenly stood up. Morrow was reaching for his .38 when the shotgun blast hit him full in the face. He died instantly. Robard could hear Anne Morrow's screams as he disappeared into the darkness.

47

The newspapers ran several stories about the killing of Alfie Morrow and the wounding of his high-profile partner who lay in a coma in the hospital. Oliverio had undergone surgery to remove a small-caliber bullet lodged near his brain. There were pictures of Anne Morrow with the two children and another of Florence Oliverio sitting in her living room with a picture of her son on the table beside her. Oliverio's wallet, found beside him in the parking lot, was empty of cash but robbery was ruled out when his partner was shot dead two hours later. Loose speculation about who may have been responsible for the shootings was rampant. Both men had worked on cases involving organized crime figures. There were no suspects, but the department was checking into every case the detectives had worked on during the past three years.

Frank Clifton was horrified when he read the accounts of the shootings. He knew Robard must be involved. He telephoned the hospital and was told Oliverio remained unconscious and in critical condition.

He called Margaret, who worked as a nurse for a family physician in Ridgefield.

"I'm sure it was Robard. He said he was watching me. He's completely out of control. We may be in danger now."

"But he thinks he needs you to help him."

"His thinking is irrational. He's capable of anything. I think we should go away for a while. Even if it means taking Bobby out of school."

"Surely the police will get him now."

"Don't count on it. I should go to them and tell them what I know."

"But you've given them everything. Surely, others in the department must know what's going on. You said you thought you could trust those two officers. But you might not be able to trust others. My big worry is what the publicity would do to Bobby."

They agreed to talk about it at home after work.

The yellow school bus geared down and came to a stop in front of Bobby Clifton's house. The door opened and he jumped to the pavement, carrying his books and a bright blue lunch box. He ran into the house through the front garage and within minutes he was out on the back deck with his fishing rod and a can of worms. He disappeared from view behind the trees near the front pond. He didn't notice the glint of sun on the binoculars halfway up the wooded hill on the other side of the pond. Robard adjusted the focus as the boy walked to the second pond. He removed a fat worm from the can and baited his hook, then opened the bale on his reel and, with a neat flick of his wrist, made a perfect cast. Robard panned from the boy toward the house. Panning in the other direction, he paused a few seconds on the boy reeling in his line, and focused on a dense thicket in a small cove out of the boy's view. He kept the binoculars trained on the shrubs until he saw the small patch of red. Under cover of the brush, Robard made his way around the rear of the pond toward the thicket. His breathing was labored by the time he reached the cove.

The boy was out of view around its point. Robard pulled aside several freshly cut branches and uncovered a red fiberglass dingy and a pair of high rubber boots. He removed his shoes and slipped into the boots. Stopping to catch his breath every few seconds, he pushed and dragged the boat to the water's edge. He pushed it out a few feet and climbed in. The pain in his belly was intensifying. He unclasped the short paddle from the side of the dingy and paddled toward the mouth of the cove.

Bobby was startled when he saw the boat come into view. He was in the middle of a cast and he failed to release his line which came to an abrupt stop in midair, causing the worm to rip free and plop into the water several yards away. The boy stood staring.

"Hi, Bobby," yelled Robard with a wave.

"Who are you?" asked the boy, wondering how this stranger and his boat came to be in his pond.

"Jack Mills," Robard said with a smile. "Your dad and I are good friends."

"How did you get out there?"

"I've been around the corner here waiting to surprise you. How do you like it?"

"Like what?"

"The boat. It's yours."

"Mine!"

"Yes. It's from your dad. He had me sneak it in here while you were at school."

"But where's dad?"

"Oh, he'll be home at his usual time. He asked me to bring it out because I have a half-ton truck."

Bobby's parents had warned him about talking to strangers. But this was different. This was his dad's friend.

"Geez, my own boat!"

Robard paddled the dingy to within a few feet of the boy.

"Pull me in and you can test it out."

The boy reached out and grabbed the bow, pulling the boat to shore.

"Geez, I'll really be able to catch the big ones from

that. I always see them jumping out in the middle in the summer.''

''Get in, we'll give it a try.'' The boy reeled in his line.

''Can I bring my fishing rod?''

''Of course. And your worms.''

''My very own boat,'' said the boy, stepping in.

''There's just enough room for two if I sit toward the back,'' said Robard. He used the paddle to pole the dingy away from shore. He paddled to the middle of the pond. His belly was burning. He stopped paddling.

''Want to try it here?''

''Oh, yeah! Great!''

Robard held out the can and Bobby reached for a worm. He baited his hook and made a short cast.

''I don't have to cast too far when I'm out here,'' he said, pleased with his good fortune. He didn't get a bite on his first two casts, but sitting in his new boat lessened the disappointment. ''They bite a lot better in the summer.''

''May I try a cast?''

''Sure. Here, go ahead.''

''It's a nice outfit.''

''Sure is. My dad bought it for me for Christmas. It cost a lot. I'm takin' it to my friend's cottage in the summer.''

''You're a lot better at this than I'll ever be. Can you show me how it works?''

''Sure,'' said Bobby. ''You open the bale like this and hold the line with your finger. Then you lift your finger and let the line go in the middle of your cast. It's a little tricky.''

Robard flicked open the bale, gripping the loose line with his index finger like the boy showed him. He moved the rod behind his head, and started it forward. Two-thirds of the way through the motion, the rod and reel slipped from his grasp and splashed into the water, sinking slowly beside the boat.

''My rod!''

Robard made a feeble swoop with his hand but missed it.

"Oh, damn! I can see it going down, but I'm afraid I can't swim."

"I can swim. My best rod. I'll get it."

"I'll lean on the opposite side when you go in. That way the boat won't tip over."

Gripping the edge of the dingy, Bobby lowered himself, fully clothed, into the water."

"It's pretty cold," he said, shivering as he released his grip and went under after the rod. Robard shifted to the side of the boat where the boy was. After several seconds, Bobby surfaced with the rod upraised in one hand.

"I've got it!" he shouted, kicking toward the boat, using his free hand to help propel him. Robard reached out as if to help but as the boy came closer he seized his shoulders and with a powerful push, forced Bobby under. The boy struggled to reach the surface, but Robard, now using both hands, held him under. The burning in his stomach intensified. *Drown the snake . . . drown.* The dingy rocked and bounced as the boy fought fiercely. The sound of the rod banging against the bottom of the boat was muffled by the water. *Drown the snake.* Robard held the boy under long after the struggling had ceased. The pain in his belly eased. When he released his hands, the boy's body floated up, arms and legs askew, the fishing rod still in his hand.

Robard paddled smoothly to the small bay and pulled the dingy ashore. He dragged it through the brush to the half-ton truck parked on the deserted dirt trail behind the pond. Using a thick evergreen branch, he brushed over the tracks left by the dingy on the shore.

Frank Clifton couldn't find his son when he went to look for him at the ponds. He called his name. It was their custom that he join the boy for a few minutes of fishing after work and before dinner. He was probably with his friend Teddy or one of the other neighborhood kids. But Margaret said she had seen him go out with his fishing rod. He was about to return to the house when he spotted Bobby's shirttail just above the surface in the middle of the pond. He ran to the shore.

"Bobby! God, no!" Frantically, he stripped to his underwear and dove into the cold water of the pond. Reaching the boy, he turned him over, hooked Bobby's chin in the crook of his left arm, and swam strongly for shore. "Please be all right. Don't die on me."

Clifton carried his son to the grass beyond the shoreline. Laying him on his back, he shoved two fingers into the boy's throat to ensure the air passage was clear. One hand held the nape of Bobby's neck while the other rested on his forehead, tilting the head back. He forced Bobby's mouth open, pinched his nostrils shut, and breathed deeply and steadily into Bobby's lungs. Each time the lungs filled he paused to watch the chest fall as it emptied of air. He continued the procedure with no response.

Through the kitchen window Margaret Clifton saw her husband working on Bobby and ran to the pond. "What's wrong?" she screamed. "What happened to him?"

"I found him in the water. In the water . . ."

"He's not moving!"

"Get me some blankets and call an ambulance."

"He's—"

"Do it now!"

Clifton continued his frantic efforts to revive his son, his mind racing. How did Bobby get so far out in the pond? He must have swum out. That had to be it. But the water was so cold. His line must have snagged, so he went out to free it. Why? *Breathe, Bobby. Please breathe. You're all we have. You're our life.* There was no pulse and the boy's face was the color of concrete. Later, the doctor realized he must have known all along that the boy was dead; it was the father, not the doctor, trying to will life into him.

48

Clifton was relieved to see Margaret sleeping peacefully in the hospital's psychiatric ward. He shuddered at the thought of her contorted, puffy face hours before at the funeral home. It happened shortly after the pale funeral director, an angel of death in his black suit, entered the room where Bobby lay in an open coffin. The director looked at his watch.

"It's time now for friends of the family to leave," he said somberly. "The family will have one last look at Bobby before we close the coffin."

Friends filed from the room, leaving Margaret and Frank standing silently by the coffin. He held her arm tightly. She'd been weeping and crying hysterically for three days. He felt her shaking and when he saw her wild, darting eyes, he knew she was about to snap.

"*He's not dead!*" she cried. "*Not dead at all. He's sleeping. Sleeeeeping!*" Clifton tried to console her. With a strength that astonished him, she pushed herself free. She had the look of a wild animal.

"*That's not Bobby! He's sleeping. At home sleeping. Do you hear me? It's not him.*"

"I want an ambulance here now," said Clifton to the funeral director.

"She's upset; perhaps a nice cup of tea in the sitting room?"

"I *said,* get an ambulance!"

"Yes, sir."

"How long will she sleep?" Clifton asked Dr. William Hunter, head of the hospital's psychiatric unit.

"I gave her a strong sedative. She'll be out for several hours."

"I appreciate your coming out like this, Bill."

"Glad to. I'm very, very sorry about Bobby. Such a tragedy."

Hunter was a tall, square-jawed man just approaching sixty. "Come on over to my office," he said, putting his arm around Clifton's shoulders. "You look like you could use a drink."

They talked after the psychiatrist poured the drinks.

"I suppose it's too early for a prognosis? Can you give me the possible scenarios?" Clifton asked.

"Well, her initial reaction was one of denial. She's refusing to accept what is manifest reality. Deluding herself. Denying that Bobby is dead."

Clifton lowered his head, pursing his lips.

"Maybe we shouldn't talk about it just yet, Frank. You've got your own grief to deal with."

"No. I'd like to know."

"Okay. . . . I'm sure one part of Margaret's mind possesses the knowledge that Bobby is gone, but she's nevertheless persuaded herself that in fact he's alive. Inevitably the truth will crash in on her. It must. Not facing it is something that cannot sustain itself indefinitely."

"But if it should?"

"Extremely unlikely."

"But if it should?"

"It would drive a person into greater and greater insanity. But I don't think Margaret's made that way. Sooner or later she'll have to accept the fact of Bobby's death."

"And then?"

"Then she may go through a period of profound grief. She'll think there's nothing left to live for, that the world is an empty and bitter place. She'll need a lot of support and love. You're going to have to be very strong."

"How do you treat it?"

"Sodium amytal for the denial. It's a disinhibiting agent."

"And for the grief?"

"Lots of support from you; and from me as her psychiatrist. And a catharsis. An emotional outpouring. Vomiting up emotions being held tightly inside."

They went through half a bottle of scotch before Clifton felt he was drained enough, tired enough, to sleep at the hotel near the hospital. "I've got the funeral in the morning. Will you look after Margaret?"

"I've got a nurse with her through the night and they're to notify me the minute she awakens. Don't worry, I'll stay with this until she understands and accepts."

Clifton craved sleep, but he lay awake for hours in his hotel room reliving his discovery of Bobby's body by the pond. When sleep finally came, it was restless and punctuated by terrifying nightmares. His head felt like a caldron of simmering blood with pale pink steam rising and constantly building pressure, but never enough to blow the lid off.

The nightmares began with the clone's birth . . . the wizened face . . . the chalky, yellowed skin. Margaret looked on, first fearfully, then accusingly. The clone's dull eyes came alive, piercing him—the doctor, his creator. It snarled, its upper lip curled and stretched over a row of rotting teeth. Clifton covered the clone's face with one hand, slime oozing between his fingers. His other hand grasped the umbilical cord, pulling it tight around the clone's neck in a noose. The small form squirmed and twisted, fighting for air. His hand sank farther into the mush as he pulled tighter, using the head for leverage. The clone emitted a prolonged grating, hissing sound, a deathbed gasp. Then there was silence. When the thrashing ceased, the doctor eased his grip on the umbilical cord. Slowly lifting his hand, the slime sticking to it like a spider's web, he exposed the face. It wasn't the lifeless, pulpy mass he expected. The snarl remained in place and the defiant eyes mocked him—still alive.

The dream shifted to the nursing home lawn. The night was black. He was pushing Robard ahead of him in the wheelchair. The guard dog flew at them, fangs, first bared, and then sinking deeply into the clone's thigh. The wheelchair tumbled over and over, bouncing wildly in slow motion as the animal pulled the listless form to the pavement. Large chunks of bloody flesh dangled from the razor teeth. The doctor retreated with the gouged, bleeding clone held tightly against his chest. He stumbled toward the ranch wagon. Margaret was inside. She locked the doors and began screaming at him: *Fool! Fool! Damn fucking fool!*

Now he, the doctor, dressed in hospital whites, sat at the head of a long banquet table in a cavernous room. He was the guest of honor. Fifty doctors, his peers, were seated around the table. All eyes were fixed admiringly on him. At the opposite end of the table, breaking the ring of white-clad figures, was Margaret, beautiful in a green velvet gown and double string of glistening pearls. Waiters in tuxedos poured champagne. The mood was jovial. They were there to honor him. There was a standing ovation, intensifying as two elegant waiters approached with an imposing covered silver serving tray. They placed the tray in the center of the table. The ovation was thunderous. The doctor sat proudly, but trying to be humble. A waiter lifted the cover from the tray.

There were gasps of revulsion. The applause stopped abruptly. A foul-smelling green bile spread from the tray to the white linen tablecloth. In the center of the tray lay the clone, its wizened face grotesquely distorted. Like a fish out of water, it convulsed and writhed in its own bile and excrement. In the clone's gnarled hand was an oversized hypodermic needle, clearly labeled

MORPHINE. The hand rose and fell in a feeble attempt to puncture its own fleshless arm. Hitting brittle bone, the needle broke off. Margaret was standing—pointing, accusing, shrieking: *Fool! Fool! Damn fucking fool! Fool! Fool!* The others joined in until it became a deafening, rhythmic chant: *Fool! Fool! Damn fucking fool!*

Frank Clifton awoke trembling and soaked in perspiration. He reached for Margaret before remembering she wasn't there. It took him a while to get back to sleep. The nightmares returned. He was back in the banquet hall. The jeering chant continued. This time, Vince Oliverio stood beside Margaret, clenched fist raised and stabbing toward him: *Fool! Fool! Damn fucking fool!*

49

The doctors and hospital staff treated the old Italian woman with deference and affection. She had been there every morning since the day her son was shot. During the first three weeks, as Vince lay in a coma, she wept and rocked slowly in the green vinyl chair beside his bed, her rosary wrapped tightly in her wrinkled hands. Always she wore a black kerchief, heavy black cotton dress, black stockings, and low-heeled black shoes. She was seventy-seven and she'd been dressing that way since the death of her husband twenty years before.

He had no way of knowing it, but when Vince Oliverio instinctively jerked his head just as Robard fired the shot into his temple, it saved his life. The movement caused the small bullet to miss his brain and hit his temporal bone instead. The resultant swelling damaged the association tracts which serve as communication links between the left and right hemispheres of the cerebrum.

They are believed to be the seats of human memory, reasoning, and learning. Doctors removed the bullet after Vince regained partial consciousness, but it wasn't until the sixth week that he recognized his mother and realized he was in a hospital. Since then he'd struggled to lift the curtain shrouding his memory. He pushed himself, searching for the key that would explain the dizzy spells and flashes of searing pain in his head. With the help of family, friends, and visiting police officers, he began to piece his life together, but there were still a lot of blanks. The details of the attack itself remained in the dark recesses of his subconscious. When they mentioned Alfie Morrow's name, he had a vague recollection that they had once worked together. No one told him Morrow was dead. Oliverio's supervisor, John Sadowski, in a panic with his best man in a coma and his hand-picked successor in a grave, visited him three or four times a week. The day after Oliverio regained consciousness, Sadowski came to talk to him, but Oliverio didn't recognize him. It was several weeks before Oliverio had improved enough for a second attempt.

"We want to get the bastard, Vince," said Sadowski.

Oliverio nodded, a sharp pain momentarily blurring his vision.

"Trouble is, it was dark," Sadowski continued. A couple of residents spotted him running from the scene, but they couldn't tell us a thing, except that he was tall and drove away in a dark, late-model car. Try to remember if you can. We think he had you in your car. We found a lot of smudges on the rear door, probably gloves, and both doors were open on the driver's side. You were running from him when he shot you in the hip."

Oliverio reached down and brushed his hand against his heavily taped hip. He would probably have a limp, the doctors told him. The bone had been shattered. An operation, maybe two, would be needed. A metal pin would have to be inserted. Oliverio struggled to concentrate, to remember.

"We went through your files to see if you were working on something that might be connected to this.

We didn't come up with anything. You and Alfie were working late on something a few months back. I asked you about it, remember?"

"Alfie?"

"Yeah, Alfie. Alfie Morrow, your partner."

Oliverio was bewildered.

"I can't . . . can't seem to remember. I keep trying, but nothing . . ." His voice trailed off. Sadowski's impatience passed quickly. The doctors had warned him it could take months, even years.

"Listen, Vince, I don't want you to overdue it. I'll drop by on Thursday after work. We'll talk some more then."

It was during their fourth conversation a week later that Oliverio, for the first time, clearly remembered his partner. "Has he been in to see me? I know I'm still confused quite a bit of the time."

Sadowski was sitting beside the bed with one arm resting on the mattress. He glanced over at Florence Oliverio, knitting quietly in the corner.

"I don't know if I should tell you this or not, Vince. I don't know if you're ready for it, but you've got to know. Alfie is dead."

Oliverio seemed confused.

"He was killed the same night you were hit. He was shotgunned. The killer probably used a different weapon to throw us off, to make us think yours was a mugging. Your wallet was cleaned out, but we think that was a ruse. My two best men don't go down within three hours of each other without a connection. The guy was waiting for Alfie when he came out of the house. He was on his way down here after finding out you'd been shot. They hit him in his own driveway."

"Alfie's dead?"

Sadowski nodded.

"Were we together when we got shot? I—I don't remember."

"No, Vince, you weren't together. Now, concentrate on what I'm saying. We think the guy grabbed you in Bay Ridge on your way home after a meeting with Alfie. Alfie's wife said you two were meeting in a bar some-

where about something important. We think this guy
was in the backseat with a piece at your head. You tried
to run and he shot you in the hip. You tried to drag
yourself up, but he was right on you and put one in
your temple. I called Alfie to tell him you were hit. His
wife said he ran out of the house and she heard the
shotgun blast. She found him down in the driveway. He
was dead before the ambulance arrived.''

"Alfie's dead. Jesus," said Oliverio, tears welling in
his eyes.

"Now, Vince, you gotta remember. It's the only way
we'll get the fuckers involved in this." Sadowski's voice
level had risen slightly and Florence Oliverio looked at
him sternly. He flashed a feeble smile and continued,
his voice softer.

"Can you remember what it was you and Alfie were
working on? I know you were on the Lazaro thing, but
we shook down every fucker connected with it and
couldn't come up with a thing. Can you remember what
you were working on?''

"I'm sorry, John. I keep trying, but . . .''

Sadowski rested his hand on Oliverio's shoulder. "I
know you're doing your best, Vince. The doctor says it
could take a while. Even if you can remember where
you and Alfie met, that would help. We could find witnesses. If the mob's involved in this, we've gotta
know.''

Sadowski rose to leave. He said goodbye to Florence
and paused at the door. "Just one more thing, Vince.
Do you know anything at all about cloning?" Oliverio
looked at him blankly. "Just checking. Some guy called
a few weeks after you were shot. Said he was a doctor
but wouldn't give us his name. He started babbling
about Elliot Brodie and clones.''

"Sorry, John, I don't know.''

"Well, at first I thought he was a cop hater or a
ghoul, but I think he was just a wacko. Rest easy, Vince.
I'll catch you later.''

50

Calvin Ritchie III loved his wife. But she was two thousand miles away on their Arizona ranch; she'd never know. The effect of the wine and liqueurs and the passion and beauty of the young woman lying on top of him on the wide bed dissolved all remnants of guilt. He'd worry about the guilt later. His first marriage ended because of other women and he'd vowed to himself he wouldn't stray when he married Joan Gantry. Until now, thirteen years into his second marriage, he'd kept that promise.

The woman in bed with him had Grace Kelly looks. This was the second time in three weeks he'd been with her. They first met at a noisy cocktail party in New York City after a meeting of his oil company's executives and senior government officials. He was taken by her looks. Whenever he looked up, she seemed to be there. When she smiled at him, he gathered the courage to approach her. They talked for twenty minutes and he invited her for dinner. She told him she was a government legal secretary and part-time model. She was a college graduate and hoped one day to become an actress. Ritchie thought she was elegant. A lot of class. He was flattered

that she was interested in him. He got an erection after
their hands touched momentarily during dinner. There
was an awkward silence in the taxi in front of her Park
Avenue apartment building, broken when she leaned
toward him and brushed her damp lips lightly against
his. She thanked him for dinner and pressed her telephone number into his hand. He returned to Arizona
vowing never to call, but he couldn't get her out of his
mind. And now, three weeks later, they were making
love in her bed. Twice they had intercourse and twice
they showered together.

"You're driving me crazy," said Ritchie huskily. He
was lying on his back as she slowly kissed and tongued
her way down his chest and belly. She raised herself to
her knees and, with her hands caressing his testicles,
she lowered her mouth to his penis. He moaned softly.
She insisted on leaving the lights on and his pleasure
was heightened when he looked down to see her mouth
working over him, something his wife would never do.

Behind the soundproof, mirrored wall, Robard adjusted the focus on the zoom lens and continued snapping pictures, as he'd been doing since the couple
arrived at the apartment. He had paid the woman five
thousand dollars, with another ten thousand to follow.

Robard was sitting on the hassock in front of the low
glass table in his apartment. He smirked as he studied
the old publicity shot of Joan Gantry stapled to the inside cover of one of the two file folders on the table in
front of him. Thumbing through the file, he paused at
photographs of Gantry and Elliot Brodie together on
a yacht and at an exclusive Hollywood restaurant. He
paused again, his eyes flashing hatred, over a newspaper
clipping with a photo of Calvin Ritchie III and his new
wife, Joan Gantry. He closed the folder, slammed it to
the floor, and went into the bedroom. He dropped his
bathrobe to the floor and lay naked on the bed. The
only light in the room was cast by a black-and-white
John Wayne western on the television.

• • •

The first oversized enveloped arrived at the sprawling Ritchie ranch two weeks after his return from the second New York trip. It was addressed to Joan. She was knitting her husband an Irish wool sweater as a Christmas gift when the maid brought the mail to her. As was her custom, Joan divided the mail into three neat piles: personal mail, household bills, and George's business mail.

She thought the brown envelope addressed to her was probably junk mail, but she saw it was sent airmail from New York and opened it first. Inside was a four-by-six-inch photograph of her husband entering a restaurant with an attractive young blond woman. She stared at the photo and smiled. George and his little pranks, she thought. But when, after three days, he made no mention of it, she brought it up over dinner.

"I received your little gift," she said, smiling.

"What gift?"

"You know very well."

"No, I don't. What?"

"Come on. The photograph. You and the blond girl."

"I'm sorry, I don't know what you're talking about," said Ritchie nervously.

"All right, play it to the hilt. I'll get it."

Ritchie didn't know what to expect. His wife returned with the envelope and dropped the photo on the table beside him.

"Trying to make me jealous?" she asked.

She could see by his reaction that his surprise was genuine.

"You mean you didn't send it?"

"No. I . . . ah . . . I didn't send it."

"Then it must be a prank."

"It has to be."

"But you *do* know her?"

"Yes, of course. She's with the federal Department of Energy."

"You look so surprised."

"Well, I don't remember anybody with a camera."

"What were you doing with her?"

"The meeting dragged on, so we carried it over to the restaurant."

"Just the two of you?"

"No. Of course not. There were, ah, seven or eight of us."

"You didn't tell me about it."

"There was nothing to tell, just the continuation of a meeting. I wonder which one of those bastards had a camera. I don't think it's very funny, sending something like that to you."

"I thought it was hilarious until I saw how nervous it made you."

"Be reasonable, darling, something like this would make anybody nervous. You know I don't give a darn for anyone else."

"You're right. Somebody's idea of a bad joke."

The second photograph arrived two days later. Ritchie and the blond were kissing in a close embrace in the backseat of a New York taxi. Joan Ritchie was furious when she telephoned her husband at his Phoenix office.

"I just received another photo of you and your blond necking in a taxi," she said coldly. There was momentary silence.

"I . . ."

"Just a business associate, right?"

"I dropped her off at her apartment and she kissed me," blurted Ritchie. "We weren't necking."

"It looks like a lot more than a goodnight kiss."

"I'm going to get to the bottom of this. I'll talk to you when I get home. Somebody's trying to destroy us."

Ritchie telephoned the woman's New York office and was told that she was a temporary employee who had quit after working three weeks. A recording told him her apartment telephone was no longer in service. He contacted the building superintendent. "She signed a year's lease but cleared out after a month," he said. "Forfeited her deposit."

"Did she leave a forwarding address?"

"Nope. And her previous address was a phony."

Ritchie was frantic. Screw around once in thirteen years and this is the result, he fumed. It had to be blackmail. But why hadn't he heard from her before she sent the photos? He'd kill the rotten bitch. Shouldn't have gone out with her. Should have suspected.

The third photo arrived the next day and Joan Ritchie cried in her room for an hour when her husband admitted he'd had an affair. The photo was a side view of him sitting on the edge of the bed and the blond walking toward him. Both were naked. Ritchie tore the photo into small pieces and flung them into the fireplace.

"I'm begging you to forgive me," he pleaded. "I swear it was the only time and I promise on my mother's grave it will never happen again. You know I love you more than anything else in the world. I was nothing until you came into my life. I'd give up everything I own for you."

Ritchie told his wife the full story as she continued to weep. He initially thought it must be blackmail, but there'd been no request for money.

"Don't you see?" he pleaded. "It's a setup. The whole thing. Somebody wants to destroy us. We've had a perfect relationship. A perfect marriage. I've never been so happy. I don't know why I did it. I was weak and stupid. I should have known, the way she came on to me. Please, darling . . . please try to understand. From now on, you can come with me whenever I go out of town. I'll do anything you want. Anything. I promise it will never happen again. I can't bear the thought of losing you."

Joan Ritchie, remembering all the good years together, decided to forgive her husband. There was, after all, no comparison between those years and the lonely years with Elliot Brodie.

Robard knew Joan Ritchie well. She was honest, loyal, and forgiving. But she was also prudish, a carryover from her strict Baptist upbringing. He knew that she might forgive Ritchie after she received the third photograph, but the fourth would break her. There'd be no forgiveness. He waited two weeks before mailing it.

Joan Gantry recoiled when she saw the familiar brown envelope with the New York postmark. Her first instinct was to burn it without opening it. She put it aside unopened and stared at it long after sorting through the other mail. Reluctantly, she reached for the envelope and opened it with a brass letter opener. Before her, in perfect focus and full color, was the sight of her husband's penis engulfed by the blond woman's mouth.

Vomit seeped through Joan Gantry's fingers held tightly over her mouth as she ran to the bathroom. She moved out of the ranch that afternoon and saw her lawyer the next day.

51

Frank Clifton decided they would move to Florida. Margaret's progress was negligible and he came to realize she might never get over their son's death. Her depression absorbed her life. She was unable to sleep without medication. She was in and out of the hospital and at home she was sullen and morose. Her despondency pervaded their lives. Clifton had never been outgoing and he had few friends at the cancer clinic in White Plains. He spent his days worrying about Margaret and he became bored with his research. His fellow scientists found him more and more insular and they began questioning the state of his mental health.

Margaret couldn't bear to look at the ponds behind the house. The memories were too painful. Clifton, in addition to the guilt he felt for not being able to save Bobby and for not imposing strict rules about fishing without adult supervision, also had to deal with the strain of Margaret's continuing illness. He was finding it more and more difficult to meet that challenge. And, unsaid but always there, was the dread over what Robard might do next.

The police had listened patiently to Clifton when he attempted to tell them his story, but they could find nothing in either Oliverio's or Morrow's files to substantiate it, and when they brought the doctor to the hospital for a face-to-face meeting with Oliverio, the policeman had no idea who Clifton was. After talking to Clifton's fellow researchers, the detectives heading the investigation into the shootings concluded that the doctor was suffering a mental breakdown following the death of his son. They found it difficult to believe that the doctor didn't have a single piece of paper to back up his claims.

"I gave everything to Detective Oliverio," he explained. "I wanted the whole thing out of my life."

The detectives promised they would continue to investigate his claims, but Clifton felt they were only humoring him.

When Margaret began spending more time in a White Plains hospital than she did at home, Clifton put their Connecticut house up for sale and moved into an apartment near the hospital. And when she showed a marked improvement and was released from the hospital, he decided it was time to make the move to Florida.

Clifton had not heard from Robard since before the policemen were shot. There had been no new murders or bombings reported in the press and he hoped the clone was dead.

52

MAY 1981

Robard opened one eye and focused on the clock beside the bed. Eight-thirty. He had a severe headache and his coated tongue felt thicker than usual. The fucking booze. A skinny arm reached for the top drawer of the beside table. He needed the needle. He'd forgotten about the woman asleep beside him. His movement caused her to stir. He changed his mind about the drawer and turned to look at her. Fucking whore. She lay on her stomach, her head turned away from him. He aimed a bony heel at her legs and kicked out.

"Owww! What the hell . . ." The woman rubbed her eyes and turned to look at Robard. "What d'ya think you're doin'?"

"Get your ass out of here."

"Aren't you a real gentleman."

"You've been paid. Now get the fuck out."

"Do you mind if I at least wash up?"

"Do it in your own hovel."

"Christ! What a nice guy."

Flinging back the covers, she slipped out of the bed

naked. Her dress and underthings were draped over a chair at the end of the bed. She stared down resentfully at Robard as she dressed.

"You don't have to take it out on me just because you can't get it up."

Goddamn, he thought. She was right. I didn't fuck her. I'm turning into a fucking junkie.

"You blamed it on the booze last night," she said, buttoning her dress. "You want to give it another try now? Half price?"

"I told you to get out."

"Okay, okay. Jesus, you're nasty."

She slammed the door when she left the apartment. Robard pulled himself up and sat on the edge of the bed. He stared in disgust at the needle tracks surrounded by ugly bruises and welts. He opened the drawer of the bedside table and reached for the red rubber catheter, knotting it around his left arm just above the elbow. He removed a morphine ampule from the drawer, snapping the neck off and placing it on top of the table. He needed it badly. The pain was starting. His gut was burning. Removing a disposable syringe from its cellophane wrapper, he thrust the needle into the morphine vial, drawing back the colorless fluid. Holding the syringe in front of him, he watched as a glistening drop formed at the tip. He pulled the catheter tighter, flexing his forearm as he opened and closed his hand. The veins are shot, he thought. Beyond the unsightly discoloration at the crook of his elbow, he found just enough vein to attempt penetration. His forearm lay flat on the table, palm upward. He steadied his right hand, which held the syringe, by pressing his elbow forcefully against the table. He punctured the skin and a thin column of blood backed into the syringe, mixing, in swirled patterns, with the colorless fluid. He squeezed the plunger downward until the chamber emptied. He let the syringe refill with blood and again pumped it into his vein.

The rush hit him like the blast from a jet exhaust. His heart pounded like a kettle drum and his vision sharpened. Emptying the chamber a third time, he sighed and withdrew the needle. Let the dream come. He was ready.

Robard knew he was hopelessly addicted, but he much preferred that to the pain of the morning seizures. He progressively needed to increase the dosage. In his drugged state he was unable to fight the spasms that took over his body every morning, but they did not hurt. Now he went with them and when it was over, he rocked his body back and forth in the fetal position. At the same time the drug helped with the pain, it heightened the intensity and emotions of the dreams. Always he was underwater, swimming blindly. The snake would appear, cold against his chest, slithering toward his throat. Then there was endless struggle grasping blindly, to fling it from his body.

Robard knew he was killing himself. He cursed Frank Clifton. He had to find him. It was his only hope.

53

It had been a year since Vince Oliverio was shot. Although his limp would always be noticeable, the strict physiotherapy regimen had paid off handsomely. The constant pain in his hip was reduced to occasional twinges, usually when the weather was cold or damp. The doctors warned he would probably have problems with arthritis in his later years.

Oliverio had also spent months in speech therapy. He sometimes stammered but his speech was no longer slurred. The migraine headaches continued to be bothersome but his doctors prescribed strong medication which knocked them down in twenty to thirty minutes. He was beginning to function better and better but he continued to be plagued by short episodes of blurred vision.

It pained Sadowski to see his friend suffering through his rehabilitation. Oliverio would be coming back to work in January. His supervisor hoped that his return would aid in his recovery, but he was skeptical. Vince had undergone a personality change as result of the head wound and his incredible memory had deteriorated. His memory for distant events, even from childhood, was flawless, but he couldn't remember most of the cases he'd worked on. And he was still unable to unlock from his memory the sequence of events leading to the shooting episode. A year now, and he couldn't recall a damn thing. His family doctor suggested he see a psychiatrist.

"I don't believe in shrinks," he protested.

"Have you ever been to one?"

"No. But I saw enough of them in the courts."

"Well, it's up to you. But they'll never get the guy who shot you unless you can remember what happened. I talked with John Sadowski. He's convinced you had to have seen your assailant. Maybe even talked to him. Why else would both the driver's door and the passenger's door be found wide open with you lying on the ground a few yards away? He must have been in your car with you."

Oliverio nodded grimly. Sadowski had given him the same pitch. But how could they expect him to remember the shooting when he couldn't even remember traveling to Italy with his mother? He'd seen the photographs over and over, but it wouldn't come back to him. And when his mother showed him the Christmas photos of the woman he was once engaged to, he had no memory of her. But he had been devastated when Florence told him that his old friend, Martin Butler, and his wife were dead.

Florence did her best to help her son fill in the pieces. She spent hours with him at a time. She told him about the late-night meetings with Alfie Morrow in the basement. And how she thought it must have been important because they were both so serious. She didn't like to disturb them. Yes, she said, there were a lot of papers around. On the table and on the bar. And he had brought his old fingerprint comparator out of storage and set it up. She'd seen him and Morrow using it more than once when she brought them coffee. His mother held psychiatrists in less regard than he did. She called them sorcerers. It was Sadowski who finally convinced him it was worth a try.

●   ●   ●

"You're suffering from what we call retrograde amnesia," the psychiatrist told Oliverio. "It's a failure to remember an event or events preceding a temporary loss of consciousness, usually the result of a head injury."

"I know what I've got. I can't remember because I was shot in the head. What I want to know now is, how do I get my memory back? I have total recall of some events but not of others."

The psychiatrist smiled.

"I was warned that you might be somewhat aggressive. I understand you don't think fondly of my profession. I must say, there are times when I share your sentiments."

"Sadowski's got a big mouth."

"This sort of amnesia can involve the unconscious suppression of a painful experience and everything remindful of it. And from reading your background reports, you've certainly had your share of painful experiences."

"I was engaged to be married to a woman who was director of a nursing home in Pennsylvania. She came to New York to visit me and I don't remember a damn thing about it. Now, explain that if you can. My partner's six feet under. Poor bastard left a wife and child. For months I didn't even know who the hell he was."

"You certainly have a lot of suppressed anger. It's good that you're getting it out." Oliverio looked at him skeptically. "Have you talked to the woman?" the psychiatrist asked.

"His wife?"

"No, the woman from Pennsylvania."

"No. She's dead. Fell down some stairs at work or something."

"Well, as I said, this sort of amnesia can involve the unconscious suppression of a painful experience and everything that reminds you of it. . . ."

"Yeah, yeah. I got that."

The psychiatrist made three attempts to restore Oliverio's memory by establishing associations with the past through suggestion. When that didn't work he tried light hypnosis. Oliverio was able to bring forth shadowy images: a car in a large vacant parking lot; an old man on a bed in a room; a glass; a drink smashing on a patio; weeping willows and a pond. All strands with nothing connecting them.

"I think you're getting there," said the psychiatrist. "We should go into deep hypnosis. I think that might do the trick."

"I'll have to think about that."

54

Robard was above 96th Street when he cut into Central Park on the west side. He felt a sense of power, a sense of mission, in his new steel-toed boots. He hadn't walked more than a few minutes when he came upon a derelict lying on a park bench near the footpath. As he drew nearer, he could see it was an old man. An empty wine bottle lay on its side in front of the bench. The man was on his back, a piece of cardboard folded double for a pillow. Robard stood over him. It was cold but the man was bare-headed, with tufts of white hair jutting in every direction. He wore a long, tattered gray overcoat and the worn soles of his shoes were separated at the toes. The burning in Robard's stomach intensified. He looked in both directions along the path and, with a powerful tug, pulled the man to the ground. The derelict murmured something in his stupor but the heavy steel toe struck his temple and he was silent. A second kick crushed his ribs. *Kill the snake. Kill it. Kill it.* The kicks took on a rhythm of their own. When they stopped, Robard briefly studied the crumpled form beneath the bench. He walked off without a backward glance, feeling sublimely peaceful.

Several unsolved beating deaths of derelicts occurred in the park over the next three months.

55

"I can't think of a single individual who has contributed so much to law enforcement in this great country," said John Sadowski, his booming voice carrying too loudly through the hall's public address system. In full uniform, complete with gold braid, he was the last of twelve speakers. There was sustained applause from the two hundred policemen, dignitaries, and their guests.

The roast beef dinner was held in an American Legion hall. Florence Oliverio, wearing an orchid which was pinned to her black dress as she entered the hall two hours earlier, wiped away a tear. She was sitting beside her son at the long head table on the elevated stage. Below them, the invited guests sat in rows of tables along each wall. Two tables near the front had been reserved for the press. Television cameras were set up in front of the stage. Huge photographs of Oliverio hung on the walls with banners proclaiming WE'LL MISS YOU VINCE.

"Although Vince is officially retiring—with full pension, I might add"—applause—"we'll still be seeing a lot of him. He's agreed to make himself available as a consultant whenever we need his wide-ranging experience." More applause. "And now, Vince, if you'll come up here, I've got something for you."

Oliverio was given a standing ovation as he limped to the podium. Television lights flooded the stage and flashbulbs popped. The applause went on and on. He was honored but he knew they pitied him. Limping. A goddamn cripple. He didn't want to retire and they all knew it. He stood beside Sadowski. The applause was deafening. Oliverio fought the tears. Tears of gratitude, tears of sadness, and tears of anger. He forced a smile and waved to the audience. They presented him with another gold badge in a fine leather case. He thanked them and then it was over.

He knew how it would go. They'd talk about what a wonderful party it had been and what a great guy he was. They'd call him into the office from time to time over the next couple of months. Then faces would change, people would be transferred, and they'd forget about him. Oliverio had seen it all before. It was the way of things. A former colleague, now in the private security business, had asked him to join his company. He might take him up on it. What else did he know?

After the presentation, a six-piece orchestra was set up in a front corner. Tables in the middle of the floor were pushed aside to make room for dancing. Two cash bars at the end of the hall did a brisk business.

Police doctors said the blurred vision was probably a permanent condition and that was the reason Oliverio was being forced into early retirement. That's what they told him, but he knew there was more to it. It was the change in personality, a result of his head wound, that caused many fellow officers to think he wasn't exactly "right." Hadn't he had problems relearning how to use the laser? And it was embarrassing for the teacher to now be the student. He was fifty-nine years old but he felt more like seventy-five.

Oliverio vowed he wouldn't feel sorry for himself. He would step up his physiotherapy sessions and he would return to the psychiatrist for deep hypnosis. He owed it to Alfie Morrow and perhaps to others, like Ellen McKinnon, buried somewhere in his memory. Most of all, he decided, he owed it to himself.

56

Robard had seen the newspaper and television coverage of Vince Oliverio's retirement. He concluded the cop was brain damaged; that was the reason there had been no public revelation that Elliot Brodie's clone was on the loose killing people. It was also a possibility that maybe Oliverio just didn't have the proof to back up any claims. That bothered Robard; what if there was proof lying around somewhere? Or what if the shitass cop tried to pressure Frank Clifton to go public?

Robard watched the Oliverio house in Bay Ridge for more than a week. He would have to make his move during daylight hours. Oliverio didn't once leave the house after dark and when he went out for his daily walks he always had a dog with him. It was a two-year-old white and tan bulldog sent to him on his retirement by his former British colleagues. He had grown attached to the dog, whose friendly temperament belied his stubborn defiant look, a result of the undershot jaw com-

mon to the breed. The dog was patient around
Oliverio's nephews and nieces and never snapped at
them, even when harried and harassed. The dog's name
was Bull and they made an odd couple on their daily
outings, Oliverio with his cane, and the dog, with its
low-slung body and broad chest, in a rolling walk beside
him on a leash. They followed a daily routine; an hour
walk in the morning and another in the early evening.
In the afternoon, they accompanied his mother on her
daily walk around the block. Once a week, on Saturday
mornings, the dog was left behind while Vince and Florence did the weekly grocery shopping. On Sundays,
when the weather was right, Vince let Bull run free at
Dyker Beach Park.

His bedroom was cool, but as soon as Oliverio raised
the blind and opened the window he knew it was going
to be a scorcher of a day. He didn't mind the heat; it
was better for his hip, which ached when the weather
was cold. He gathered his daily medication, pills from
the six bottles on top of his dresser, and swallowed
them with the fresh orange juice his mother left for him
each morning. In the basement, he worked out with
free weights to keep his muscles toned. Later, he and
Florence had coffee and a light breakfast on the back-
yard patio while Bull sat on his haunches, watching
expectantly.

There was air-conditioning in the bedrooms, but
Florence kept the downstairs cool by drawing the blinds
and drapes in the heat of the day. Bull growled content-
edly and nuzzled Oliverio's leg as his leash was snapped
to his collar. It was not yet nine, but they could feel the
warmth of the sun as they set off down the street.

Robard rounded the corner and walked toward them.
He could feel the weight of the pistol, with its silencer,
in the right pocket of his tan trench coat. Oliverio first
noticed him at a distance of two hundred yards. He
thought it odd that the thin man was wearing a coat,
considering the weather. He chuckled at the thought
that he might be a flasher. Oliverio thought he saw light-

colored gloves as the man's hands disappeared into his pockets. Couldn't be. But maybe . . . ?

He felt uneasy. The distance between them was shrinking quickly. They were twenty feet apart when Oliverio saw the bulge in the right pocket of the man's trench coat. Bull began to growl. The man raised his head for the first time. There was a familiar look about the piercing dark eyes that Oliverio couldn't place. He was also unmistakably an addict. The right hand started to move out of the pocket. Oliverio instinctively moved to raise his cane, but a look of panic crossed the man's face and he walked quickly past, head down. Turning to watch the man, Oliverio saw a marked police cruiser coming toward him. The car pulled up next to him at the curb. It was Sadowski.

"Hi ya, Vince. I was hoping I'd catch you."

"Nice to see you, John," said Oliverio, looking beyond the cruiser at the quickly retreating figure in the trench coat.

"Who was that?"

"Nobody . . . nobody. What's up, John?"

"Dave Meyers from ballistics is taking early retirement. Some of the guys are taking him to lunch today at P.J.'s. We'd like you to come along."

Sadowski didn't want his old friend to think he was being forgotten and Oliverio appreciated it.

"It would be nice to see the guys."

"Great. I'll send a car around for you at eleven-thirty."

Oliverio had conflicting feelings when he stepped out the elevator on the eighth floor of the Police Academy. There were a few new faces but enough familiar ones to make him feel at home. Some of them shouted greetings; others came up to shake his hand. They were clustered around him in front of the bulletin board when Sadowski came out of his office.

"Okay, you assholes, back to work. We're goin' to lunch."

As they turned to leave, Vince spotted the composite

drawing on the bulletin board. He was certain it was the man he'd seen on his street.

"What's this guy wanted for, John?"

"We think he's the one who's been killing the winos and derelicts up in the park. Several witnesses say a guy who looks like this has been hanging around up there. Why? Do you know him?"

"No . . . no. Just wondering."

57

Margaret and Frank Clifton settled into a routine that was not altogether unpleasant. St. Petersburg's reputation as a popular winter resort, enhanced by three hundred and sixty days of average annual sunshine, swelled its population in the winter months and many visitors from the northern states returned to live there when they retired. As the influx continued, the price of real estate spiraled upward. But with the profits from the sale of their home in Connecticut, the Cliftons had been able to purchase a comfortable two-story house on a secluded lot in Palm Harbor fronting on the Gulf north of St. Petersburg.

The doctor was again engaged in cancer research, seeking genetic clues to explain why some forms of cancer were more likely to be inherited than others. The ultimate aim was to isolate high-risk cases, to aid early detection and treatment. The small private laboratory he worked for was affiliated with, and operated out of, the University of Tampa. The campus, with its fine Moorish architecture, was an island of serenity for Clifton.

The move to Florida had produced the first positive

signs that Margaret was recovering from the depression that had consumed her since Bobby's death. Clifton was convinced he himself would have suffered a mental breakdown if they hadn't moved away. Still, they kept to themselves. Invitations to dinner parties and local events dried up as Clifton's fellow scientists tired of his lame excuses. He wanted to scream out to them that his wife had been ill, that she wasn't ready. That the joy in their lives, their only son, had been taken from them forever. But he suffered in silence, and knew that he and Margaret were thought to be snobs.

Until Bobby's death, Margaret had been a voracious reader. Clifton was relieved to see she was renewing her favorite pastime—even though initially she seemed obsessed with self-help books. Eventually, she returned to her usual fare: biographies, poetry, and potboiler detective novels. On weekends they walked the shore or took drives, exploring the Gulf Coast.

To avoid the oppressive heat of the upcoming summer they arranged to rent a bungalow on Nantucket Island for July and August. They planned a leisurely drive to Woods Hole, Massachusetts, where they would catch the ferry to Nantucket. But that was more than two months away.

58

It had only been two weeks, but Vince Oliverio felt comfortable smoking a pipe. It was something he had always wondered about. He had never smoked cigarettes and chided friends and relatives who did. But there was something romantic about a pipe. Perhaps it was memories of the old men puffing away while they watched the bocce games at Dyker Beach Park. Perhaps it was the paraphernalia and the ritual that went with pipe smoking. One thing he quickly learned: It was an expensive hobby. If you were going to be serious about it, one pipe was useless.

Julius Vasco, the pipesmith he visited for advice, told him six pipes was the minimum requirement for a dedicated pipe smoker. "Why six?" asked Oliverio, dismayed. "When one gets hot, you let it cool and use another. You let them rest. Clean them. Rotate them. Treat them well, like a good thoroughbred, and they'll be good to you. And forget about pipes with filters. They're for amateurs. Good pipes don't need filters." If he followed the pipesmith's advice it would have cost him several hundred dollars, even more if he chose Vasco's handmade masterpieces. Until he determined if pipe smoking was for him, Oliverio, the novice, would settle for two pipes—with filters. "The customer is boss," said Vasco sullenly.

Two pipes and a box of filters. That was the beginning. There were also pipe cleaners, a jar with a seal to keep the tobacco from drying out and losing its aroma, a leather pouch to carry tobacco when smoking outside the house, another pouch to carry the pipes, an ashtray with a cork knob in the center to knock loose stubborn ashes, and a pipe companion. "A pipe companion?" queried Oliverio. Vasco generously produced one. A two-inch instrument, with three retractable appendages, in its own leather pouch. In the center was a tobacco tamper and on one side, a small blade for scraping the inside of a pipe bowl. On the other side was a stoker—a thin metal probe, like an oversized toothpick, for digging out ashes.

"What about tobacco?" Oliverio asked apprehensively. "I want something mild that smells good."

"Virginia is the one," decreed Vasco.

Oliverio's visit to the pipesmith cost him two hundred dollars. The pipe, for now, was a prop, but Oliverio was considering its long-term possibilities.

It was past midnight and his friends and family would surely think he was off the deep end if they could see him sitting there smoking a pipe on a bench in Central Park above 96th Street. It was a dangerous place to be; so dangerous the cops called it the DMZ. He leaned down and patted Bull, who lay on the ground at his feet. This was his fifth night in the park this week. He wouldn't tell his mother where he was going, only that he would be home late. She worried initially, but after the third night she'd concluded he was seeing a woman and stopped questioning him. Twice over the five nights, undercover cops had warned him he could get mugged or worse. Didn't he know that for the past year there was a maniac loose in the park? He was tempted to flash his gold detective's shield but decided against it. It might get back to Sadowski, who would tell him he belonged in Bellevue, entering the park at night without a weapon. He had had to turn in his gun when he retired. Although Oliverio had never really liked guns, and he knew most of the killer's skid row victims had been kicked to death, he was also certain the man he had seen on his street in Bay Ridge had been carrying a pistol.

He wasn't entirely defenseless; he had Bull. One look at the dog or one sincere growl was enough to send would-be muggers on their way. And beneath his London Fog raincoat, Oliverio wore his old NYPD-issue flak jacket. In his hands he held a butane lighter and a can of lighter fluid. He had spent hours modifying and testing them in his den. They would do what he wanted them to do. Whenever anyone approached he held the lighter in one hand and tilted the can as if he were pouring in fluid. He wondered if he was wasting his time. The killer hadn't struck for three weeks. There was no guarantee he would strike again and if he did, it might not be in the park. Three of his seven victims had been killed on skid row streets away from the park. Oliverio was playing a hunch and he was prepared to give it a few more nights. He didn't look the part of a drunk, but he hoped his cane and light-colored coat would make him a good target.

Bull growled before Oliverio heard the footsteps. He unconsciously bit hard on the stem of his pipe when he saw someone approaching in the shadows. The height and build were about right. This time the trench coat was black. He felt his stomach tighten. The nearest lamppost was forty feet away and much of its light was blocked by trees that left only scattered patches on the path.

Robard saw the figure on the bench and as he moved closer he saw the cane, the dog, and the glow of the pipe. Not the type of target he was looking for. He was going to ignore them and walk past the bench, but he hesitated. Jesus Christ! It's him! The cop! He looked around frantically. Was it a setup? He couldn't see anyone. It had to be coincidence. A gift.

Oliverio always released Bull's leash as soon as they entered the park. The dog was on his feet.

"Stay," whispered Oliverio.

Robard hadn't planned to use his gun, but he always carried it with him. Now he pulled it from his pocket. He was at the bench in several swift strides, the pistol trained on Oliverio's chest.

"I didn't think this would take two meetings."

Bull growled and appeared ready to lunge.

"Stay!" commanded Oliverio, eyeing the intruder's steel-toed work boots.

"If he moves, I'll shoot him."

Oliverio ordered the dog to sit. He had trouble getting the word out because of the pipe in his mouth. Using the hand holding the lighter, he set the pipe on the bench.

"We didn't really meet the other day," said Oliverio calmly. "I think you were about to introduce yourself when the police car made an appearance."

"That's not what I'm talking about, shitass."

"You mean we've met another time?"

"I guess you don't recognize this," said Robard, nodding toward the revolver.

Oliverio looked at him blankly.

"I know I don't look the same," said Robard. "I've lost ten or fifteen years."

"I don't understand."

"I'm the one who shot you. You dumb fucker. I don't know how I messed up at that range. Your thick fucking wop head, I suppose."

"And Alfie, my partner?"

"He walked right into it. That was easy."

Oliverio was desperately trying to calm himself. He felt a migraine coming on.

"Why?" he asked. "Why us?"

"And that bitch at the nursing home and that big dumb cop and his wife."

"Why? Why?"

"You don't fucking remember? I don't believe it. You *did* have everything with you in the car. And you don't remember a thing?"

"Nothing." Oliverio was desperately curious, but his main concern was staying alive.

Robard began to laugh. He stopped suddenly. Oliverio knew it was time to act.

"You'll go to the grave knowing fucking nothing," said Robard, raising the revolver.

The can of fluid resting on Oliverio's lap was pointed upward toward Robard and the lighter was aimed in the same direction. The fluid hit Robard's shoulders and the bare skin of the left side of his neck as he pulled the trigger. At the same time, the flame from the lighter shot out, igniting the fluid that continued to spew from the can. As the bullet ripped through Oliverio's raincoat and struck the flak jacket, knocking his upper body hard against the bench, the upper left side of Robard's coat was ablaze. Robard screamed in agony as his free gloved hand beat at the burning flesh on his neck and the left side of his face. Bull's teeth tore at his leg and trousers.

Oliverio's adrenaline was pumping as he fought to get his breath. It was a small-caliber pistol and the flak jacket had done its job. The wind was knocked out of him and he would have a nasty bruise, but he knew he was all right. Robard fired wildly, but missed Bull. Oliverio called off the dog.

Robard rolled, screaming, on the ground until the flames on his shirt were out. Oliverio would never forget the inhuman moans or the glimpse of burned flesh on the left side of the man's neck and face as he disappeared, running north along the dirt path.

59

I'm the one who shot you. You dumb fucker. . . . He walked right into it. That was easy. The words were haunting Oliverio. Why couldn't he remember? He played the incident on the street and the confrontation in the park over and over in his mind. What did he know that made the killer want to come back to finish him off? He was considered a threat even though he was half crippled and retired. He was aching to know why.

The impact of the bullet created a massive bruise on the upper right side of his chest. It took six weeks for the tenderness and discoloration to disappear. He had parked his car on a side street on the night of the encounter in the park, but he was in such pain he and Bull had to take a taxi home. In his basement den that night, he sat with ice packs on his chest and called every hospital, trauma center, and clinic to see if a tall thin man had sought treatment for burns to his upper body. None had.

Oliverio had decided that if the killer sought treatment, he would inform Sadowski and have him picked up. Otherwise, he would keep the events of the night to himself. He had to know why the killer wanted him dead and why he killed all the others.

Oliverio didn't know the extent of the burns inflicted on the man who shot him, but his gut told him he would probably survive, so there was a good chance he would seek revenge. Thinking of his mother, he bought and registered a new .38. He kept it in his bedroom and carried it with him whenever he was out walking.

The spark of recognition when his eyes met the killer's on the street that day near his home was encouraging to Oliverio. He had stopped seeing the shrink months before, when the hypnosis wasn't working. He had been told he was resisting. But there were other shrinks. He would find the best. And the NYPD would pick up the tab.

Dr. Jonathan Zaritsky, considered unorthodox by his fellow psychiatrists, was a firm believer in hypnosis. He was short, with penetrating dark eyes and long, flowing black hair, combed to one side at the front. He had no time for small talk. Oliverio liked his abruptness. Zaritsky prodded the former policeman to talk about himself. Oliverio did not tell him about his encounters with the killer on the street and in the park. After two sessions they were ready to begin hypnosis.

"You want to help yourself," said Zaritsky, "but you have an abiding distrust of people in my profession and, more importantly, you've always been your own man and you fear that hypnosis will rob you of that control of self. You're afraid you'll say things that will make you appear weak. You also have the false impression that deep hypnosis will put you in a comatose state. That's just not so. If your brain wasn't functioning, what would be the point in attempting therapy? You have a distorted view of hypnosis, as do most people, because of the garbage you read in the newspapers or see on television. You see subjects being hypnotized on stage and making fools of themselves, but that is all

rigged for the audience. You cannot remain in a hypnotic state unless you find it such a pleasant experience
that you don't want leave it. You also have a fear that
once under hypnosis there may be a foul-up and you
will never come out of it. That too is false. Even if
you were under and I told you to open your eyes but
you didn't, that would not mean you were in some sort
of permanent trance. You would either open your eyes
when you felt like it, or you would have a snooze and
wake up as you would normally do.''

Everything Zaritsky said sounded logical to Oliverio.
He was convinced that if anyone was going to help him
unlock the buried memories in his mind, this was the
man.

"I can't guarantee that we'll be able to recover the
missing pieces in your memory," said Zaritsky. "You
are very lucky to be alive at all. And the reality is, a
trauma of that severity, involving the brain, may have
permanently wiped out those memories. That's the negative side. On the positive side, some images did come
forth in your earlier attempts at hypnosis.

"Initially, we'll use regression to see if there are any
incidents far in your past that may serve to trigger something that will help us. Because of the physical severity
of your wound this will be a long process. And as I
pointed out, it may not work.''

60

Andrew Smythe, who supplied Robard with codeine and morphine, was a sixty-year-old physician who lost his license to practice medicine in 1976. The American Medical Association found him guilty of unethical conduct after numerous complaints of sexual harassment by former female patients. Those complaints also earned him eighteen months in a state prison. Upon his release, he found work as a sales representative for a pharmaceutical company and in his off hours he did his own dispensing. His prices were high. His best customer over the past five years was Robard Anthony Bryce. The man was eccentric and demanding, but he always paid and always with cash. Smythe had never asked, but he was convinced Bryce had recently undergone plastic surgery. The marks weren't obvious, but he was looking younger.

Smythe lived alone in a house in a quiet neighborhood in Queens. He also kept a Manhattan apartment under an assumed name. It was from there that he conducted his private business and entertained prostitutes. His stay in prison was not an experience he wished to repeat. He rented two parking spots in the underground

garage at his apartment building and used two cars and
a disguise to protect his double life. Only once had he
conducted business from his home. It was on a winter
night in 1980 when Robard pounded on his front door,
demanding the supply of morphine that hadn't been
delivered to him as promised. Smythe ushered him into
the house, away from the prying eyes of his neighbors.

"How did you find me out here?" he asked, obviously shaken.

"Did you think I would do business of this sort without knowing all about you? You are not Robert Malone,
you are Andrew Smythe. You used to be Dr. Andrew
Smythe and you spent a year and a half in prison for
trying to fuck your patients. And now you're trying to
fuck me."

"How long have you known?"

"I knew before I ever did business with you."

"But how—"

"Never mind that. Where's my fucking morphine?"

"I . . . I . . . The shipment was late. I'll have it for
you tomorrow."

"Why didn't you tell me?"

"I didn't get a chance. I didn't think a day would
matter."

"It matters to me. Just remember that. It always
matters."

Smythe did remember. He was never late with a delivery to Robard again.

It was one-thirty in the morning when Smythe opened
his front door in response to the frantic knocking. He
was appalled when he saw the condition Robard was
in. He recognized the smell of burned flesh.

"My God! What happened?"

"Just fucking help me," rasped Robard through gritted teeth. "Morphine . . . morphine . . ."

"You should be in a hospital."

"No fucking hospital!"

●   ●   ●

Robard paid Smythe thirty thousand dollars for treating his burns. For three weeks he took up residence in the spare bedroom of Smythe's home, injecting massive amounts of morphine to fight the pain. The most severe burns were to the left side of his neck, shoulder, and left hand. Burns to his left biceps, back, and the left side of his face were less severe.

"The burn on your neck is second degree," explained Smythe. "It will require skin grafting. The same with your left hand."

"That means a hospital?"

"Yes."

"No hospital!"

"Let me explain to you what will happen. I'll start with the neck. The burns have damaged your neck muscles. That's one strike against you. Now, without a skin graft on the burn itself, scar tissue will begin to form and it will contract and shrink to a fraction of what it was. This will result in a deformity. The combination of those two factors means that there will likely be a limitation in the movement of your head. A skin graft would reduce both the deformity and the limitation of movement.

"As for your hand, you obviously used it to try to beat out the flames of your burning clothing. You've charred the pulps on the tips of your fingers and the palm. Again, without a skin graft, contraction of the scar tissue will leave your hand deformed. You will be unable to fully extend your fingers."

Robard thought of the severe burns, to the hands and chest, suffered by Elliot Brodie when his plane crashed.

I'm not going to a hospital and I'm not having skin grafts."

Smythe, a trained physician, knew his greatest challenge was to ward off bacterial infection. It is such infections that most often lead to the death of burn victims; an open, raw burn area can permit a constant loss of protein and red blood cells, resulting in a severe drain on a person's resources and a retarding of the healing process.

The night Robard arrived, Smythe gave him a morphine injection and applied ice packs to the burned areas. In the morning he canceled his appointments and picked up the supplies he needed to treat Robard.

He washed the burns with an antibiotic solution and removed all loose skin except for a large blister on Robard's neck. Using a sterilized needle, he punctured the blister but left the overlying skin to protect the raw area beneath. He then applied two layers of an antibacterial, nonadherent dressing, four layers of gauze, and a layer of cotton-wool. Over all of that he applied a bandage which he taped along the edges to healthy skin. After four days he changed all but the first part of the dressing and a week later changed the entire dressing.

Smythe was amazed at Robard's tolerance for morphine and codeine, which kept him in a blissful stupor. At the end of the third week there was no evidence of infection and the burns were healing nicely, although Smythe could already see the scar tissue beginning to contract on the neck and hand. He drove Robard to his apartment and left him with a supply of calamine and lanoline cream to apply to the burn areas. He also left him the usual supply of morphine and codeine.

61

Twice a month for thirteen months, and now today was the day Vince Oliverio was to face his past. Dr. Zaritsky believed it would happen. He had prepared his patient well. With a combination of traditional therapy and hypnosis they had dissected his life before and after "the incident," as they had come to call the shooting. In the process, they had become close friends.

"We're going to deepen the trance more than we've ever done before," said Zaritsky when Oliverio came into his office. "I canceled all my other appointments, so we've got all afternoon and longer if we need it."

"I'm ready as I'll ever be," Oliverio said with a sigh.

"Okay, Vince. I want you to sit in the straight-backed chair beside the desk." Oliverio complied. This was something new. He usually lay on the couch against the wall. "Now, take a deep breath and slowly exhale. Empty your lungs."

Zaritsky stood in front of the chair and held one open hand, fingers extended, inches from Oliverio's forehead. "I want you to keep your head still and, with your eyes, watch as I move my hand slowly down in front of your face. When it disappears from view I want you to let your eyes close."

Oliverio's eyes blinked slowly once and closed.

"Very good, Vince," said Zaritsky in his low, soothing voice. "Now I want you to relax your entire body. That's good. Your eyelids are so relaxed you know you can't open them. Test it for yourself. Make sure you can't open them." He could see movement under the eyelids, but they didn't open. Oliverio was in a prehypnotic state.

Zaritsky sat beside his desk, facing Oliverio. He set the metronome on the desk in motion. It began its rhythmic clicking sound. "I want you to visualize the pendulum of the metronome, Vince. Back and forth . . . back and forth . . . very relaxing. Now, Vince, I want you to talk about the den in the basement of your house. Tell me about how you fixed it up and everything that's in it."

Over the next forty minutes Oliverio, with Zaritsky's occasional prodding, described in minute detail the construction of the den and everything in it.

"That was very good, Vince. Now I want you to concentrate on the sound of the metronome. Each click is helping you to get more and more relaxed. . . . Now I want you to go back in time. You are down in your den. You're sitting in your favorite barber's chair. Your mother is upstairs . . . remember. Someone's in the den with you. It's your partner, Alfie Morrow."

Zaritsky could see there was rapid eye movement under Oliverio's lids. He was visualizing himself and Alfie in the den. They were staring at the fingerprint comparator. Clearly, he saw a name on the corner of the screen: Elliot Robard Brodie. It came back in a rush. His brain could barely keep up with the pictures. The print cards from Martin Butler, Brodie's prints on the wall, scars, age creases, endless files, the nursing home, Dudley, and Ellen . . . Sweet Ellen; her house; her bed; New York; their lovemaking, their plans.

Zaritsky watched the tears flood down Oliverio's face. He was having an abreaction, replaying the missing parts of his life as if he were there. The emotions, the clothing, the conversations, the sounds and smells, and the actions. Everything was being replayed exactly as it was. The eyes remained closed. He was fishing with Martin Butler, sitting by the campfire. Ellen is dead. Martin is dead. He and Alfie with Frank Clifton at his house; at the bar in Connecticut. . . . And then, the darkened street . . . the clone, the steel silencer against the back of his head. Oliverio clenched his fists and gritted his teeth and his body twisted in his chair as he saw himself rolling to the cement. His breathing grew louder and more labored. Zaritsky sensed he was trying to elude his would-be killer. Oliverio could see the townhouses when he heard the first shot. The doctor watched as Oliverio's upper body turned wildly and both hands clutched his damaged hip. Now the gunman was on him. and his head jerked to one side.

Oliverio was drenched in sweat and his body was trembling when Zaritsky began to bring him out of the hypnotic trance. "Now, Vince, you will be able to consider this entire episode at will in your subconscious mind and it will not disturb or upset your conscious being whether you're asleep or awake. You will feel refreshed when you awaken."

62

It was early on a pleasant Sunday evening when Margaret and Frank Clifton arrived home in Palm Harbor after a day trip south along the coast and to Cabbage and Mullet keys. As they turned into the driveway, they saw someone sitting on the lawn with his back propped against the side of the garage.

"Somebody's there," said Margaret.

"I see him."

"He looks filthy."

As they drew closer Clifton could see it was a shabbily dressed, unkempt teenager. He slowed the car, opened the glove compartment, and removed a small revolver, which he held in his lap.

"What are you doing?" whispered Margaret.

"I'm not taking any chances," replied Clifton. He had purchased the gun soon after they arrived in Florida. The rising crime and murder rates in the state, particularly in Miami, had created a purchasing frenzy for guns, and Clifton caught the fever. People had to defend themselves, he said. You never knew when a crazy from the south might suddenly appear and try to rob you or kill you. That's what he had told Margaret, but she knew the real reason.

"He's probably a runaway, spaced out on drugs."

"What are you going to do?"

"He looks harmless, but I'm not taking any chances. I want you to go into the house and stay by the telephone. If I yell, call the police."

"Maybe we should back right out of here and call them now."

"He's not moving. He's probably passed out. If he wanted to rob us, he wouldn't be sitting out there in broad daylight." Clifton stopped the car in front of the garage door. "Just go into the house. I'll handle it."

Margaret quickly left the car, unlocked the front door, and entered the house. She pulled aside the drapes and watched her husband get out of the car, his light blue nylon jacket draped over his right hand and the small pistol. He walked slowly out of sight to the side of the garage.

The youth's eyes were closed. Clifton noticed his head was at a peculiar angle and he was wearing a white silk scarf around his neck. His faded blue jeans were threadbare at the knees and his open plaid shirt revealed a grimy T-shirt. He was pathetically thin and the shirt hung loosely on his frame. A small, soiled, black canvas bag was slung over one shoulder. Clifton noticed the deformed clawlike left hand as he positioned himself in front of the sleeping figure. "Hey!" he said, gripping the pistol. "This is private property."

The youth opened his eyes and raised his head. It was then that Clifton saw the unsightly flat white scar on the left side of his face and it was then he realized the person before him was Robard: dissipated and much younger, but unmistakably Robard. He stepped to the side, startled.

Robard's upper body swiveled when he turned toward the doctor. It was apparent to Clifton the clone was unable to turn his head without turning his shoulders and he saw fear and helplessness in the sunken eyes.

"You!"

Robard nodded, pushing himself up from the ground. Clifton was astounded. The clone looked no more than fifteen and his body had shrunk several inches. His incredible growth after birth had been medically inconceivable. So had his youthful appearance the last time the doctor saw him in White Plains. And now this.

"Let's walk," said Clifton, surprised by the sternness in his own voice. Robard was so thin his head appeared out of proportion to his body. They walked along the driveway, away from the house.

"Why did you come here? I should call the police."

"I'm sick. You were supposed to help me and you didn't."

Clifton was surprised at how much the voice had changed since he last saw him.

"You shot those policemen."

Robard looked at him blankly. Clifton eyed the canvas bag.

"What's in there?"

"Just my clothes. Everything's gone. All the money. I think I'm dying. You've got to help me."

There was desperation in his voice.

"You've been abusing drugs all along, haven't you?"

Robard held his left arm protectively against his body. Reaching out, Clifton grasped the arm and raised the shirtsleeve.

"What a mess!"

The inside of the arm was a mass of bruises and puncture marks.

Robard pulled his arm away.

"Is the other one the same?"

"Yes. I can't help it. I can't stand the pain."

"You're still having those seizures?"

"Yes, every morning. And I have these dreams at night. Like they're so real. I don't know who I am anymore and I forget lots of things. Like you told me about those policemen, right? Well, I think you're right, but I don't really remember. It's like it maybe happened in a dream or something. I'm not saying I didn't do it, but, ah . . . I think they were after me or something. See that's not, like, really clear. But the dreams at night. Like I'm staying with my uncle Victor in California. That was after my mother died. I hang around the studio with him all the time.''

"What studio?"

"Where they're making movies. My uncle did writing for them.''

"What was your uncle's name?"

"I told you, Victor. Victor Brodie."

"Do you remember the nursing home in Pennsylvania?"

"I think I dreamt about that once."

"What did you dream?"

"An old man with a cane or something."

"So you're telling me you don't remember shooting the policemen or the other murders?"

"I told you I remember some things, but I don't know if they were just dreams or something.''

"How is it you remember me? How did you find me?''

"I wrote down about you and how you were supposed to help me. But then I couldn't find you for a long time. A guy I know on the street helped me. I wrote out your name and he found out where you lived from the, ah, Medical American . . .''

"American Medical Association."

"Right. Yeah. So I hitched a ride down here."

"What's wrong with your neck and hand? You've been burned on the side of your face.''

"I think somebody did it to me in the park."

"What park? Did what to you? What are you talking about?''

"Like he set me on fire or something. With his lighter.''

Clifton looked at his hand and pulled the scarf away from his neck. "Those are hypertrophic scars. You didn't have a skin graft. Who treated you?''

"Smythe. He used to be a doctor. I wouldn't go to the hospital. I don't go to hospitals.''

The ugly scarlet scar on his neck was thick and hard. The skin contracture had forced his head to tilt to the side. Surgery would be required to release the contracture, allowing more movement of the head, unless the scar had been there too long and the damage was permanent.

"When did this happen?"

"I don't know."

"What do you mean, you don't know?"

"I can't remember."

Clifton didn't know whether to believe him. If what he said was true, the accelerated age reversal was affecting his mind as well as his body. He was remembering Elliot Brodie's youth and quickly forgetting his own past.

"What happened to all the money?"

"It's gone. They made me leave where I lived and I've been on the street. The drugs cost a lot too. You've got to help me."

"Have you had a fix today?"

Robard nodded.

"What are you on?"

"Heroin."

"Where did you get it?"

Robard clutched his canvas bag.

"There's only enough for a couple more days."

"What do you expect from me?"

Robard looked at him, confused. "Can't you stop the pain? Then I might not have to take the drugs."

Perhaps he no longer realizes he's getting younger, thought Clifton.

"Can I stay with you, Frank?"

It was the first time Robard had used his name and it caused a tremor to run through his body.

"The first thing we have to do is get you cleaned up. There's a very good clinic in Tampa. I'm going to take you there right now."

"It's been very bad for me, Frank. The pain . . . you have no idea."

Clifton had Robard wait in the car while he went into the house. Margaret, who had been watching from the window, met him at the door.

"What does he want?"

"It's Robard."

"What? But he's just a boy."

"I tried to explain to you that he was getting younger."

"My God, are you sure?"

"I'm sure."

"But I . . . I never imagined it was like this."

"Nor did I."

"Are you going to call the police?"

"No. He's sick. Somebody burned him badly. His hand and neck are deformed. He's a physical mess. A heroin addict."

"My God!"

"I'm driving him over to the drug clinic in Tampa."

"What about those murders?"

"It appears he doesn't remember much of what he's been doing."

"He could still be dangerous."

"He's a lot more pathetic than dangerous."

"Just be careful. Addicts can be very unpredictable."

"I'll have this with me," said Clifton, exposing the revolver under his jacket.

In the car, Clifton removed the remainder of Robard's heroin supply from his bag.

On the pretext of assessing the extent of the deformity of Robard's left hand, Clifton arranged for X rays at the Tampa clinic. What he was actually looking for was the presence of epiphyseal cartilage between the shaft and the ends of the long bone of the left arm. That type of cartilage ceases to exist after it is transformed into bones and a person stops growing. Although Robard was shrinking rather than growing, the X rays revealed a layer of epiphyseal cartilage normal for a young teenager. The rate of Robard's reverse aging convinced Clifton there would be more and more of the cartilage as his bones diminished in size. If age reversal continued, the entire skeleton would gradually soften and the bones would consist partly of cartilage or fibrous tissue.

Doctors at the clinic put Robard on a two-week regi-

men of methadone. The synthetic opiate was itself addictive, but there was much less trauma withdrawing
from it than from heroin. At the end of two weeks, the
clinic's medical counselors decided Robard was ready
to go cold turkey. He was locked in a tiny room with a
stainless steel bed built into the wall and rounded at the
edges. There were no pillows or bedding; only a stainless steel sink and toilet. He spent much of his time
vomiting or attempting to vomit. Clinic staff kept a
close eye on him through the clear Plexiglas door, the
only entrance to the room. Stomach cramps came with
the vomiting, a typical withdrawal reaction. But on the
morning of the second day, the clinic staff became
alarmed when Robard's body jerked to the fetal position
and went into spasms. A doctor was summoned and he
entered the room with two attendants.

"Should we sedate him?"

"No," said the doctor. "Just see to it he doesn't in-
jure himself. This is very unusual. I've never seen a reaction like this to methadone withdrawal."

"Maybe he was on something else, too."

"Nothing showed up in his tests."

Robard lay on his side, his arms rigid, except for the
slight crook in his burned arm. The tilt of his head was
exaggerated more than usual and his pupils were wildly
dilated. He began snarling like an animal, teeth bared.

"Watch his head doesn't hit the wall."

One attendant held his shoulders, another his calves.
Robard struggled fiercely. Without warning, his legs
snapped straight out, catching an attendant just above
the knee and knocking him backwards against the door.
The attendant cried out in pain.

"He's as tight as a spring," said the other attendant.

The legs began kicking out rhythmically.

"*Kill it! Kill the snake!*" screamed Robard. "*Get it
off! Kill it! Kill . . .*"

63

In the fourteen months since hypnosis revealed the secrets locked away in his subconscious, Oliverio, with Dr. Zaritsky's help, divided the lost memories into segments and talked most of them out in great detail. His amnesia had not allowed him to grieve properly for the loss of Ellen, the Butlers, and Alfie Morrow. Zaritsky warned that the enormity of the tragedy could overwhelm Oliverio if they didn't proceed with caution.

"Taken all at once, it would be too much for anyone," he had said. "You've lost a fiancée, two longtime close friends, and your partner."

Memories of Ellen McKinnon and her death caused the most suffering for Oliverio. He couldn't reconcile himself to her loss.

"I know it's probably too late in life to have a romantic relationship of any substance," Oliverio told Zaritsky. "I can handle that. What I can't handle is the injustice of such a young, decent, warm person having her life snuffed out like that."

"You're certain she was murdered?"

"Yes, I'm certain. He laughed about it when he told me."

"Who?"

"The guy who shot me. He told me he did it. I was sure of it."

"Have you told the police about it?"

"There's no point. He may not even be alive. He's the one I saw on the street."

He told Zaritsky about the encounter in Central Park.

"That was the last that you saw of him? He ran off in flames?"

Oliverio nodded.

"But how do you know he's dead?"

"I said *probably* dead. I told you that's one area I don't want to go into. But I assure you, it's nothing I'm hung up over. It's just something I'm not ready to talk about."

Oliverio debated telling Sadowski the full story but decided against it. Maybe someday. Without proof, who would believe him? He was still having migraine attacks and blurred vision. They came on without warning. Sadowski had witnessed them. It was a bizarre, nightmarish story and if he told it they would think he was nuts: Elliot Brodie's clone on a murder spree, getting younger and younger. If somebody who'd been shot in the head came to him with a story like that, he'd never believe it. He went through every file and scrap of paper in his den looking for something, anything, that might not have been in the material taken from him by Robard. Anne Morrow also allowed him to go through Alfie's papers. All he found was a telephone number for Frank Clifton. He tried the number, but it was out of service.

64

Knitting was Margaret Clifton's latest passion. But now that the boy was living with them, not all of her sweaters and scarves and socks would go to local charities. As his age and size diminished, she was obliged to take in his clothes and sew or knit new ones. He was a child now, younger than the age Bobby was when he drowned. The boy's presence made it easier for her to accept Bobby's death and deal with the sorrow. Perhaps there was some good, some spiritual purpose, for Robard's existence. It gave her a warm feeling to see him playing with other children. Thinking of Bobby made her think of the water and she looked up until she spotted Robard among the other children. Children could be cruel and she knew they made fun of the boy's deformed hand and neck, but she protected him as much as she was able.

It was reassuring to see the municipal lifeguard keeping a close eye on the children in the water. A line of floating white markers, strung together, cordoned off an area considered safe for swimming. Margaret sat on a folding aluminum chair under the shade of a palm tree at the edge of the beach.

She watched Robard paddling the inflatable toy boat and went back to her knitting.

It had become a game with Robard, propelling the boat ahead as straight and as fast as possible while switching the plastic paddle from side to side. It was a difficult challenge because the boat was so light and it tended to veer wildly with each stroke of the paddle. His deformed hand made it that much more demanding. Robard beat furiously at the water. He hated the doctor. The woman hated him too, he thought. The doctor was mean to them. He wished he'd go away and never return. He wished he was dead. *Dead! Dead! Dead!* He chanted the word under his breath, the paddle picking up the pace to match the rhythm. A child's voice intruded on his trance.

"Hey! Hey you!" yelled a fair-haired, freckled boy of six or seven. He was standing near the shore, the water to his knees.

Robard stopped paddling and stared at him.

"That sure is a nice little boat. You can sure make it go fast." Robard paddled closer to shore. "Boy, I sure would like to try that."

"You can try it," said Robard. "But I can't go in any closer, so you walk out."

"I don't know how to swim too good yet. My mother doesn't want me to go out too deep."

"It's not too deep. The boat's rubbing the bottom."

The boy started out from the shore. He was chest deep when he reached out for the boat, but with a quick reverse stroke, Robard moved it out of his reach.

"Stop the boat, it's goin' out too far."

"C'mon, Bobby. C'mon, you're almost there."

"I'm not Bobby. I'm Jamie." The boy was up to his neck when Robard moved the boat away a second time. "Don't go so far! I can't reach."

"You can reach, Bobby."

"I'm *not* Bobby!" Robard's eyelids began to flicker.

"It's a present for you, Bobby. I'm your daddy's friend."

The frightened boy lunged at the boat, gripping its side. Robard released his paddle and pushed the boy's head underwater. The boy lost his grip and was thrashing wildly.

The lifeguard ran to the boy and pulled him, coughing and spitting, to shore. The boy ran off crying. The lifeguard then went out to Robard, who was staring at him coldly.

"What the hell do you think you're doing?" he demanded. "You could have drowned him."

Margaret heard the commotion and ran to the water's edge.

"What's wrong?" she asked.

"Does he belong to you?"

"Yes."

"Well, he just tried to drown a young kid here."

"We were just playing," said Robard innocently.

"I was watching you. That's no way to play." The lifeguard turned to Margaret. "If I ever see him pull another stunt like that, he's banned from here. He could have hurt that child." He walked off before she could respond. Robard ran to Margaret. She put her arm around his shoulder and kissed the top of his head.

65

Frank Clifton was thumbing through a magazine on the back deck. Margaret sat beside him, knitting at a furious pace.

"Frank?"

"Hmmm?"

"Have you noticed he's not reading anymore?"

"Pardon?" he said, lowering the magazine.

"I said, he's not reading anymore."

"Oh?"

"Haven't you noticed?"

"No, I haven't."

"I'm worried about him."

"It's not as if we're preparing him for the university."

"He should have the same opportunity as other kids his age."

"He's not like other kids."

Margaret scowled at him.

"Why don't you talk to him?" he suggested in a conciliatory tone.

"I've tried. I've even offered to help him. He lets me read to him, but he won't read himself."

"You can't do any more than that. If he won't listen to you, he certainly won't listen to me."

"Well, I have done something," she announced. "I called an agency and hired a tutor to help him with his reading. A woman will come to the house three afternoons a week."

"Look, we've already had to move once since we arrived here. Prying neighbors weren't enough; now you're going to have somebody right here in the house, three times a week. If she's stays on for any extended period, it'll be obvious to her something's drastically wrong with him."

"I've thought about that," she said smugly. "We can change agencies every month or so."

"This isn't that big a place." Clifton was skeptical. "Have you talked to him about it?"

"Not yet. But I'll explain to him that it's for his own good."

Soon after Robard moved in with them, Clifton realized he'd made a mistake. At the time, he didn't know what else to do. Robard went off drugs as he promised he would, and he really had nowhere to go. Clifton told him it would be up to Margaret. She was adamantly opposed but agreed to meet with him. It was at that meeting, at a restaurant where they had lunch, that Clifton realized how manipulative the clone was. His warm smile immediately disarmed Margaret and it was impossible for her to relate the young teenager to the repulsive creature from the Staatsburg house.

Initially, during Robard's daily seizures, Margaret left the house, but as his body continued to shrink and his age regressed, she stayed with him, cradling his head in her lap. She spoke soothingly to him, ignoring his guttural cursing during the seizures. Robard no longer knew what it was he wanted the doctor to do for him, but he felt deep resentment toward him.

•   •   •

Mrs. Green, the tutor, was a retired elementary school teacher in her early sixties. She wore a baggy, dark brown dress. She was plump and bespectacled and her steel gray hair was tied in a bun. The agency advertised her as one of its very best.

"I've explained that you're here to help him," said Margaret. "I've set up a room off the den as a miniature classroom. My husband is a doctor involved in cancer research. He's at work."

Mrs. Green was impressed.

"You realize I must have privacy with the student?"

"Of course. I'll introduce you to him and then I'll go about my business."

Robard was seated on a padded stool at a card table set up for him as a desk. He eyed the woman as she entered the room.

"Robard, this is Mrs. Green." Margaret smiled. "She's going to help you with your reading."

"Hello, young man," said the woman warmly.

Robard was silent.

"Say hello to Mrs. Green."

"Hello, he said, his voice barely audible.

"You'll find he's somewhat shy at first."

"That's understandable."

"Well, I'll leave you two now. Good luck with the lesson."

"So, young man, you're having problems with your reading?"

Robard stared at her coldly.

"Now, you mustn't be afraid to speak up," she said, removing several thin books and note pads from her briefcase. Robard was silent. "Young man, I must insist you speak up."

"Shitass," he said softly.

"*What?*"

"I said, shitass."

"That is not very nice language, coming from a young boy. Where in heaven's name did you hear such words?"

"Cunt!"

"Stop it! This instant!"

"Whore."

"I'll not tolerate this."

"Fucking dried up old whore."

Mrs. Green lashed out at Robard with a thin text-book, striking a glancing blow off his shoulder.

"Cocksucker!"

Mrs. Green was on her feet, jamming her books into her briefcase. "In all my years of teaching, I've never been treated like this. You are a sick, evil boy with a sewer mouth. You ought to be ashamed of yourself and so should your mother. Such filth!"

"Such filth," mimicked Robard. "Such dirty, rotten, fucking filth."

"I'll speak to your mother about this and I shall never return."

"Good fucking riddance."

Mrs. Green startled Margaret when she rushed into the kitchen and announced she was leaving.

"Never in my life have I been so insulted. That boy is foulmouthed and evil. A drunken sailor wouldn't use such language. I think it's high time you found out who his friends are. He must get it from somewhere."

Margaret watched helplessly as the woman slammed her car door and drove off. She found Robard sitting in the den with his head buried in his hands on the card table.

"My God! What happened in here?"

Robard slowly raised his head. He appeared to be on the verge of tears.

"What happened?"

"She . . . I . . . I couldn't read. I was scared and . . . and she hit me with a book."

"She *hit* you?"

Robard nodded, lowering his head.

"What was she saying about bad language?"

"I dunno. I couldn't read and she hit me."

Margaret called the agency to complain about Mrs. Green, but the agency defended the teacher, insisting there must be a misunderstanding. They promised to call back after they talked to Mrs. Green. Half an hour later the director of the agency telephoned to defend the teacher. Margaret was extremely agitated when she related the entire incident to her husband over dinner. Clifton had no doubt that the tutor's version of events was the correct one, but he kept his thoughts to himself. He was concerned by the apparent deterioration in Margaret's mental state. He didn't want to upset her. He eyed Robard several times during the meal and each time the boy lowered his eyes.

Robard was in bed and the dishwasher was humming in the kitchen. Clifton approached his wife at the sink and embraced her. He felt her stiffen.

"That woman's conduct didn't seem to bother you a bit."

"What's there to say? She quit and that's it."

Margaret pulled away from him.

"You don't even care, do you? Can't you see he's a helpless child?"

Clifton shrugged. He would be sleeping on the couch in the den that night, something he'd been doing often of late.

66

Clifton could see Robard was already a bit groggy. He'd be out cold in another half hour or so. The babysitter would arrive in ten minutes. Perfect timing. The doctor had carefully planned the evening. He and Margaret hadn't been out of the house alone, without *him,* for more than eight months. Margaret's whole life revolved around Robard and he was determined to break that cycle. The clone's conduct with the tutor convinced Clifton that Robard could never be trusted alone with a babysitter, so he decided to mix a sleeping compound with Robard's dessert.

Margaret checked her appearance in the hallway mirror.

"All set, darling?"

"Ready as I'll ever be. Seems so strange to be all dressed up. It's been so long, I'd forgotten what it's like."

"We'll have a ball."

"I'm just worried about leaving him with a sitter, after that awful experience with the tutor."

"But you said it wasn't his fault."

"It wasn't. I'm just worried the babysitting agency will send us a bad apple too."

"Don't worry, darling, it couldn't happen twice in a row."

The babysitter, a cheerful, blond, blue-eyed high school junior, arrived on schedule. Her father dropped her off. Clifton greeted her at the door.

"Hi," she said with a bright smile. "I'm Patti Skrypek." Margaret and Frank introduced themselves and they prepared to leave.

"We should be back by midnight," said Margaret. "There's lots to snack on in the refrigerator. Just help yourself."

It was a romantic evening with a fine dinner and dancing afterward, but Clifton sensed his wife's thoughts were on Robard. It helped when he insisted she call home. She was beaming. No problems. After the call, Margaret was more relaxed, but as the evening wore on she became distracted once again. She rushed into the house the moment he pulled up in front. The babysitter was watching television.

"Is he all right, Patti?" asked Margaret.

"Just fine. He went to bed early. He's sound asleep. He was very good. No problem at all." Margaret went to Robard's room. The boy was sleeping soundly. She paid the babysitter and Clifton drove her home.

"Well, what do you think now?" asked Margaret on his return. "You heard what the sitter said; no problems at all. Just like any normal child."

"I think it's great," he lied. "Now I'll tell you what we're going to do. Our lab and the university are having a hoity-toity dinner and dance in a couple of weeks and I think we should go."

"Oh, Frank, that sounds great. Tonight was wonderful, but I wasn't totally relaxed. I guess I was worried about leaving him alone."

The doctor had decided he must get Margaret out of the house as often as possible. If it meant drugging Robard, that's the way it would have to be. It was all he could think of to counteract her obsessive, unnatural relationship with the clone. The child was her whole life. It was a house of cards that would, he knew, soon collapse.

Next to leaving Bobby alone at the pond, Clifton's greatest regret was telling Margaret about Robard and allowing him to live with them. By now, he was convinced, she might have fully faced up to Bobby's death and carried on with her life. Instead, her mental state was tenuous as she watched the clone deteriorate day by day. The accelerated age reversal would, he concluded, soon end in Robard's death and he dreaded the effect it would have on her. He had no idea what form the death would take. But he wanted to be prepared, to have a plan.

Clifton was dismayed when Robard pushed aside the butterscotch pudding, his favorite dessert. He discounted the possibility that the boy had seen him stir the sleeping compound into it. It was simply bad luck. He'd eaten more of the main course than usual. The doctor was worried, but there was no backing out. He must get Margaret out of the house. She'd talked about it all week. She bought a new dress, her first in four years. Perhaps Robard would eat the pudding soon after they left. But what if the babysitter should happen to eat it? He'd tell her the boy was on a special diet and he could eat the dessert later if he wanted it.

Patti Skrypek arrived half an hour early. Clifton went to Robard's bedroom, where he was watching television. The boy had been in a sulky, resentful mood all day. The doctor knew it was jealousy.

"I want a word with you."

Robard ignored him.

"Margaret's been looking forward to this and I don't want anything to mess it up. Understand?"

"What do you mean?"

"You know damn well what I'm talking about. You've been playing your game and getting away with it for a long time. You've got her conned, but you can't con me. I think you're an evil little bastard. I know what went on with the tutor and I don't want a repeat.''

''I don't know what you're talking about.''

Clifton was taken aback. Maybe Robard didn't know. His mind was regressing every day. But why, then, did his attachment to Margaret remain so strong? Maternal instinct, perhaps? It wasn't adding up. How could the clone feel resentment toward him if the feelings and experiences of previous days were lost to him? He concluded there had to be some residual memory. Could it be explained scientifically? The doctor had given up trying to make scientific sense out of any of this. The one abiding truth, at least in his mind, was that the age reversal was DNA connected and was a process operating exactly the opposite to Cockayne's syndrome. He'd read what precious little there was on the syndrome and it continued to amaze him that a human body was capable of such radical change in such a short time period.

''What I'm saying is, I don't want this girl hassled.''

Robard mumbled something Clifton didn't hear. Clifton moved towards the boy aggressively. ''What did you say?''

''I said, when are you going to help me? You promised to help me. And I hardly have any of the things I had before. Where's my pony gone?''

''You've never had a pony.''

''I did too.''

It was at times like this that Clifton began to question his own sanity. None of this could be true. It was all a terrible dream and at any moment he would wake up beside Margaret after working the night shift as an intern at Massachusetts General Hospital. There would be no Elliot Brodie. The problem was, the dream didn't end. And here he was telling an eight-year-old boy, Elliot Brodie's clone, not to give the babysitter a hard time. It was all madness.

Robard was staring at him coldly. Clifton wondered what confusion, what evil, filled his thoughts. By his estimates, Robard would die within the year. He had difficulty comprehending that the clone had no recollection of either of his lives—as Elliot Brodie the eccentric recluse or as his vengeful, murderous replica. The questions bombarded the doctor's mind. How acute were the memories of Robard's childhood as Elliot Brodie? Both Brodie's parents had died before he was eighteen. Did he have memories of them? If so, were they negative or positive?

Like his body, the functional ability of Robard's brain was shrinking. The only constants were the morning seizures and the deep resentment he felt toward the doctor.

Clifton hadn't seen Margaret so relaxed since before Bobby's death. She joked with people she had just met; she laughed a lot; she danced. She was alive. It was he who was on edge, wondering what awaited them at home. Watching Margaret talking animatedly and having such a good time, he wished he could freeze the moment, wished it would always be like that. He mourned for his dead son, their child of love, and he hated Elliot Brodie for the misery he'd wrought on their lives. And, as always, he blamed himself. Nobody forced him to accept Brodie's deal. It was ego and greed. He'd sold his soul to the devil.

On the drive home Margaret moved closer to him and rested her head on his shoulder as he drove. They agreed they would definitely do this more often. It was after one when they arrived home. Clifton waited in the car while Margaret went in to pay the sitter, but he ran from the car when he heard his wife scream. The living room was in a shambles, with furniture overturned, lamps broken, and the television screen smashed.

Patti was on the couch, her eyes swollen from crying. Her blouse was torn and there were ugly red scratches on her neck and upper chest. Margaret was hysterical. Robard wasn't in his room and she demanded to know where he was. "In the kitchen," sobbed the girl. Clifton got there before his wife. Robard, his eyes wild, strained to free himself from the chair to which he'd been tied with the cord from the clothes iron which was dangling at the side of the chair. A towel was tied tightly over his mouth. Margaret rushed to untie him.

"How could she do this to a child," she cried.

Clifton was furious. The illusion of normalcy had been smashed. He returned to the living room to comfort the young girl.

"Why is she screaming at me?" she sobbed. "He tried to kill me."

"Don't listen," he whispered. "She's hysterical. I know it's not your fault. I'll get you out of here. We shouldn't have left him with you."

Margaret was sitting on the kitchen floor, rocking Robard in her arms, when the doctor returned to the kitchen. Patti stood in the doorway, holding a corner of her torn blouse to cover herself.

"She *hit* me!" screamed Robard.

"You shut your vile mouth," ordered Clifton, fists clenched.

"But Frank," cried Margaret, "look at what she did."

"Look at her, for Christ's sake, Margaret. Just look at her. What the hell does it take?"

The girl, sobbing uncontrollably, ran from the house. The doctor followed her out and calmed her down. On the twelve-mile drive to her home, she related the events of the night.

"I was watching TV and he suddenly came in and just started swearing at me and calling me awful names. For no reason. And he wouldn't stop. I kept telling him to stop, but he wouldn't. Then I decided to ignore him and he attacked me. Like . . . like a wild animal, kicking and biting me. Like, I do track and field at school, but he was so strong. He ripped my blouse and scratched me. He's young, but it was like, I thought he was trying to do something sexually. And then, like, he was trying to strangle me. Finally I pushed him off and I ran into the kitchen. He followed me and I pushed him down and sat on him. He was kicking me and finally I got him tied up with the cord from the iron. I didn't know who to call. I tried the number your wife gave me. It rang and rang, but nobody answered. My parents are out late tonight and my brother's gone for the weekend. I didn't know what to do, so I just waited until you came home.''

"I've been worried about him for some time," Clifton said. "He's never done anything as bad as this, but he's become more and more irrational of late. We're going to have to get him psychiatric help. As you saw tonight, the strain on my wife has been incredible. She's not able to think clearly. I'm very sorry he chose tonight to go over the edge.''

In front of her home, Clifton removed four twenties from his wallet. "I'll pay you double your rate for all your trouble, Patti, and here's an additional forty to replace your blouse.''

"It's too much. It didn't cost that much. I couldn't take all that.''

"Please take it. I insist." She took the money reluctantly. "We'll probably have to commit him to a hospital. I'd appreciate it if you didn't say too much about this, other than to your parents. It's going to be difficult enough as it is. I hope you understand.''

"I understand, Dr. Clifton.''

67

Clifton was sitting bare-chested on the small patio behind the modest home at Port Richey a few miles north of Palm Harbor when he heard a car pull up in front. He went to investigate. It was a taxi. Vince Oliverio climbed out of the rear seat. He was using a cane. They stood staring at each other as the taxi pulled away. Oliverio thought the doctor looked like a beaten man— old beyond his years and weary. But then the former policeman was much thinner, and frailer, than when Clifton last saw him. The doctor didn't recognize him until he spoke.

"I had a hard time finding you, Frank. I'm sorry about your son."

"You're okay? You remember?"

"Took a while, I'm afraid. I had to go to a couple of shrinks. A lot of hypnosis."

"I called you and went to see you in the hospital, but you didn't remember me."

"A bullet in the head will do that."

"I tried to tell your department what you were working on, but they thought I was crazy. Can't blame them, I guess. Everything I had was in the diary and documents I gave to you. Couldn't prove a thing. Nobody seemed to know you were working on it.''

"That was my fault. Too much pride. We wanted to break it ourselves. I had everything with me when I got shot. He took it all. He was watching us in the bar when we met you.''

"Bobby's death was very difficult for us. My wife is still not over it. I guess she never will be. We moved down here to forget and to get away from it. I'm working at a small private cancer research lab at the University of Tampa.''

"I know. Isn't that what you always wanted?''

Clifton nodded. "If only I'd done that from the beginning. . . . Instead I get involved with a madman.''

"I've been around a few days, Frank. I was wondering if you'd heard from him again. Then I saw the child . . . the burn scars.''

"You know about that?''

Oliverio nodded and related the encounter with Robard in Central Park.

"He never really told me what happened when he came here. His hand and neck were deformed. He wasn't properly treated.''

"It's like a bad dream. I wanted his ass so bad. He killed a lot of people. My people.''

"There's not a day goes by that I don't think about it.''

"When I saw your wife with him, I couldn't believe it. I know you told us what was happening, but it's just so unreal.''

Clifton nodded grimly.

"How long do you give him?''

"Months at most. I don't know what will happen to my wife. She's in bad shape as it is.''

"Does he still have those seizures?''

"They're not as intense, but he still has them. I'm convinced they were dreams from the womb. I think everybody has them, but we have trouble recalling them because of oxytocin. That's the principal hormone in a woman's body that induces contractions during birth. The going theory is that oxytocin also induces amnesia. That's certainly the case with laboratory animals. There's no reason the same couldn't hold true for humans. It would explain why birth and womb memories are buried so deeply in the subconscious. In his case, it was as if the umbilical cord, the snake, was Elliot Brodie's bloodline. Taking him over. Choking off his own identity.''

"Were you able to figure any of this out, Frank? Medically? Scientifically?"

"The only constant seems to be that everything that's happening to him is an exact reversal of normal growth. Except that it's at an accelerated pace. But I have no idea what triggered it. Whatever it is, it caused accelerated growth at birth. Then there was the long stable period where he lay comatose. And then something kicked in to reverse the whole process. If we had a film of his insides, and you ran it in reverse, you would see a speeded up, but accurate, picture of normal human growth. If you ran the film forward, the way you're supposed to, everything would be backwards.

"In the womb, a baby's skeletal structure, initially, is not made of bones but of fibers and cartilage in the shape of bones. It's difficult to explain, but eventually growth hormones increase the size and numbers of cells which enlarge and lengthen the bones. And there is a calcification process which gradually hardens them. Growth hormones also promote the growth of body tissues and organs and thickens the skin. We're not sure exactly how it works, but the growth hormones promote protein formation and speeds up the movement of amino acids out of the blood and into cells. All of this enhances normal growth."

"I'm afraid you've lost me, Frank. I can't sort things out as well as I used to."

"What I'm saying is, all those normal growth mechanisms in the clone are completely reversed and they're operating at an accelerated pace. It's like a car speeding down a one-way street in the wrong direction."

Oliverio could see Clifton was becoming agitated.

"I know this hasn't been easy on you, Frank."

"If only I hadn't been working that night in Boston. . . . If only I'd been stricter about the pond with Bobby. . . . If, if if!"

"You can't blame yourself for the boy's death. It wasn't your fault."

"I shouldn't have let him near the pond without one of us being there."

"It wasn't an accident, Frank."

"Wha . . . what do you mean?"

"I wasn't going to tell you this, but I can see it's probably better that you know."

"Tell me what? What do you mean, it wasn't an accident?"

"Before he shot me, he told me he was going to kill your son to get back at you for talking to us."

Clifton was devastated.

"I'm sorry, Frank. Maybe it was a mistake to tell you. But I hope, now, you'll stop blaming yourself."

The doctor folded his arms against his body, as if trying to hug himself. He closed his eyes and bowed his head as he rapidly rocked his upper torso back and forth. Oliverio could see by the swell of Clifton's jawbone that he was gritting his teeth. When he regained his composure they talked a while longer. Oliverio told him he'd been forced to retire from the police force. Then they stood silent for several minutes until Oliverio's taxi returned.

"I told him to come back for me. I'll be on my way. I just had to know."

Margaret pulled into the driveway as Oliverio was turning to leave. She passed them and stopped in front of the garage. She lifted Robard from the safety seat. Oliverio walked slowly toward the taxi. He turned one last time to stare at the child. For an instant it seemed the child's eyes were the eyes of an adult—penetrating, evil. Oliverio nodded his head and entered the taxi.

"Who was that?" asked Margaret.

"Uh . . . dunno. Wrong address."

"The groceries are in the trunk. Would you mind taking them in?"

"Ah . . . sure . . . sure."

68

JUNE 1989

The anxiety was more acute than usual as Frank Clifton drove home from the clinic, and it wasn't just the hellish traffic and the heat. Robard's weight had dropped to below seven pounds, despite Margaret's continuous efforts to get food into him. She had convinced herself the age reversal would cease and the clone would begin to grow as a normal child and everything would be right with the world. Frank continued to live the lie for her sake. He even pretended to care about the child. But he knew the sham, the hypocrisy, was about to end. He prayed that she would consider Robard's death a mutual loss and that she would turn to him to share her grief and pain. But another scenario haunted him. What if Margaret blamed him for the death? The death of her beloved replacement child. He had no way of gauging; her mental state was too volatile. He was drained and emotionally battered by the tension, isolation, and uncertainty of the past few years.

He was driving by rote, wondering how he was able to function day to day. Each day had become a gray blur. Every morning he awoke before Margaret, who had regressed since the incident with the babysitter. She refused to go anywhere without the child and she was again dependent on sleeping pills and valium. Robard slept in a crib beside their bed. Clifton checked on him each morning. He remembered, long ago, ignoring Margaret's pleas to remove the life supports when the clone was born in the Staatsburg house. He was too principled then.

Where were his principles now? Now it was he who wanted the clone dead and Margaret who was desperately, by force of will if nothing else, trying to keep him alive. Clifton wanted an end to the morning seizures when Robard, enveloped in Margaret's arms, screamed and wailed, out of control. It was the doctor who now found the daily attacks intolerable. It was he who left the house for long walks until they were over. His worst fear was that Robard would die in Margaret's arms during one of the seizures. He'd decided that morning that he would tough them out with her from now on. No more walks. No escape. He had to be there when the end came. He secretly kept a hypodermic needle and a strong sedative hidden in the night table beside their bed. When the time came, he would put Margaret under for several hours. His plan was to dismantle the crib and burn it in the fireplace along with everything else that belonged to Robard. Whatever wouldn't burn would be put in a plastic garbage bag. He'd already quietly removed from the house all the belongings and toys that Robard no longer used. The clone's body would be wrapped in a blanket and covered with newspapers and trash in another garbage bag. Two bags, filled with trash, had already been set aside in the garage. When death came, he would put all of the bags in the trunk of his car and drive eight miles to the county dump and leave the bags among the tons of garbage waiting to be bulldozed under as part of a land reclamation scheme. Eventually the site would be covered with earth and concrete to form the base for a large housing development. As a precaution, the doctor ensured there was nothing in the garbage bags that could lead back to them. No credit card receipts. No junk mail. Nothing with a name or address. Clifton had driven to the dump several times. His plan, he felt, was barbaric, but he saw no alternative. He would be there when Margaret came out of sedation. His path was clear. If she was unable to accept the loss, he'd inject her again and have her institutionalized until she was well. One way or the other it would be a new beginning, their last. They would move again, perhaps to California.

Clifton left the car in the driveway and went to the front door. It was locked. He tried the rear entrance. It, too, was locked and Margaret was not on the deck. Probably out for a walk with the stroller. He used his key to enter the house. He loosened his tie as he entered the kitchen. He called out to Margaret, but there was no response. Too nice a day to stay inside, despite the heat. He prepared himself a ham and cheese sandwich and washed it down with a glass of milk. He went upstairs to the bathroom. He preferred it to the one off the kitchen. He urinated and washed his hands. Pulling off his tie, he entered the bedroom to undress, anticipating a cool shower. He turned toward the bed. His eyes focused on the scene and his brain registered it. And then he screamed. Soundless at first and then inhuman and shattering—an excruciating scream of eternal anguish and stark terror.

Margaret lay nude on her back. It wasn't difficult to see it was her, for her face was serenely still, her eyes closed. There were tiny beads and narrow rivulets of blood in the delicate hollow of her throat, splashed there from another source, spreading like a river across her once unblemished body and ending in streams running off both thighs. Her calves, ankles, and feet were, like her face, untouched.

The trained medical eye saw the bloodied, sharp steel butcher's knife on the blood-soaked white sheet beside her. It was, he knew, responsible for the single brutal slash from the vagina, deep through the womb and abdomen, to the breasts. And the small motionless form—

the clone, Robard—barely visible, face down in the ab-
errant, blood-filled cavity. And Margaret's hands, frozen
in an obscene death clutch at the cavity's edge. The
medical eye surveyed it all, but the medical brain
couldn't determine if the hands were there as an invol-
untary response to the carnage wrought on the body,
or if they were there to broaden the cavity, to make
room.

His screams filled his brain until the raw red flashes
became a bottomless black hole . . . and then oblivion.

69

The soothing motion of the rocking chair continued strong and steady as Vince Oliverio read *The New York Times'* account of the Florida deaths. An autopsy revealed the woman wasn't pregnant as first surmised. The blood types were different. It wasn't her baby. The baby's identity was unknown. It was a newborn with just the slightest remnant of an umbilical cord. The baby asphyxiated in the woman's blood. Her husband, a forty-nine-year-old doctor, was being assessed at a mental institution. It seemed he came upon the grisly scene and the shock turned his hair prematurely white. He was now in a deep catatonic state. Police found no evidence of an intruder. There were no fingerprints on the weapon. They had no answers. They simply didn't know.

Vince Oliverio continued rocking. They'd retired him early, but he knew. Oh yes, he knew, all right.

epilogue

The morning sun came streaming through the tastefully decorated apartment. On a mantel over the living room fireplace was a framed wedding photograph. The bride and groom were Maria Brazao and Doug Bradford.

Maria stood at the window, looking out at the park, two stories below, where her eight-year-old son was playing with his friends. She smiled and nodded when he looked up at her. He knew it was time. His shoulders slumped as he walked from the grass toward the building. The antique clock on the mantle showed nine-thirty when the boy entered the apartment. He went to Maria on the couch. She cradled him protectively in her lap as if he were a young child. He sobbed as his body tightened into a fetal curl. After a few seconds, his legs straightened rigidly and his arms went stiff at his sides, fists clenched. The spasms continued for more than an hour.

Maria and her husband had been to several specialists. Epilepsy was ruled out, along with every other known ailment. Perhaps, they said, it was psychological, like bed-wetting. Perhaps it stemmed from negative birth or womb memories. It would pass. The child would grow out of it, they had said. But the seizures continued.

Maria's husband didn't know the child wasn't his. She had conceived the boy during the brutal, illicit love-making with the stranger who had stolen her will. Perhaps, she thought, her son's affliction was God's way of punishing her.

Maria held her son closely. She kissed the soft curly hair at the back of his neck. Once the seizures stopped, everything would be just fine.

About the Author

BRIAN VALLÉE is a graduate of Michigan State University's school of journalism.

Between 1962 and 1978 he worked as a reporter-columnist for several newspapers in Canada, the United States, and England.

Until 1989 Vallee was a producer with the Canadian Broadcasting Corporation's award-winning current affairs program, *the fifth estate.* He was associate producer of the ninety-minute documentary *Just Another Missing Kid,* which won an Oscar at the 1983 Academy Awards.

His 1986 non-fiction book *Life With Billy,* about an abused wife who took the law into her own hands was a bestseller in Canada and was published in the U.S. in 1989.

Vallee lives in Toronto and spends his summers at his cottage in northern Ontario, where he is working on his next novel, entitled *Incubus.*

A poacher is stalking Kenya's Aberdare National Park...
and animals aren't his only prey.

EDGE OF EDEN
by Nicholas Profitt

The natives call him Fisi, the hyena; they say he is an ex-
mercenary, a torturer, a witch doctor. They say he takes
men's lives and men's souls. They say that anyone who
tries to stop him will not come out of the forest alive....

Peter Odongo is the police inspector assigned to investigate Fisi and his heavily armed band of poachers. Adrian
Glenton is the former big-game hunter Odongo hires to
lead a small team of native warriors and trackers on a
jungle manhunt. While Odongo explores a trail of corruption that leads from the bush into the highest corridors of
power, Glenton and his handful of men will pursue Fisi
down a wilderness trail of grisly death. In the midst of the
most spectacular scenery in the world a battle for the
survival of the land and its precious wildlife is raging. And
for the men who are hunting an uncannily elusive killer,
the most dangerous enemy is the one lying in wait...for
them.

Nicholas Profitt takes us into a new heart of darkness in
EDGE OF EDEN. On sale in June wherever Bantam
Falcon Books are sold.

AN237 -- 5/91

THE GOLDEN ORANGE
by Joseph Wambaugh
The *New York Times* Bestseller

When forty-year old cop Winnie Farlowe lost his shield, he lost the only protection he had. Ever since, he's been fighting a bad back, fighting the bottle, fighting his conscience. But now he's in for a special fight. Never before has he come up against anyone like Tess Binger. She's a stunningly beautiful, sexually spirited three-time divorcee from Newport Beach - capital of California's Golden Orange, where wallets are fat, bikinis are skimpy, and cosmetic surgery is one sure way to a billionaire's bank account.

When Tess Binder's father washed up on the beach with a bullet in his ear, the coroner called it suicide. Tess saw it as a sign of things to come, and now Winnie Farlowe finds himself being drawn deeper into her world and into the heart of the Golden Orange, where death awaits around every turn.

"[Wambaugh's] laserlike descriptions of orange county are worth the price of admission" -- *The New York Times Book Review*

The Golden Orange, the new novel from Joseph Wambaugh, available in May wherever Bantam Books are sold.

AN238 -- 5/91